IRIS AVENUE

IRIS AVENUE

Pamela Grandstaff

Books by Pamela Grandstaff:

Rose Hill Mystery Series:

Rose Hill

Morning Glory Circle

Iris Avenue

Peony Street

Daisy Lane

Lilac Avenue

Hollyhock Ridge

Sunflower Street

Viola Avenue

Pumpkin Ridge

ISBN-10: 1453671153
ISBN-13: 978-1453671153

For Betsy

CHAPTER ONE - Sunday

Ray Caliban slid a hunting knife into the holster on his belt, where it would be hidden by the bottom of his leather jacket. He glanced down at his alibi, who was sleeping off the knockout drug he'd slipped her the night before. As he left the motel room behind the Roadhouse Lounge he looked around for other potential witnesses, but it was that time in the morning when even the hardcore partiers were unconscious, and there were no early risers at the Roadhouse Motel.

Ray was amped up on methamphetamine. His days all seemed to be twenty-four hours long on meth, and he hadn't slept for three. Ostensibly a bartender at the Roadhouse, Ray was actually an illegal drug distribution rep, and the bar was his district office. He made enough to support his own habits, keep up the Harley, and pay for some female company whenever he wanted it.

Ray left the parking lot and walked down the narrow lane that led to the railroad tracks by the Little Bear River, about a hundred yards behind the Roadhouse. He crossed the tracks and slid more than walked down the steep hillside to where an old fishing shack stood next to the river.

Ray scanned what was left of the snow for footprints or tire tracks but saw none. He drew out his knife before he checked to be sure the shack was empty. He returned it to the holster while he scanned the riverbank and hillside on each side of the water.

The only sounds he could hear were the rushing water and the wind in his ears. This part of the river featured shallow rapids over a rocky bed. The current was swift and deadly in the middle, but there were deep, dark, still places along the bank where trout were known to hide.

It was a clear, beautiful morning in early March but the sharp wind made it feel like February.

As time passed, his ears began to sting from cold. He repeatedly tipped up on his toes before setting his heels back down and opened and closed the snap on the knife holster. He lit a cigarette with shaking hands. The previous murders he'd committed were reactions to sudden turns of events, fueled by adrenaline and the need to survive. He didn't like having all this time to think about it beforehand.

A flash of bright color on the other side of the river caught his attention. A man emerged from the thick underbrush on the steep hillside there and slid down to the narrow riverbank, causing a small avalanche of dirt and rocks. Ray realized that when the man called the night before he hadn't specified on which side of the water he would appear, and had assumed when he said 'by the shack' he meant this side. Ray didn't know of any other shacks, he didn't have a boat, and it appeared this man didn't either.

The man across the river cupped his hands around his mouth and shouted something, but Ray couldn't hear for the rushing water. He focused his full attention on the man, who was now waving his arms, pointing, and shouting, Ray couldn't figure out what he was trying to communicate. It seemed to Ray as if he was indicating Ray should stay there and the man would somehow cross over.

What the man was actually pointing to was the person who was creeping out of a huge drainage pipe in the hillside behind Ray. This man had a knife and was stealthily approaching Ray's back.

The person creeping up behind Ray had also been waiting for the man across the river. This person had no compunction about killing Ray, who was simply an obstacle to be removed, a complication to be eliminated; the next move in a brutal game. Thus he didn't hesitate when he reached his victim; he seized and dispatched him before the man had time to react.

Within minutes the riverbank by the fishing shack was deserted, and the man across the river had fled. Ray tumbled and rolled through the freezing cold rapids until he reached a calm stretch of water, where he floated on his back, his body turning in lazy circles as he went downstream. His eyes were wide open, but he could no longer see the brilliant blue sky.

CHAPTER TWO - Monday

Rose Hill Police Chief Scott Gordon sat at his desk and considered the last box of evidence related to the murder of postmistress Margie Estep. During the investigation into that crime twenty years' worth of stolen mail was discovered in her attic crawlspace. Margie's killer was in prison awaiting trial; the evidence pertinent to the case was with the district attorney. With the Pine County Sheriff's permission, Scott had been returning the rest of the purloined mail to its proper owners. He had made appointments with everyone who had stolen mail and was awaiting his last visitor this morning.

Miranda Wilson, known as Mandy, worked at Fitzpatrick Bakery during the day and the Rose and Thorn bar at night and was the live-in girlfriend of Scott's best friend, Ed. Mandy had a twelve-year-old son named Tommy who was the town's only paper carrier. Mandy had been one of Margie's extortion targets, and Scott held before him the ammunition Margie had used in that blackmail attempt.

Mandy crept into Scott's office, her big green eyes wide in her pretty face. Mandy's long blonde hair was wound up in a messy knot on top of her head, and she wore a Fitzpatrick Bakery sweatshirt with jeans and sneakers.

"Hey, Scott," she said in her Chattanooga twang.

Scott got up, closed the door behind her, and gestured for her to sit.

"Thanks for coming in, Mandy," he said. "I wanted to give you the letter Margie stole from you."

"Did you read it?"

"I had to," Scott said. "I read every piece of mail that had been opened when I was trying to figure out who killed her."

Scott handed the letter to her, and she read it silently, moving her lips as she did so. When she finished, there were big tears in her eyes, and her face was flushed.

"Do we have to talk about it?" she asked.

"No," Scott said. "This isn't officially any of my business. As your friend, I'd like to know why you don't want your mother to know you're alive and well. It seems like she's gone to a lot of trouble to find you."

"It's complicated," Mandy said.

"How could Margie use this to try to blackmail you?"

Scott could tell Mandy was struggling with her fear, so he let the silence play out. Finally, she said, "When you went through the mail she took did you find anything for somebody called Melissa Wright?"

"I did, but there's nobody by that name in town that I know of. I still have the letters."

"Well, I know her. You can give 'em to me."

"Who's Melissa Wright?"

"I can't tell you, Scott. It ain't exactly a legal situation."

"Then you should discuss it with an attorney."

"I can't afford nothin' like that."

"Then maybe Father Stephen could help."

"I ain't Catholic," Mandy said. "I ain't nothin' religious. Them church folks seem nice enough in church on Sundays, but they're mean as the dickens everywhere else, and it don't seem to matter."

"Father Stephen says church is for imperfect people learning to do better."

"When that preacher looks at me I feel like I done something wrong even if I ain't."

"Delia and Ian love you, Mandy, why don't you confide in them?"

"I hate to let 'em down," Mandy said. "They been so good to me, givin' me a job and a place to live. They're like family."

"What about Ed?"

"I ain't tellin' Ed and you better not neither."

"Tell Hannah then, or Patrick. Someone you trust."

"Can I have the other mail?"

"I can't give you mail that doesn't match the name on your driver's license."

"Well, don't give it to nobody else," Mandy said as she rose from her chair, tucking her letter into her back pocket.

"Mandy, please let someone help you deal with this, whatever it is."

"I appreciate your advice, Scott, but I'll handle it."

After Mandy left, Scott did some Internet sleuthing. He knew Mandy came to Rose Hill from Florida, and he'd heard her talk about St. Petersburg, so he ran a search for the name Melissa Wright in St. Petersburg, Florida. What he found surprised him. He called the St. Petersburg Police Department, and after proving he was who he said he was, they referred him to someone at the Treasure Island Police Department.

Treasure Island had a small staff, and luckily there was someone still working there who remembered the case.

"Melissa Wright died in a house explosion eleven years ago," the officer told him. "Her husband was a local drug dealer who was cooperating with an undercover investigation into a methamphetamine production and distribution ring. We found him tied up and shot in the head in a dumpster near the airport. A day later there was an explosion at the house he'd been renting. His wife and two men were killed."

"How was she identified?" Scott asked. "Dental records?"

"No," the man said. "A neighbor identified the body."

"What was the neighbor's name?"

"Let me look," the man said, and Scott held his breath until the man said, "Miranda Wilson. When the police arrived Miss Wilson was on the scene, and an officer spoke to her. She stated she heard the explosion and ran over to see if she could help."

"What caused the explosion?"

"They'd built a meth lab. They were bright enough to make the drug but stupid enough to blow themselves up doing it."

"Were there any other deaths around that time with the same M.O. as the husband?"

"Several," he said. "It was a bloody housecleaning by a local drug lord, and it seemed like we found a body every other day."

"Any criminal background on Miranda Wilson?"

"Do you mind to hold?" the man asked.

"Not at all," Scott said. "I appreciate the time you're taking."

When he came back on the line, the man said, "Nothing on Miranda Wilson. I've got her profile if you want to run a background check. I can also e-mail the incident report to you if you want."

Scott took down the Social Security number, gave the man his e-mail address, and thanked him. Within the hour Scott had a copy of the newspaper account of the explosion as well as the notes from the case file. Scott read the newspaper account with growing interest.

"Sunday morning at approximately 4:12 a.m. Melissa Wright, the wife of the late Dallas Wright, was killed in a house explosion at 1118 Sixth Street East on Treasure Island, west of St. Petersburg. A source within the police department, speaking on the condition of anonymity, said that based on their preliminary investigations, the Pinellas County sheriff's department suspects the structure housed a methamphetamine lab. Three victims were killed in the fire, including Mrs.

Wright. Authorities are withholding the names of the other two victims pending notification of their families.

The officer's notes corroborated the newspaper account and included the names of the other two victims, who both had outstanding warrants for a number of drug-related crimes. It was also noted that Miranda Wilson left the area shortly after being interviewed at the scene, and was believed to no longer be a resident of Florida.

Scott got out the letters written to Melissa Wright. There were three, and they were all from the same P.O. Box in St. Petersburg, Florida. One had been sent every year on the same date for three years. Scott checked his notes. The date was the same as the anniversary of the explosion that killed Melissa Wright. Each had the same message scrawled on white copy paper: "Someone is looking for Miranda." The letter Margie used to blackmail Mandy had been sent six months ago, three months after the last Melissa Wright letter.

Scott e-mailed the officer in Florida, thanked him, and then made one further request. The officer e-mailed a scan of both Melissa Wright's and Miranda Wilson's driver's licenses. After he printed out both IDs and compared them, Scott felt sick inside. Both women were very young, pretty blondes. Scott knew one of the women very well, having been served donuts and coffee by her every morning for the past several years. He was just surprised to find Mandy's face on Melissa Wright's driver's license.

After debating with himself for a few minutes, Scott ran a background check on Miranda Wilson. He found her St. Petersburg, Florida records, and the live birth of her baby boy recorded twelve years earlier in a local hospital. There was no record of a marriage, and the father was listed on the birth certificate as "unknown."

Ed Harrison waded through the celebrity gossip magazines, bras, panties, and damp towels that were draped over every fixture in his only bathroom, and found his good safety razor in the tub, along with what seemed like forty different kinds of shampoos, conditioners, bath gels, and lotions.

He took a few deep breaths as he changed the blade and cleared enough space so he could shave over the sink. Mandy had written "I love you" on the mirror with lipstick, and it took glass cleaner and elbow grease to get the waxy red letters off the glass so he could clearly see the irritated expression on his stubbly face. He had a housekeeper who cleaned every Friday, and this was only Monday.

"You got yourself into this," he said to his reflection. "You might as well make the best of it."

After he finished shaving and was cleaning the sink, he heard someone in the house and opened the bathroom door. Mandy was walking down the hall, and when she saw him, she jumped back and gasped.

"What're you doing home?" she asked. "You like to scared me to death."

"Tommy was in the bathroom so long this morning I didn't have time to shave," Ed said, noting how agitated Mandy seemed. "Why are you home?"

"I forgot somethin'," she said, but she didn't look him in the eye as she said it. "I gotta get back to the bakery now before Bonnie has a fit."

"See you later," Ed said as she disappeared out the door.

Mandy waved but didn't say anything.

Ed was confused. Anytime they parted or reunited he usually had to peal her off limb by limb, and then wipe off all the lipstick she left on his face. He returned to the bathroom, gathered up all the damp garments and towels, and threw them in the laundry hamper. The magazines he threw in the trash.

Scott put his feet up on his desk, wadded up a scrap of paper, and shot it toward a wire mesh basket in the corner. He and his friends Ed and Patrick played basketball for the Rose Hill Thorns, one of the Pine County Men's League teams. Although Scott was barely six feet tall, he was a serviceable defensive player. His shooting stats weren't worth writing home about, but he could still hustle up and down the court and pass to those who did shoot well. It was eleven o'clock in the morning and practice wasn't until seven o'clock, so Scott had several hours to kill with nothing to do.

Rose Hill had been quiet for the past couple weeks, which suited Scott just fine. There had been four murders in the small town over the past few months, where previously the most serious crimes Scott had investigated involved domestic disputes or vandalism. Scott had almost been corpse number five; his hair was starting to grow in around the scar on the back of his head caused by an iron-skillet-wielding murderer. That person was locked up in the mental health unit of a federal prison, unlikely to be released anytime soon.

Up until a few weeks ago, Scott would have spent any free time he had preoccupied with what Maggie Fitzpatrick was doing. He would have walked down to Little Bear Books to pester her for attention. He still loved Maggie, but they had experienced a serious rift in their burgeoning relationship. Nowadays he was keeping his distance, hoping that leaving her alone would eventually cool her anger. He also hoped that when enough time passed, she would forgive him for what he'd done.

Ed walked through the station into Scott's office and regarded the wastebasket full of paper balls.

"There's more in than out," he said. "That's an improvement."

Scott swung his feet off the desk onto the floor as Ed sat down in a chair across from him.

"What's up?" Ed asked him.

"I'm officially done cleaning up after Margie," Scott said. "Now maybe everything and everyone in this town can get back to normal."

"Did you ever find out why she was blackmailing Mandy?"

Scott hesitated before he spoke.

"I can't discuss that with you," he finally said. "You'll have to ask Mandy."

"Fair enough," Ed said. "I figure it's probably something that was no big deal to anyone except Mandy."

Scott balled up another piece of paper and shot it toward the basket, but Ed deflected it.

"Since you don't have anything to do," Ed said, "you can help me find a new car."

"You feeling alright?" Scott asked him.

"I'm serious. I've never actually purchased a car. In college I walked or took the bus; after I married Eve, I drove her car. I've been driving Dad's truck since he died."

"Did the old rust-bucket finally give up the ghost?"

Ed's father's ancient truck was built before seat belts and airbags were invented, and you could hear it coming from a few blocks away.

"It still runs, but I'm carrying Mandy and Tommy around in it now, and I need something safer with more room."

"Like a minivan."

"No," Ed said. "Don't even think that."

"So, an SUV?"

"No gas guzzlers. I've been reading about hybrids. I've got a report on the best ones to buy."

Ed pulled a folded piece of paper out of his pocket and handed it to Scott. Scott unfolded it, looked it over, and nodded.

"Looks like you've done your homework," Scott said. "I'd be glad to help, but you should probably talk to Patrick. He knows way more about cars than I do. He helped me buy my Explorer from some guy up at the ski resort; got me a good deal."

"Patrick's still mad at me for tripping him up under the net last week."

"He'll be over that by now. Ask him."

Ed looked as if he didn't want to, but he accepted his folded paperback and said he would.

"How's it going?" Scott asked him.

Ed shrugged.

"The dog's happy. Everyone's feeding Hank because no one can remember whose turn it is, so he's getting fat. Tommy's still quiet, but he seems fine. I enjoy having him around. He's developed into a fierce Scrabble opponent."

"You've left out the most crucial roommate."

"She's great; it's me who's the problem. After Eve left, I had this quiet, peaceful life. Now, suddenly I'm sharing a bed and a bathroom with Mandy, and we're eating every meal together. I've lost all my privacy."

"There are compensations, I imagine."

"Oh, yeah, absolutely. It's just taking me some time to adjust."

"She's crazy about you. She seems happy."

"I know," Ed said. "I don't know what's wrong with me. Too set in my ways, I guess."

"Maggie used to say that, too," Scott said. "That was one of her excuses, anyway."

"I guess you heard she and her mother went to see Brian in prison," Ed said.

Brian was Maggie and Patrick's oldest brother. They also had a brother named Sean.

"Brian and Maggie started screaming at each other, and she and her mother were escorted out of the facility," Scott said.

"I feel sorry for their mother," Ed said. "It's getting harder and harder for Bonnie to believe it's all been a big misunderstanding."

"Easier I guess for Maggie to write off a brother than Bonnie to write off a son."

"Kind of like Maggie wrote you off?" Ed said.

Scott shrugged, said, "I did what I did, and now I'm paying for it. I'm not mad at her for being sore about it. I just miss her."

"Have you talked to her?"

"We run into each other on the street, and she's polite. She doesn't look me in the eye, but at least she doesn't sock me in the nose."

"It's a small town."

"Yep, and we both have to live in it."

"Is it too soon to talk about other fish in the sea?"

"I don't have a line in," Scott said. "One would have to jump out of the water and land in my boat."

The station's front door opened and county sheriff's investigator Sarah Albright came in. Ed greeted her and left.

"Hey," Sarah said to Scott. "You got a minute?"

"Sure," Scott said and motioned for her to sit in the chair Ed just vacated.

Sarah Albright was an ambitious violent crimes investigator for the county sheriff's office. She had worked with Scott on the recent murder investigations in Rose Hill. After putting up with her abuse for several weeks, Scott finally called her out on the constant sexual harassment and barrage of put-downs she dished out at every turn. She came to see him in the hospital after he was attacked and they agreed to call a truce; since then Sarah had been acting in a much more professional manner. Scott found out through the grapevine that Sarah had been reprimanded and was attending some re-training classes.

"Your ex-girlfriend's brother escaped from prison yesterday," she said.

Scott almost jumped up, his impulse being to run straight to Maggie's side. He sat back in his chair as he remembered he would no longer be welcome.

"How did that happen?"

"His cellmate stabbed him. He lost a lot of blood and was unconscious when they took him in an ambulance to the hospital. On the way, a tire blew out. The guard got out of the ambulance; Brian overpowered the medic, brained the guard with a fire extinguisher, and escaped into the woods next to the interstate. Lots of crap hitting the fan over this one, as you can imagine."

"Any county folks involved?"

Sarah grinned, saying, "Nope. All state police. You can bet some heads will roll."

"They don't think he'll come here."

"No, not likely. I thought I ought to let you know. I thought you might want to inform the family."

"I appreciate that. Thanks."

"I hear from my friends in D.C. that the feds are back in town."

"About Brian?"

Sarah shrugged, saying, "Could be about Theo."

Theo Eldridge had been the first murder victim in Rose Hill this year, back in January. During that investigation, Maggie uncovered evidence that Theo was blackmailing a few high powered politicians and prominent local citizens. Scott discovered Theo was also involved in a dog breeding scam and drug trafficking. The feds collected all the evidence Scott and Sarah had gathered, left town, and no one had heard another thing about the investigation.

"I was thinking of getting some breakfast while I was over this way," Sarah said. "You're welcome to join me, purely professionally, of course."

Even though she was an attractive, petite brunette with dark eyes and a sexy self-confidence, Scott was turned off by the constant contempt she displayed for his job, his town, and all the people he cared about. Since they called a truce, she hadn't said anything the least bit objectionable, but still, he could tell she wanted something more than his professional attention. He wasn't about to encourage her lest she fall off the wagon completely.

"I guess you haven't heard the diner closed," Scott said. "The owners moved to Florida. You can still get something at the bakery or the bookstore."

"I didn't know that," Sarah said. "That's too bad. You want to split a donut?"

"No, I better get back to work. Thanks again for stopping by," he said. "I'll let the family know about Brian."

Maggie's brother Patrick Fitzpatrick worked at their Uncle Curtis's service station every morning, so Scott left the police station, crossed Rose Hill Avenue, and walked down the block to see him. The March sky was bright blue with no clouds in it, but the wind still felt arctic. In Rose Hill, the month of March was ordinarily a cold, gray, slush-and-mud-fest, with only the occasional spring preview day to brighten things up. Today was one of those brightened-up days.

Patrick was talking to a young woman as he filled the tank of her expensive sports car.

"You should come to the Thorn this Saturday," he told her. "Scooter Scoley and the Snufftuckers are playing."

"No, thanks," the young woman said. "My idea of a good time is not listening to a bunch of old geezers playing fiddles and banjos."

"Ah now, you gotta love the bluegrass music," Patrick told her. "It's the music of our people."

"Your people, maybe," she said. "It sounds more like a cat fight to me."

"You've wounded me to my core," Patrick said, clasping his hand to his heart and staggering back. "I may never recover."

Patrick's crooked grin was enhanced by bright blue eyes and a strong cleft chin. The young woman seemed torn between putting him in his place and enjoying his attention. After she paid him, Patrick leaned down in the driver's side window and said something to her Scott could not hear. Her face flushed a deep pink in response.

"I'll think about it," she said.

Scott waited until the girl drove away, and Patrick waved to her as she went.

"These young kids don't appreciate their musical heritage," Patrick said, as he pretended to throw a basketball to Scott, who pretended to catch it and throw it back.

"She's an Eldridge College student," Scott said. "She's probably from someplace a lot more sophisticated than Rose Hill."

"Practice tonight," Patrick said, pointing a finger at Scott. "If you're late I'm gonna make you run sprints 'til you puke."

"Don't worry," Scott said, following Patrick into the station, where a couple of old coots sat by the gas fire, smoking and gabbing. Patrick's beagle Banjo looked up from where he lay on a bed in the corner and wagged his tail at the sight of his adored master; Patrick ignored him.

Scott pointed to the office; Patrick nodded and then led the way. Once the door was closed on the tiny, grubby space, which smelled like motor oil and gasoline, Scott told him about his brother Brian. Patrick listened with no expression, although a nerve jumped in his temple and Scott could see he was clenching his jaw.

"They don't think it's likely he'll come here," Scott said.

"My brother often does the unlikely," Patrick said.

"Do you want me to tell Bonnie?"

"No," Patrick said. "I'll tell my family; you go tell Ava."

"Will do."

"Thanks for letting me know," Patrick said, and Scott rose to leave. Patrick opened the back door of the office for him so he could exit via the alleyway behind the station.

"I'm sorry about all your family's trouble, Patrick," Scott said. "If there's anything I can do ..."

"I'll let you know."

"You want me to keep an eye on Ava's place?"

"That's none of my business. You can work that out with her."

Ava was the wife Brian had abandoned many years before, leaving her alone with their two small children. Afterward, with the Fitzpatrick family's help, Ava restored her rundown Victorian home and turned it into a bed and breakfast. Patrick had stepped in as a surrogate father to Ava's two children and had fallen head over heels in love with his beautiful sister-in-law. Scott was one of the few people who knew about their affair.

Scott found Ava in the kitchen, cleaning up after her guests' breakfast. As always happened, Scott's breath caught in his chest at the sight of her, and he felt a little lightheaded. Ava had that magical combination of perfectly proportioned facial features, a dancer's body, a glowing complexion, and the serene, self-possessed demeanor that gives some women a sort of star quality. She underplayed her beauty by dressing plainly, but she still had a striking effect on people, who often stared and bumped into things as she passed by. She smiled as Scott entered the kitchen through the back door, and he felt his heart skip a beat.

"Hi Scott," she said. "Where've you been?"

"Just working, you know," he said, and felt like an idiot who can't think what to say to a pretty girl.

"Sit down here, and we'll catch up," she said and poured him a cup of coffee. "I haven't seen you in awhile. How's the head?"

"It's okay," he said as he sat. In addition to his recent head wound, Scott was also prone to migraines.

"I know you and Maggie are on the outs at the moment," she said, "but you and I are good friends. I won't let you drop me."

"I won't, I promise," he said. "Ava, I have some bad news."

Ava Fitzpatrick had come to expect bad news over the past couple months. After Theo Eldridge was murdered back in January, the reading of his will revealed a large bequest left to Ava, and the town gossips were still working overtime on that scandal. Patrick was at one point a suspect in Theo's murder, and Ava had ended their relationship in order to protect him.

Ava's husband, Brian, who'd been missing for over six years, turned up next, threatening to kidnap her children if she didn't pay him off with Theo's bequest. Shortly thereafter he fled town, abandoning the child he'd had with a second wife he was suspected of killing. His ex-drug supplier and an FBI agent visited Ava shortly thereafter, one with dire threats and the other with lots of questions.

Ava cooperated with the FBI in order to get Brian apprehended, but not before she coerced him into signing over guardianship to her of the infant son he abandoned in Rose Hill. The six-month-old baby was the spitting image of Ava's own redheaded son Timmy, and it seemed to Ava that he was meant to be her child.

Unbeknownst to anyone but her attorney brother-in-law Sean, Ava was in the process of mortgaging her bed and breakfast in order to pay off Mrs. Wells, the gray-haired drug titan to whom Brian owed half a million dollars. Mrs. Wells had offered to knock off ten percent if Ava delivered Brian to her, but Ava decided to cooperate with the FBI instead.

So, when Scott told her he had some bad news for her, Ava wasn't surprised.

"Are my kids okay?" she asked him, glancing at the crib in the corner of the kitchen, where the baby they were calling "Little Fitz" lay sleeping peacefully.

"The kids are fine. This is about Brian."

"What's he done now?"

Scott told her what he knew, and she grew weary-looking as she listened.

"He'll come here or contact me," she said. "The FBI will be back before nightfall, you watch."

"Sarah says the feds are already in town."

"That's great," Ava said. "My kids were just beginning to feel safe sleeping in their own beds."

"I'll have Skip and Frank keep an eye on your place."

"Thank you. Please tell them to watch the school, too."

"I'll make sure the principal and the teachers know. We'll keep them safe."

The oven timer dinged. Ava rose, took a tray of muffins out of the oven, and put two on a plate for Scott. She still wore a cast from breaking her wrist rescuing Little Fitz but didn't seem to favor that hand or feel any pain from using it.

"Scott, I know I probably shouldn't be asking you this, but do you know how I could go about getting a gun?"

"No, Ava, not with kids in the house. I won't let you."

"I know, I know," she said. "But I don't feel safe."

"Would it help if I stayed here at night?"

"Scott, that is so sweet, and even though I probably shouldn't, I'm going to take you up on that offer. People will gossip about it, but I can't afford to worry about how things look anymore. If you don't mind doing it, I won't mind what people say."

"I don't mind at all. I only have Duke to feed, when he bothers to come home at all. I ought to warn you, though; he'll probably follow me here."

"Don't worry about that cat. He walks with Timmy and Charlotte to and from school sometimes, and I feed him on the back porch. I hate to make you sleep on the sofa every night, but my rooms are all booked."

"I don't mind the sofa, and that way I can come and go and not disturb you and the kids."

Ava gave him a key to the back door, along with a hug and a kiss on the cheek.

"You'll eat like a king," she said. "I'll make sure you have a good breakfast every morning and a good dinner every night."

"That won't be necessary," Scott said, but he was already looking forward to it.

Ava's hug and kiss kept him warm all the way back to the station.

County Animal Control Officer Hannah received a call to come out to the Roadhouse, and when she got there, she found a big, burly dumpster service driver sitting on the bumper of his truck, crying. He was holding something against his chest, down inside his jacket.

"Hey, buddy," Hannah said as she approached him. "Are you okay?"

The man looked up at Hannah through red eyes, his cheeks stained with tears.

"I don't understand people," he said.

"Me neither," Hannah said. "Did you call about a dog?"

He pointed at the garbage dumpster sitting between the Roadhouse and the motel behind it.

"Somebody dumped a litter of pups in there. Who does something like that?"

Hannah patted him on the shoulder.

"I know, buddy," she said. "I know."

He sniffed a little and wiped his eyes with the back of a grimy hand.

"You got one of those pups in your jacket, there?" she asked him.

"Yeah," he said. "The other ones are dead."

He held out his jacket so she could look down at the tiny black pup he cradled there.

"Look there," she said. "You saved one."

"I can't keep her," he said. "My wife's allergic."

"I'll find her a good home," Hannah said.

"You won't kill her," the man said. "I won't let you take her unless you promise."

"Listen, little girls this cute are easy to find homes for. Before you know it, this dog will be chasing squirrels all day and sleeping inside every night. I promise."

The man carefully lifted the pup out, and Hannah tucked it inside her jacket.

"I find all kinds of awful stuff in dumpsters," he said. "I even found a dead guy once, but that didn't bother me nearly as much as this."

A man came out of one of the motel rooms behind the Roadhouse, and when he saw the dumpster driver, he stopped in his tracks. He looked familiar to Hannah, and not like someone she'd ever want to meet alone behind the Roadhouse, even in broad daylight.

"What's going on?" he said as he approached.

He looked to Hannah like one of the biker gang members who hung out at the bar, which was notorious for violent fights and drug traffic. Even though it was cold outside, he was wearing a sleeveless muscle shirt and combat fatigue pants. Hannah could see tattoos on almost every visible inch of skin, and anything on his head that could be pierced was. He even had little horn-like bumps installed above his forehead on each side of his bald head. The effect was as satanic as he intended it to be. Hannah shivered a little and was glad to be standing next to a bigger, more tender-hearted guy.

"There's nothin' going on," the driver said. "I found something in the dumpster, is all."

The devil man's eyes widened.

"What in the hell are you talking about?" he said.

"None of your business," the dumpster driver said, and when the devil man started toward them, the driver stood up to his full height.

"You don't scare me," the devil man said and drew a knife out of a sheath on his belt.

Hannah started backing up with the idea that she would run to her truck and call the police.

"Then maybe this will," the driver said, and produced a small handgun out of his jacket pocket. He pointed it at the man's horned head and cocked it.

This stopped the devil man in his tracks. He put the knife back in its sheath and held up both hands.

"Hey man," he said. "None of my business, like you said."

They watched him go in the back door of the Roadhouse.

"He'll be back with friends," the driver said. "You better get on out of here."

Hannah didn't need any more encouragement. She thanked the man and ran back to her truck with the puppy whimpering against her chest. As she left the parking lot, she saw the horned man coming out the front door of the Roadhouse with two guys who were even bigger and scarier looking than he was. Hannah watched in her rearview mirror as they jumped out of the way to avoid being mowed down by the dumpster driver's huge truck. She wondered if they would follow him. She also wondered what was in the dumpster that had the devil man so worried.

Maggie Fitzpatrick was standing in front of the checkout counter in Little Bear Books, talking to Jeanette, her second in command.

"I need your grandson to take a look at my computer," Maggie said. "Since we upgraded I've been getting weird results when I run my financial reports."

"Jeffrey's got school until two forty-five," Jeanette said. "But I'll let his mother know he should come here before soccer practice."

"Can't we get him out of school?" Maggie asked.

"He's fourteen, Maggie," Jeanette said. "He can't miss school to work on your computers."

"Maybe he could get class credit for the work," Maggie insisted.

"I don't think so."

"I've been paying him but not that much. Maybe I should give him a raise."

"He does it for the discount," Jeanette said, "and because his grandmother works for you. Maybe you should give me the raise instead."

Maggie looked so stricken that Jeanette laughed.

"You should see your face, Maggie. You're as tight as a tick."

"I know," Maggie said, shaking her head. "My mother did that to me. That woman could squeeze two cents out of every penny."

Since Maggie couldn't do the bookkeeping she wanted to do she went over to the family's bakery to see if she could help out there. Maggie's bookstore ran better without her nitpicking the staff to death, and Jeanette had everything well in hand, so she could afford to be flexible with her schedule.

She arrived at the bakery right after Patrick told their mother that Brian had escaped from prison. Bonnie, pale and shaky, left to go tell Fitz, their father. Maggie was worried about her mother, but couldn't go with her and leave the bakery unattended.

Maggie called her cousin and best friend Hannah and asked her to please come to the bakery as soon as possible. She didn't dare tell her the news over the phone, as the scanner grannies in town listened in on cellular and cordless phone calls using their police scanners. They were mostly harmless, isolated by age or illness, and looking for excitement by listening in to other people's lives, but Maggie didn't underestimate the negative effect of their gossip.

Hannah's mother Alice, who worked the eight-to-four shift in the bakery, came back from a short break and Maggie got her caught up.

Alice's response was, "Well, why on earth didn't they shoot him rather than let him escape? He may come back here and kill us all in our sleep."

Maggie rolled her eyes as she turned away. Her Aunt Alice was ditzy and prone to say tactless things, but Maggie overlooked her for Hannah's sake.

When Hannah arrived, Maggie told her what was going on.

"Your brother is like a comic book villain," Hannah said. "No bars can hold him!"

"Seems like it," Maggie said.

"Maybe he's half man, half water vapor. When cornered he evaporates, and then reappears out of a puddle somewhere nearby."

"Hannah."

"I'll have to think of a good comic book name for him. I know I want the word 'red' to be in there somewhere."

"Watch it," Maggie warned.

Brian and Maggie both had the red, freckled coloring of their mother's Scottish side of the family, while their brothers Sean and Patrick had the blue eyes and dark hair of their father's Black Irish side.

"Keep your curls on," Hannah told her. "Something to do with pirates, maybe."

When Brian tried to kidnap his son Timmy, the young boy had described his would-be assailant as looking like a pirate, with long red curls, a beard, and an earring.

"Brian the Red," Hannah said. "Or Slippery Brian, the Red Pirate of Rose Hill."

"Too long," Maggie said.

"Redbeard!" Hannah said. "Like Bluebeard only red."

"Bluebeard killed his wives."

"Accuracy is the hallmark of a good comic book name."

"Don't joke about it," Maggie said. "It feels wrong."

"Alright," Hannah said. "I'll work on another one, but it won't be half as good if it's not accurate."

Maggie helped her Aunt Alice prepare for the lunch rush, and Hannah rang up customers. Hannah tended to eat more baked goods than she sold, so they had to keep an eye on her. Even though Hannah was tiny and skinny, she ate like a lumberjack.

"Have you used any of that makeup I bought you?" Alice asked her daughter. "It's supposed to erase the lines you have around the eyes."

"No, mother," Hannah said. "You know I don't wear makeup."

"Well," Alice sighed, "a mother can continue to hope, I guess. I had four boys before I had you, and if I'd known you wouldn't like girly things I probably wouldn't have bothered."

Maggie gasped, but Hannah just laughed.

"After I threw that fit at the first pageant you put me in you should have drowned me in the river," she said.

"I don't know why you say such awful things," her mother said. "You know I didn't mean it that way."

Maggie shook her head in disbelief, but Hannah shrugged it off as her mother went back to the kitchen.

"She thinks Claire and I were somehow switched at birth, even though we were born a year apart."

Claire was their cousin, daughter of Uncle Ian and Aunt Delia Fitzpatrick, and she, Hannah, and Maggie had always been close growing up. Claire was a girly girl and worked as an assistant to a famous actress on movie sets around the world. It only sounded glamorous, according to Claire, who suffered through long months on difficult location shoots babysitting her demanding boss. She came home about once a year and lived in California when she wasn't traveling.

"Have you heard from Miss Claire?" Hannah asked Maggie.

"I get e-mails occasionally, but she hasn't called in awhile."

"Last I heard she was in Istanbul," said Hannah. "Where is that, by the way?"

"Turkey."

Hannah looked unenlightened.

"Next to Greece," Maggie said, pointing to an imaginary map on the counter. "There's the Mediterranean, then Greece, Turkey, Syria, Iraq, and Iran."

"That's scary; why would you film a movie so close to a war zone?"

"Because the story takes place there, I guess."

"Yeah, but can't they build a pretend Turkey in California, on one of those lots? It seems like it would save a lot of money."

"Claire says spending money is what directors are good at, not saving it."

"She also says everyone in Hollywood sleeps with everyone else," Hannah said.

"She should know," Maggie said

"Meow, cousin. I'm telling her you said that."

A group of customers came in, and the lunch rush began.

Ed Harrison sat at his desk in the Rose Hill Sentinel newspaper office, his finger poised over the "Enter" key on his computer keyboard. He'd finished designing a website for the weekly paper, had proofread it multiple times, and was about to publish it on the Internet. It was a momentous occasion for the paper as well as for Ed, the third generation owner. The subscription base and advertising sales for the printed paper barely supported the business and Ed's few personal expenses, and it had finally become evident that a change must be made.

Ed couldn't imagine how a website could take the place of the weekly paper, let alone support the business. Some of the older local business owners had balked at paying additional fees to have ads on the Internet version of the Sentinel, but the younger generation of business owners who had websites jumped on board. Ed was planning to launch the thing today and hoped it wouldn't be a huge failure or ruin what was left of his print business.

Ed's grandfather had started the Sentinel, and Ed's father brought him up to take over the business. Now Ed was bringing it into the twenty-first century, albeit a little behind the curve. His father had done his own typesetting and operated a printing press up until the day he keeled over with a heart attack.

Ed, who was working on a Philadelphia daily paper at the time, came home immediately, made arrangements for his father's funeral, and impulsively decided to take over the Sentinel. He purchased a computer and the requisite publishing software and then engaged a local printing company to publish the little weekly.

Ed made the paper his whole life, just like his father had, and his wife left him, just like Ed's mother left his father. Ed quickly settled into the same ruts in which his father traveled every day: he did the same job, lived in the same house, drank the same beer while he sat on the same stool in the same bar, and drove the same truck. Over the years he had transformed from an energetic, promising young journalist into the middle-aged caretaker of one of the town's most sacred cows.

Ed clicked on the button that published the website and exhaled the breath he hadn't realized he was holding. Mandy came in and swooped down on him with a big smooch and a hug from behind. This was more like the affectionate greeting he was used to.

"Hey, good lookin'," she said. "How's my baby today?"

"Same as I was a little while ago. Why aren't you working?"

"I got some time off so I could run some errands. I told you 'bout that, but you weren't listenin'. Got yer nose stuck to that computer all the time."

"I launched the website today."

"That's great! Are you gonna add a celebrity gossip page?"

"I don't think that's quite right for the Sentinel."

"I'm tellin' ya, it's the only thing people read on the Internet. My favorite part's the blind items and the pictures of the crazy outfits."

"Hopefully people will read the news online as well," Ed said, "or I may have to go to work at the Rose and Thorn alongside you."

"Don't you worry, honey," she said. "It'll do great, I just know it. You're the smartest man I know, and you know exactly what you're doin'."

Ed wished he felt that confident.

Hannah came in and greeted Mandy, who sailed out, blowing Ed a big kiss as she went.

"Oo la la," Hannah said. "It's still the honeymoon suite in here, I see."

"What can I do for you, Hannah?" Ed asked her.

"I came to see Hank, not you," Hannah said, and walked over to look at the big black lab, who was asleep on a red cushion by the gas stove.

"No more dogs, Hannah," Ed said.

"Now, why would you jump to that conclusion?" Hannah asked him, as she stooped down to rub Hank's belly. "I just wanted to stop in and see my old buddy. He's getting awfully fat, by the way. He could use a friend to play with."

"I jumped to that conclusion because I know you so well," Ed said. "What is it this time?"

"It's a lab mix," she said. "She's so sweet and perfect for you."

"The last time you said you had a lab mix that was perfect for me, it was two percent lab and ninety-eight percent vicious killer."

"This is different. You've got to come see her; she's over at Drew's."

"Hannah, no. Even if she's wonderful, my house is bursting at the seams as it is."

"Alright," Hannah said. "I'll have to throw her in the kennel with the stone-cold killers and hope she survives. I found homes for all of Theo's dogs, you know."

"Everyone knows," Ed said. "On your own time with county resources."

"She'll keep Hank company, and really, two are no more trouble than one."

"I can't take on any more responsibility," Ed said. "Housebreaking would just about do me in."

"That's okay," Hannah said, backing out the door. "You've got enough on your plate. I understand."

Ed sighed deeply, then got up and put on his jacket.

"Stay," he told Hank, who didn't even open his eyes.

When Tommy arrived at the newspaper office at lunchtime, he found Ed typing on the computer keyboard with one hand while cradling a small black puppy against his chest with the other.

Ed handed the puppy to an ecstatic Tommy and said, "If you want her, you'll have to take full responsibility. You'll have to feed her and make sure she gets outside in time to poop and pee, every hour until she learns to hold it. I can keep her while you're in school, but otherwise, she'll be your problem."

Tommy took the puppy from Ed's arms, and it whimpered a bit.

"Where'd she come from?" Tommy said as he cuddled her up under his chin.

"Hannah found her," was all Ed said.

"I'll take good care of her," Tommy said.

Mandy came in with a big smile that disappeared as soon as she saw the puppy. She gave Ed a pointed look.

"Do I get to vote, or has this decision already done been made?" she asked.

Tommy looked up in a panic, but Ed shrugged and met Mandy's irritated look with a cool one of his own.

"If you don't want Tommy to have the dog, he can't have the dog," he said.

"I'll take care of her," Tommy pleaded. "Please, Mom."

Mandy and Ed locked eyes for a long moment.

"Thanks a lot, Ed," she said. "Like I could say 'no,' now."

"Tommy has promised to look after her," Ed said. "It will be a good experience for him."

"Good thing, because I ain't cleanin' up after it," she declared. "You better make sure it don't chew up none of my shoes, neither."

"I will; I promise," Tommy said.

"You better take her out and see if she needs to pee," Ed told him.

As soon as the boy left, Ed said to Mandy, "I know I should have consulted you first and I'm sorry. Please don't take it out on Tommy."

Mandy embraced Ed and snuggled up under his chin.

"That's alright," she said. "We're still findin' our way 'round each other."

Ed hugged her and kissed the top of her head.

When Tommy came back in, he was smiling from ear to ear.

"She peed and pooped."

"Grab a plastic grocery bag and go pick it up," Ed said.

Tommy made a face.

"That's what it means to be a responsible pet owner," Ed told him. "Anything that comes out of that dog you clean up."

Tommy nodded and fetched a grocery bag out of the office kitchen.

"I'll go to the grocery store and get her some food after you go back to school," Ed told Tommy when he came back. "She's too little to eat Hank's food."

"I gotta get to work," Mandy said to Ed. "Don't forget you have basketball practice at 7:30 and Tommy needs help with his homework. You boys be good."

She kissed them both and left.

Tommy ate and then went back to school. Ed took the pup down to the IGA to pick out some chow.

Morris Hatcher stopped in at the Fitzpatricks' Service Station right before Patrick left to go to his afternoon job at the Rose and Thorn. "Hatch," as he was known, was a homely car mechanic who had been Hannah's high school boyfriend. He worked at a service station in Fleurmania, a town so small it made Rose Hill seem like a metropolis.

Patrick embraced Hatch and clapped him on the back.

"I can't believe my eyes," Patrick said. "I didn't think Marvin ever let you off the chain up there."

"That mean old sumbitch up and died on me this past weekend," Hatch said. "Can you believe that?"

"Well, he wasn't exactly a health nut," Patrick said and invited Hatch inside out of the cold wind.

Station owner Curtis Fitzpatrick greeted Hatch warmly and offered him a seat by the stove. The old coots had toddled off home for lunch, so they had the place to themselves except for the mechanic, Lester, who was working on a car in one of the two service bays.

"I can't believe Marvin lived as long as he did," Curtis said when they told him. "He had that sugar problem and drank like a fish."

"He was a big man," Patrick said, "around the middle and at both ends."

"Yep," Hatch said. "Had himself a heart attack. His wife said he was yelling at some politician on the TV and just fell over."

"What's going to happen to the station?" Curtis asked.

"Well," Hatch said. "That's what I came to talk to y'all about. I was hoping you'd want to buy it."

"Nah," Curtis said, shaking his head. "You know as well as I do that selling gas doesn't make much money, and at least we've got the tourist trade. Fleurmania isn't on anyone's way anywhere."

"We do alright," Hatch said. "I get a lot of repair business from the Mennonite church and the Sugar Creek mine. If I had the money, I'd buy the place myself. Slim Nida said he'd drive the wrecker for me and his wife Edith could work the front office."

"Can't you get a loan?"

"Not without a down payment. I could pay the payments, but not the twenty percent down."

"How much does the widow want?"

"A hundred grand."

"Lordy day, son," Curtis said. "That old station's not worth that. Don't you let Melvin's old lady hornswoggle you."

"It's not just the building," Hatch said. "It includes the oil company contract, all the equipment, the wrecker, and the tire and battery business."

"You should get that appraised. I still think she's cheatin' ya."

"So you really ain't interested?" Hatch asked.

"No, son, I haven't got twenty grand to play around with, and I can't afford to take the risk. I've got no debt right now, and I aim to keep it that way."

"What about you, Patrick?"

"If I were gonna spend a hundred grand," Patrick said. "I'd buy the old Woolworths building, expand the bar, add a proper stage, sound equipment, and a dance floor. Sorry, Hatch."

"Well, it was worth a try," Hatch said.

"Now, if you need work I'd love to have you over here," Curtis said. "We get more than enough business to keep two mechanics busy, and I can always use another tow driver in the winter."

"I appreciate that," Hatch said. "I'll keep that in mind; I will."

Hatch stood up to go, and Patrick offered to buy him a beer at the Thorn.

"No, I got my sister's child in school up at home, and I like to be there when he gets off the bus," Hatch said. "You tell Hannah I said hi."

"I'll do it," Curtis said.

After Hatch left, Curtis shook his head and sighed.

"That poor boy never had a chance. I pulled what was left of his daddy's truck up out of a ravine after he wrecked it; he was soaked in whiskey and dead on arrival. Then his mama died of cancer and left him with all those kids to raise. Ian and I offered to take them in, but Hatch said he wasn't raised to accept any charity."

"Maggie said the oldest girl's got mixed up with drugs," Patrick said. "It's her boy Hatch is raising."

"It doesn't seem fair," Curtis said. "Hatch was a good boy and he just never seemed to catch a break. Marvin should have left him that business. They didn't have any children, and you know Hatch probably never missed a day of work in twenty years."

"Maybe he'll come work for us," Patrick said. "I'll run out there and ask him again in a week or two."

"You know I love my son-in-law," Curtis said, "but that Hatch would have been an excellent addition to our family. Hannah was heartbroken when he quit school. Just think if he hadn't done that he'd probably be working here with us now."

"For cheap, like me," Patrick said.

"You heard from Sam?" Curtis asked him.

Hannah's husband Sam was Patrick's best friend.

"No," Patrick said. "But he'll be back."

"I don't know if that marriage is going to make it," Curtis said.

Patrick was silent, watching Hatch pull out of the service station parking lot in a beat up truck that nevertheless sounded like it possessed a finely tuned engine under the hood.

"Sam always comes back," Patrick said.

"That he keeps leaving her is the problem," Curtis said. "I know he had a bad experience in the war, and I know he has things to overcome, but there's only so much a woman can be asked to bear. I'm afraid my girl's at the end of her rope."

"Hannah's tough," Patrick said. "She'll be alright."

"Every woman's got her limit," Curtis said. "Most men don't realize that until it's too late."

CHAPTER THREE - Tuesday

Hannah left Fitzpatrick's bakery and drove the animal control truck out to Bear Lake to look for a stray dog reported near there. She stopped at a small convenience store called "Roush's Bait Shop," which sold more beer than bait. There was a group of old men huddled around the ancient coal stove inside, smoking and chewing the fat, just like at her dad's service station. They all knew Hannah, of course; before she quit smoking, she used to join them on many a cold, snowy day.

Owners Fred and Fanny Roush were working behind the counter. Fred was running the register and Fanny was deep frying fish and chips for a lunch order. Fanny motioned Hannah back around the counter.

"Hi, honey," Fanny said. "The fella who reported the dog said it had a collar but no tags and was real friendly like. It's hanging around the roadside picnic spot between here and Fleurmania."

Hannah thanked her but declined the free order of french fries Fanny scooped up for her. Her stomach felt queasy. She bought a package of hot dogs to use to catch the stray.

Hannah had run into Hatch several times over the years. Fleurmania wasn't in Pine County, but nevertheless, it was a small community out in the same neck of the woods, and Hatch was a fixture. Hannah kept track of him through local gossip, and she knew pretty well at all times what was going on with him. When he passed her truck at the roadside picnic area, he turned around, came back, and parked his truck nose to nose with hers.

"Hey, you!" he hollered over the hill, to where Hannah was trying to coax a dog to come to her using a hotdog as bait.

"Hey yourself!" she hollered back. "You know this dog?"

The dog in question was a hound mix with big long ears and a dopey expression. He was standing on the other side of a shallow creek. Hannah could tell he was tempted by the smell of the raw hotdog but didn't like the look of the loop lead she was holding. Hatch came half-walking, half-sliding down the hillside to stand next to her.

"I think that's Hollis Marcum's pooch," he said. "Now, what's that dern dog's name?"

Hannah threw the dog a little piece of hotdog. The dog gobbled it up and looked interested in having more. She broke off another piece and threw it to the side of where she was standing, hoping to at least get him on her side of the creek.

"I'll run up and call Hollis," Hatch said. "If it's his I'm sure he'll come down and fetch him."

By the time Hatch returned Hannah had the dog on the lead and was dragging him up the hill.

"Come on, Randy!" Hatch said, and the dog leaped the rest of the way up the hillside, pulling Hannah toward Hatch.

"Thanks," Hannah said.

"Hollis is on his way," Hatch said. "He said he just left Friendsville, so he'll be here in about a half hour. You want me to take him back to the station?"

"I don't mind to wait," Hannah said. "I have to fill out a report to justify my mileage, and I'll need him to sign it."

"I'll wait with you if you don't mind," Hatch said. "It'll give us a chance to catch up."

Hannah put the dog in one of the compartments on her truck and then sat with Hatch in the cold sunshine, on top of a picnic table. Hatch pulled out a rolled up pouch of chewing tobacco and stuffed a little wad in between his cheek and gum.

"I keep meaning to give this up, but at least it keeps me from smoking," he said.

Hatch told her what was going on with his sisters and brothers, and about keeping his nephew. He told her about Marvin dying, and wanting to buy the station.

"I need twenty thousand dollars down to get the loan," he said. "It might as well be twenty million. It seems a shame that an honest man can't get ahead, and there's my sister's man covered up in money from selling drugs."

"You ever hear about some big drug ring involving Theo Eldridge and the man who used to live with Maggie?"

"Sure have. They got this old lady what bankrolls the whole operation, likes to slit people's throats and throw them in the river when they make her mad. Did you know your cousin Brian has a price tag on his head?"

"Same old lady?"

"One and the same. If he's smart, he'll get as far away from here as possible, pretty dern quick."

"How did you know he's escaped? I only heard that this morning."

"I hear stuff, you know," he said, and shifted uncomfortably.

Hannah looked at Hatch and saw the gawky sixteen-year-old kid he'd once been. He had long, silky black hair back then and now it was a buzz cut. He looked older and tired.

"You doin' alright?" Hatch asked her. "Yer old man treatin' you right?"

"We're fine," Hannah said. "We still live on the family farm, and Sam works out of an office there, doing computer stuff. I keep busy rounding up these old dogs."

"You know I heard tell of a man raises dogs to fight over in Blacknell Furnace. I don't cotton to that, no ways. You want the address?"

Hannah got out her notebook and took down the information.

"Now, don't you go over there by yourself," Hatch warned. "They're a rotten bunch what tend to shoot first and ask questions later."

"I won't be called in until after they're arrested," Hannah said. "I just take custody of the dogs when it's all over."

"Well, like I said, I don't cotton to it."

"Thanks, Hatch," Hannah said.

When the dog owner arrived, Hannah had him sign the official form before she brought Randy out of his container. The dog seemed glad to see him. She waved to Hatch and the dog owner and got back in her truck. She'd let herself get chilled, so she let the heater warm up the cab before she started back to Rose Hill.

As she waited for the cab to warm up, she thought about Hatch and wondered how it was Hatch knew Brian had escaped when it was still supposed to be a secret, and how he knew so much about the drug ring his sister's boyfriend was involved with.

She wondered what her life might have been like had she married him instead of Sam. She'd have helped him raise all those kids, for one thing. They may have had some of their own. She could easily picture him on the farm, and working for her dad, which was their plan before he broke up with her.

Funny, she thought, how life can turn out completely different than how you think it's going to. In high school, Sam Campbell was the star athlete who dated the prettiest cheerleader. Hannah didn't think he even knew she was alive.

When Sam returned from the war with a broken body and spirit, the pretty cheerleader quickly decided this wasn't how her life should turn out. Hannah was a waitress at the Rose and Thorn around that time and served Sam beers whenever Patrick, Ed, and Scott could convince him to come out with them. He didn't say much but was never rude to her. He sat with his wheelchair situated so that his back was to the wall, keeping one eye on the door at all times. He seemed painfully uncomfortable in his own skin.

After he'd been home a few months, Sam started working out with the wrestling team at the high school. The coach had been Sam's coach, and he and Patrick conspired to get Sam involved in "helping out" with the team. Hannah observed his mood began to improve and he started talking and laughing a little more.

One night in the bar Hannah and Patrick were giving each other the usual hard time about something, and Sam said to Hannah, "I don't remember you being such a smart-ass in high school."

Without thinking, Hannah retorted, "I don't remember you being so short."

You could have heard a pin drop in the few seconds of silence between the moment the words left her lips and when Sam threw his head back and laughed a deep belly laugh. There had been tears in his eyes when he stopped.

"I needed that, Fitzpatrick," he said to her afterward. "Thank you."

Hannah decided right then to make it her life's mission to keep Sam laughing, and had eventually won his heart through her efforts.

Sam had undergone many years of therapy, both mental and physical, in order to recover from losing both his lower legs below the knee in an attack on his convoy outside Kuwait. He persevered through a strong will to survive and with the support of his loyal friends Patrick, Scott, and Ed.

After completing physical therapy, Sam returned to college on the GI Bill and graduated from MIT with a degree in Information Technology. After a few years working as a contractor he started a network security consulting business he ran from his home.

Sam had a genius IQ and a fierce determination. Nonetheless, he occasionally succumbed to dark bouts of depression that strained the bonds of their marriage. About a month earlier Hannah had found a body in the deeply packed snow at the Rose Hill Winter Festival. Sam blamed himself for not being there doing the work Hannah was doing when she made her gruesome discovery, and for not being physically able to get to her when she needed him. After days of bitter fighting with Hannah, and suffering from a vicious combination of self-pity and self-recrimination, Sam had gone on a "business trip," and had not been in touch with his wife since.

Hannah spent part of the afternoon crawling under a house on Lilac Avenue, retrieving some feral cats. The mother cat was a skinny gray she-devil who hissed and screeched at Hannah. Once she was in a crate, Hannah scooped up her two blue-eyed kittens: one gray-striped and the other gray like her mama.

The homeowner agreed to look after the kittens until Hannah could find homes for them, even though Hannah was well known for leaving kittens with people temporarily and then never returning to pick them up. Hannah took the mother cat and kittens to Drew's veterinary, where she left mama to get spayed and the kittens to get wormed and inoculated. Tired, dirty, wet, and cold, Hannah then headed home.

Wally and Jax, the housedogs, met Hannah's truck at the top of their driveway. The farm lay in a rolling valley surrounded by hills, off Hollyhock Ridge Road, about ten crooked miles from Rose Hill. Hannah rubbed and patted her dogs as she walked out to the kennel where she kept her "inmates." She only had room for six dogs and often found that many strays in a week. Hannah had thirty days to find each dog a home or place it in a no-kill shelter before the county sent the local vet on rotation to put it down.

Hannah had a fair success rate and was always looking for homes for the dogs that were well-behaved enough to place. Rose Hill was also infested with feral cats, which seemed to multiply faster than Hannah could catch, spay or neuter, and release them. There were a dozen feral cats in her own barn, and she tipped out some chow for them before she fed and watered the canine prisoners.

The four inmates currently incarcerated in her barn were pit bulls rescued during a raid on a dogfighting ring. Two of the dogs had been well-behaved enough to place in homes. The more severely injured dogs had been put down.

Hannah had been trying, with no success, to socialize these last four survivors so that they, too, could be placed in homes. They were like ticking time bombs, unfortunately, poised to go off in a frenzy of sharp teeth at the slightest provocation. Although she pretended otherwise, Hannah knew her socialization program for them was a complete failure.

After she exercised the dogs and cleaned their kennels, Hannah trudged back to the house, followed by Jax, a husky mix, and Wally, a border collie. There were no messages on the answering machine and no e-mails from Sam on her computer. She turned up the heat and made herself a meal of scrambled eggs and toast, then gagged at the smell of the eggs and dumped them in the dog bowls instead. She sat at the kitchen table, eating dry toast and drinking some hot, sweet tea, thinking about what she was calling her "calendar problem."

For a few weeks now, Hannah had thought she might be pregnant, something she first began to suspect when looking at her kitchen calendar right before Sam left. From the start of their marriage, Hannah wanted babies, as many as she could pop out. Although they never used birth control she never got pregnant.

Tests taken early in their marriage revealed there was nothing in her physiology that would prevent her from having a child. She didn't have the heart to ask Sam to be tested. After he returned from the war he'd spent a long, difficult time in a hospital, and had come home dangerously depressed. Hannah was afraid if it did turn out to be his fault they couldn't conceive he would fall into another deep depression. So they didn't talk about it. Hannah's periods were not regular, and she sometimes skipped one, but never three in a row.

Hannah went upstairs to take a shower. After she stripped, she looked at her belly in the mirror. It looked as flat as ever. Her breasts were tender like they were right before her period. She'd been an emotional mess recently, but that could be because she found a dead body a few weeks ago, and then her husband left her.

As she showered, she let herself imagine being pregnant and thought it couldn't come at a worse time. She wasn't sure where Sam was or if he was coming back. She certainly didn't want him to come back because she might be pregnant. She tried to imagine what her life would be like without Sam and with a baby. She'd have to leave the farm, for one thing, and move into town, where she had family who could help. Furthermore, she couldn't imagine crawling under a house to rescue kittens when she was eight months pregnant.

After her shower, Hannah went to the computer and looked up the contact information for Sam's former MIT roommate, Alan Davidson. They had stayed in close contact, and Alan visited them every summer. He had an engineering degree and was the founding partner of a company that designed prosthetic devices–a career inspired by his college roommate. Sam had said he was going to Boston on business, and Alan lived outside of Boston, so it wasn't exactly a wild guess.

He answered on the second ring.

"I've been expecting your call," he said.

"Is he staying with you?" Hannah asked.

"Yep," Alan said.

"Is he with you now?"

"Nope," Alan said. "But I'm in a meeting. Can I call you later?"

"Sure," Hannah said and disconnected the call.

About an hour later Alan called her back.

"Okay," he said. "Since you called me first I'm not breaking any friendship codes or anything."

"Heaven forbid," Hannah said. "Too bad my husband's not as concerned about his marriage vows."

"You knew how he was when you married him," Alan said. "I warned you myself."

"Thanks for reminding me."

"He did come up here to work for one of his war machine clients, which I think is kind of ironic, considering how poorly they protected him in the Gulf."

"I'm well aware of your political beliefs," Hannah said. "I've heard you two argue about them enough."

"He finished that job a few days ago, and now he's taking some time off."

"What's the mood?" Hannah asked. "Prince of Darkness or Superhero?"

"A little of both. He sees his counselor every day, so that's positive, right?"

"No, that's great, really. Thanks for looking after him. Do you think he's planning to come home anytime soon?"

"Yes, I do. I think he's doing this so he can come home."

"What's that supposed to mean?"

"I don't want to betray his confidence, but I can say that he wants to make certain improvements before he comes home, and he's working hard to make those improvements so that when he does come home, things will be better."

"You suck at keeping a secret. Does this mean he intends to be walking when he comes home?"

"Possibly."

"You know I don't care about that."

"But he does, Hannah. That's the thing. He needs to do it for himself."

"But he's tried this before; it's so painful for him."

“The types of prosthesis we use now are a hundred times better, Hannah. Plus he’s had all this time for his knees to heal and build up muscle tissue. You’ll be amazed at what we can do now, and how comfortable these are for him. We’re working with the manufacturer to make a special cleat attachment that will keep him from slipping on the snow and ice.”

Alan’s voice became excited, as it always did when he talked about his work.

“We have ones with snowshoe attachments. We have skis he can use. I’ve got clients with less limb structure than Sam who run track, and they compete against fully limbed runners.”

“I’m sure it’s all great, Alan, and I appreciate you helping Sam. I just don’t think our marriage can survive another setback.”

“I honestly think it will be okay this time. I plan to come down with him and make any adjustments that need to be made. I won’t let him fail.”

“Listen, you can move in with us if you want. I need all the help I can get.”

“That bad, huh?” Alan asked her. “How are you doing?”

“I don’t know,” she said, her voice faltering. “Not good.”

“Can I give you some advice?”

“For all the good it will do,” she said, sniffing.

“Listen to me. You have to take care of yourself. You have to do whatever it is you need to do to be healthy, strong, and happy, and let Sam do this thing he needs to do. Then when you get back together, which I have no doubt you will, you’ll both be strong, healthy, and happy, together.”

“Can you cross-stitch that on a pillow for me?”

“I mean it.”

“Thank you, Mr. Davidson. You are, like, the best guidance counselor, like, ever.”

"Give those dogs a big hug for me."

"I will."

Hannah hung up and looked down at her tummy.

"Are you hungry?" she asked the unconfirmed baby. "What would you like to eat?"

She listened intently, and could only hear the tick of the clock on the kitchen wall, the wind whistling around the house, and the whoosh of the gas furnace coming on.

"Pretzels? I love pretzels too!" she told her tummy. "Whattaya say we keep 'em down this time?"

Scott found Mandy working at the Rose and Thorn. She was laughing when he walked in, but her face fell when she saw him. There were only a couple of customers sitting at the bar, so Scott and Mandy sat down in a booth near the door (as far away from Patrick as possible), and Scott handed Mandy the print-out of the driver's licenses. Tears welled up in her eyes.

"This looks real bad, I know," she said. "Are you gonna arrest me?"

"Just tell me what happened," Scott said. "If I can help you, I will."

"I should've left town," she said. "As soon as I knew Margie had the letters."

"Was Miranda Wilson Tommy's mother?"

Mandy nodded.

"Was she involved with drugs?"

"She was a crackhead."

"Was he mistreated?"

"She didn't hurt him; she just didn't pay any attention to him. Their next door neighbor could hear him cryin'; said it'd go on for hours. One day I went over to the house, walked past all of them sittin' around, high outta their minds, picked him up, and took him home with me. She didn't care."

"How did you meet her?"

"She showed up with them losers my husband was hanging out with, a bunch of drug addicts. They got this big idea they was gonna make meth, said it was easy money. They went through the first batch instead of selling it."

"Was the baby in the house with the lab?"

"He was. Miranda didn't care about nothin' but the crack pipe and the meth. Our neighbor, Consuela, helped me take care of Tommy; she would've reported Miranda to social services, but she employed illegals in her business and didn't want them to get sent back to Mexico."

For once Scott was glad for the loud Irish folk music Patrick liked to play because it gave Mandy and him some privacy.

"Tell me what happened, step by step."

"Dallas dealt some drugs to an undercover cop and got arrested. He told the cops he would testify against some big-time dealer to get out of it. They let him go, and I figured sooner or later somebody would knock him off for squealing. Early one morning not too much later we heard the explosion."

The words were pouring out of Mandy like it felt good to have them out. Scott stayed silent and waited for her to continue.

"I knew the cops would put Tommy in foster care. Miranda was a foster kid, and she told me how awful people treated her. When the police got there, I told 'em it was Melissa Wright who died. It just come outta my mouth before I knowed what I was sayin'."

"They believed you?"

"They must've. The man wrote down everything I said and asked me to come in later and sign something."

"But you didn't go."

"Before the police came I broke into Miranda's car. She'd left her dang purse in there. I knew it was a sign I was doin' the right thing. I had her ID and her baby. Consuela lent me some money and promised to keep in touch in case someone came snooping around asking questions."

"Why did you come up here?"

"My mama died when I was little, and my aunt raised me up in Markleysburg. I was fourteen when I run off to Florida with Dallas. After the explosion, I thought I'd come back up here, and she'd take us in. We got clear up there before I found out she was dead. We didn't have nowhere else to go. The car broke down on the four-lane north a here and the state police called Curtis to tow it to Rose Hill."

"And Ian and Delia took you in."

"You know their little boy died when he was younger. Their daughter had gone to California, and they let me and Tommy stay in their house and me work at the bar until I could pay for the car repairs. After a while, I got to like it here and thought why not stay?"

"No better cover than living with the chief of police."

"These people been nothin' but good to me all these years, Scott. In my heart, I know I done the right thing by Tommy."

"So Consuela sent you the letters addressed to Melissa?"

"I paid her back the money I borrowed and kept in touch with her. I guess Miranda's birth mother started looking for her. She's got some disease and is gonna die soon, so she wants to see Tommy."

"What're you going do about that?"

"Tommy doesn't know none of this; now Margie's dead nobody knows about it but you, me, and Consuela."

"Margie sent a letter to Ed before she died, but he said he never received it."

"Lucky me," she said.

Out of the corner of his eye, Scott could see that Patrick was about to yell at Mandy to get back to work, so he gave Patrick a pointed look and shook his head one quick shake. Patrick looked irritated but left them alone.

"I guess you gotta do something," Mandy said.

"You broke the law," Scott said.

"Tommy would've died in that explosion," Mandy said. "We both would have. Or she might've sold him to somebody to pay for drugs. I saved that baby's life, Scott. That's gotta count for something."

"You assumed someone's identity and kidnapped a child, Mandy. I know you had good intentions, but if Miranda's mother discovers what you did, she could have you arrested and take custody of Tommy."

"She gave Miranda up for adoption when she was just a baby," Mandy said. "Maybe she wouldn't know the difference."

"I guess there's a slim chance you could talk to her mother, tell her what happened, and maybe come to some agreement with her."

"You don't believe that."

"I think it's unlikely," Scott said. "But she has a right to know her grandson before she dies."

"If I took him and ran away, would you hunt us down?"

"Running away's not going to solve anything," Scott said. "She found you here, didn't she?"

"I could go back to being Melissa," Mandy said.

"Except the Social Security office would wonder why a dead person was suddenly earning wages."

"I hadn't thought of that," Mandy said.

"Are you using Miranda's Social Security number now?"

"I ain't never filed a tax return," Mandy said. "I get paid in cash, and I pay in cash."

Scott wished he didn't know Mandy was employed illegally by the Fitzpatrick family. Since Theo Eldridge was murdered, Scott had discovered the more he found out about what went on in Rose Hill, the less he wanted to know.

"Did you use Miranda's ID to get a driver's license here?"

"You might as well lock me up for that, too," Mandy said. "I also used it to get Tommy's birth certificate so I could sign him up for school."

Scott reflected that Mandy had been fortunate to land in a small town where everyone took her at face value and trusted what she said was the truth. After the Fitzpatricks took her under their wing, she was as good as one of their family.

"Tommy had to get a Social Security card to work at the paper," she said. "I think that's how she done found us."

"I'm not going to lie to you," he said. "This is a mess."

"I know it," she said, her eyes filling with tears.

"I need more time to think this through," Scott said. "Meanwhile, you tell Ed about it. Between Ed and me, we'll help you figure out what's the best thing to do."

"He's not gonna wanna have anything to do with me," Mandy said. "You know him. He's big on the truth tellin'."

"He cares about you, and he'll help you," Scott said. "Thank you for being honest with me, Mandy. Promise me you won't run off and do anything stupid."

"Where would I go?" she shrugged. "As far as the world's concerned I'm dead."

Scott stood up as the two customers left.

"You must think being a waitress means making the customers wait," Patrick called from behind the bar. "I guess what I really need in here is a worktress."

"Put a cork in it," Mandy said. "I'm coming."

Maggie Fitzpatrick put down the book she was reading after realizing that even though she'd been going through the motions of reading for several pages, her thoughts were elsewhere. The sun had gone down behind the hills on the other side of the Little Bear River, so she turned on lights as she went down the long hallway of her apartment, which was on the second floor of the building she owned that housed her bookstore.

Her kitchen was at the end of the hallway, with french doors and a cast iron balcony that overlooked the alley behind her building and the backyards of the big houses on Lilac Avenue. Looking out the back window into one of the big houses, she could see preparations for a dinner party taking place, with candlelight reflecting off sparkling glassware. In another house, she could see a woman working in a kitchen while a child did homework at the table.

Maggie looked at her own kitchen, a gleaming stainless steel and granite showplace that had been installed by the previous owner. Maggie only used one gas ring to heat water for tea and one shelf in the glass-door fridge to keep milk cold for her cereal. There were no provisions in the house to cook an actual meal. Maggie couldn't see the point of buying a bunch of groceries to cook for one person.

She picked up the phone, dialed PJ's Pizza, and gave her usual order. In about twenty minutes the delivery person buzzed to alert her, and she ran down the steps to open the door.

"Hey Paulie," she said, surprised to see the owner making the delivery. "Julie making you work tonight?"

"Most of my delivery kids have that stomach virus that's going around," he told her, as he handed her the box. "I'm afraid they'll infect the whole town if I let them go out when they're sick."

"I appreciate that," Maggie said. "I certainly can't afford to be sick."

Paulie hesitated, obviously wanting to say something else.

"What?" Maggie asked him. "Didn't I give you enough money?"

"No, that's not it," he said. "I want to ask you something, but I don't want to make you mad."

"I'm not promising anything," Maggie said.

"Well, I know you and Scott aren't seeing each other anymore, and I was wondering if I could fix you up with my brother Tony."

Tony Delvecchio owned an insurance agency in town and had never married. One of the middle children of four brothers, he lived at home with his parents, diminutive Salvador and the statuesque Antonia.

"I thought Tony had a girlfriend in the city."

"He hasn't been going to see her lately, and we think they may have broken up. He's very private and doesn't talk about that kind of stuff. He never brought her home to visit, so we don't think it was ever serious."

"That's nice of you, Paulie, and I certainly like Tony, but I'm just not looking for anyone right now."

"Keep him in mind, though. He's a good guy, and we'd all like to see him settle down. My family thinks the world of your family."

"Thanks, Paulie, I'll keep him in mind. Tell Julie I said hi."

The Delvecchio and the Fitzpatrick families owned several businesses in Rose Hill. Sal had been a close friend of Maggie's father for many years. Paul and his wife Julie were the P and J in PJ's Pizza. Paulie's brother Matt had taken over the local grocery store when their father retired, his brother Sonny owned the hardware store, and Tony had the insurance agency.

A marriage between the two families had always been a much-desired wish of both sets of parents. Maggie, being the only single female Fitzpatrick left in Rose Hill since Hannah married and Claire went to California, was probably seen as the natural choice for Tony.

Maggie took her pizza back up to her apartment, walked down the long hall to the kitchen, and placed it on the table, all the while thinking about Tony Delvecchio. He'd been several years ahead of Maggie in school, and although she knew him well enough to make polite conversation, and sat near him and his mother every Sunday at Mass, she didn't know him all that well. The thought of going out on a date with anyone made Maggie shudder, but still, she had to admit Tony wasn't a bad choice for her. He would understand about her crazy work hours and family responsibilities in a way many men would not. His mother was a fierce Gallic Amazon, but she'd always had a soft spot for Maggie. It was a pleasant diversion from thinking about Scott, with whom she was still so angry, or Gabe, whom she didn't want to think about at all.

Ed went to the Rose and Thorn to check in on Mandy at around ten o'clock, only to find the bar empty and her crying in Patrick's arms. As soon as she saw Ed, she pulled away, and Patrick went to the back room.

"What's going on?" Ed asked her.

"I'm just having a bad day," Mandy said. "Don't mind me."

"What happened?"

"Nothin'," she said. "I don't wanna talk about it."

"Except to Patrick."

"When you and me talk honest it don't always go so well."

"You have to be able to confide in me," Ed said. "Or we can't have a relationship."

"You do whatever you got to do," Mandy said. "I got a right to keep some things to myself."

"I don't understand what's going on," Ed said. "But whatever it is, I don't want Tommy to get hurt."

"Everybody gets hurt," Mandy said. "I don't want Tommy goin' around thinkin' nothing bad can ever happen. That won't prepare him for nothin'."

"You're really not going to tell me what's going on?"

"Nope," Mandy said. "And I guess me and Tommy will just have to live with the consequences."

Some customers came in, and Mandy wiped her eyes with her apron.

"Could you yell at me later?" she asked. "I need to get back to work."

Ed considered confronting Patrick, then decided it would only upset Mandy more. He left the bar and walked back toward home, not seeing anything that surrounded him.

"Hey," Scott said, and Ed realized he'd just walked past his best friend.

"Sorry," Ed said.

He stopped, and Scott caught up with him.

"What's going on?" Scott asked. "You look like you've got the weight of the world on your shoulders."

"Something's going on with Mandy," Ed said. "And for some reason, she can tell Patrick but not me."

"I wouldn't make too much of that," Scott said. "They've known each other a long time. They're more like brother and sister than anything."

"No," Ed said. "She was crying, and he was holding her, but it wasn't like you'd hold your sister."

"What do we know?" Scott said. "Neither of us has a sister."

"Let me put it this way," Ed said. "I would not have been surprised if the next thing Patrick would have done if I hadn't interrupted them was kiss her."

Ava was expecting an FBI agent, so when one showed up at the back door with a suitcase, she wasn't surprised.

"Agent Brown," she said as she opened the door to him.

"Hi, Ava," he said and smiled at her.

"I'm booked up," she said, refusing to be defrosted by his familiar manner.

"I have a reservation," he said. "It's under James Randolph."

"Oh," she said. "I see."

He followed her through to the front parlor, where she checked in her guests. She went through the motions of checking him in without saying a word. He seemed comfortable enough with her silence, and she wasn't willing to waste her hostess chit chat on him. She showed him to his room, the tiny single with a three-quarter bath in the attic. He was so tall that he could only stand up straight in the center of the room.

"If you need anything, press zero," she said. "I'll pick up."

"Could I possibly have some coffee?" he asked.

"Of course," she said, reminding herself he was a paying guest. "I'll brew a fresh pot."

Agent Jamie Brown had shown up in Ava's kitchen one night the month before, while her husband was still at large. It was right after she'd been threatened by Mrs. Wells, Brian's drug supplier, that if she didn't cough up half a million dollars within thirty days, something bad would happen to her children. Jamie was a tall, handsome man with dark eyes and hair, and he seemed kind and friendly, but the information he brought her was horrible and hard to believe.

Jamie had asked for her cooperation in the federal investigation, and Ava knew she had no choice. He knew things he could only know if Ava's home and phone were bugged. They struck a deal that allowed her to get custody of Little Fitz and Brian was apprehended. Although Jamie treated her with compassion and delicacy, once Brian was behind bars, Ava hoped never to see the agent again.

When Jamie came downstairs, he had on jeans and a sweatshirt with "ARMY" printed on it. Ava poured him a mug of coffee and offered him a plate of muffins, cheese, and grapes.

"Thank you so much," he said. "I've been driving all day and didn't take the time to stop and eat."

Ava softened a little toward him as her innate graciousness was stimulated, and she replenished the plate as soon as he finished all she'd offered.

"I guess you heard," he said, in between bites.

"Oh, yes," Ava said. "I've been expecting you."

"Have you seen or heard from him?"

"No."

"How's the baby?" he asked her.

"Fine. He's upstairs sleeping," she said, gesturing to a baby monitor on the kitchen counter.

"They've officially declared his wife's death a homicide," Jamie said.

"You said before you expected they would," she said evenly, determined not to reveal anything by her expression. "But you didn't tell me how it happened."

"He took her scuba diving and came back without her. He reported her missing, and after they found her remains, he stayed long enough to get the death certificate so he could collect the life insurance. The police in Bimini were tipped off that he'd taken out a large insurance policy on her right before she died, but he fled with the baby before they could bring him in for questioning.

"The woman traveling with him, who was caring for the baby, had been working as a housekeeper for the wife, who was very wealthy. She's back in Bimini now, and she was able to tell the police a lot of what happened before and after they fled. Evidently, Brian cheated on the wife, she threatened to divorce him, he talked her around, and then they went scuba diving. The housekeeper said there was a prenup, and if he cheated he got nothing in a divorce."

"So he killed her for the insurance money."

"The authorities think so."

"He abandoned the baby. He might have died."

"If not for you," Jamie said.

"Are you only investigating Brian because of what he did in Bimini?" Ava asked.

"No. That's someone else's investigation."

"Then why are you here?"

"To talk to you about Mrs. Wells."

Ava said nothing, just looked at him with as blank an expression as she could muster. She realized she was gripping the baby monitor so hard her fingertips were white. She took a deep breath and willed herself to stay calm.

"I know you applied for a home equity loan of half a million dollars, Ava, and I know that Brian owes Mrs. Wells that much. I'd like you to tell me about that."

Ava felt her body start to tremble although she willed it to stop. She could feel a lump forming in her throat and tears stung her eyes.

"My children are my reason for living," Ava said. "I won't risk their lives because you want to catch a drug dealer."

"Mrs. Wells is much more than a drug dealer, Ava. If we don't put her behind bars and break up her business, there will be more death and destruction in this region than you can imagine. You may not know it, but there's a war going on, a battle for territory, and she needs to show her enemies just how powerful she is. She'll kill as many people as she has to just to make that point."

"I just want to pay her off so she'll go away."

"But she won't go away," Jamie said. "She'll come back for more money, or worse, for favors. You'll never be free. You can't even run away. She'll threaten every person in this town that you love. She's a sociopath. She has no conscience, no scruples."

"Why don't you arrest her?"

"We want to be sure our case is a slam dunk, and that takes time. We are so close, and if you cooperate, it will happen even faster."

"What about my kids?"

"We won't let anyone harm your children," Jamie said.

"Those are just words," she said. "They don't mean anything."

Jamie put his hand over Ava's, which rested on the kitchen island.

"I promise to personally do everything I can to ensure that you and your children are safe. Between the two of us, we can accomplish that."

Ava felt as if the decision to cooperate had already been made, and all she could do was go along with it.

Scott knocked on Ava's back door just then, and Ava let him in. He looked from Ava to Jamie, who stood and offered his hand while Ava introduced them. Scott shook the agent's hand, and took a seat at the kitchen island, accepting the coffee that Ava offered.

"I trust Scott," Ava told the agent. "I won't help you unless he's involved."

"I know all about Chief Gordon," Jamie told her, and then to Scott, he said, "I was planning to bring you on board tomorrow, but we may as well get you up to speed tonight."

Maggie closed the front door of Fitzpatrick's Bakery and locked the door behind her. The streets of Rose Hill, which had felt so safe to her for most of her life, now seemed to be made up of places in which someone could hide and then jump out at her when she least expected it. She walked in the middle of the street instead of on the sidewalk, down two blocks and then left on Marigold Avenue toward the high wall that separated the Eldridge College campus from the town.

Her parents' house was the last one on the block, and all the lights were on inside. As she opened the front door, she happened to look back and saw the town's only police cruiser coming down the street. Her first thought was that Scott was following her to make sure she was safe. Her second was that it was more likely the police were keeping an eye on her parents' house in case Brian decided to come home.

Inside, her father, known as Fitz, along with her Grandpa Tim, and Uncles Curtis and Ian were watching the news on television. Her father glanced at her briefly but didn't seem to see her, and her Grandpa Tim winked.

Uncle Curtis nodded to her and Uncle Ian grabbed her hand as she walked by. She leaned down to kiss him on the cheek.

"Brian's escape hasn't been mentioned on the news yet," he murmured.

In the kitchen her mother, Bonnie, eyes swollen, skin blotchy and a tissue clutched in her hand, was sitting at the kitchen table with Aunt Delia.

"Do you want tea?" Delia asked Maggie, who shook her head and sat down across from her mother.

"Your last words to him may well be those spoken in anger," Bonnie said, glaring at her daughter. "Not many mothers can boast of having been kicked out of a prison, but I can, thanks to you."

Delia clasped Maggie's hand under the table and squeezed. Maggie bit back what she wanted to say and asked instead, "Have the police been here?"

"The state police were here," Bonnie said. "They said Brian is considered armed and dangerous."

"Has Scott been here?"

"He's at Ava's," Delia said. "He's going to stay there until Brian is found."

Maggie felt a sharp stab of jealousy but was determined no one should see.

"That's good," she said. "At least we'll know they're safe."

"As if he would harm his own flesh and blood," Bonnie said. "I guess I'm the only person who still believes a man is innocent until proven guilty."

Maggie, who knew way more about what Brian was capable of than their mother, resisted the temptation to enlighten her on her firstborn son's greedy and murderous impulses. She could tell that far from consoling her mother, she was only agitating her, so she got up to leave. Of course, that was wrong, too.

"Don't mind us," Bonnie said. "We'll let you know when they shoot your brother down like a rabid dog. I'm sure it will be in all the papers if you're interested. Will you be able to make the time to come to the funeral, do you think?"

Maggie walked out the back door, and her Aunt Delia followed.

"She's beside herself," Delia started, but Maggie interrupted.

"Don't even try," Maggie said. "She only becomes more who she is when she's upset. This is when I get to see how she really feels, as if I didn't already know."

"I'm so sorry," Delia said as she hugged her. "You're a good girl, Mary Margaret, and you've been good to your family. She knows that. I don't know why she can't acknowledge it."

"I was late getting here because I was running the bakery she walked out of this morning."

"I know."

"Will I need to open it tomorrow?"

"I'll find out and let you know."

"Has anyone called Sean?"

"He's coming as soon as he can get away; it may be tomorrow or the next day. It's complicated, he said, but he'll be here."

"That should please her. She likes him."

Delia shook her head.

Maggie walked down the alley next to the wall that separated the college from the town. She walked all the way to the college entrance on Rose Hill Avenue without worrying about anyone jumping out at her. She thought the way she felt right now she could tear a man apart with her bare hands if he so much as looked at her funny. She walked around the block behind her store and went upstairs to her apartment without looking in on the staff. She was afraid of what she might say if anyone spoke to her.

The phone was ringing in her kitchen, and she ran down the hall to answer it but was too late. When she checked her voice mail a few minutes later, there was a message from Scott.

"Hey Maggie, I know we aren't on the best of terms right now, but if you need anything, I hope you know you can call. It doesn't have to mean anything. I just want to help if I can. Bye."

Maggie rested her forehead against the kitchen wall for a moment, wishing she could crawl through the telephone toward his warm, familiar voice. A pre-recorded voice asked her if she wanted to delete the message. She saved it.

The bar wasn't busy, and only the local stalwarts were left come closing time. Mandy locked the front door after the last one tottered out, and Patrick began to put the chairs up on the tables so she could mop.

"You gonna tell me what's going on?" Patrick asked her.

"Nope," she said.

She went to the restroom to fill the mop bucket, and Patrick followed her.

"Ed being mean to you?" he asked. "I'll kick his ass from here 'til Sunday."

"No," Mandy said with a sigh. "Ed's not bein' mean to me."

"It ain't that time of the month, is it?" Patrick asked. "I got the calendar marked wrong if it is."

"No!" Mandy said and flicked water at him from the faucet in the utility sink.

"C'mon, Mandy," Patrick said. "You were pretty upset earlier. You knocked up or something?"

"No," Mandy said as she dunked the mop in the rolling bucket and pushed it past Patrick out into the bar. "I'll figure it out myself. Don't you worry 'bout it."

Patrick performed all the tasks of closing up the bar: counting the money in the till, locking the deposit and the base funds in the safe, and then gathering the trash to take to the dumpster. Mandy put on her coat, and they left by the side door. He locked the door, hefted the trash bags and flung them in the dumpster in the alley behind the bar. He walked with Mandy down Iris Avenue and stood outside Ed's house with her. She seemed reluctant to go inside.

"If this isn't working out," Patrick told her, "you say the word, and I'll have you moved back in your trailer in no time."

"I thought you liked living there," she said.

"Oh, I'm not moving out," Patrick said. "I'll just make room for you and Tommy."

"No thanks," Mandy said. "I told you, don't worry 'bout it. I can take care of myself."

"I mean it," Patrick said as she walked down the path to the front door. "Just say the word. I won't even beat him up if you don't want me to."

Mandy shook her head and then waved as she let herself in the door. Ed was sound asleep in the recliner in front of the television. He woke as she turned off the TV.

"Hey," she said.

"I waited up," he said.

"I'm beat," she said. "Do you mind if we leave it until tomorrow?"

"Let's leave it altogether," Ed said. "I was just jealous when I saw you and Patrick. You have a right to your privacy and your own friends."

He stood up and wrapped her in a bear hug, then kissed the top of her head.

"I don't have to know everything," he said. "But if I can help in any way, I hope you'll let me know."

Mandy said, "Okay."

Later, after Ed was sound asleep in bed, Mandy went into the bathroom and looked at the letter again. When Margie confronted her with the Melissa Wright letters and this one, she'd felt like a cornered criminal, desperate to keep her secret safe.

All Margie demanded was that Mandy pretend to be her friend in return for her silence. Mandy put her off for a long time until finally, Margie threatened to reveal what she suspected. When Margie disappeared after mailing several poison pen letters, Mandy was worried. When Hannah found Margie's body in a snowdrift at the Winter Festival, Mandy was ashamed at how relieved she felt.

Later, lying in bed beside a snoring Ed, Mandy stared at the ceiling and let the tears roll down onto the pillow beneath her head. The old feelings of desperation and despair returned, and she wondered what she could do. The problem was she'd been Miranda for so long she'd almost forgotten what it was like to be Melissa. Lying in the dark, crying softly to herself, she remembered.

When Scott knocked on Ian Fitzpatrick's front door, the recently retired police chief answered right away. Scott knew that Ian was a night owl, and through the window, he'd seen the flickering blue glow of the television in their living room.

"Come in, come in," Ian said. "It's good to see you, son."

Scott entered the modest house Ian shared with his wife Delia and followed his former boss to the kitchen. Ian filled the tea kettle and turned on the gas ring.

"Sorry to come by so late," Scott said. "I'm in a tough spot, and I need to talk it through. I hope you don't mind."

Ian put two mugs on the table and dropped a tea bag in each. He sat down across from Scott and took the lid off the sugar bowl.

"I'm always glad to help you, Scott," he said. "What's on your mind?"

"While going through the mail that Margie stole, I found out something about Mandy, something serious enough that Margie was blackmailing her over it."

"Is this about Melissa Wright?" Ian asked.

Scott sat back in surprise as the kettle began to whistle. Ian got up, turned off the gas ring, and poured hot water into each mug.

"You know about that?"

Ian sat back down and put several teaspoons of sugar in his mug.

"Do you really think I'd let some stranger come into my house, sleep under my roof, and break bread at my table if I hadn't thoroughly checked her out beforehand? Her story was flimsy, and she was obviously scared of something or somebody. I got in touch with the Pinellas County Sheriff, and he told me all about it."

"He knew?"

"He lived a few blocks away. He heard the explosion and got there right after it happened. He knew who Melissa was, knew who her husband was. They had all been under surveillance for months. He knew she'd taken the child out of the house and that she wasn't involved in the drug business."

"Did she know he knew?"

"No," Ian said. "She thought he believed her story. He knew what would happen to her and the kid if he took them in. He made a judgment call. I probably would have done the same."

"And you never talked to her about it."

"No need to. I kept a close eye on her, but she never made a false move. She's a good mother to Tommy and a darn hard worker. We may have given her a home, but she's earned everything else she has."

"Under the table, of course."

"Not exactly," Ian said. "I include her wages in with Delia's, and then Delia gives her cash. That way I pay the IRS and the Social Security office, and no one's the wiser."

"It didn't bother you to be covering for her all this time?"

"You have to consider a person's character in context. That girl may not be the sharpest knife in the drawer, but she's got good moral fiber, an exemplary work ethic, and a steel backbone. She was under extraordinary pressure and did the right thing by that boy. I don't regret it for an instant."

"I worked for you for six years," Scott said. "But I didn't know how hard this job could be."

"You're doin' fine," Ian said. "The spirit of the law sometimes comes into conflict with the letter of the law. I prefer to think of law enforcement as more of an art than a science."

"There's a woman claiming to be Miranda's mother who's looking for her. She knows she's here in Rose Hill."

"I thought Miranda was an orphan."

"This woman is looking for the child she gave up for adoption. She's dying and wants to meet Miranda and Tommy before she dies."

"Probably wouldn't know there'd been a switch," Ian said.

"Probably not."

"Well, keep me informed," Ian said. "If I can help her out I'll be glad to. Poor, motherless child."

Scott told Ian about the feds being in town investigating Mrs. Wells.

"She's a piece of work, that one," Ian said. "No soul in her, if you ask me. If she's cornered, she'll kill anyone that gets near her. If Ava's agreed to testify, she's in danger. I don't want Delia over there in the middle of this, but I'm sure my wife will continue to do as she pleases."

"I'm staying at Ava's until this is over," Scott said. "I'll keep an eye on things."

"That'll get the scanner grannies' knickers in a twist," Ian said. "The phone lines will be burning up with that bit of information."

"How come you never cracked down on them?" Scott asked.

"If you want to know something," Ian said, "or you want something to get known, you couldn't ask for a better instrument. They're better than a bullhorn on Rose Hill Avenue."

Scott thanked Ian and walked on down Iris Avenue to Pine Mountain Road, and then turned left and walked up to Rose Hill Avenue. From the corner, he could see the light on in Maggie's apartment. He stood there on the corner and watched until it went out. Then he went to Ava's.

CHAPTER FOUR - Wednesday

Malcolm Behr showed up at the station bright and early, as Scott was enjoying the blueberry muffins and thermos of hot coffee Ava had prepared for him that morning. Malcolm was the town's fire chief and a hairy beast of a man who most people referred to as "Bear."

"You got plans this morning?" Malcolm asked him.

"Nothing that can't be rearranged," Scott said. "Why?"

"Mean Mann just called me. It seems he's got the Corps of Engineers and a special wildlife agent coming down to break up a beaver dam that's blocked Raccoon Creek where it empties into the Little Bear; it's causing some flooding. Mean's got an abscessed tooth and has to have emergency dental surgery, so he wants me and you to oversee the project."

"It must have killed him to call you," Scott said.

"I notice he didn't call you."

"He may hate me just marginally more than he hates you. You should be flattered."

Lieutenant Colonel Harlan "Mean" Mann worked for District One of the State Division of Natural Resources Law Enforcement and was one of the most thoroughly unpleasant men Scott had ever met. He delighted in catching people hunting or fishing out of season and then torturing them during the time that it took the state police to arrive. Mean would not even refer to Hannah, the county domestic animal control officer, by name; he preferred to call her "that female dog catcher" instead. If it were up to Mean, every stray dog or cat would be shot on sight, and there would be no need for an animal control officer.

"I've heard about the Fitzpatricks' latest troubles," Malcolm said. "I'm guessing the ratio of law enforcement to citizens in Rose Hill is high enough right now that you're free to go for a look-see."

Scott had no doubt the scanner grannies had informed Malcolm that Deputy Frank was in the station, Deputy Skip was patrolling Rose Hill in the station's only official car, the feds were watching Ava's bed and breakfast, and the state police were filling up any leftover space.

"I need to go home and get my waders," Scott told him.

"Better bring some dry clothes too," Malcolm warned him as he left the station. "Once we get above the second dam Cal's taking us the rest of the way in his boat, so we're both liable to end up in the river."

Scott met Malcolm and Cal Fisher at the bottom of Pine Mountain Road, which ended in the Little Bear River. Cal Fischer was a certified rescue diver and volunteer firefighter. When Scott arrived, Cal greeted him in a friendly manner, but a little nervously as well. During a recent murder investigation it had come to light that Cal sometimes removed the barriers at the bottom of Pine Mountain Road in order to back his boat into the water, and then cross the river with his dog, a shotgun, and a spotlight, to hunt deer out of season.

The late postmistress Margie knew about this practice and had threatened to tell Mean, who would have enjoyed getting Cal fired from his day job as security guard at the power plant, as well as dismissed from the volunteer fire brigade. In a lucky twist of fate, Mean had burned the letter without opening it because it had no return address, which to his suspicious mind meant that it was probably from terrorists.

With Cal's boat hitched behind his SUV, they drove north from Rose Hill until they reached a river access road above the second dam. Flooding of the Little Bear was controlled by a series of aging stone dams built by the Civilian Conservation Corps during the Great Depression.

The dams were losing integrity every year, but the funds to repair them were always sacrificed during the annual state budget cuts.

"I used to go frog-gigging in Raccoon Creek with my brother Hamish," Malcolm said as they set off in Cal's boat. "We once caught the mayor's wife skinny dipping there with the organist from the Methodist Church."

"Peg Machalvie?" Scott asked.

Cal chuckled.

"They were both three sheets to the wind, singing 'Shall We Gather at the River.' "

"Did the mayor ever find out?" Cal asked.

"Not unless she told him," Malcolm said. "She never could look me in the eye after that. When my mother died, Peg gave me a fifty percent discount on the whole funeral package."

Scott shook his head, saying, "I can't believe that."

"No, it happened," Malcolm said. "Ask Hamish. My only regret about the incident was that it took place before Peg had her boob job."

When the men arrived at the mouth of the creek, they were amazed at the size of the beaver dam, which must have been thirty feet wide and rose six feet out of the water. It extended out into the Little Bear far enough that it was catching a lot of debris. The creek had breached its banks behind the beaver dam, and the low-lying fields on either side were flooded.

There was a group of men standing on the shore, and Curtis Fitzpatrick had backed his wrecker down to a nearby dock, as close as he could get without taking a chance of sliding into the river. One of the men on shore was dressed in a wetsuit, just like Cal had on underneath his parka and coveralls. Cal cut the engine and threw a line to Curtis, who was standing off to one side, looking amused. As soon as they were close enough, Curtis tied up the boat, and the three men jumped onto the dock.

"They're arguing about the best way to do it," Curtis told them. "The man in the rubber suit is worried about hurting the beavers, and these other guys are worried about the possibility of flash flooding downriver once this thing is broken up. The man in the red jacket is the property owner on this side of the river. He plants sorghum in these fields, and he wants his topsoil to stay where it is."

Scott and Malcolm nodded appreciatively.

"Are you worried?" Malcolm asked Curtis.

"Naw," Curtis said with a wink. "I'm being paid by the hour."

The man in the wetsuit entered the water and submerged. Cal stood on the shore, holding a line attached to him. He was only down for a minute or so, but it was peacefully quiet onshore as everyone paused and watched. Scott saw a disturbance beneath the surface on the other side of the dam, and two beavers swam away toward the middle of the river. One of them smacked the water with its tail, and the sound echoed off the nearby hills.

There was a frenzy of movement where the diver had entered the water, and he came up thrashing. Scott's first thought was that he'd been attacked by beavers defending their home. Cal pulled on the line and assisted the man out, and he hurriedly pulled off his breathing apparatus and mask.

"There's a dead guy down there," he said, and then took a few steps across the soggy bank and vomited.

Cal was the one who got called whenever a drowning victim needed to be recovered, so he calmly shed the clothes he wore over his wetsuit, put on his equipment, and gave Malcolm the other end of his line before he waded in. Scott's reaction to dead bodies was more like the first guy's, so he was dreading what came back up. Scott checked his cell phone and saw he had no service. He asked Curtis if he could use his wrecker radio to call in and was glad for an excuse to walk away from the action.

"I never get used to this," Scott told Malcolm after he finished his call and returned to the bank.

"Me neither," Malcolm said.

Cal came back up with the body of a man. It was obvious from the state of it that it had been through some sort of trauma, either before or after it went in the river. They pulled it onto the bank and rolled it over. Lifeless eyes stared at the sky, and it was plain to see the throat had been slit from ear to ear. The absence of blood or a bad smell helped Scott keep his nausea under control.

"Time to call Sarah," Malcolm said to Scott.

Scott glanced up at Curtis, who was crossing himself.

"Can I use your radio again?" he asked Curtis.

Curtis led the way.

"You recognize him?" Scott asked Curtis, as he climbed into the passenger side of the wrecker cab.

"Nope," the older man said. He shook his head, started the engine, and turned the heater way up.

"He looks a little familiar to me," Scott said. "But I can't place him."

"I was afraid it was gonna be Brian," Curtis said, and Scott was taken aback to see the older man wipe his eyes and blow his nose on a big white hankie he took from his back pocket.

"I'm so sorry for what your family is going through," Scott told him. "We're keeping a close eye on Ava and the kids."

Curtis nodded and cleared his throat.

"You do a lot for this family that's never acknowledged," he said to Scott. "We appreciate all you do; we just don't always say."

Scott was touched by that, and it helped salve some of the wounded feelings he'd been having since Maggie had banished him from her life. Although everyone in the

Fitzpatrick family made a point of still being friendly, he was no longer invited into their homes or kept abreast of the latest family gossip.

Scott called the county dispatch, thinking that although this was yet another murder in close proximity to Rose Hill, it was far enough outside the city limits that he wouldn't have to be involved. This was a relief. He'd had enough murder and the subsequent services of county investigator Sarah Albright to last him a lifetime.

The proverbial tall, dark, and handsome man walked into the bookstore. He was dressed in a black trench coat over a gray suit, white shirt, and dark red tie. He approached Maggie with a wide smile as if they already knew each other well. Maggie felt a blush creep up on her face and sighed to herself over her body's lack of subtlety when she was embarrassed by special attention.

"Maggie Fitzpatrick?" he inquired.

"Yes," Maggie said. "Can I help you?"

He kept smiling at her as if they shared some private secret, and delicious as that prospect was, Maggie also felt some apprehension.

"I think so," he said and handed her his card.

"James R. Brown, Federal Bureau of Investigations" it read.

"That's a really lousy cover name," Maggie said. "You might as well use John Smith."

He kept smiling at her as if she was some dear old friend whose rude comments amused him. His eyes fairly twinkled with good humor.

"Unfortunately, James Randolph Brown is my real name," he said. "Although I'm hoping to marry someone with a more interesting last name so I can hyphenate it. Something like 'Fitzpatrick-Brown.' Do you think that would help?"

Maggie thought some Aztec god name would be more appropriate for him, something like 'Hotzytotl.' The man was seriously dreamy, with cheekbones that made her think there was some Native American ancestry in his background.

"I'm guessing this is about my brother," Maggie said.

"I'm sorry, it is," the man replied.

Maggie looked around the bookstore, which had several customers in it.

"I'm covering someone's break right now," she said. "Would you mind to wait until she gets back? We can go to my office."

"I never mind to wait in a bookstore," Agent Brown said with a smile. "That coffee smells good. Can I get you one?"

"No, thanks," Maggie said.

He smiled at her again, and Maggie thought he must be an excellent agent; a man that handsome and charming, she thought she might tell anything he wanted to know.

When Jeanette came back, Maggie told her she had a meeting, and her staff member regarded the agent with appreciation.

"Publisher's rep?" the older woman asked.

"Something like that," Maggie said.

"I'd buy anything he's selling," Jeanette said.

The agent was looking through a copy of the latest Rose Hill Sentinel while sipping a latte in the cafe.

"This is great," he said and gestured with his drink.

"Benjamin is my best barista," Maggie said. "Can we do this in my office?"

"Sure," he said and brought his latte with him into Maggie's small, messy office.

Maggie cleared a chair for him next to her desk and shut the door, so they would have some privacy. The man looked around and nodded with approval.

"In my wildest retirement fantasies, running a place like this is high on the list."

"You're better off keeping it a fantasy."

"Why's that?"

"The profit margin on books is practically nonexistent. I can't compete with online booksellers or big box prices, so I have to rely on sidelines and touristy stuff. The café does a good business, and the college textbooks are a pain in the behind, but they bring in the students who buy the coffee. Unless you're independently wealthy or just plain crazy, Agent Brown, I wouldn't recommend it."

"So, why do you own one?" he asked.

"It's genetic," Maggie said. "This is what Fitzpatricks do. I was working in my parents' bakery before I was big enough to see over the counter; I stood on a milk crate."

"I've had croissants from there; they're delicious."

"Please sit down, Agent Brown," Maggie said.

"Please, call me Jamie," he said.

Jamie took off his overcoat, and Maggie hung it on a hook behind the door. He smelled like spicy vanilla aftershave. They sat down, and Maggie waited for him to begin. He took out his federal ID and showed it to her.

"Just so you know I am who I say I am," he said. "You know why I'm here, obviously. We're interested in your brother's disappearance as related to an investigation we're undertaking, and I'm hoping you're willing to share what you know."

"I'm wondering if I should have a lawyer present."

"I've already spoken with your brother Sean and your sister-in-law Ava, and if you'd like to call either of them to check me out, I understand completely."

"I'm going to be honest with you, Jamie. The most important thing in the world to me is my family. I'll do anything to protect them. My brother Brian has lost the privilege of being called family. If you've already talked to Ava and Sean, you know all the reasons why. I don't know what else I could tell you."

"I understand you have a letter," he said, "from Gabriel Cortez."

Maggie felt sick. She'd expected all sorts of questions but nothing that involved Gabe. Jamie was looking at her compassionately. Maggie knew she would have to share it sooner or later, and later might include a subpoena. She got up and went to the back wall of the office, opened the safe, and then used a key that only she possessed to open a locked box inside the safe.

The letter, from her ex-boyfriend Gabe, had only recently come into her possession after being hidden in Margie Estep's attic for seven years. Part of the reason she and Scott weren't speaking was that he found the letter and didn't immediately give it to her; she found it after he accidentally dropped it. The other reason was detailed in the letter itself.

The paper was now creased and somewhat tear-stained. Jamie treated the letter with care as if he understood how precious it was to her, and he took his time reading it.

When he finished, he said, "I'd like a copy."

Maggie had a small fax/printer/copier in her office and made a copy for him before returning the letter to the box in the safe.

"I've met him," he said. "He seems like a nice guy."

"Who, Scott?"

"No, your ex. Gabriel."

Maggie felt like she'd been punched in the gut.

"When did you see him?" she asked.

"Last week, in Florida."

"I didn't know what happened," Maggie said. "He just disappeared one night. I don't even know if he's telling the truth in the letter. It turns out I didn't really know him at all."

"He said when I saw you to tell you he's truly sorry he hurt you."

Maggie felt tears well up. Even though she thought she'd cried all she could over Gabe, she continued to find fresh grief with every revelation.

"He's getting out," Jamie said.

"I thought he got ten years," she said.

"He's been a model prisoner, and he's agreed to help us with our investigation in exchange for an early release."

"Where will he go when he comes out?"

"Mrs. Crawford has agreed to let him stay with her."

"Lily Crawford?" she asked. "How did Lily get involved?"

"She's agreed to be responsible for him. She even offered to put up any bond necessary."

"But why would Lily do that?" Maggie asked.

Maggie reflected that Lily knew them both well, and had been fond of Gabe, but not as anything more than a dear friend and neighbor. If Jamie knew more, he wasn't saying.

"When will he be here?" she asked.

"In a few days," Jamie said.

"Great," Maggie said. "Whether I like it or not."

"I know this is hard for you," Jamie said. "I hate to be the one to bring you news that upsets you."

"Is there anything else?" Maggie asked him. She wanted him to go so she could think.

"You saw your brother in prison before he escaped," Jamie said.

"Yes," Maggie said. "He was worried someone inside was going to kill him. He said there was a price on his head."

"Did he mention any names?"

"He said someone named Mrs. Wells was paying for the hit. He said even though Ava was paying back the money he 'borrowed,' it was personal between them. She wanted revenge."

"Anything else?"

"He said he was sorry about what happened to Gabe."

"He apologized?"

"Oh, not to me, or to his wife and kids, or anyone else in our family. No, Brian doesn't think we count, for some reason. But he said Gabe wasn't involved in what he did, just happened to be in the wrong place at the wrong time, and took the fall for it."

"Have you heard from Brian since he escaped?"

"No. I figure he's long gone from here, don't you?"

"We don't know."

"If he contacts me I'll let you know. I wouldn't help him."

"I got that feeling," Jamie said.

"It's like living in my own personal soap opera," Maggie told him. "I just wish it would end."

"Would your parents help him?"

"Of course," Maggie said. "They still think it's all some huge mistake. We haven't told them everything, trying to protect them. I don't want them to be hurt any more than they already have been."

"It will all come out at the trial, you know. What about your brother Patrick?"

"He wouldn't help Brian. He'll tell you anything you want to know."

"Is there some particular reason Patrick and Brian don't get along?"

"Same as with me," Maggie said. "Brian's a jerk."

"Your sister-in-law seems anxious that Patrick not be involved."

"She's just trying to protect everyone," Maggie said. "There's no reason for you not to talk to Patrick."

"Can you think of any place Brian might go to hide?"

"No," Maggie said. "Up until a few weeks ago, I hadn't seen or heard from him in over six years. Can I ask you something?"

"Sure."

"You seem too nice to be a fed."

"Is that a question?"

"How does somebody decide to be an FBI agent?"

"I was a paperweight for a long time," he said.

"A paperweight?"

"I sat at a desk, papers came and went, and I stared at a computer all day every day. I went to lots of meetings. I was really bored."

"Then what happened?"

"I applied for more active duty."

"When was this?"

"About five years ago."

"How many cases have you been on?"

"Just this one."

"For five years?"

"It's complicated; there's a long history and a widespread network. Careful, methodical work is more likely to bring about the desired result."

"Not a lot of gunplay, then."

"No," he laughed. "No shoot-outs so far. Just a lot of interesting connections and coincidences."

"Which you can't tell me about."

"No, sorry."

"I get the feeling you know a lot more about me than I think. Am I paranoid?"

"I do know a lot about you. You're a pivotal person in this case. Your brother, ex-boyfriend, sister-in-law, and the police chief you dated are all involved in some way. I recently got to see the video of your meeting with your brother in prison."

"So there was no reason to ask me about it."

"Sorry, I have to corroborate facts. It's part of my job."

"What part of me telling off my brother inspired you most?"

"Well, your passion, for one thing. I thought, 'I'd hate to be on the wrong side of this woman.' But I also thought, 'What a woman to have in your corner.'"

"You said Scott was involved. Not in a bad way, I'm sure."

"He's not in any trouble."

"He's a good man," Maggie said. "You can count on him."

"I can understand why he might bend the law a little for you. I might have done the same. I take it that relationship is over?"

"Yes," said Maggie. "No use dragging him down with us."

"Are you quite sure about that?" Jamie said.

"I finally quit fooling myself," Maggie said. "There doesn't seem to be any point in believing my life is ever going to be normal or my family any saner. If you know all there is to know about us you must agree."

"A lot of families are weird and crazy."

"Rose Hill definitely has a higher percentage. You'll find out I'm right."

"Well, here's my card," Jamie said as he stood up. "Please call me if you hear from Brian or think of anything that might be helpful."

"Are you undercover? Do you want me to say you're a book rep?"

"I don't mind people knowing who I am, but please don't share what we talked about."

"No problem."

Jamie put on his coat and then stuck out his hand to shake Maggie's. His handshake was warm, strong, and set off some alarm bells in Maggie's own department of defense.

"It's been such a pleasure to meet you," he said. "I'm sure we'll cross paths again before this is all over. I'm looking forward to it."

He gave her a warm, knowing smile that implied the pleasure wasn't purely professional. Maggie blushed again.

After he left, Jeanette stuck her head inside the office.

"That was a damn fine looking man. I hope you bought a lot of whatever he's selling."

"I did," Maggie said. "I bought the whole package."

Hannah received a call from Caroline Eldridge, begging her to come out to her house and evict some raccoons. A self-determined spiritualist explorer, Caroline had inherited the lodge from her older brother, the recently murdered Theo. It was a stone and timber Craftsman era mansion that sat high atop a ridge between Rose Hill and the ski resort town of Glencora, overlooking Gerrymaine Valley and Bear Lake. The snow was still thick on the ground up there, and the temperature was always ten degrees lower than in Rose Hill.

One of the Buddhist monks currently staying at the lodge answered Hannah's ring outside the heavy front door. She was surprised to find he was a man about her size, with light, freckled skin, hazel eyes, and wire-rimmed glasses. His head was shaved, but Hannah could tell his hair had been a mousy brown, much like her own. The incongruence of the camouflage-print thermal underwear shirt and leggings he wore underneath his bright orange robe was disconcerting at first. He also had on heavy wool hunting socks with his sandals.

The man bowed deeply with his hands in a prayer formation in front of him. This was Hannah's first experience with a monk of any persuasion, and she wasn't quite sure what to do. Caroline had told her on the phone that she shouldn't talk to them, but how in the world could she communicate what she wanted?

"Hiya," she said finally after they each bowed to each other a few times. "Is Caroline home? She said there was a raccoon family living in the ceiling of the garage apartment. I'm going to try and catch them for her."

The monk backed toward the kitchen, bowing continually. Hannah followed him. As soon as they entered the kitchen, he disappeared into what used to be the dining room. As he opened the door, Hannah could hear chanting, and the scent of sandalwood incense wafted in.

Caroline was sitting at the kitchen table, her head in her hands.

Hannah cleared her throat.

"Oh, Hannah," Caroline said as she looked up.

"You okay?" Hannah asked.

"I'm fine," Caroline said. "It's nothing a few days of warm weather wouldn't cure."

"It won't be warm up here until June," Hannah said. "You may need to take a vacation before that."

"I can't go anywhere while the monks are here," Caroline said. "There's too much to do, and I have to take care of them."

"How long are they staying?"

"Who knows?" Caroline said with a sigh.

"That's a pity," Hannah said.

"Oh, no," Caroline said. "It's a privilege to have them here; any inconvenience to me is far outweighed by the greater good. I'm not suffering at all; suffering is just an illusion."

"Are the raccoons you called about real?" Hannah asked, "Because I can't justify the mileage on imaginary ones."

"They're real and extremely noisy," Caroline said. "I don't want them harmed in any way, just relocated, if possible. They're keeping Petula and Sven awake at night, and heaven knows we all need our sleep; we get so little of it as it is. Not that I'm complaining. Some yogis go for months without sleep or food. I'm not quite that evolved yet. It helps that I'm vegan even though I'm considering becoming a fruitarian. It's just that there is so little organic fruit available and you have to be sure it fell off the trees naturally and wasn't removed forcibly; fruitarians consider that murder. You can't be sure of the cruelty-free purity of the fruit when it's shipped in..."

"That's all really interesting," Hannah interrupted. "But I need to get started if you don't mind. I have a humane trap I can set up, and once they're caught, I'll relocate them somewhere else. We need to figure out how they got in, though, and seal it up."

"Sven will do that," Caroline said. "He's handy. Have you met Petula and Sven? They're from Stockholm. I met them at a conference in Seattle. They're both Reiki masters and have completed all but the most secret levels of a Sacred Energy Medicine course I was involved in for a while. They're working for me to earn money to pay for the last module. Once they complete the training, they'll be able to manipulate the electromagnetic field that surrounds us, that connects us all. It's powerful magic and not just anyone can do it; you have to be born with the gift. Not many people understand the importance of the electromagnetic field. Did you know cell phones interrupt the radar that bees use to navigate? That's why they're disappearing at such a fast rate. It affects humans and animals as well, but most people aren't sensitive enough to detect the changes in the atmosphere..."

Hannah wondered if maybe Caroline was starved for someone to talk to. The simplest question seemed to trigger a chronic bout of verbal diarrhea. Hannah's attention wandered to the decorations tacked to the walls of the kitchen. One, in particular, caught her eye.

"Um, Caroline," Hannah said, as soon as Caroline stopped long enough to take a breath. "Who's the monster guy?"

She pointed to a large poster on the wall featuring what looked like a fierce, blue man-beast with long, pointy teeth holding a large wheel with his long, pointy claws. Each section of the wheel between the spokes had a little scene of Asian characters in different situations, some of which looked pretty dire.

"That's Yama, holding the wheel of time," Caroline said. "He's a Tibetan Buddhist deity who protects Buddhists. He was a monk who planned to meditate in a cave for fifty years in order to achieve enlightenment. In the last month of the forty-ninth year, robbers brought a stolen bull into his cave and cut off its head. When they realized Yama had seen them do it, they cut off his head as well."

"No wonder he looks so mad."

"Yama put on the severed bull's head and terrorized all of Tibet. Finally, Manjushri, Bodhisattva of Wisdom, manifested as an even scarier deity and defeated him. Yama then became a protector of Buddhism."

"It looks like he's holding one of those View-Master disks like we had when we were kids."

"That's the karmic wheel of life. The six realms represent samsara, into which beings are reborn. The nature of one's existence is determined by karma, and these are the stages a soul goes through before reaching enlightenment."

"I thought Buddhists were all peaceful and laid back," Hannah said. "That scene right there looks more like hellfire and brimstone."

Caroline looked at Hannah as if she were an idiot.

"If you want to learn more, I'd be glad to lend you some books," Caroline said. "The monks teach a course of study in Zen Buddhism here at the lodge if you're interested."

"No, but thanks anyway," Hannah said. "I'm currently blacklisted at Sacred Heart and the Methodist Church. No use pissing off the Buddhists as well."

"It's very interesting..." Caroline began, but Hannah interrupted, "I'm sorry I can't chat longer, but I need to get started."

Caroline went to her office to get the key to the garage apartment, and then got sidetracked by a phone call. Hannah looked around the room. The monk who had answered the door came back in, bowed to Hannah and then stood quietly nearby, placid and calm.

"So, no talking, huh?"

He smiled kindly at Hannah and nodded.

"Now, see," Hannah said, "that alone would keep me from being a good monk. I like to talk too much."

The man continued to smile benevolently.

"I thought all of you would be Asian," Hannah said. "I guess that was small-minded of me, thinking every Buddhist would look like the Dalai Lama. You actually look more like my brother Quinn. We always wish Quinn would sit still and shut up for a few days."

There was a small poster held by magnets on the refrigerator titled "The Five Hindrances," and Hannah gestured to it.

"Things to watch out for?" she said. "Like the seven deadly sins?"

The man nodded.

She read out loud, "Sensual Desire, Ill-Will, Sloth, Worry, and Doubt."

The monk nodded again.

"Sounds more like Caroline's to-do list," Hannah said.

The man's eyes twinkled, and Hannah thought she detected the telltale signs of suppressed laughter.

"Careful," she said. "You'll have to say ten Hail Buddhas if you laugh."

Caroline came in with the key, and everybody bowed to everybody all over again.

"Thanks, so much," Caroline told Hannah as she handed her the key. "I appreciate your help."

"Anytime," Hannah said as she went out. "I'll bring the key back in a bit."

As Hannah removed the humane trap from the back of her truck a large, dark sedan came up the curving drive and parked in front of the lodge. Hannah dawdled so she could see who was in it. She was surprised to see bank president and political ass-kisser Knox Rodefeffer exit the vehicle and hurry up the steps to Caroline's front door.

Knox was a large, ungainly man with blinding white capped teeth and an unconvincing toupee. Although she personally found him horribly unattractive, Hannah had heard that his sexy secretary was also his mistress. Knox loved to name-drop his political connections and brag about his trips to Washington, D.C. If Rose Hill was a small pond, Knox was one of the biggest bottom feeders.

Hannah wondered what business he had with Caroline Eldridge, and concluded he must be trying to get Caroline to put money in his bank, or to write a big fat check to one of his political cronies. Caroline had pledged to provide a match for a grant application Hannah and Drew were writing, to start a feral cat program and build a no-kill animal shelter. Hannah hoped Caroline hadn't forgotten about that and thought she might mention it again before she left.

Hannah set a trap for the raccoon family and then poked around the eaves until she found where they were getting in and out. She took the key to the apartment back to the lodge house and saw that Knox's car was gone.

When she rang the doorbell, a different monk answered. This man was tall with cocoa-colored skin and warm, friendly brown eyes. He too wore the camouflage undergarments that seemed so bizarre underneath the orange one-shouldered robe. He backed bowing to the kitchen and Hannah followed. He led her through the kitchen to Theo's old study where Caroline Eldridge sat staring at a stack of paperwork that looked like contracts.

"Sorry to bother you," Hannah said.

Caroline obviously hadn't heard her enter the room; she jumped, startled, and quickly covered up the paperwork.

"No bother at all," she said.

Caroline's eyes darted back and forth from Hannah to the paperwork on the desk. She offered Hannah some herbal tea, and Hannah, whose terminal nosiness compensated for her dislike of healthy food, accepted. As Caroline led her back into the kitchen, she started talking again. Hannah sat down at the kitchen table, plopped her elbows on top, and rested her chin on her hands. She knew she might as well get comfy.

"I'm hosting the monks because their temple burned down in a California wildfire and their abbot died," Caroline said. "The woman who'd been taking care of them basically dumped them on my doorstep and ran back to California. She said they did nothing but meditate, chant, eat, and sleep. I thought they would be easy to take care of."

"Like a large bowl of Buddhist fish," Hannah suggested, but Caroline wasn't listening.

"The actual amount of work involved is overwhelming," Caroline said. "I hired staff to take over most of the household work. That's made a huge difference, but an expensive one. I hate bookkeeping or anything to do with finances, but I finally sat down this morning with a calculator and a stack of bills, and I can't continue on this way indefinitely. Sacrifices will have to be made."

Hannah thought to herself, 'There goes my grant match.'

"But what can I give up?" Caroline said as she poured hot water over what looked like a handful of dried sticks and leaves. "I'm not giving up Callie; she's a vegan chef and prepares all the meals, plus she does all the shopping and cleaning up afterward. I'm not giving up Petula; she cleans the lodge and washes all the sheets and towels, which in itself is a full-time job. And I'm certainly not getting rid of Sven; he takes care of the grounds and keeps all the vehicles running, including the snow blower and the truck with the plow blade. I can't do this without them."

Caroline poured Hannah a cup of tea from a pretty porcelain teapot and sat opposite her at the table. Hannah considered the vegetation floating in her cup and decided not to risk it.

"I thought you had a big trust fund," Hannah said. "Didn't Theo leave you some money?"

"Theo's bequest will be tied up in probate for at least a year," Caroline said. "The majority of my family trust payments are pledged to other charities."

"What will you do?" Hannah asked, mustering up her most sympathetic look.

A quiet rustling sound and a slight stir of the air caused them both to look up, and they saw one of the monks standing in the doorway opposite. He bowed to Caroline and Hannah. Caroline turned, then rose and responded in kind.

The monk handed Caroline a note, which she read to herself.

"Fine," she said, although Hannah detected more than a little irritation in her tone. The man bowed his way back the way he came in.

"It's a list of more supplies they need," Caroline said as she sat back down. "Please excuse me while I say a quick positive affirmation to release the negative feelings I'm having."

"Sure," Hannah said. "Knock yourself out."

"I am one with the universe," Caroline chanted. "Omni padme ohm."

She repeated this several times before she opened her eyes and took a deep breath.

"Feel better?" Hannah said.

"I expected when I offered to host the group that I'd spend my days meditating and chanting with them," Caroline said. "Unfortunately there's more to do than there are hours in a day, and by the time my chores are done I'm too exhausted to meditate without falling asleep."

"So kick them out," Hannah said. "You tried, and it didn't work out. They're grown men; they should be able to look after themselves."

"This is a test," Caroline said. "I need to let go of my ego's need to be rewarded in some way for my efforts. I need to be more selfless. I need to let go of my attachment to outcomes."

"They need to let go of their attachment to being waited on hand and foot," Hannah said, "while you pay the bills."

"I need to meditate on this," Caroline said. "My inner guide will tell me what to do."

"How do you do that, exactly?" Hannah asked. "Meditate, I mean."

"I'll show you," Caroline said.

She kicked off her clogs, retrieved a special cushion, and sat cross-legged on the floor.

"I clear my mind of my left brain chatter," she said. "I repeat my mantra, over and over; the first part with each breath in, the second part with each breath out. I picture a pinpoint of light in my solar plexus, and concentrate on growing it with each breath until I fill my entire body with radiant white light."

Caroline narrated her progress as Hannah watched. She described the light radiating out from deep within her rib cage, slowly moving outward, growing brighter and stronger as it spread throughout her body. She'd got only as far as her elbows and knees when she was interrupted again.

"Excuse me," someone said.

Caroline sighed and opened her eyes. The interrupter was Petula, the female half of the tall, blonde

Scandinavian husband and wife team who looked after the house and grounds.

"I'm so sorry to bother you, but one of the upstairs toilets has overflowed," she said. "I turned off the water supply at the base, but there's a huge mess. Sven's in Rose Hill picking up supplies, Callie's shopping for groceries, and I have the rest of the bedrooms and bathrooms to clean before they break for lunch. Could you help me?"

Caroline took a few deep breaths and stretched her neck to each side before she rose and accepted the mop and bucket Petula was holding.

"Are you angry?" Petula asked her, with real fear in her voice.

"No," Caroline said, "of course not. Anger is a poison and an obstacle to enlightenment."

"I hated to interrupt," Petula said, "but if I get off schedule now I'll never get caught up."

"It's no problem," Caroline told her with a tight smile. "I appreciate all you do. I am blessed by your work. Namaste."

Petula crept out, and Hannah offered to help. Caroline seemed sincerely grateful as she accepted the offer.

As Caroline mopped up the sewage that covered the bathroom floor, Hannah carried the buckets to the nearest working toilet. She could hear Caroline muttering something.

"What's that you're saying?" Hannah said.

"My loving-kindness mantra," Caroline replied. "It helps me remember to love myself and have compassion for others."

"If I were you I'd be chanting the bus schedule back to wherever they came from," Hannah said.

Maggie Fitzpatrick walked across the street from her bookstore to the grocery store to pick up some milk for the cappuccino bar. Inside the small store, she was surprised to see Anne Marie Rodefeffer, who had been in a serious car accident back in January. After Anne Marie woke up from her coma and was recovered enough to travel, her husband, Knox, whisked her away on a cruise, which he seemed to keep extending.

It was no secret Knox had rabid political aspirations. Anne Marie, with her drug problems and penchant for seducing college boys, had been a constant source of embarrassment to her husband. Although he had an airtight alibi, he was still suspected of arranging for his wife's accident.

"Maggie!" Anne Marie called out to her, in a much more friendly tone than she'd ever used before.

The tall, attractive blonde ran over to Maggie and gave her a tight hug, which surprised her. Before her accident, Anne Marie had always snubbed her or looked down her nose at Maggie.

"Hi Anne Marie," Maggie said. "When did you get back?"

Anne Marie was built like a tall, thin fashion model, and usually dressed like one. Today, however, she wasn't decked out in designer rags but was casual in jeans, turtleneck, and a ski parka. Maggie had never seen her dressed down this much, sans perfect hair and makeup, and gawked a little. Anne Marie's hair was still streaked blonde, but instead of being arranged in an artfully tousled and shellacked helmet, it was pulled back in a simple ponytail. She wore none of her chunky jewelry or oversized, insignia-encrusted handbags, only a gold crucifix on a chain and a cloth tote bag.

"I know Knox told everyone I was on a cruise, but since I found the Lord I don't lie anymore," Anne Marie said. "I was actually in a rehabilitation facility for my sex, drug, and alcohol addictions, and it was the best thing that ever happened to me."

Maggie heard an inner warning bell go off at the mention of "the Lord," but she was trapped between Anne Marie and the refrigerated dairy case so she couldn't escape. She'd heard rumors about Anne Marie going to rehab a few times before, but the transformation she seemed to have undergone this time was striking. Her eyes were sparkling, the color was high in her cheeks, and she was beaming a little too intensely. She was also standing too close, and the effect of all her bright energy was somewhat overwhelming.

"I'm so glad you feel better," Maggie said. "We were all worried about you after your accident."

"You know, I don't remember a thing about it," Anne Marie said. "And it's just as well. I'm a new person now. Like the song says, 'I was lost, and now I'm found.' The old Anne Marie died and was born again, praise the Lord."

"Well, you certainly look different," Maggie said. "Really well, I mean to say. Healthy."

"I won't lie to you, Maggie," she responded, grabbing Maggie's hand and clutching it. "I was headed for Hell, as low as I could go; there was nothing I wouldn't do. Since I found our Lord Jesus Christ, I only need His love and His word to be fulfilled. I'd love to sit and talk with you about it. I want to share my story, and bring as many other people to the Lord as I can."

"Maybe some other time," Maggie said. "I need to get back to work. We ran out of milk, you see..."

"You have to take the time, Maggie. It's more important than anything else you could be doing. You being Catholic, well, you need to know the truth about how dangerously close you are to being banished to the eternal fire pits of Hell for following pagan papist teachings. You have to come to the true Jesus in the right way before it's too late."

Over Anne Marie's shoulder, Maggie could see Fran, the checkout clerk, making the cuckoo sign.

"Okay, Anne Marie, that's all I can take today," Maggie said. "We're going to have to respect the right to choose our own religion and practice it without judging each other."

"I can't respect your false idol worship, Maggie. The judgment of your sins will come by fire, and all the believers in heathen religions will feel the flames of God's wrath. Truly this shall come to pass unless they give their lives to Jesus Christ Almighty and serve only Him. It is only by being born again into Jesus's one true faith that you can be saved and not perish in the eternal flames of damnation."

"I'm going to go now, Anne Marie. You take care."

Maggie hurriedly paid Fran for her milk and left the store, worried Anne Marie was going to follow. But Anne Marie had already accosted someone else and was busy trying to save that person's soul.

Maggie thought she'd seen the last of Anne Marie that day, but she was wrong. Less then an hour later Maggie was sitting in her office, up to her neck in invoices that needed to be paid, when Jeanette tapped on the office window. She gestured urgently for Maggie to come out into the store.

When Maggie came out of her office, she saw Anne Marie playing tug of war with a scowling ten-year-old boy. They were pulling so hard on a book that the binding was coming apart. Several other books were splayed out on the floor of the children's section.

"It's for my book report," the boy said. "My teacher assigned it."

"It's blasphemy!" Anne Marie said. "It's the work of the devil!"

Maggie saw red.

"Stop it!" she yelled at Anne Marie, who dropped her end of the book. The child fell over, and Jeanette helped him up.

"Maggie, we have to start with the children," Anne Marie said as she came toward her, hands out in a pleading way.

Her pupils were dilated, and Maggie could have sworn she was high. A group of people had gathered to watch, and Maggie motioned for Anne Marie to follow her back to her office.

"Sit!" Maggie said as soon as she had the woman inside with the door shut.

"Those books teach witchcraft and black magic," Anne Marie insisted as she sat down. "Our children are open conduits for Satan. You must be strict in their teaching to save them from becoming tools of the devil."

Maggie wanted to say 'those books encourage children to read and use their imaginations,' but she knew it was useless to argue with someone who was mentally ill. Instead, she held up one finger to indicate Anne Marie should wait, and with the other hand she called the bank and asked for Knox.

Anne Marie slouched back in her chair and pouted when she heard Maggie ask to speak to her husband.

"Knox is an unrepentant sinner, a fornicating liar, and he cannot stop me from doing the Lord's work," Anne Marie said but stayed seated.

"Knox," Maggie said when she got him on the line. "Your wife is in my store disrupting my business, and you have exactly two minutes to come get her before I call Scott."

"I'll be right there," he said and hung up.

"Anne Marie," Maggie said. "What kind of rehab did you go to that you learned all this religious information?"

"It wasn't the rehab. Those sinners were as godless as their watered-down talk of a 'higher power.' The Lord led me to meet Reverend Cowbell there. He's a righteous man of God who was forced into treatment. Some evil, soulless children made false accusations against him and practiced their witchcraft on the congregation of his church."

"Was he accused of abusing the children?"

"He was persecuted by their heinous lies. Satan spoke through them when he saw how powerful and righteous Reverend Cowbell had become. Children are more susceptible than we realize. You have to be strict with them and beat the devil out of them, if necessary. Reverend Cowbell was trying to save the children, not harm them."

Maggie thought Reverend Cowbell was lucky the judge chose rehab over prison.

"How did you get involved with the reverend?"

"I had a spiritual experience when I was in my coma. I saw Jesus, and He spoke to me. No one in our group at rehab would accept that Jesus spoke to me; not the counselors, not the other sinners; no one but Reverend Cowbell. He realized he'd been sent there to guide me, to help me accomplish what Jesus wants me to do."

"What did Jesus tell you to do?"

"He said it wasn't my time to go, that I had to come back and help people."

"Couldn't that be interpreted in a lot of ways? Couldn't you volunteer at a food bank or raise money for cancer research?"

"I don't expect you to understand. Reverend Cowbell was sent by Jesus to guide me. He saw the Jesus light that shines in me. Jesus sent me back to save the world and Reverend Cowbell is going to help me do it."

"What does the reverend think you should do?"

"I'm going to help him start a new church. He wants me to be his conduit to the Lord's almighty power. Many may rise up against us, it has been prophesied, but we will persevere. When we die, we will ascend to heaven to be with the Lord!"

Maggie could see how someone like the rich and mentally vulnerable Anne Marie might appeal to someone like Reverend Cowbell, with her ability to help him realize his spiritual ambitions while transcending a particularly difficult and expensive legal situation.

"Well, you are special, Anne Marie, there's no doubt about that. I'm glad you're off the drugs and feeling good. However, if you come in here again and cause a ruckus, I'm going to have to ban you, and if you cause any problems after that, I'll have you arrested."

Knox appeared at Maggie's office door, breathless, his face covered in beads of perspiration.

"I'll pray for you," Anne Marie said to Maggie as Knox opened the door. "You're on the wrong road, asleep at the wheel, and I only hope you'll awaken before it's too late."

"I'm so sorry," said Knox, his face flushed as much from embarrassment as physical exertion. Maggie was impressed. Knox Rodefeffer was unaccustomed to both aerobic exercise and making apologies.

"Come along," he told his wife.

Anne Marie grabbed Maggie's hand in an iron grip and squeezed her eyes shut. Maggie tugged but could not get free. Anne Marie moaned some words Maggie could not understand. Knox tried to pry Anne Marie's hands off Maggie's but failed. Maggie felt the heat from Anne Marie's grip increase until it felt unbearably hot. Anne Marie opened her eyes, but Maggie could tell she wasn't seeing anything in the room.

"Your sin is pride," Anne Marie said in a low voice. "You must forgive those who have sinned against you. Beware the serpent that appears as an angel."

"Stop it!" Knox hissed at Anne Marie, who looked at him with venomous hatred.

"Your sins are legion," she told her husband. "Your corruption makes the angels weep. Your harlot stinks of your rutting lust. I can smell it every time I'm near her."

"That's enough," Knox said, as he took her by the arm. Miraculously, Anne Marie went with him, docile as a lamb.

Jeanette had cleaned up the mess in the children's section and stuck her head in Maggie's office.

"What was that all about?" Jeanette asked.

"Poor Anne Marie," Maggie said. "She's gone off the deep end."

Maggie couldn't even muster up enough schadenfreude to call and laugh with Hannah about what happened; it was just too sad. She started to call Scott but remembered she was still mad at him. She sighed instead and went back to her invoices. Anne Marie's words reverberated in her ears, however, and she found it hard to concentrate. When she thought about people she needed to forgive, she immediately pictured Gabe and Scott. When she thought about charming snakes, funnily enough, it was Agent Jamie Brown who came to mind.

CHAPTER FIVE - Wednesday/Thursday

Ed Harrison heard about the body being pulled out of the river and rushed to the scene with his camera. By the time he arrived the county morgue van was there, and they were zipping up the body bag. Scott allowed him to look at the corpse, but not to take photographs of it.

"I know him," Ed said. "His name's Ray. He's a bartender at the Roadhouse."

Sarah was there, and she shoved everyone aside to get to Ed.

"When did you last see him?" she asked and clicked on her handheld tape recorder.

Ed was taken aback, but after a glance at Scott, who nodded his head, he answered.

"Last summer. He plays on their softball team. He's their right fielder."

"Last name?"

"I don't remember. I have it on the team roster at the office."

Sarah nodded at Scott.

"Take him back to his office, get that name, and call me."

Scott nodded, gritted his teeth, and turned to Ed.

"Will you give me a ride?"

"Sure thing," Ed said, looking amused at his friend being bossed around so thoroughly, and hating every moment of it.

Malcolm Behr stayed behind, waiting for Sarah to say if they would be allowed to break up the beaver dam. It may have been a murder site, but it was also a serious flood threat. According to the National Weather Service, there was a warm front on the way, and it was bringing foul weather. If the snow base in the mountains melted rapidly, and if something wasn't done about the beaver dam, the ensuing deluge would endanger Rose Hill.

As soon as they were bumping up the muddy track that led from the river to the main road, Ed cleared his throat.

"I didn't tell Sarah everything," he said.

"Why not?"

"I wanted to talk to you first."

"I thought maybe it was because she accused you of killing Theo Eldridge," Scott said.

"That's the kind of thing that's hard to forget."

Ed had been the one to find Theo's body, and subsequently, Sarah made him her number one suspect.

"So spill it," Scott said.

"A few weeks ago I went to see Phyllis out at the Roadhouse to find out to whom she'd rented her trailer. I got this notion that Brian was hiding out there, and it turned out he was. Ray overheard me talking about Brian, and he followed me outside afterward. He said there was a price on Brian's head for stealing half a million dollars of some drug kingpin's money. He said the reward was fifty grand, and he hinted that he would like to collect it."

"Did you know Brian escaped from prison?"

"I heard the scanner granny gossip but there's been nothing on the news and no law enforcement agency will confirm it."

Scott told him as much as he knew from talking to Sarah.

"They have dogs and every uniform from the county to the National Guard out looking for him, but he seems to have disappeared."

"He's good at that."

"I'm thinking maybe Brian tangled with Ray and killed him," Scott said.

"Wait a minute, here's another thing Ray said to me," Ed said. "When I asked who the kingpin was he said it was someone who ate guys like Theo Eldridge for breakfast, and that he would tell me who, but he didn't want me to end up floating down the Little Bear with my throat cut."

"Way, way off the record I can tell you that 'kingpin' is actually a woman named Mrs. Wells. She probably sent someone to kill Ray."

"For helping Brian?"

"Or over some other drug-related business."

"Should I have told Sarah all this?"

"Probably. Don't worry about it. You can always say you remembered later. There's an FBI agent in town I'd like you to talk to. That's also off the record, by the way. Not for print."

"You're making it very difficult for me to practice my profession."

"If I didn't trust you I'd just say, 'no comment.'"

"Like everyone else I call for confirmation," Ed said. "If I could print uncorroborated gossip, I wouldn't have any problem filling my columns."

"Remember your journalistic integrity," Scott said.

"Oh, I do," Ed said. "It's what's keeping me from paying the light bill."

Ed found Ray's last name on the softball roster from the previous summer. Scott called Sarah and gave her the information, but didn't add all that Ed had told him. He wanted to talk to the federal agent first. Scott left Ed at the newspaper office and walked up Pine Mountain Road to Ava's bed and breakfast. Maggie's Aunt Delia was working the front desk, and Scott noticed she was looking tired.

"Hey, Delia," Scott said as he approached the front desk, "are you feeling okay?"

I don't think I can do this much longer," she said. "I'm helping out at the bakery and the pub, and my own house is a filthy mess."

"Doesn't Ava have anyone else to help her? What about those girls she hired?"

"With all that's going on she doesn't want to put the girls at risk," she said, with a pointed look.

He didn't know how much Delia knew, but it seemed as if she knew quite a bit.

"Ah, I see," Scott said. "Maybe Ava should close for a while."

"Oh no," Delia said. "Everything has to look normal; as if I can remember what normal looks like. Since Theo Eldridge died, this whole town seems to be coming apart at the seams."

Scott was taken aback by Delia's pessimistic tone. She was usually the one who bucked up everyone else.

"Don't let this make you sick," Scott said. "I'll have a word with Ava."

"Don't bother," Delia said. "She's got her hands full with that FBI agent."

"Agent Brown is here to protect Ava and the kids," Scott said.

"He's definitely keeping her under close surveillance," Delia said.

"As long as Brian is out there somewhere, we all have to be on our guard, but Ava may be in real danger."

"I understand you're staying here nights."

"Only until they catch Brian," he said. "I'm sleeping on the couch."

"Mmm hmm," Delia said. "You be careful, Scott. I love Ava, but she has a way of taking advantage. Be careful you don't end up in the same boat as Patrick."

Scott was further surprised by this comment. Not many people knew about that affair.

"It's just for her safety, nothing more," Scott protested. "Ava didn't ask me to do it, I offered."

"Of course not," Delia said. "She never has to."

Before Scott could interpret this comment, they were interrupted by a guest entering through the front door. Delia waved Scott back toward the hallway to the kitchen, saying "They're back there."

When Scott entered the kitchen, he found Ava and Jamie seated close to one another at the kitchen island, drinking coffee and talking in low voices. Ava jumped up when Scott entered the room. Jamie's face was inscrutable, but Ava looked embarrassed. This expression was immediately replaced with a warm smile, and Ava greeted him with a brief but tender hug and a kiss on the cheek.

"Scott, I'm so glad you're here."

Scott decided he shouldn't take to heart anything Delia said when she was so tired. Ava was a naturally warm and friendly woman, and no one should read anything more into it than that. He did feel a little buzz whenever he was in Ava's presence, but he assumed every man did.

"Delia seems a little frazzled," Scott said. "Isn't there anyone else who can cover the desk so she can go home?"

"Oh no," Ava said. "I feel so awful. I'll go up and take over. You two can talk."

Ava lifted Little Fitz out of his high chair, where he had been carefully picking up rings of oat cereal and trying to put them in his mouth. The baby waved a pudgy hand and garbled some sounds as Ava carried him out of the room.

Scott told Jamie about Ray's body being found and what Ed had said. Jamie didn't respond with either words or a change in facial expression. Instead, he excused himself, grabbed his coat, and left through the back door.

Scott helped himself to the coffee left in the pot and had just taken a long sip when Delia came back to the kitchen, putting on her coat. She patted Scott on the arm and said, "I'm sorry I was so grouchy. I know you're only helping out."

"You're tired," Scott said. "Go home and put your feet up."

She waved as she went out.

Scott foraged around in the kitchen and found some leftover blueberry muffins. He sat at the kitchen island to eat his snack. Ava came back with the baby and smiled at him.

"I'm glad to see you're making yourself at home," she said. "It's so good to have you here."

Scott felt an inner glow at Ava's kind words and lovely face. It was nice to be appreciated for a change.

Maggie left the bookstore by the back door and was momentarily stunned to find that her vintage VW Beetle wasn't parked where she always left it. It took her a moment to process its absence and return to the bookstore.

"Mitchell," she addressed her second best barista, a charming college student with dreadlocks and multiple piercings.

"Yes, ma'am," Mitchell responded, having been raised by a mother who prized good manners over conservative haircuts and undecorated facial features.

"Did Patrick borrow my car?"

"Not as far as I know," Mitchell said.

Maggie went to her office and called the Rose and Thorn. Patrick said he hadn't borrowed it. Maggie couldn't think of anyone else who would take it without asking. She called Curtis, and he confirmed her fear. Her extra key wasn't hanging on the pegboard in the service station office. There were some other things missing as well, including the petty cash and his cell phone.

She dialed the police station and was informed Scott was out. She left the bookstore and walked quickly to her sister-in-law's bed and breakfast, intending to ask her what she thought of the possibility that her husband-on-the-lam could have burgled the service station and stolen Maggie's car. She rushed in the front door and down the hallway only to be stopped short by the little scene currently being played out in the kitchen. Scott was sitting at the kitchen table with Little Fitz in his arms, feeding him a bottle of milk. He had a cloth diaper hanging across his shoulder to use as a burping pad. He was talking baby talk.

"What are you doing?" Maggie said a little louder than she meant to.

Scott looked up at Maggie and smiled.

"Feeding my little man," he said.

"Where's Ava?"

"Frank took her to pick up the kids from school," Scott said. "I offered to babysit."

Maggie had been avoiding Scott as much as possible, and when she couldn't avoid him, she'd tried to make their interactions as brief as possible. She knew he was staying nights at Ava's while Brian was on the loose, but she wasn't prepared to find him so domestically entrenched in her sister-in-law's home. So comfortable looking. So at home.

"My car's been stolen," Maggie said, crossing her arms in an attempt to control her temper.

"Patrick probably borrowed it," Scott said in the same soft tone he'd been using to coo at the baby. He said it to the baby as if he was talking to Little Fitz and not Maggie.

"I called him. I also called Uncle Curtis. The extra key to the bug is gone plus Curtis is missing some money and a cell phone. He thinks Brian was there."

Scott jerked his head up and looked at her. Finally, she felt like she had his full attention.

"You're sure no one else could have your car? Drew maybe, or Hannah?"

Drew was the local veterinarian who Maggie had briefly dated.

"Drew has never borrowed my car, and Hannah would ask me first."

"Okay, call Skip and report it stolen. Tell Curtis to do the same. Skip will let the state and county know about it."

"Aren't you going to do something?"

"Skip can handle it, Maggie."

Maggie was used to Scott jumping up and helping her whenever she had a problem. She didn't like this new behavior. She didn't like Scott sitting in Ava's kitchen looking like he belonged there. He was looking at her with a frank, "like it or lump it" look she'd never seen before. It made her feel cold inside. It made her feel alone.

"Fine," she said and left the way she came in.

"Your Aunt Maggie doesn't like the taste of her own medicine," Scott told Little Fitz, as he lifted the baby up to his shoulder and patted his back. "She doesn't like it one bit."

Little Fitz responded by spitting up everything he'd just eaten.

After Ava came back, Scott waited until the kids were settled in the family room before he told her about Maggie's visit. Scott thought Ava would be preoccupied with the idea that Brian might have been in town, but instead, she asked him, "Are you still in love with Maggie?"

"I do love Maggie," Scott said. "But she's still tangled up in her feelings for Gabe."

"You know if it weren't for the fact that you've been so good to me, I'd never butt in," Ava said. "But it seems to me you shouldn't have to convince someone to love you. She'd be lucky to have you."

"Well, thanks, Ava," Scott said. He could feel his face get hot and knew he was blushing.

Ava placed her hand on one side of his face and kissed the other.

"If I were a single gal," she said, "I'd never let you get away."

Patrick pulled up in front of Ed's newspaper office in a robin's egg blue Volvo station wagon. Ed came out, and Patrick tossed him the keys.

"Kept in a garage for fifteen years," Patrick said. "It belonged to the man's mother; she died last year, and the estate was settled this week. He started it up every so often and kept the oil changed, but there are hardly any miles on it. He brought it to us this past weekend to get it ready to sell. Curtis said to tell you he would waive the commission if you pay for the oil change and new air filter."

"This is great, Patrick," Ed said as he got in the driver's side.

"These cars are known for their safety ratings," Patrick told him from the passenger side. "Let's take it for a spin."

Once around the block was enough for Ed. He went home to get his checkbook and then met Patrick back at the station. He left a check for the car with Curtis and then drove it over to the bakery. Bonnie, Delia, and Mandy came out to see it.

Mandy wasn't as excited as he expected her to be.

"It's old," she said.

"It is," Ed said. "That's why I got such a good deal."

"So you already done bought it?" she said.

"Well, yeah," Ed said. "It has really low mileage, and it's a safe car. I want you and Tommy to be safe when we drive. You hate it?"

"I'll get used to it, I guess," she said.

Ed realized he'd made yet another decision on their behalf without consulting her.

"I guess I should have let you see it first," he said. "I thought it would be a great surprise."

"Well, I'm surprised, alright," she said and looked at the car in distaste.

"You want to drive it?" he offered.

"No, thanks," she said and went back to the bakery.

"It's a lovely car," Bonnie said.

"She's young," Delia said. "She probably imagined a red sports car."

"It was the sensible thing to buy," Bonnie said.

"She'll come around," Delia said.

Ed thanked them, but he didn't feel any better.

Brian Fitzpatrick winced as the VW Beetle he'd stolen from his sister jerked and sputtered up a rutted, muddy track rarely used outside of hunting season. The self-inflicted stab wound he'd made was oozing blood, and every pothole and rock felt like another knife being inserted into the same wound. He was in trouble, not from bleeding too much, but from the infection he knew was going to develop in the deep gash that had not been stitched up.

As soon as the car crested the ridge of the hill, he checked for a cellular signal and was relieved to find he had service on his uncle's phone. He pressed the numbers he knew by heart, and when the party he was seeking got on the line he made his request short and to the point. He also reminded the recipient what would happen if his request wasn't followed to the letter, and right away. He gave directions and then ended the call.

Back in the VW, he steeled himself for two more agonizing miles of narrow track, muddy where the sun shone on it and icy where it didn't. He had to stay alive long enough to come up with a new plan and get as far away from Rose Hill as possible. It would be nice to have a big wad of cash as well, but right now he would settle for some painkillers and a safe place to sleep.

The hunting cabin the Fitzpatrick family owned was located on the outskirts of the land Curtis had deeded over to Hannah and Sam when they got married. It was in a remote location only approachable by a logging road that started on Hollyhock Ridge, wound through the State Park, and ended in another state.

Brian's father Fitz had been the keenest hunter of the family, but since his accident, he could barely make it to the fridge for a beer and back to his recliner. Brian, Patrick, and Hannah's brothers had all used the cabin as a place to seduce girls and hold the occasional drinking party when they were teenagers. Brian had used it to seduce several women during his marriage to Ava. It hadn't been used by anyone in many years.

Brian parked the VW down the muddy track a hundred feet beyond the cabin, back in among some large rhododendron bushes, and dragged some snowy brush over to cover it. He was relieved to find the cabin empty and boarded up, with a "no trespassing" sign on the door. He broke in through a back window.

Inside he found some matches in a plastic bag in a drawer, cleaned off an oil lamp that still had oil in it, and lit the wick before placing the protective glass column back over the top. He didn't dare make a fire in the fireplace, for fear the smoke would draw attention to his hiding place. Instead, he reconnected the gas line to the stove, opened the valve and lit the pilot lights. The family had mineral rights to this land, so there was no meter for gas service. He lit the oven and left its door open to heat the room.

Although still weak from the loss of blood, Brian made his way down over the hill behind the cabin to the spring house to get some water. He had to use a rock to break up the thick ice that had formed around the steady trickle of clear, clean water. He filled two plastic milk jugs and then struggled up the hill with them.

There was coffee, sugar, and whiskey in the cupboard, so while he warmed some water for coffee, he cleaned his wound with the whiskey. The pain was so intense he almost passed out. He made a dressing out of some paper towels and duct tape and covered the gash, which was bleeding again.

The hot sweet coffee tasted good and warmed him inside, but he was so weary it did nothing to revive him. He lay down on the bottom bunk in the back bedroom, and although he told himself he must stay alert, he fell deep asleep.

It was a struggle to wake up when he heard the crunch of tires on snow and footsteps on the back porch of the cabin. His heart was pounding as he peeked out the window, and his relief was a cold sweat on his skin as he opened the door for the visitor he was expecting.

"I've helped you this one time, but I won't do it again," his visitor said an hour later, as he prepared to leave. "Do what you will."

"I won't need you again," Brian said. "By this time tomorrow, I'll be long gone from here."

"Eventually you'll have to face the consequences of your actions. None of us gets away with anything, not in the larger sense."

"I'm not spending the rest of my life in prison. I'd rather die."

"Heaven help you, then."

Brian listened as the engine started and the four-wheel drive struggled out of the muddy driveway. As the sound of the vehicle faded away, Brian took stock of his situation. He had Maggie's VW, a cell phone with no charger, and $40 he stole from his Uncle's service station. He knew Curtis left the side door open for the mechanic while he went to the bakery to get his breakfast.

He'd waited in the bushes behind the station until he heard Curtis go whistling down the street, and then he'd slipped in the side door that led into the car service area. He'd hoped to steal one of the cars in the lot outside, but the customers' keys were no longer kept on pegs in the service area.

A quick check of the office had revealed a brand new safe; no doubt purchased after Brian's last robbery of the station a few weeks before. Maggie's VW key was still hanging on the pegboard, however, so he grabbed that, a cell phone left on the desk, and all the money in the petty cash bag kept in the top drawer. On his way out of the garage, he took a pair of coveralls and some gloves.

As Brian warmed his front side before the open oven door, he wondered if he could count on his visitor not to rat him out. He wanted to spend the night here, in the cabin, and then leave before light, taking the muddy track all the way to the other end, where he hoped he could escape unseen into Maryland, and see about exchanging Maggie's car for another. After that, his plan was to get as far away as possible as fast as he could.

Brian took some scissors into the bathroom. He took a handful of his long red curls, now matted with sweat and dirt, and cut them off at the scalp. He cut off all his hair as close to the scalp as possible before he shaved his head with one of the disposable razors he found in the medicine cabinet. Then he cut off his beard and mustache before he shaved his face clean. He didn't spend much time admiring his clean-cut, younger-looking face in the mirror. He needed to erase any distinguishing characteristics that made him stand out in a crowd.

He swept up the hair, put it in a plastic bag along with his prison garb, took it outside, and threw it over the hill. He found an old backpack and filled it with a blanket, some towels, the rest of the disposable razors, the whiskey and the provisions his visitor had brought. He dropped the backpack and the jugs of water by the back door.

He was exhausted. Despite the painkillers his visitor had delivered, he was still suffering from the pain of his wound. He was afraid to lie down and sleep for fear his recent visitor had alerted the police to his whereabouts. All he could think of was that he must get away.

The few weeks he'd spent in the county lockup and then the state penitentiary had been the worst weeks of his life. He knew he wasn't tough enough to survive prison. The bullying that worked so well with women and those weaker than him had no effect on the cold-blooded killers in the state pen. He didn't think he could bear to do what he would have to in order to survive inside. The feds were willing to work with him on the length of his sentence in order to get what they wanted out of him, but Brian had decided that what he wanted was no sentence. There was no going back now.

Brian heard a noise outside and was relieved to see it was only a buck nosing around the porch of the cabin. He knew he wasn't going to be able to sleep in the cabin and feel safe, but he needed to get some rest in order to get through the next few days. He weighed his options as far as alternative places to bunk down were concerned. When the solution came to him, he thought he might have just enough energy left to get there.

Hannah woke up to the house dogs barking at three in the morning. She pulled on some clothes and hurried to the kitchen, thinking maybe Sam had come home. Although the dogs were carrying on at the back door, she couldn't see anyone out there. The parking area next to the house was covered with a new, pristine layer of snow, and against the porch light, she could see more snow was falling.

"What are you guys barking at?" she asked.

The dogs were hysterical to get outside, which probably meant they'd seen a deer or a fox. Hannah decided to let them out so they could run off their energy. They took off toward the barn and Hannah locked the door behind them.

Since she was wide awake now, she poured herself some juice and fired up the computer that sat on a desk in the pantry off the kitchen. This was where Hannah kept track of her household bills and corresponded with people via e-mail. She was surprised to find an e-mail from her husband.

"I'm so sorry in so many ways for so many things that an e-mail just won't cut it," he wrote. "I'll be home to apologize in person this week. I hope you'll let me stay. I miss you. Love, Sam."

If Sam thought she would be thrilled to hear from him and thankful he was coming home, he was sadly mistaken. She felt only bone-deep exhaustion and a sense of dread.

Hannah looked at the calendar and thought of all the things she needed to do between now and Sunday. She had to work at the food pantry at the church later this morning, and then assist Drew with some vet clinic surgeries in the afternoon. Thursday the county vet was coming to execute the prisoners; that was a hard day to get through so she hadn't scheduled anything else. She had planned to set humane traps all over Pine County on Friday, and then scoop up the feral cats she caught and deliver them to Drew to spay and neuter on Saturday.

Drew was coming out to the farm on Sunday to help her write a grant proposal for money to expand her kennel facility and start the feral cat program. Congressman Green had promised the mayor they could have government-funded Vision workers assigned to the project if they got the grant. This was all supposed to happen in between any calls she received about stray dogs, garbage-raiding possums, or home-invading raccoons.

She could imagine herself canceling all that and sitting at home waiting for Sam, not knowing if he would show up. She could also imagine him e-mailing her late Sunday night to tell her he was sorry but he wasn't ready to come home. It had happened before, and she'd felt like a fool. She wrote and re-wrote her response several times before she got down what she thought she wanted to say.

"Sam – if you do come back this week you are welcome to stay here at the farm. I have a lot to do so I may not be here when you arrive. Call me on the cell when you get home or to let me know if you change your mind. We will talk when I see you, Hannah."

She clicked on "send" and pictured her response flying up and over the mountains to the little town west of Boston where Sam's college roommate Alan lived. She couldn't imagine him sleeping in Alan's guest room, or doing anything he must have done since he left home. In her mind, as soon as he left the house and drove away, he'd disappeared, and did not exist anywhere but in her imagination, where he was suspended by whatever self-destructive impulse it was that always compelled him to run away from home.

She knew he would return full of apologies made out of the words he had to use to get back in her good graces, back in their home, back in their marriage. His promises always turned out to be as hollow and brittle as bird eggs in an abandoned nest; they were pretty to look at but crumbled under the slightest pressure.

The dogs had still not returned, and Hannah feared they were tracking a deer, which meant they might be gone awhile. They would come to their senses eventually, and then Jax's sense of direction and Wally's keen intelligence would help them find their way home.

'If no one shoots them first,' Hannah thought. She put on her coat and grabbed a flashlight before sticking her feet down in the snow boots that stood next to the side door. It was cold outside, but not bitterly cold. Mercifully the snow was falling straight down in big fat flakes, not blowing sideways like piercing needles.

She called for the dogs and whistled, but only heard the kennel dogs bark in response. She followed her dogs' tracks to the outbuildings and saw they had circled the shed where Sam kept his four-wheeler and tools. The door was ajar, and Hannah felt a little frisson of fear as she realized her only means of protection had just run off into the woods. There were no human footprints in the newly fallen snow outside the shed, only paw prints, but the dogs were definitely on the trail of something or someone. Hannah slowly opened the door the rest of the way and pointed the flashlight inside. The four-wheeler and wagon Sam used to do chores on the farm were inside, along with all his tools, but nothing seemed disturbed.

Hannah shut and bolted the door behind her as she left the shed. She followed the dog tracks on out to the barn, which Hannah was relieved to see was bolted and locked with the padlock. She pulled her keys out of her coat pocket, unlocked the door, and went in to check on the inmates. They were restless, so she decided to let them out for a breath of fresh air.

The four pit bulls currently on death row had been raised to fight and thus far had resisted all her efforts at socialization. Because they were so vicious, she had to let them out one at a time into an outdoor pen connected to each kennel by a sliding door. She was about to let the first one out when she heard footsteps crunching in the snow outside the barn. All four of the dogs started growling, a deep menacing sound.

Hannah made a quick decision. She climbed on top of the kennel that held the pit bull she was about to let outside, and instead of unlocking the door to the outside pen, she unlocked the door that opened into the barn. She lifted the pen door a few inches, and the dog sniffed and scratched at the opening. She hadn't turned on the lights in the barn, so other than a night light and her flashlight all was in darkness. When the footsteps reached the entrance to the barn, Hannah shone her flashlight in the face of the person standing in the doorway. The dogs erupted in a frenzy of barking.

"Take one more step, and I'll let this dog loose!" she yelled. "He'll tear you to pieces!"

The pit bull in the kennel below her started lunging against the kennel door, foam flying from a mouth full of wicked looking teeth. Hannah shone her flashlight down on the frothing, scarred muzzle of the dog below her, and when she tipped the light back up at the door, the man had disappeared. Hannah thought she could hear running steps in the snow, but the dogs were barking so loud she thought she might have imagined it. She dropped the kennel door back down, secured it, and then climbed down.

"That was an awful thing to do to you, and I apologize," she told the dog, and then let him out the back of his kennel into the penned area outside.

She heard the dog rush to the far end of the enclosure and lunge against it, the chain-link fence ringing under his onslaught. His snarling made him sound like a beast straight out of hell.

'That ought to make an impression,' Hannah thought.

Hannah cursed herself for coming outside without a gun or a cell phone. She hadn't even locked the door of the house behind her. Her housedogs were who knows where on the trail of some deer, or lured into a trap by the intruder, and she was stuck in the barn with only four vicious dogs for protection. There was no way to lock the barn door from the inside.

After she exercised each dog, Hannah closed the barn door and locked herself in her barn office. She searched the room for some sort of weapon, and almost cried in relief when she found an old taser in the bottom drawer. It had an unreliable safety setting which made it dangerous to leave in the glove box of her animal control truck, and she'd intended to get it repaired.

She turned it on and found it still had a charge. She thanked her lucky stars for her own procrastination. There was no phone connection in the barn, and her cell phone was in the kitchen, recharging. She needed to get from the barn to the house in order to call for help but had no way of knowing where the intruder was.

Hannah was torn between staying right where she was or trying to get to the house. She cleaned the frosted glass of the office window on the back wall, which faced the long driveway down to the farm, and cupped her hands in order to see outside. In the light from the motion detection lamps on the side of the barn, she could see the footprints of the intruder going from around the back of the barn to the front and then retreating in the same direction. But then to where? They didn't seem to lead to the house, but what if he was waiting around the corner of the barn for Hannah to make a run for it?

The dogs had calmed down. She knew they would alert her if anyone entered the barn. She wished one of the inmates was friendly enough to put on a leash, but there wasn't one she could trust not to turn on her.

Hannah turned on the milk house heater and sat down in the old horsehair-filled armchair that sat across from its twin. She and Maggie often retreated to this clubhouse to discuss problems and gossip, and it was where she kept the county animal control files.

It was also where Hannah came to smoke back when she still smoked. She desperately wanted a cigarette right now and knew if she looked hard enough she could find one; but if she was pregnant, she wasn't taking any chances with the baby. This thought helped her make up her mind. She would stay put until daylight came or until her dogs came home.

She looked up at the ceiling of the office and spoke out loud.

"You gotta help me out here, man," she said. "I need your help."

At four o'clock in the morning, Maggie woke up worrying about Hannah. She grabbed the phone and punched in her cousin's number before she was fully awake, and when no one answered after the tenth ring, she jumped out of bed and pulled on some jeans.

Ordinarily, she would call Scott and ask to borrow his SUV, but that no longer seemed like a viable option. Instead, she threw on her coat and snow boots and quickly walked several blocks through the newly fallen snow, down to the trailer park where her brother Patrick was living.

All the while she called Hannah over and over on her cell phone. Her brother was cross at being awakened, having gone to bed a couple hours previously, but he didn't hesitate to get dressed and drive Maggie out to Hannah's, only insisting they take his beagle with them.

"Otherwise he'll wake up the neighborhood with his howling."

Banjo was one of the foster placements Hannah had made from the pack of dogs included in Theo Eldridge's breeding scam. The dog was so attached to Patrick that he howled pitifully whenever the man left his sight for longer than five minutes. Banjo spent all day in the service station, all evening in the Rose and Thorn, and slept at the foot of Patrick's bed at night. Patrick didn't seem to mind him, and it had become customary to see the dog following him everywhere he went.

Banjo sat between Patrick and Maggie in the cab of the truck and seemed to enjoy getting to go somewhere. Maggie had only told Patrick she couldn't find Hannah, and now they speculated on where she could be or why she wasn't answering her home phone or cell phone.

"Maybe Sam came home," Patrick suggested.

Maggie was calling again.

"If someone called as many times as I've called she would answer. It's the middle of the night. She's got parents, brothers, nieces, and nephews. She would answer."

"She shouldn't be staying out there all by herself."

"Well, if her stupid husband would quit running off she wouldn't be."

"He's been to hell and back," Patrick said. "He's got post-traumatic stress disorder. She knew that when she married him."

"She was in love with him. She couldn't imagine what it would be like long-term."

"I think I know Sam," Patrick said. "But I don't, not really. I'd do anything for him, and he for me, but I wouldn't say we're close like we were in high school. He keeps himself to himself."

"Maybe he's gone off the deep end. Speaking of which, have you talked to Anne Marie since she got back? I had to throw her out of my bookstore."

"Anne Marie came into the Thorn and tried to convince Ian to quit selling alcohol. He had to call Knox to come get her."

"I'm beginning to think everyone in this town is crazy, not just our family. Who could ever have believed Brian would do what he did?"

"I'm just glad he didn't go to Mom and Dad's house."

"He won't get far in my car," Maggie said. "The voltage regulator is about to go, and if you run it faster than fifty miles per hour the whole car shakes so hard you think it's going to fly apart."

"It's time you retired that thing and let me get you something more reliable. I found a car for Ed that..."

"You don't think Brian would go to Hannah's," Maggie interrupted, and they looked at each other in horror at the thought.

"Hold on, Banjo," Patrick said.

Maggie gripped the dog's collar as Patrick put his foot down hard on the gas pedal.

Bonnie Fitzpatrick arrived at the family bakery at four o'clock. She turned on the ovens and tied on her apron before taking the chilled croissant dough out of the walk-in fridge. She assembled all the ingredients necessary to make the croissants, cinnamon rolls, and doughnuts that were the staple of her early morning offerings.

She thought she could probably do the work in her sleep and did, in fact, feel half asleep as she went through the motions. She'd loaded the trays of cinnamon rolls into the proofing box when she heard a knock at the front door. It was Ed and Tommy.

"My coffee maker finally bit the dust," Ed said. "Could I prevail upon you to make some coffee for us?"

"Come in, come in," Bonnie said. "I could use a cup myself. But Tommy shouldn't be drinking coffee. I'll make him some nice hot tea."

Ed didn't point out that tea had as much caffeine in it as coffee. In Bonnie's mind, children did not drink coffee; they drank hot sweet tea with a splash of milk in it.

Bonnie put a filter into one of the two commercial coffee makers behind the counter and then spooned ground coffee into it. She asked Tommy if he would grind some more beans for her, and he did as he was told. His mother worked there each day, and Tommy helped out almost every day after school, so there were few tasks he hadn't done before. Ed sat down on one of the stools at the counter that ran around the perimeter of the bakery.

"I was sorry to hear about Brian," Ed said.

"I appreciate you not putting that shameful business in the paper," Bonnie said.

"It didn't happen in Rose Hill," Ed said, "and it hasn't officially been reported to the public yet. I don't print rumors, and I don't like to hamper the police."

"I don't know what I'll say when it's known," Bonnie said. "With a son who's broken out of prison and turns out to have a second wife and a child no one knew about."

"I don't know why Brian did what he did, but he's still innocent until proven guilty."

"Thank you for that," Bonnie said. "I know the people in this town, and there's bound to be many a tongue wagging already, although no one's been brazen enough to ask me about it."

Ed didn't think anyone was brave enough to ask Bonnie about her son Brian, lest they suffer the wrath of her legendary temper. So fearful were people of Bonnie's temper that she didn't have to actually do anything except raise an eyebrow and look as if she might fly off the handle. The fact that she was known to have done so in the past was enough to put the fear into anyone.

"Brian gave you another fine grandchild," Ed said.

"He did," Bonnie said. "He's the spitting image of Timothy at the same age. Just as feisty, too. Wants to hold his bottle all by himself and sits up already."

Bonnie gave Ed a paper cup of coffee with a lid and the same but tea for Tommy. Bonnie then surprised Tommy by giving him a hug and a kiss on the cheek before he left.

"I consider you a fine grandchild of mine as well, even though we aren't kin," she told him. "Don't you ever forget that. We may be a family of horse thieves and graverobbers, but we'll always take you in when you're cold and hungry. Did you eat this morning?"

"I did," Tommy said. "Ed fixed me oatmeal."

"That Ed's a good fella," Bonnie told him. "Mind you do what he tells you."

Tommy smiled and waved goodbye to her and Ed followed him out, thanking Bonnie for the coffee.

As Bonnie watched them go, she felt tears well up and a lump form in her throat.

"None of that," she said.

She wiped her eyes, cleared her throat, and got back to work.

When Patrick and Maggie came over the ridge top on the long rutted driveway that led from Hollyhock Ridge to Hanna's farm, the truck slid sideways on a combination of slush, ice, and newly fallen snow. The lights were on in the farmhouse and in Hannah's office in the barn.

"The dogs aren't coming to greet us," Maggie said. "Where are the dogs?"

They could hear the kennel dogs barking, and Hannah's animal control truck was in the driveway. As they bounced and slid down the final yards to the farmhouse, Maggie had her seat belt off and door open before the truck came to a full stop.

"Hannah!" she yelled as she ran up the wheelchair ramp to the side door that led into the kitchen.

She flung open the storm door, opened the door into the kitchen, and yelled again. There was no response. The lights were on in the kitchen.

Maggie checked all the rooms on the first floor except Sam's office, which was always locked up tighter than Fort Knox. She ran upstairs and checked all those rooms as well. No Hannah. There was a cellar under the house that you could access via a door outside, and Maggie's intention as she left the house was to go there. Instead, when she exited the house, she heard the kennel dogs barking their heads off.

When Maggie got to the barn, she found Patrick in the barn office with Hannah. Maggie grabbed Hannah in a quick bear hug. They both started to cry and then laughed at each other for crying.

Banjo was having a barking contest with the pit bulls in the kennels, although Banjo sounded more like "Olp! Olp! Olp!" and the inmates sounded more like "we want to kill you and eat you!" Pretty soon Banjo began to howl, and the pit bulls began to howl along with him. It was an eerie, lonesome sound. Patrick yelled at them to shut up.

"Let them do it," Hannah said. "They're all going to die tomorrow, anyway."

Hannah started to cry again, and Maggie hugged her. Patrick carefully took the taser out of Hannah's hand, switched it off, and laid it on the desktop.

"What are you doing out here?" Maggie asked her as she let go.

Hannah dried her eyes on her pajama shirt and told them what had happened. Patrick went out to look for footprints, taking Hannah's flashlight and the taser with him.

"I could kick you for coming out here without your cell phone," Maggie said.

"I know, it was really stupid. What in the world are you two doing out here so early?"

"I woke up worrying about you and called."

"What time was that?"

"Around four."

Hannah looked up at the ceiling and shook her head.

"What?" Maggie asked her.

"Nothing," Hannah said, wiping new tears away. "Looks like I'm going to start going to church with you and your mom."

"What brought that on?" Maggie asked. "And where are Jax and Wally?"

"They ran off after something, probably a deer. Fat lot of help they are."

"Did you see the person?"

"Briefly. I don't think it was Brian. This guy was cleanly shaven. I don't think I'd know him again if I saw him."

"When you didn't answer, I thought maybe one of the inmates got you."

"It was probably some lost hiker or hunter. I probably scared him more than he scared me."

"I can stay out here with you from now on."

"I heard from Sam."

"And?"

"He says he's coming home this week."

Maggie struggled to suppress all the mean things she wanted to say.

"I know," Hannah said. "You don't have to say anything."

Patrick came back with Banjo right on his heels.

"The snow has covered up the footprints," he said. "There's no one in any of the outbuildings. Whoever it was is long gone."

"She doesn't think it was Brian," Maggie said.

"Whoever it was just missed being a pit bull breakfast," Hannah said. "Come on in and get some coffee. It's the least I can do."

CHAPTER SIX - Thursday

When Scott got to work at eight o'clock, Sarah Albright was waiting out front in a county car. She was scowling, her brow furrowed and her mouth turned down at the corners. Scott greeted her, let her in, then turned on the lights and turned up the heat. He took off his coat and set his thermos and bag of warm muffins on his desk before seating himself across from her.

"What can I do for you, Sarah?"

"You can tell me what's going on with the federal investigation you're involved with, and what Ray's murder has to do with it."

"I don't know that Ray's murder has anything to do with a federal investigation. Why do you think it does?"

"Because the bureau just jerked the case out from under me, that's why."

"You're always so busy, why would you mind?"

"Because I know there's something big going on, and I want in on it. If there's an important case brewing in my jurisdiction, I want a piece of the action and some credit when it all goes down."

"Don't you still have friends at the bureau? Why ask me?"

"Because I know you're cooperating with them and I want in."

"Why would you think that?"

"I know it, and you know it. So do me a favor and introduce me to the agent and tell him or her that I'm exactly who they need to have involved."

"I'll tell you what I'll do. The next time I see a real live FBI agent, I'll tell him or her all about you."

"Look, Scott, I know we got off to a rocky start. I haven't always taken your feelings into account when we collaborated in the past. I'm working very hard to honor our professional relationship while keeping appropriate boundaries and respecting your right to disagree with me. Can't we work together as a team to solve this problem?"

"You're saying all the right things, Sarah, and I can tell you've been paying attention in class, but you have to practice what you preach. I said if I see any FBI agents I'll tell them about you, and then it's up to them. That's all I can do."

Scott could see she was really pissed off and frustrated, but she was hamstrung. Now that she'd realized, due to an intervention on the part of her supervisor, that insults and intimidation were not an appropriate communication style in every situation, she had to struggle against her urge to let everyone have it when they didn't immediately jump when she said they should.

"Do you want to get some breakfast?" she asked.

Scott gestured at his coffee and muffins.

"I'm all set. Thanks for stopping by."

"You want to know what we found in Ray's post-mortem, don't you?" she asked.

This was a more effective sweetener, and Scott was tempted.

"I do want to know, but I've got nothing to trade for the information."

She stood up to leave, and Scott thought that meant she was going to refuse to share what she knew in order to punish him. Right before she got to the door, she turned.

"He was killed upriver about twenty miles, next to an old fishing shack down behind the Roadhouse; there was blood on the river bank there. It looks like whoever killed him hid in a drainpipe set in the side of the hill. Our killer was an amateur; he left cigarette butts all over the place. He must have slipped up behind Ray, slit his throat, and pushed him into the river. The water level is so high right now his body slid over two dams before he was caught in that beaver dam. His Harley is still parked at the

Roadhouse, but no one reported him missing. They all thought Ray was off on a bender somewhere."

"Any leads on the killer?"

"We sent the cigarette butts over to the state lab for DNA analysis before the feds intervened. You know as well as I do it takes months to get those back."

"Autopsy done?"

"Done, but not filed. Unofficially I got confirmation he was hopped up on speed or meth. Big sharp knife made a cut so deep he was dead before he hit the water."

"You think he was meeting Brian?"

"It's a possibility. You tell your fed buddies I have some good insights into the whole situation. I'd be a real asset to their investigation."

"If I see one, I will."

"Right."

Sarah left Scott in deep thought. If Brian killed Ray, why wouldn't Brian use his Harley to get as far away from there as possible? Why come all the way to Rose Hill to steal Maggie's car? Was there something else Brian wanted to do before he left? And if so, what was so important that he would risk being arrested in order to stay and finish it? Scott hoped it wasn't to take revenge on his wife or his brother, or whomever Brian blamed for his current predicament.

Malcolm Behr came in, and Scott poured him a cup of coffee.

"How goes the beaver dam business?" Scott asked him.

"The feds won't let us touch it," Malcolm said. "Meanwhile, that warm front is almost here, and the guy that owns the fields on either side is threatening to break it up himself."

"What did the Corps of Engineers say about the dams between here and there?"

"That they should have been replaced thirty years ago."

"That's no surprise."

"I've got all my volunteers on call twenty-four seven, and the Corps has put a monitor on the water level. If that thing breaks up, we may have a disaster on our hands."

"What can I do to help?"

"Keep your radio handy," Malcolm said. "If something happens we'll need to evacuate Lotus Avenue immediately; maybe Marigold as well."

"Does the mayor know?"

"He's excited about it; he wants a hydroelectric dam, and he thinks if the old ones break we'll get one."

"Do you think the Little Bear is big enough to support that?"

"I don't know. But I wouldn't be surprised if the mayor broke up the beaver dam himself just to find out."

Jamie entered the kitchen so quietly Ava didn't notice his presence until she turned around. She jumped, startled.

"Jamie," she said. "You scared me."

"Sorry," he said. "Bad habit."

"It's okay," she said. "I'm feeling kind of jumpy."

"One of our agents is coming today to work the front desk," he said. "Her story is she's researching her ancestry through the city records and is willing to work the front desk to pay for her stay."

"That's clever," Ava said, summoning up a vestige of a smile for him, but it didn't reach her eyes. "Will she be wearing a false nose and a wig?"

"I think it will help," Jamie said, ignoring her question. "I know you're worried about your aunt. Terese's one of the best people I have, and she can help with the kids. Do you have a room for her?"

"Yes," Ava said. "I'm telling anyone who calls that I'm fully booked even though I have vacancies. No sense in endangering my guests as well as my family. You can fill up every room with agents for all I care. The more the merrier."

"I know this is difficult, Ava, but it will all be worth it. We have to gather enough evidence and enough people willing to testify in order to ensure Mrs. Wells and her accomplices go to prison for a long time. You're a key witness to this investigation. Without you, I'm not sure we could succeed."

"I've meant to ask you, what does Lily Crawford have to do with Mrs. Wells? I saw her out at Lily's farm a few weeks ago when I took the kids sledding. I just recently remembered where it was I'd seen her. How is Lily involved in this?"

"I can't answer that, Ava."

"I'll ask her myself, then."

Jamie shrugged.

Ava slammed the sheet pan she was drying down on the counter and was gratified to see him jump.

"Lily is someone I trusted," Ava said. "I've known her all my life. Now I don't know who I can trust. You expect me to tell you everything and trust you with all our lives, but you won't tell me anything!"

"I'm sorry. I know this is horrible for you. I can tell you this: you are as safe at Lily Crawford's house as you are here."

"Which may mean not at all."

Jamie smiled at her and Ava turned her back on him. When she turned back around he was gone. Ava rubbed her aching, cast-covered wrist and wondered if she had damaged it. She called Doc Machalvie, and he told her to come right over.

"It looks fine," he said while looking at the x-ray.

"When can you take it off?" she asked him.

"Three more weeks," he said. "We have to be sure it's fully healed."

"It makes everything harder to do," she said. "Plus I have to wrap it in plastic every time I take a shower or wash dishes. It's probably covered in germs, and I hate exposing the baby to that."

"How is the little fella?"

"Delia's got him today. He's doing really well. He's getting some teeth, so that's making him cross, but other than that he's great."

"Bring him over to see me next week," Doc said. "Now that he's fully recovered from his respiratory infection we need to get his immunizations up-to-date."

Ava stood and gathered her things in preparation to leave.

"You heard Brian escaped," she said.

Doc hesitated as if he was deliberating over saying something. Then hugged her and kissed her on the forehead.

"Don't you worry," Doc said. "They'll catch him."

The young woman who showed up with the story about researching her ancestors was a credible actress. If she hadn't known it was all a lie, Ava would have believed everything she said. Ava reflected that she needed to start assuming everyone she met might be pretending to be someone they were not and that everything that was said could be a lie.

Ava took Terese up to her room, where she left her suitcases, and then took her back downstairs to show her how things were done at the front desk.

"You're welcome to use the computer and the phone," Ava said. "We won't be taking any more reservations for a while, so you don't need to know how to do that. Tell anyone who calls that we're booked up through May, but take their information if they want to be on a cancellation call list."

"You should mark your reservation book to match that information," Terese said. "Right now it shows vacancies."

“Then that can be your first duty,” Ava said sweetly, but her voice had an edge to it.

“Aren’t you worried about losing money by turning away customers?” Terese asked.

“I’m more worried about them being murdered by a psychopathic drug pusher,” Ava responded, and the woman didn’t even pretend not to understand.

“I’m so sorry about all this,” Terese said under her breath and looked at Ava with real pity in her eyes.

“Make yourself at home,” Ava said as she walked away. “There’s coffee in the kitchen and spare ammo in the linen closet.”

Maggie was determined to stick to Hannah like glue the rest of the day, although Hannah insisted she was fine. Patrick went back home to get some sleep and Maggie hung out in Hannah’s kitchen while her friend showered and dressed for the day. Afterward, they spent some time exercising the inmates.

“I’m ashamed of myself for using these dogs as a weapon,” Hannah said. “Letting them kill a person would’ve been worse than making them fight each other.”

“I’d have done the same thing,” Maggie said.

“That doesn’t make it right,” Hannah said. “I gotta tell you I don’t know how many more executions I can take.”

“You did everything you could to rehabilitate them,” Maggie said. “You could never trust them. It would be like leaving loaded guns lying around.”

“I know that, and yet who are we to decide it’s time for them to die? The yahoos who trained them to fight will get off with a fine and very little jail time. These dogs got the death penalty.”

“It’s all backward.”

“I know I say this every month, but I think I may hang it up. I don’t think I can keep doing this.”

"Then who will save the dogs that can be rehabilitated? Who will do the foster placements? Who will relocate the groundhogs, possums, and raccoons? What about the feral cat project? That's going to be a huge undertaking, and you'll finally have help. What about the no-kill shelter? That's always been your dream; you can't give up now."

"It's not even the euthanasia that's so awful, although it is. The vets who do it are good people, and they do it humanely. It's how quiet the kennel is afterward. That quiet does me in."

Maggie hugged Hannah with one arm, and they left the barn.

Hannah showed Maggie how to plow the driveway using a blade attached to the four-wheeler.

"I want one of these!" Maggie shouted as she took her first turn and scraped the driveway down to mud.

"Not so deep," Hannah called out. "I'd like to keep the gravel if you don't mind."

When she was through Maggie hosed off the four-wheeler, dried it with some rags kept for that purpose, and returned it to the shed. When she entered the house, she found Hannah taking clothes out of the dryer in the kitchen.

"What's next? Should we go look for the dogs?" Maggie asked her.

"No, they'll come home eventually. Kind of like my husband."

Maggie held her tongue, which took an effort.

Hannah drove Maggie home.

"I'll be over to the food pantry as soon as I'm presentable," Maggie said, gesturing to her matted red curls and hastily assembled attire.

Maggie went up the back stairs of the bookstore and let herself in the apartment. Her voice mail light was blinking so she called in. She had two messages. The first message was from her mother, wanting to know where in the world she was; did she forget she promised to cover for Mandy from ten to two? Maggie glanced at the wall clock and saw that it was 9:45. She called Hannah to tell her what was up and Hannah told her not to worry, she could handle the food pantry on her own.

Maggie did not have time to shower, so she twisted her long red curls into a messy knot on the back of her head. She washed her face, brushed her teeth, and put on some clean clothes. She was five minutes late to the bakery.

"Nice of you to drop by," was her mother's terse greeting, even though Maggie brought her a cappuccino.

Maggie knew better than to answer, and instead, she took off her coat, slipped the neck loop of a long white apron over her head, tied the long tails behind her waist, and washed her hands.

She'd been working in the bakery most of her life, so she immediately fell into the rhythm of waiting on customers: ringing up sales, making change, taking phone orders, washing and re-washing her hands, using fresh food service waxed sheets to pick up baked goods, and bringing out fresh stock from the kitchen. When Scott walked in, she was so worn out she didn't have the energy to be rude to him.

He sat at the counter, and she poured him some coffee.

"Patrick told me what happened this morning at Hannah's," he said. "You should've called me."

"There was no crime being committed. I was just worried."

"Is Hannah okay?"

"Yeah, but I'm going to stay with her until Sam comes home. That may be this week sometime."

"That's good news. Anything I can do to help?"

"Find my car."

"There's no sign of it yet. If it was Brian who took it, he's probably long gone by now."

"Then why are you still staying at Ava's?"

"Because we don't know for sure where Brian is."

"Why didn't Ava ask someone in our family to stay? Why does it have to be you?"

"You sound jealous," Scott said. "I wonder why."

Her mother came out from the kitchen, and Maggie gave Scott a look that said: "shut up."

Bonnie looked from Maggie to Scott and back before smiling at him and saying, "It's so good to see you, Scott. Can I interest you in a ham and cheese turnover or a corned beef and cabbage pasty?"

"I'd love a pasty," Scott told her. "But you better make it to go. I have places to go and people to see."

Bonnie wrapped two pasties in waxed paper and put them in a bag, then poured him a cup of coffee to go. She refused to accept any money. Scott waved to them as he left, but Maggie refused to look at him.

"You need to have your head examined," Bonnie hissed at her daughter as soon as the door shut behind him. "You won't find a better man in this town, let alone one that's willing to marry your sorry hide. What's wrong with you?"

"You wouldn't understand."

"Oh, I know all about what he did. Ran your man out of town on a rail and lied to you about it. Saved you from the rotten bastard, is more like it. Would you rather have born the shame of living in sin with a man who sold drugs to children? Folks would have thought you knew about it, would have thought you were doing the same. Would that have been a better life than the one Scott is offering? You answer me!"

Maggie untied her apron and threw it on the floor as she left the bakery.

"You know I'm right!" her mother yelled at her.

The door shut behind Maggie and Bonnie scowled at it.

"I should've waited until she'd finished her shift," Bonnie said. "Now I've got no help until Alice gets here at two."

After Maggie left the bakery, she went straight to the food pantry behind Sacred Heart Catholic Church. What used to be a garage next to the alley behind the church was now a collection and distribution point for volunteers, who sorted donations and packed the boxes that were delivered to families in need.

Hannah was unpacking a recent delivery.

"Where's your coat?" she asked Maggie, who went straight to the gas stove to get warm.

"I had a fight with my mother and left it in the bakery. She probably took it outside and set it on fire."

"You and your mother fighting, what a surprise. What was it about this time?"

"Nothing. I don't want to talk about it."

"Fair enough. You can start with the canned goods."

Maggie did as she was told, weeding out the canned goods from the boxes and bags of food that had been donated, and sorting them by contents on the shelves.

"I can't do anything right," Maggie said.

"Mmm hmm," Hannah said.

"What I decide to do with my life is none of her business."

"Uh huh," Hannah said.

"If I don't want to marry Scott Gordon, I don't have to marry Scott Gordon."

"Has Scott proposed to you lately?"

"No, but you know what I mean. Scott came in, and she just had to make a comment."

"You and your mother are like bleach and ammonia: fine separately, but toxic when combined."

"She won't let up," Maggie said.

"She's right, that's why."

Maggie turned on her cousin.

"Whose side are you on?"

"Yours, of course, but I'm sorry, she's right. Scott did a stupid thing seven years ago, but for all the right reasons, and you need to get over it before Ava snags him right out from under your nose."

"Ava's not trying to snag him. He's only staying there until they catch Brian."

"Yeah, uh huh, just like your brother Patrick was only helping out until Brian came back. You saw how that turned out."

"You think Scott is in love with Ava?"

"Not yet, but you keep rejecting him and making him feel bad about himself, and keep giving her enough opportunities to tell him how wonderful he is..."

"You think Ava would do that?"

"Please! Ava's had a lot of people fooled for a long time with her Miss Perfect act, but not me. All she has to do is bat her lashes and tell a man how big and strong he is and he falls for it. Brian fell for it and married her; Theo must have fallen for it, or he wouldn't have left her all that money; Patrick fell for it, put his life on hold for seven years and now what does he have to show for it?"

"She broke his heart," Maggie said. "I thought she really loved him and was just protecting him after Theo was murdered. You think she was just using Patrick, and now she'll use Scott the same way?"

"She needs someone to hold her hand and play daddy to her children. So, let's see, who's available? Who's feeling sorry for himself? Who would appreciate all the good food and flattery she dishes out? Who's always ready to ride in on a white horse and save the day? I'm only surprised it took her this long to get around to Scott."

"Scott is Patrick's friend," Maggie said. "He knows Patrick is still in love with Ava. Scott wouldn't do that to Patrick."

"You need to wake up and smell the testosterone, sister. I can hear her now: 'Oh, Scott, you're so manly and I feel so safe in your arms. I'm so weak and defenseless, and you're so strong and brave.'"

"She is good at playing on people's sympathies."

"I keep telling you she's the queen of this town's pity party, but you always defend her."

"She's a great mom."

"People can be more than one thing at a time. They can be good in some ways and conniving and evil in others."

"He did look very much at home there the other day."

"It's not too late," Hannah said. "But it soon will be."

"If Scott would rather be with Ava, then so be it. I'm not going to stand in their way."

"Pride won't keep you warm at night, cousin."

Maggie was reminded of Anne Marie's weird prophecy about how pride was her sin, and she should forgive those who had sinned against her.

"Anne Marie is crazy," Maggie said.

"Okay," Hannah said. "What's that got to do with anything?"

Maggie shook her head.

"Nothing. I don't want to talk about it anymore."

"So you keep saying."

Maggie's head was whirring with thoughts while she shelved the canned goods. She pictured Scott holding Little Fitz in Ava's kitchen. She pictured Ava and Scott having breakfast together every morning. She pictured Scott and Ava alone at night after the kids had been put to bed.

"Scott can't father children," Maggie said. "That's one of the reasons he and his ex-wife split up."

"I remember," Hannah said.

Maybe it would be the best thing for Scott to end up with Ava, Maggie thought. He'd get the family he always wanted, and Ava would appreciate everything Scott did. She wouldn't bark at him and find fault with him all the time. It now seemed to Maggie that this was what was going to happen. Scott would be happier with Ava than with her. Tears welled up in Maggie's eyes. She wiped them on her sleeve and sniffed.

"Are you crying?" Hannah asked her.

"No," Maggie said.

"Then you should definitely get that eye-leaking thing looked at," Hannah said and handed Maggie a box of tissues. "It's not a done deal, you know. You could still win him back."

"No," Maggie said. "He could have a family with her that he couldn't have with me."

"That's not true," Hannah said. "You can adopt as many rug rats as you want."

"No, this is for the best," Maggie said.

"Don't forget Ava is still married to your brother Brian."

"Somehow I don't think that's going to be for much longer. If Brian doesn't wind up dead before this is all over, I think Ava will get an annulment."

"Can you get one of those if you have kids?"

Maggie shrugged.

Father Stephen entered the garage and Maggie hurriedly wiped her eyes.

"Ladies," Father Stephen said. "Am I interrupting? Maggie? Are you okay?"

"Yes, Father," Maggie said. "I just had a fight with my mother. We'll both get over it."

"Do you want to come to my office and have a chat?"

"No, thank you. I'm fine."

"What about you, Hannah? I haven't seen you in the congregation for a long time."

"I'll be there this Sunday. I was just telling Maggie that this morning."

"That's great!" Father Stephen said. "I look forward to seeing you."

He thanked them for volunteering and left the garage.

"I'm pretty sure it's a very bad sin to lie to a priest," Maggie said.

"I wasn't lying. I told you this morning I'd be there, and I will. When do you get there, around ten-ish?"

"If you want to be there on time, which, if you're sitting with your Aunt Bonnie, you better be."

"I'll be there, you'll see. Has it changed much? All I remember is stand-up-sit-down-kneel-get-back-up-sing-rinse-and-repeat."

"It hasn't changed. Why this sudden religious conversion?"

"I don't know. Maybe I caught that thing Anne Marie has."

"I hope not," Maggie said. "One crazy queen of righteous salvation is enough in this town."

Hannah and Maggie packed up the last of the meal boxes that Elbie, the church van driver and handyman, would take to the families scheduled for deliveries.

"We barely covered the list," Hannah said as she surveyed the almost empty shelves of the food pantry they had just filled and depleted.

"I'll ask Ed to put an ad in the paper," Maggie said.

"Have you seen his new website?" Hannah asked. "It's good."

"He did it himself. I'm thinking about hiring him to make one for the bookstore."

"That's a good idea. Maybe I could get him to do one for my feral cat project."

"Have you submitted the grant proposal?"

"Not yet. Caroline pledged to put up the matching funds, but we don't have a check yet. If she follows through, the mayor says we're a shoe-in to get the grant."

"Well, she's got the money."

"And I placed all her brother's dogs for free..."

"On your own time, using county resources," Maggie finished. "Yes, Hannah, I know. You only tell everyone that every day."

"She owes me."

"Yes, she does."

Elbie Midkiff came in and greeted them, saying, "Hello, girls."

Elbie was a retired mine maintenance worker who did electrical, plumbing, and miscellaneous repair work for Sacred Heart Church. He drove the church van that brought people to and from services if they were unable to get there on their own. He also delivered the food pantry boxes on Mondays and Thursdays.

He sat down in a rocking chair by the gas stove, took out his pipe and a rolled up packet of tobacco. Maggie and Hannah sat on overturned milk crates and watched as he went through his ritual of emptying and filling the pipe. He didn't then light it, but clenched it between his back teeth, crossed his arms, leaned back, and got started on the latest gossip.

"I just got back from taking them monks that were staying with Miss Caroline up to the Pittsburgh Airport."

"She got rid of the monks?" Maggie said.

"She did," Elbie said. "They were the quietest passengers I have ever conveyed anywhere. If it weren't for Miss Callie, I would've been starved for company."

"Callie went along for the ride?" Hannah asked.

"Miss Callie is going with them all the way to Portland, Oregon. There's a monastery up there that's agreed to take 'em on, and she's going to work there in the kitchen. She has a degree from a culinary institution, she says. She is what you call a vegan, and vegans don't eat meat, nor eggs, nor drink a drop of milk, on account of that's considered cruelty to animals."

"Is she happy to be going?"

"Well, you know, that gal was disinclined to say anything untoward about anybody, but I got the idea she wasn't too happy at Pine Lodge."

"Really?" Hannah said. "Why's that?"

"I guess Miss Caroline is sorta nervy and het up most of the time. She likes things a certain way but doesn't want to be bothered with the details. Miss Callie also thinks Miss Caroline's got her religions a mite mixed up, on account of she doesn't want to settle on just one."

"When I was up there Caroline was complaining about the snow, saying how she wanted to go somewhere warm," Hannah said. "I bet she takes off before long."

"I was coming to that," Elbie said. "Miss Caroline is taking Mrs. Anne Marie Rodefeffer out to California to visit a lady that speaks to spirits. They're leaving tomorrow."

"How did Caroline get involved with Anne Marie?" Maggie asked.

"Knox told Miss Caroline about Miss Anne Marie speaking to spirits," Elbie said. "Miss Caroline said she knew somebody out in California who could help her control that."

"Caroline Eldridge is a danger to herself and others," Maggie said. "I wouldn't put her in charge of a stinkbug, let alone another human being. Anne Marie has had some sort of mental breakdown and should be under a doctor's care."

"It all makes sense, now," Hannah said. "I saw Knox up there and wondered what he was doing. Drew hasn't said anything about Caroline leaving."

"He probably doesn't know," Maggie said. "She'll dump him right before she gets on the plane. No, I want to amend that. She'll probably take off, and then he'll get a postcard from her next fall saying she's sorry she forgot to tell him goodbye, and p.s. she's now in Bali."

"What about Petula and Sven?" Hannah asked.

"They're staying on to look after the place," Elbie reported. "Somebody has to be there when the cell phone people come to put up the new tower."

"The what?" Maggie said.

"One of those cell phone companies is paying Miss Caroline upwards of a million dollars to put a cell phone tower on her property."

"Where?" Maggie said at the same time as Hannah said, "That big fat hypocrite."

"Now, that I don't rightly know," Elbie said. "Somewhere on the property up there, and you know those Eldridges own just about everything between here and the State Park."

Hannah told Maggie and Elbie about her experience at Caroline's, and what she'd claimed about cell phone transmissions' purported effect on honeybees.

"What do you wanna bet Knox is involved in that, too?" Maggie said. "All that land is supposed to be protected. It would take some shady legal maneuvering to get around that."

"He was out there," Hannah said, "and after he left, when I went back in, she was reading contracts."

"Poor Drew."

"I bet Drew doesn't know about any of this," Hannah said. "He was telling me yesterday about his plans to renovate the barn out at Pine Lodge and put his practice in it. He has a whole business plan drawn up and blueprints of the layout. He's excited about it."

"This is classic Caroline behavior," Maggie said. "He won't know what hit him."

"I hope she writes that big check for my feral cat project before she goes," Hannah said.

"Don't count on it," Elbie said. "Miss Callie said Miss Caroline's been living on credit cards and they haven't been paid for weeks."

Hannah and Maggie parted ways after Elbie left with the food pantry deliveries. Maggie went back to the bookstore, and Hannah crossed Rose Hill Avenue and then Pine Mountain Road to get to the veterinary clinic.

Drew's newest receptionist was Dee Goldman, a former nurse married to lawyer turned dairy farmer Levi Goldman. They owned a company called Pumpkin Ridge Farm, which sold organically produced eggs, poultry, and dairy products to area grocery stores.

Dee and Levi had come to Pine County from Princeton, New Jersey. They were part of the "back to the land" movement of the late sixties and early seventies, a few of those who stayed once the romance of the idea wore off.

"Hello, lady," Dee said when she saw Hannah. "Drew said you'd be here this afternoon. How are ya? How's that handsome husband?"

"I'm just peachy. How in the world do you have time to work here with all you guys have going on out at the farm? Bonnie said you were building a new dairy."

"Well, I told Levi it was the new dairy or me. I'm almost sixty years old, and I'm tired of working so hard. He said if I got a job that would pay for my replacement I could retire."

"Some retirement."

"Hey, this is a piece of cake compared to the farm. I'm still taking care of the house, but I have been kicked by my last cow. That didn't come out right, but you know what I mean."

"I sure do. They seem nice, but they're secretly waiting for you to let your guard down."

"Well, I guess if I were pregnant all the time I'd be grouchy too."

"How do you like the job?" Hannah asked, to change the subject.

"I love it. It's warm, it's inside, and Drew is the easiest guy in the world to get along with. I forgot what it was like for someone to tell me 'thank you.' He appreciates everything I do."

"I bet he does. Your predecessors were all idiots, every one of them. How do you feel about assisting with surgeries?"

"My nursing skills are rusty, but I'm used to doctoring cows and chickens. I should be able to learn it pretty quickly."

"You don't need a dog or cat on the farm, do you?"

"We're just as covered up in feral cats as anyone in this county," Dee said. "Our old dog died this past winter. I don't know if you knew that or not."

"No, I didn't. I don't have any good farm dogs right now, but I'll be on the lookout for one for you."

"It's got to get along with cats, can't chase the cows, and can't kill the chickens."

"I'll find something. I always do."

The bell hanging on the front door rang, and Caroline came in.

"Dee, hi! Hannah, hi!" she said. "How is everybody?"

Drew came out. They embraced and kissed.

"Look, Hannah, it's true love," Dee said. "Aren't they precious?"

Hannah said nothing but observed them closely. She quickly decided Drew didn't have a clue what was coming. Anne Marie came in behind Caroline and was introduced to everyone. She shook hands with Dee and Drew, and then said, "Of course, I know Hannah," as she shook Hannah's hand.

Her hand was warm to the touch, and to Hannah's surprise, Ann Marie held on and didn't let go. She looked off over Hannah's shoulder, and her eyes seemed to go out of focus.

"Something's wrong with Anne Marie," Hannah said. "I think she's having a seizure or something."

"She's fine," Caroline said. "Just relax and go with it."

"What's she doing?" Dee asked, and Caroline shushed her.

"She's in a trance state," Caroline said. "She's a conduit for the higher planes of consciousness."

Hannah was pulling hard on her hand now, but Ann Marie could not be detached. Hannah was about to kick her in the shins when Anne Marie spoke in a low, sonorous tone.

"With child," she said. "All will be well with the son. The mother and father were together in many past lives and still have lessons to learn together in this life."

"Stop her," Hannah pleaded with Caroline. "I don't like this."

"Listen to her," Caroline said. "You're privileged to have the opportunity to communicate with your guiding spirits."

"I want her to stop," Hannah said.

"Caroline," Drew said. "Hannah shouldn't have to humor her if it makes her uncomfortable."

"The mother is here to care for the beasts of the field and forest," Anna Marie interrupted. "When she petitions the source, assistance will always come."

"That's good news," Caroline said.

"Ask for a lotto number," Dee suggested in a loud whisper.

"Caroline," Drew said. "This can't be good for Anne Marie. Don't you think we should..."

"Don't take them all. Leave some to maintain the balance," Anne Marie said.

"Leave some what?" Dee asked.

"Thanks, Anne Marie!" Hannah said loudly, snapping the fingers of her free hand in front of the woman's transfixed face. "You can wake up now!"

"Don't break the trance," Caroline said. "It could be dangerous."

"Caroline," Drew said. "I don't think this is what you think it is."

"The vessel needs to eat," Anne Marie said. "Feed the vessel."

Anne Marie's face went pale; she let go of Hannah's hand and fainted. Drew and Caroline caught her and laid her on the hard bench in the waiting room. Caroline cradled her head while Drew ran to get the smelling salts.

Hannah shook the hand that Anne Marie had clutched so tightly. It was bright red and hot like it had a fever. She felt a little woozy, herself.

"That was some show," Dee said as she came back with a cold, wet cloth. "I've heard about this kind of stuff, but I've never seen it before. Is she okay?"

"She's fine," Caroline said. "She needs to eat something. You heard her, 'the vessel needs to eat.' Anne Marie hasn't been cared for properly, and her gift has been abused by people who wanted to take advantage of it. I'm going to see that she gets the proper care and training so that she can use it for its intended purpose."

"What's that?" Drew said as he came back into the room.

"To help people, of course," Caroline said. "And to teach us what the universe wants us to learn."

Drew broke the capsule and waved it under Ann Marie's nose. She immediately revived. Dee gave her the cloth, and Anne Marie wiped her face.

"Wow, that was a strong one," she said. "Was I out long?"

Hannah was hanging back, holding her sore hand, and Anne Marie looked right at her.

"You're going to have a son," she told Hannah. "And he's going to be funny, just like you."

Everyone looked at Hannah.

"Sorry," Hannah said, although she could feel her face flush. "I don't know what you're talking about."

Anne Marie continued to look at Hannah with a smug smile on her face while everyone else looked at Anne Marie.

"Let's get you something to eat," Caroline said and helped Anne Marie up from the bench. "Can you walk?"

"Yes, I'm fine," Anne Marie said, still looking at Hannah with that strange smile.

"We're going to run over to the bookstore and get something to eat, want to come?" she asked Drew.

"I can't," Drew said. "I have patients."

Caroline waved goodbye to everyone and led Anne Marie out. Hannah put her hands behind her back as Caroline pulled Anne Marie past her out the door.

"Are you okay, hon?" Dee asked Hannah.

"Yeah, I'm fine."

"Don't put too much stock in anything Anne Marie says," Drew said. "I personally think she's mentally ill and should be treated by a doctor."

"Then why is Caroline taking her to California?" Hannah asked, and then clapped her hand over her mouth.

"She's not," Drew said. "Where'd you hear that?"

"From a very reliable source," Hannah said.

"She isn't going anywhere," Drew said. "She's taking care of the monks."

"They left this morning," Hannah said.

Drew looked like he'd been hit by a bad news bus.

"Has Caroline given you the grant match check?" Hannah asked him.

"Yes, it's in my office safe."

"I'd get that in the bank right away, if I were you," Hannah said. "Just to be safe."

Drew looked at Hannah and then at the door through which Caroline had recently exited.

"She wouldn't do that to me," Drew said.

"She might," Hannah said. "She's done it before."

"I'll be right back," Drew said, and took his coat off the rack by the door as he went out.

"Wow," Dee said. "I've been living out on the farm too long. This town living is where all the action is."

"It is, don't kid yourself," Hannah told her. "Rose Hill is not the sleepy little town everyone thinks it is."

"Is she psychic? Did you believe anything she said?"

Hannah shook her head but didn't answer.

"Is Caroline dumping Drew?"

"I think so, yes. And that information came from a source I trust more than any guide in the spirit world. That gossip came from Elbie Midkiff."

"Then it must be true," Dee said. "Elbie's always right."

Hannah left the veterinary office, crossed the street, and ran into Scott coming out of the bakery with a bag in his hand.

"What'd you get me?" she asked, as he swung the bag up out of her reach.

"Get your own donuts," he said. "These are mine."

"C'mon," Hannah said. "I only want a bite."

"I know better," Scott said. "This whole bag is one bite to you."

"Hey, I heard you found some dead guy floating down the river."

"Something like that," Scott said.

"You need me to look into that for you?" Hannah said.

"No, I think Sarah can handle this one," Scott said.

"Tiny Crimefighter, you mean," Hannah said. "She's also known as the crime-fighting kitten or the pointy claw of the law."

"It's a county case," Scott said. "And that's fine by me."

"Who was the guy?" Hannah asked.

"His name was Ray," Scott said. "He was a bartender at the Roadhouse. It was probably drug-related."

"Hey," Hannah said. "I was up at the Roadhouse the other day, and there was some shady character who was worried I might be snooping in their dumpster. Maybe the murder weapon is in there."

"What did he look like?"

"The usual nefarious biker gang member, tattooed and pierced all over, but he had these little horns on his head. He looked familiar to me, like I've seen him somewhere else."

As soon as she said the words Hannah knew what was familiar about the man.

"I gotta go," she told Scott.

"Thanks for the tip," Scott called after her.

Maggie couldn't help but overhear the argument Drew and Caroline were having in the café of her bookstore. Anne Marie sat at a table, sipping her chamomile tea, openly listening as if it was every bit her business. Maggie reflected that she at least had the good manners to skulk behind a bookshelf and eavesdrop.

"When were you going to tell me?" Drew asked Caroline.

"I knew you'd react like this," Caroline said. "Even though you promised you wouldn't get too attached. Exclusive relationships are so bourgeois."

"But we made plans together," Drew said. "I was going to move my practice out to the lodge. I hired an architect; I paid him to draw up the blueprints."

"Send me the bill," Caroline said as she shrugged. "It's just money. When the universe commands, I obey. I'm supposed to take Anne Marie to California now. I'm being guided to help her."

"Just like you were guided to take care of the monks?" Drew asked her. "When that turned out to be too much hard work, you bailed on them, too."

"That was only ever supposed to be temporary," Caroline protested. "I was a bridge to help them get where they needed to go."

"I guess there's no point in arguing with you," Drew said, "when you can rationalize any selfish thing you decide to do."

"I'm not the one being selfish here," Caroline said. "I'm doing this for Anne Marie."

"Lucky her," Drew said. "Until you get bored and another whim sends you off in a new direction."

"I don't expect you to understand," Caroline said. "You're limited by your five senses at the expense of your sixth."

"Get some real help," Drew advised Anne Marie, who smiled and waved to him. "Go to a real doctor and get some medical advice. You have a mental illness, and you need medical treatment, not witch doctors and voodoo."

"Ignore him," Caroline insisted. "He's closed off at the crown chakra. He doesn't recognize any realm but the material."

"But I do recognize a self-indulgent, spoiled brat when I meet one," Drew said to Caroline. "Don't bother to keep in touch."

Drew walked out of the bookstore, and Caroline looked momentarily stung. Then she made a point of laughing, but everyone in the café looked away from her in embarrassment. Maggie escaped to her office, but Caroline found her there.

"I guess you heard that," Caroline said. "What a typical left-brain male."

"Drew is the most sensible person I know," Maggie said. "And I agree with him. You're a user and a hypocrite. Always have been, always will be."

"I can't believe you just said that. I thought we were friends."

"I wouldn't call what we had a friendship, considering you only remember me when you want something," Maggie said. "And who was it who preached to me about the evils of cell phones, who said they're killing all the honey bees?"

"Well, they are!" Caroline said. "Studies have shown that it's true. Cellular waves interfere with the bees' ability to navigate."

"So putting up a cell phone tower on the protected property your family owns squares with that belief in what way?"

"How did you find out about that?"

"Everyone knows about it, Caroline. We all know you're doing Knox a big favor by taking Ann Marie out of his way so you can get your cell phone tower request approved through his political connections. You can twist your spiritual beliefs to fit any self-serving thing you want to do. I wish I'd never wasted one minute caring about you. I don't intend to waste one more."

"Be careful, Maggie. Words can be dangerous weapons. Your toxic negativity bounces off my crystal shield back onto you. You're probably being influenced by lower plane disembodied entities."

"That's right, Caroline. I think you're full of crap so it must be the spirit cooties talking. Take your shield of craziness, get out of my bookstore, and don't come back," Maggie said, pointing at the door. "You are now officially banned."

"You shouldn't treat people like this," Caroline said. "You're creating horrible karma for yourself."

"This is your family's karma, not mine. I banned your brother and sister, and now I'm banning you."

Caroline held her head up and tried to leave the bookstore with some dignity, although it was difficult with the loopy Anne Marie in tow. Maggie slammed the door to her office.

Mitchell, who was tending the café counter, went over to the dry erase board of shame, where Maggie kept the names of those she'd banned from the bookstore. Theo Eldridge's name had been written so long ago it was faded, with parts of the letters missing. Gwyneth Eldridge's name was the latest addition, written in dark black caps at the top. Mitchell added Caroline's name up the side of the board in the only white space left.

"I heard she banned people, but I've never actually seen it done," a college student said to Mitchell. "Does she ever let them back in?"

"No," Mitchell said. "Maggie's what you might call a gifted grudge keeper. We're just glad she doesn't rule an unstable country with nuclear capabilities."

Hannah came in, and Mitchell filled her in. She went back to Maggie's office and tapped on the glass. Maggie's face was flushed in what Scott would have called a code red threat status.

"I came in to congratulate you on the Eldridge family banning trifecta," Hannah said.

"I can see why they get murdered so often," Maggie said.

Hannah closed the door behind her and sat down. She told Maggie all about the incident at the Roadhouse.

"And the reason this devil man looked so familiar," Hannah concluded, "was because he had these snake tattoos down each arm."

"Like the man in the blackmail photos we found in Theo's safe."

"It was him," Hannah said. "He was in cahoots with Theo, Phyllis, and your brother."

Hannah and Maggie had snooped around Theo's house after he died and had discovered his stash of blackmail photos, many of which they subsequently burned. The man with the snake tattoos had been a recurring player, but his face was never shown.

"We need to tell someone," Hannah said.

"And explain we know this how?" Maggie said. "We're lucky we didn't get caught when we did it; why would we confess now?'

"This guy was in those pictures with Phyllis and your brother. He was freaked out that I might look in the dumpster. He probably killed Ray and threw the murder weapon in there. I told Scott about the dumpster, but Tiny Crimefighter's the one in charge. We need to get this information to her."

"As awful as I know this will sound, Hannah," Maggie said. "I don't care that some drug dealing loser murdered another drug dealing loser."

"When I took my oath as a crime fighter," Hannah said, "I promised to uphold the law whenever it was most convenient to do so. What you're saying is this isn't one of those times."

"You're the masked mutt catcher," Maggie said. "You do the math."

"I'll have to put my superpowers to work and figure out a way to get this information into the right hands without serving jail time."

"Leave me out of it."

"I'm off," Hannah said, with her hands on her hips in her best superhero stance. "I have scanner grannies to prime and gossip to pump."

After Hannah left, Maggie sat at her desk and thought about what Anne Marie had said during her trance in Maggie's office. Could the serpent she warned Maggie about be the horned man? He certainly hadn't reminded Maggie of any angel she'd ever seen. As much as she believed Anne Marie had experienced some sort of mental breakdown, Maggie had felt something very disturbing as the woman held her hand and spoke in that weird voice. Maggie shivered, just thinking about it.

Maggie found Jeanette re-alphabetizing the fiction section.

"You're into all that new age stuff, aren't you?" she asked her.

"I'm interested in it," Jeanette said. "I like to think I keep an open mind."

"You know that thing Anne Marie did in here the other day, that trance thing in my office?"

"I knew something happened," Jeanette said. "But I didn't hear what she said."

"Do you think someone can be crazy and psychic?" Maggie asked her. "I mean, she's obviously got a screw loose, but some of what she said was so specific to me, and it felt so weird in there, all of the sudden. It was like the barometric pressure in the room changed, or something."

"I think the line between genius and madness is sometimes perforated," Jeanette said. "Maybe that goes for being mentally ill and psychic, too. Maybe she's both."

"My mother said that the gypsies used to tell her grandmother's fortune back in Scotland," Maggie said. "She believed they had second sight."

"What would your mother think of Anne Marie?"

"That she needs her head examined," Maggie said.

Ava was looking out the window in her bedroom when she was startled by a noise behind her. It was Jamie.

"Sorry," he said. "I called up the stairs, but you didn't answer. I heard you went to the doctor earlier today. I came up to make sure you were alright."

"This part of the house is off limits," Ava said. "There ought to be somewhere I can go to have a little privacy."

"I'm not your enemy, Ava," Jamie said, and to Ava's consternation, he entered the room and sat down on the edge of her bed. "I'm here to protect you and your family."

"I appreciate that, I do," Ava said. "But Scott's here most of the time. You don't need to hover."

"I know I don't have to," Jamie said. "I want to."

He was giving her a meaningful look; it was the kind of look Ava had been deflecting all her life.

"Do you always make passes at the people you're supposed to be protecting?" Ava asked him. "Aren't you afraid I'll report you to your supervisor?"

"I'm not trying to coerce you into anything, Ava; I'm just here to say what we both already know. You and I have a spark between us. I feel it every time you're near me. I know you feel it too."

"I've got enough going on in my life without you complicating it further, Agent Brown."

"We didn't plan for this to happen, but it did. You want this, you need this, and you know it."

"You're not the first man who's only known me for ten minutes but thinks he knows what I need," she said. "It's a common delusion. It can be painful to realize you've fooled yourself, but you'll eventually get over it."

"I've never done anything like this before," Jamie said. "I'm risking my job being up here right now, talking to you like this. I want to know you, Ava. Let me know you. You won't be sorry."

"You're very sure of yourself," Ava said. "I find handsome, overconfident men often turn out to be the biggest fools."

"Is it Patrick? Are you still in love with him?"

"That's none of your business."

"I can see you've got Scott wrapped around your little finger, but he's not right for you. He's in love with Maggie Fitzpatrick."

"Scott's a good friend to this family, that's all."

"So you're not attracted to me, is that it?"

Ava hesitated, and Jamie took that as encouragement. He jumped up and came over to where she stood at the window. Ava looked past him to the door.

"Scott took the older kids to their grandmother's house, and Terese has little Fitz in the parlor," Jamie said. "No one will hear us."

He took Ava in his arms, and she smiled at him.

"That's a wicked smile," he said, and for a moment she could see a glimpse of the vulnerability beneath his confident charm.

He kissed her, and the chemistry was as good as she thought it would be, had imagined it would be. She was lonely for that kind of passion, and he had it to give, she could feel it.

She broke away, saying, "I'm a married woman."

"That's never stopped you before," he said and winked at her.

Ava tried to slap him across the face, but he caught her hand and held it.

"How dare you," Ava said. "Get out of here."

Jamie smirked at her and walked out of the room, saying, "When you change your mind, Ava, you let me know. I'll be waiting."

CHAPTER SEVEN - Friday

When Scott woke up Thursday morning, Ava was standing next to the sofa in her family room, looking down at him.

"Is everything all right?" he said, as he struggled to sit up in a tangle of blankets.

"Everything's fine," Ava said and sat down on the edge of the sofa, turned toward him.

She was dressed for the day and had on her coat.

"Where are you going?" he asked her.

"I'm going to see Lily," she said. "I need you to stay here with the children until I get back."

"Why are you going to Lily's? What time is it?"

"It's five o'clock, and I'll be back in plenty of time to wake up Charlotte and Timmy. Here's the baby monitor. Little Fitz should sleep, but if he wakes up, change his diaper. If you give him his pacifier afterward, he should go right back to sleep, but you might have to rock him a little. You can handle it."

"Wait for me to get dressed, and I'll take you. You shouldn't be out alone. It's not safe."

"Agent Brown's taking me. He's outside warming up the car."

"Oh," Scott said.

"I want to talk to Lily, and I need you here with the children," Ava said. "You're the only person I feel safe leaving them with right now."

She kissed him then, not on the cheek but right on the lips. It was a brief, light kiss, but it was definitely more intimate than the cheek kisses Ava usually gave him.

"You're my rock, Scott. I couldn't get through this without you."

She smiled that warm smile, and she was so beautiful. Scott felt his body react, and he almost reached for her, but she stood up and patted him on the shoulder.

"I knew I could count on you. I'll be right back."

As she closed the back door behind her, the cold wind whipped around the corner and made Scott shiver. Through the baby monitor, he could hear Little Fitz snoring softly.

'What just happened?' he thought.

Lily was expecting Ava and swung open the door to her sunroom as Ava walked up the shoveled flagstone path. Jamie stayed in the car with the motor running. It was still dark out and bitterly cold.

"Thank you for agreeing to see me," Ava said, feeling awkwardly formal, even though she'd known Lily Crawford since she was a child.

Lily was a round, soft woman with white hair and wire-rim glasses. She was dressed in jeans and a pink sweater over a pink pinstriped blouse. Ava thought she looked like a Sunday school teacher.

"Ava, you're always welcome here, you know that. I'm an early riser, so I'm always up this time of the morning."

Ava followed the older woman into the kitchen, where Lily's basset hound Betty Lou was curled up in a basket by the gas heater, with a small cat nestled in next to her. Betty Lou wagged her tail but didn't get up, and the small striped cat curled itself into a tighter ball and covered its nose with its tail.

"She's lazier than ever," Lily said. "She didn't even run out to greet you."

"How are they doing?" Ava asked as she took off her coat.

"Happy as two peas in a pod," Lily said. "They can't bear to be separated."

Ava sat down at Lily's kitchen table and accepted the cup of coffee Lily offered.

"You have some questions for me," Lily said.

"You need to tell me how you know Mrs. Wells," Ava said. "I saw her here a few weeks ago when I brought the children out to go sledding."

"I'm sorry to say I've known Mrs. Wells for many years," Lily told Ava. "I hate to speak ill of anyone, but that woman is truly evil."

"She came to my house and threatened the children and me," Ava said, with tears welling up in her large brown eyes. "She's demanding half a million dollars she says Brian stole from her. I'm hoping if I repay the debt she'll leave us alone. Do you think that's possible?"

"Once you've dealt with her," Lily said, "she never leaves you alone. That I know from experience."

"But how do you know her?" Ava asked.

"It's a long story," Lily said. "It may not make you feel any better, but you deserve to know the truth."

Lily wrapped her hands around the heavy mug on the table before her, as if to warm her hands, and began.

"Simon and I were high school sweethearts. He got drafted, went to Vietnam, and somehow managed to survive the experience. Afterward, he went to Clemson University on the GI bill; they have a good agricultural program there. After he graduated, we got married. He said when he was over there, in Vietnam, that our dream of living on a farm was all that kept him sane.

"His family was dirt poor, but I have a small trust fund, and my parents were willing to help us buy the property. They were sure we'd get tired of it and move back to Greenville, S.C.; that's where both our families are from. Both sets of parents are gone now. I was an only child. Simon lost touch with his brother Paul, who went to Canada to avoid the draft. Simon respected Paul's choice, but Paul did not return the favor. Anyway, we were not hippies but definitely into the idea of living a peaceful, rural life.

"Simon's degree was in horticulture. He worked as a county farm agent for a long time, but the politics and bureaucracy involved made him unhappy. We had my trust fund, but he wanted to support us through work he did with his own hands. Farming is hard, and there was very little support for organic methods back then. We could barely break even when the weather did cooperate. Without me knowing about it, Simon planted a little plot of cannabis, at first just to smoke himself or share with our friends. He'd learned to like it in the service, said it calmed his nerves. I didn't like it, but I couldn't see anything wrong with it. It didn't seem to hurt Simon, and it helped when he got to remembering too much about the war.

"What he grew was very good, apparently, and when it became clear that it could be a small business, he sold some of it. Our friends smoked it like some people drank wine, just socially, but weren't into drugs in a major way. Simon built a lab in the loft of the barn, experimented with different strains, and developed a hybrid that was extremely potent plus resistant to drought and infestation.

"We belonged to a Harley riding club, and while most of the people we met through the club were harmless weekend bikers like Simon and me, we occasionally crossed paths with some shady characters. Mrs. Wells' father was the local drug dealer and a dangerous man, but we naively thought that we could have dealings with him and not get our hands dirty. Simon made a deal with Mr. Wells to sell him everything we grew as long as Simon agreed not to sell it to anyone else. We could hardly keep up with his demand. Simon devoted a whole mountaintop to it on a remote part of our property. He planted it among the rows of corn we grew for the cattle.

"It seemed ideal until we found out the kind of business Mr. Wells was actually running. He was the kind of man who would sell heroin to children. He killed people who tried to move in on his territory. He was paranoid and suspected Simon of selling to others even though he wasn't. He would show up at our house, high out of his mind, making crazy accusations and threatening to kill us.

We wanted to get out, but we were so far into it we didn't know how. Simon finally came up with what he thought was the perfect solution. He offered to sell Mr. Wells the hybrid formula and train someone else to grow it and process it like he did. In exchange, Mr. Wells would let us out of the business.

"Mr. Wells agreed. Simon went down to Mexico and trained a farmer there. After he came home, he destroyed what was left of his source stock, plowed up and razed the ground that had been used to grow it, and locked up the lab. We thought we were home free and were relieved to be. We had enough money to see us through the rest of our lives, and we were out of danger, or so we thought.

"Mr. Wells was eventually murdered, some say by his own daughter, who is now referred to as 'Mrs. Wells.' She took over his business, so of course, she knew of our connection. Soon after Simon died, Mrs. Wells came to me and threatened me. She wanted money, and she knew I had it. If Simon had been alive, we might have been able to handle her, but alone I felt there was nothing I could do but cooperate. I've been paying her a substantial amount every month since then.

"I'm down to almost nothing now, and she wants the farm. She's threatened to have me murdered if I don't deed the farm over to her. I don't care about my reputation any longer. I don't even care about losing everything. I'd go to jail if I thought I'd be safe there, but she has people everywhere, people who wouldn't hesitate to kill you for money."

Ava spoke for the first time since Lily started her story, and Lily took a sip of her coffee.

"Aren't you afraid to tell me all this? Don't you worry she has the house and phone bugged?"

"You haven't met my nephew."

"Your nephew?"

"David," Lily said. "He's probably out in the car with your friend Jamie, keeping him company. I'm as sure they're listening in on us as I'm equally sure Mrs. Wells is not."

"What are you talking about?"

"You have your new friend Jamie, and I have David. He's staying with me while he considers buying the farm."

"I don't understand. How does he know Jamie?"

"He's an agent, dear, just like Jamie. We're telling everyone he's my nephew, but he's actually from the FBI."

"So you're going to testify against Mrs. Wells."

"Yes, I am. So is Gabriel, Maggie's ex-boyfriend. So was Brian supposed to, before he escaped. So, I'm guessing, are you."

"I already knew about Gabe," Ava said. "You remember when Margie died and Scott found a stash of stolen mail in her attic? There was a letter hidden there that Gabe wrote to Maggie seven years ago. In the letter, Gabe wrote about how Scott gave him a choice to leave town or be arrested, and how Brian got him involved in a drug delivery in Florida. After they wrecked the car they were using to transport the shipment, Brian left Gabriel there, injured, to take the blame. He's been in prison all this time."

"Gabriel was a good boy," Lily said. "He just got involved with the wrong people. He's coming to stay with me as soon as he gets out, which should be any day now. I think they must be going to arrest Mrs. Wells soon if they're bringing him here."

Ava took a deep breath and let it out with a whoosh.

"I thought when Theo died and Brian went to prison things would go back to normal."

"I'm so sorry you had to be involved," Lily said.

"It's all Brian's fault," Ava said. "You didn't do anything to me."

"I'm sorry just the same."

"Thank you," Ava said as she pushed her chair back and stood up. "For telling me the truth. I hope we all survive this."

Lily smiled, but it was a tired effort.

"You have more to live for than me," she said. "At this point, I don't care to lose everything. I just want to stop her from hurting anyone else."

Ava hugged Lily briefly and then put her coat back on.

A tall blonde man with light blue eyes came in through the back door and offered Ava a firm handshake.

"I'm David," he said, "Lily's nephew. It's good to meet you."

Ava rolled her eyes and gave him a pinched smile.

"Uh huh, whatever you say. Just take good care of her."

She said goodbye to Lily and went out to the car, where Jamie was standing, holding the passenger door open for her.

"I guess you heard all that," she said.

"Watch out, Ava, your real feelings are showing. We can't have that."

"What if Mrs. Wells has people watching?" Ava asked him. "What will they think of you and me being out here together?"

Jamie pushed Ava back against the open doorway of the car and kissed her, long and hard. She eventually pushed him away with a frown.

"I guess they'll be jealous," Jamie said.

"Don't do that again," Ava said. "There's enough gossip about me going around this town as it is."

"Yes ma'am," he said, but he was grinning. "Very unprofessional of me, I know. I promise I won't do it again unless you ask me to."

"I won't," she said.

"You will. You need a man, Ava, and I'm ready, willing, and able."

"I don't need a man, but if I ever do, it won't be you."

“Listen,” Jamie said to her, still standing close. “Why don’t you leave Scott alone? I know you can be pretty ruthless when it comes to men, but he’s a good guy, and he belongs with your sister-in-law.”

“I don’t know what you’re talking about.”

“Yes, you do. I’ve been observing you for a while now, even before you knew it. You’re a great mother, a successful business owner, and an upstanding citizen in your community. You’ve played the pitiful abandoned wife for a long time now, and I don’t fault you for that; you did what you had to do to survive and protect your kids. But I think there’s a part of you that’s just about done with being a good little girl.”

“You don’t know anything about me.”

“I know more than you think. But there’s one thing I don’t know that I’m dying to. Why did Theo leave you all that money?”

“I have no idea.”

“Did Theo make a deal with Brian to take care of you financially if Brian disappeared?”

“No, that’s absurd. Brian borrowed a half million from Theo to buy drugs, and when he sold them, he paid Theo back. I saw the loan documents. It was Mrs. Wells’ half million that he lost when they wrecked the car. It was his first assignment as her courier, and he blew it in a big way.”

“Is Charlotte Theo’s daughter?”

“No.”

“Did you ever have an affair with Theo?”

“We dated the summer after Brian graduated, for a few weeks. That’s all.”

“So, you’re telling me, that because he was once in love with you, way back when you were teenagers, the richest man in this town left you a fortune.”

“I guess so.”

Ava pushed Jamie away, sat down in the car, and shut her door. She fastened her seat belt as he came around and got in the driver's side of the car. She looked away from him until they backed out and started down the driveway. Then she met his gaze. He looked amused.

"I want more agents," Ava said.

"More agents?"

"When you arrest Mrs. Wells I want agents watching my children every moment of every day. I want a bodyguard, and I don't care how obvious it is that I have one. I want a team of agents watching over my family every second until this is over."

Jamie laughed out loud, and Ava scowled at him.

"You're something else, Ava," he said and gave her a longing, sexually charged look.

"That's my price," she said.

"You've got it," he said. "As long I get the night shift."

Ava smiled at that, but turned her head away as she said, "we'll see."

When they returned to the bed and breakfast, they found Scott in the kitchen holding a howling baby while trying to warm a bottle of formula under the hot water tap.

"Thank goodness," he said and handed the baby to Ava.

Jamie was trying hard to control his smirk.

"He not only filled his diaper," Scott said, "He filled both legs of his pajamas. I never knew so much poop could come out of such a small human. And the smell! I threw his pajamas away and hosed him off in the kitchen sink. Then he peed all over everything, including me. You're going to have to bleach the whole kitchen."

Ava took the baby, popped a clean pacifier in his mouth, and thanked Scott for his help.

"Hey, man," Jamie said. "Good news: I've got some additional agents coming so you can sleep in your own bed tonight."

"I don't mind staying," Scott told Jamie. "Whatever Ava needs I'm glad to do."

"Me too, my friend," Jamie said while clapping him on the back. "Me too."

County sheriff's investigator Sarah Albright knew she had no business investigating Ray's murder, but she'd received an anonymous tip about a certain tattooed biker who may have been involved in the Theo Eldridge blackmail investigation and the murder of the Roadhouse bartender.

There was nothing she wanted more than to bring credible evidence to lay at the feet of the feds. In return, she would only ask that a kind word of praise be shared with her supervisor, who wasn't too happy with her right now.

She pounded on the door of Phyllis's motel room, out back of the Roadhouse, until she heard, "Alright already! Give me a second!"

Phyllis opened the door a crack. She looked as if she had just woke up, with smeared makeup and a deeply lined face. Sarah knew the woman was in her mid-thirties, but she looked twenty years older.

"You," Phyllis said in disgust. "What in the hell do you want?"

"Let me in, and I'll tell you," Sarah said. "Or we can use the cuffs and take you down to the county lockup for a chat."

"Hold your horses," Phyllis said and closed the door long enough to unhook the flimsy security chain.

Sarah picked her way through a thick layer of empty liquor bottles, overflowing ashtrays, gossip magazines, and dirty clothes. She used her notebook to knock a pile of dirty clothing off a chair and sat down.

Phyllis lit a cigarette and sat on the edge of her bed. Her flimsy robe covered a stained tee shirt with a picture of The Golden Girls on it and some sparkly bikini underwear.

"Alright, what?" Phyllis asked.

"It's about Ray," Sarah said.

"I don't know anything about that," Phyllis said, pointing her cigarette at Sarah. "It's like I told the state cops: Ray and me partied together the night before he died but when I woke up the next day he was gone. I remember somebody called him on his cell phone, but he didn't tell me who it was or anything about Brian Fitzpatrick. I wouldn't cover for Brian, either. That man owes me a month's rent."

Phyllis's legs were crossed, and the foot she was dangling was twitching back and forth. She was looking at Sarah through a cloud of cigarette smoke, speculatively, as if she wondered if Sarah was buying her act, but there was also fear in her eyes.

"I don't think you're involved," Sarah said. "But I do think you know who killed Ray."

"I don't," Phyllis said. "You're wasting my time and yours."

"We've got the bar bugged, Phyllis," Sarah said. "We heard you talking about it. I have it on tape."

Sarah pulled a small tape recorder out of her inside jacket pocket, showed it to Phyllis, and then put it back in her pocket. She had clicked "record" before she entered the room, in order to tape their conversation.

"You guys wear me out," Phyllis said. "It isn't enough that you hounded my son into an early grave. Why do you gotta keep trying to get me involved in things all the time? Why don't you arrest the guy who was telling me about it? He's the one who did it."

"We can't find him," Sarah said, feeling the excitement build now that her bluff was paying off. "But I knew where to find you."

"Isn't he out at the cemetery?" Phyllis asked. "Hey, do you mind if I get a drink? My head is about to bust right off my neck."

"Go right ahead."

Phyllis went to the bathroom and came back with a stained coffee cup, a child-size juice box, and a pint of vodka. She mixed herself a drink and then sat down on the edge of the bed.

"Why would this man be in a cemetery?" Sarah asked her.

"Because he works at the Rose Hill cemetery. He's the caretaker out there, the spooky grave-digger guy."

"We have someone out there waiting for him," Sarah said, scrambling to keep Phyllis talking. "But he may have taken off."

"Well, if he killed Brian he'd have the money to do it. Fifty grand, they're paying. That night in the bar he was trying to buy my services if you know what I mean. I asked him, what did he take me for? I wouldn't sleep with that creep for all fifty grand."

"I find that hard to believe."

"I do have standards, believe it or not, and he smells like cemetery dirt," Phyllis said with a shudder. "He has creepy tattoos of devil stuff all over him. He has these horn thingies under his skin on top of his head. He calls himself the crypt keeper. Crystal says he does black magic in the graveyard."

"Who's Crystal?"

"She strips at Hotter Trotters over on Route 16. She's a Wicker, you know, one of those good witches."

"You mean she's a Wiccan?"

"Yeah, yeah, one of those. She says he has an evil aura."

"Okay, great. That's very helpful. So why did he kill Ray?"

"So Ray couldn't collect the reward. Somebody tipped him off about Ray meeting Brian. Not me, though. I didn't know it was Brian who called Ray. I figured that out after I talked to the state cops."

"What did the crypt keeper say happened?"

"Brian showed up on the wrong side of the river, so he killed Ray and Brian got away."

"Who's paying the reward?"

"Now, that I don't know," Phyllis said. "And I don't want to know."

"Why did he tell you all this?"

"He was falling down drunk, is why, and trying to get in my pants. He probably doesn't even remember telling me. Least I hope not. Hey! You gotta give me police protection."

"Did he tell you his name?"

"It's Duane something, I think."

"Now, Phyllis, we're going to cut you a break for cooperating with us."

"About damn time."

"As long as you don't tell anyone I was here or what we talked about; do you understand?"

"You better keep a close eye on this place," Phyllis said. "I don't wanna end up in the river like Ray."

"If you hear from Duane, you let me know. Don't meet alone with him. It wouldn't be safe."

"You have to protect me."

"Someone will be watching this place," Sarah said.

Phyllis didn't get up as Sarah went to the door.

"You know," Phyllis said, and Sarah paused at the open door. "I used to be pretty like you."

"What happened?" Sarah asked her.

"I wasted it," Phyllis said, "on losers and users."

Hannah met the vet's van in her driveway with a wave and a heavy heart.

"Hey, Gene," she said, as the vet on rotation got out of the vehicle.

He had a new assistant with him and introduced her as Rhonda. Hannah shook her hand.

"I hope you don't take this the wrong way, but I hate to see you arrive," Hannah said.

"I understand," Gene said, and patted her shoulder. "Let's see what we have."

Afterward, Hannah offered them coffee, and they took her up on it. They sat at the kitchen table. Hannah was trembling with emotion and had to excuse herself to go throw up in the little bathroom under the stairs.

"How far along are you?" Rhonda asked when she came back.

Hannah started to deny it but then shook her head and sighed instead.

"Three months and some change."

"You're through the worst of it, I bet," Rhonda said. "The whole nine months I cried every time someone looked at me cross-eyed, but I only threw up during the first trimester."

"It's the hormones," Gene said. "My wife did the same thing."

Hannah made them coffee and served them some coffee cake, but neither wanted anything to eat.

"I think my day's bad until I think about yours," Hannah said. "You're just getting started."

"It's hard," Gene said, and Rhonda nodded. "But I ask myself what kind of a life it would be locked up in a little cage, angry and unhappy and unloved. I'd rather go to sleep forever than live like that."

"I don't know," Hannah said. "I think just to be alive, warm, fed, and able to see the sky each day is worth something."

Gene stood up, said, "Well, we have miles to go before we sleep."

Hannah shook hands with both of them.

"Congratulations on the baby," Rhonda said.

"Thanks," Hannah said, but her thoughts were on the quiet barn and her missing housedogs.

After the county vet left, Hannah worked in the house all morning, doing anything she could think of to avoid the silence of the barn. Gene and Rhonda had taken the dead dogs away, so all Hannah had left to do was sterilize their empty kennels, and she had all day to do it. She was sitting at the kitchen table, nibbling on saltines and reading the grant application instructions when she heard a vehicle coming down the long drive. She looked out to see Patrick's truck, and he leaned on the horn as soon as he started down the driveway.

When she got outside, she saw Patrick had three dogs in the cab of the truck with him; two were hers. As soon as he opened the door, Wally and Jax leaped out of the cab in a frenzy of happy barking and wagging, and almost knocked her over.

"Patrick! Thank you!" she cried.

They were muddy and stinky and covered in burrs, but they were beautiful to Hannah.

"Oh my gosh, I missed you guys!" she told them as they jumped up and put their muddy paws all over her, trying to kiss her face. "You bad, bad dogs! Let's go get you cleaned up so you can come inside."

Patrick followed her out to the barn. Banjo trotted alongside Patrick, looking proud as if he'd done this good thing all by himself.

"Where did you find them?" she asked.

"I put the word out to all the beverage distribution guys, and they must have told every bar owner and convenience store clerk in all of God's country. Last night I heard back from a man over at Bruceton Mills who said he saw the dogs on his property. He said he fed them on his back porch yesterday evening but couldn't catch them. I didn't want to get your hopes up, so I didn't call. I got up early this morning and headed over there. I stood out back of that man's house yelling my fool head off for an hour.

Sure enough, eventually they came running down the hillside, and they were glad to see their Uncle Patrick."

"That's over twenty miles from here."

"They must have gone as the crow flies. Probably still ten miles."

"How can I ever thank you? I thought I'd never see them again."

"Tweren't nothing, as the man over in Bruceton Mills said. I knew you were having a bad day today."

"You made it much better," she said and started picking burrs off Wally's matted coat.

"I guess the deed's done," he said, looking at the empty kennels.

"Yeah, got it over with early, which I always prefer. They worked with the dogs a little beforehand and agreed with me that they weren't ever going to be anyone's pets. Gene always brings them steak for their last meal."

Hannah teared up then, and Patrick cleared his throat as well.

"Where's Maggie? I thought she was going to stay with you."

"She's only called every five minutes," Hannah said. "I prefer to do these days by myself. I've got a taser in one coat pocket and my cell phone in the other. Nobody's gonna get the jump on me."

"Can I help you clean up the kennels?"

"No, but thanks. You've done your good deed for the day. You better get going to the gas station before Dad calls around looking for you."

Patrick said goodbye and he and Banjo left.

"Now, as for you rotten delinquents," Hannah told the grinning dogs dancing around her. "We're gonna have us some burr picking, some brushing, a warm bath, and then big treats in the house. I'm so glad you're back."

Maggie left the bookstore by the front door and decided on the spur of the moment to go check on her dad. She was avoiding the bakery because of her fight with her mother but didn't want to neglect her father. She knew Patrick was giving him lunch today, but Fitz liked to see his only daughter Maggie, and Maggie liked to see her Grandpa Tim, who slept most of the day and night in a recliner in the same front room as her father. Maggie walked toward the college and then down the narrow alley on the other side of the Bijou Theater known as Daisy Lane. It was a single lane gravel road that ran alongside a brick wall with ornamental iron fencing set in the top that served as the boundary of the Eldridge College campus, all the way from Lilac Avenue down to the river.

When she got to her parents' house, she saw that Grandpa Tim was sound asleep in his recliner and her father was watching a twenty-four-hour news channel. The Irish setter everyone referred to as "Lazy Ass Laddie" was sprawled out in his usual place in front of the gas fire.

Maggie bent down to kiss her father's scratchy cheek and smelled whiskey on his breath. There was a cup of coffee on the TV tray next to his chair that she bet had more whiskey than coffee in it. She said nothing about it because there was no point. The drunker he got, the more Irish her father sounded, and then he fell asleep. He might be pickling his liver, but at least he wasn't operating any machinery heavier than a recliner.

Fitz Fitzpatrick had been a tall, strong, handsome man in his youth, looking much like her brothers Sean and Patrick did now. Fitz fell off a ladder and broke some vertebrae in his back when Maggie was still in elementary school. It was a miracle he could walk at all, and he was in constant pain. Doc Machalvie kept him supplied with pain medication and Patrick kept him supplied with whiskey. It was one of those situations that everyone was aware of, and no one agreed with, but no one knew what to do about it, so they did nothing.

"Would you get me an oatmeal pie out of the cupboard over the fridge, there, Maggie? That's a good girl. Your mother thinks they're hidden up there, but Patrick keeps filling the box, so she doesn't know I'm eating them. Bring me two. I'm fair addicted to those things. They must be filled with the crack cocaine or something."

Maggie brought him two cellophane wrapped pies and refilled his coffee cup with coffee. He knew better than to ask her to tip some more whiskey in. She was her mother's daughter in many ways.

"Grandpa Tim's sleeping mighty deep this morning," she said, and as soon as the words were out of her mouth, she wished them back in. Grandpa Tim was too still. She didn't want to, but she walked over to his chair and knelt there.

"He had a rough night of it," her father said. "He's been having an awful pain in his throat where they zapped it to get all the cancer. He won't go back to the specialist, and I don't blame him one bit. They poke you and prod you, and charge you a fortune, but they're just guessing what's wrong with a body because they don't really know. He took a couple of my pain pills in the night, and he's been sleeping like a baby ever since. Don't wake him, Maggie, there's a good girl. Let the poor man sleep in peace."

Maggie lifted her fingers off her grandfather's cool wrist and took a deep breath before she turned.

"Da," she said.

"You haven't called me that in ages," her father said, "not since you were a little girl."

"Dad," Maggie said.

"Look at that rotten bastard on the TV, Maggie. He lied and cheated and stole from good, honest people in order to line his own pockets, only now he says he's found the Lord, and he's sorry. You wait until the Lord finds him. He'll find out what sorry is."

Maggie went to the kitchen and swung the door closed behind her. She dialed the bakery first; when her Aunt Delia answered Maggie breathed a sigh of relief that it wasn't her mother. She quietly told Delia that Grandpa Tim had passed away. Delia said that she would bring Bonnie home.

Maggie dialed the service station and told her Uncle Curtis, who said he would call her Uncle Ian. He also said he would tell Patrick, and they would come right over. Maggie dialed Hannah, but she didn't answer. Maggie remembered again that this was the day the inmates were to be executed, so she left a message. Then she called her brother Sean at the bank where he worked in Pittsburgh, and he said he would be there as soon as he could.

"I had planned to come home today, anyway. I'll run home and pack a bag," he said. "I should be there in a few hours."

"That's everyone," she breathed into the telephone as soon as Sean hung up.

She'd called every person she knew would say, "I'm on my way" rather than ask, "Should I come?" She thought of calling Ava but didn't. She no longer knew into which category her sister-in-law fell. Back in the front room, her father was arguing with a politician on the television.

"You're not representing the common man, you lying, thieving sack of horse manure. You're representing the lobbyist you sold your soul to," he said. "You wouldn't know a day of honest labor if it jumped up and bit you in the arse."

"Dad," Maggie said, as she stooped next to him.

"What is it, sweetheart?" he said, but he was still looking at the television.

"Grandpa Tim has died," she said. "He's passed away."

Her father looked at her with a frown and then looked over at his father-in-law.

"You're quite sure," he said.

"I'm sure. He must have died in his sleep."

"You'll need to call your mother."

"I just did."

"That's good," he said, patting her arm. "She'll take care of everything."

He took a deep swig of his coffee cocktail and considered the still body of the man who had been his friend, mentor, and companion for many years.

"If you're going to go," he said, "that's the way to do it."

He raised his cup in a salute and said, "May God rest your soul, Timothy Brian MacGregor. You were a good man, a good husband, and a good father to your daughter."

Her father drained what was left in the coffee cup and wiped his mouth.

"Cover him up, Maggie, do," he said. "You don't want your poor mother to see him all at once like that. It will give her a shock."

Fitz went back to watching his program. Maggie closed her eyes briefly, sighed, and then took an afghan and covered Grandpa Tim. She called to Lazy Ass Laddie and made him go outside in the backyard, then filled two tea kettles and put them both on to boil. She got out the canister of tea and filled the sugar bowl. She took out a new filter and made a full pot of coffee. She found her father's whiskey (behind the toilet paper rolls in the bathroom cupboard) and poured herself a shot.

"God rest your soul, Grandpa Tim," she said and swallowed the burning liquid.

By noon Grandpa Tim's body was at Machalvie's Funeral Home, and Doc Machalvie was pouring shots of Jameson's in the front room of the house. All the women who came to pay their respects brought food and crowded in the kitchen, drinking tea or coffee. All the men who showed up brought whiskey or beer and were lounging in the living room, singing old songs while they drank. Sean alternated between the two rooms, although he kept offering to go get anything that was needed in order to get out of the house.

Maggie didn't think she could bear the crowd in the house for one more minute. She was sitting on the glider in the sunroom at the back of the house, drinking coffee with a fair amount of whiskey in it. She rarely drank but felt this was one occasion that warranted it.

"Where's your drink?' she asked Hannah.

"Tea's fine," Hannah said.

"My father would say why don't you have a wee drop?"

"No thanks," Hannah said.

"You won't drink, you quit smoking, and you claim you're going back to church. What happened to you? Did you fall and hit your head? Did you lose a bet?"

"No," Hannah said. "I just feel like it's time to make a change."

"You'll be eating tofu and taking dance aerobics next."

"Don't count on it."

"I heard you got your dogs back."

"Patrick tracked them down and brought them home. They're at my mom's house, getting spoiled rotten."

Lazy Ass Laddie was sleeping at Hannah's feet, next to the beagle Banjo, who was pining for Patrick. The sunroom was chilly, but Patrick had brought out a space heater for them to use so that their fronts were warm and only their backsides were frozen.

"My brother Patrick is a fine man," Maggie said. "Sean and Patrick are both very fine, very good brothers."

"You're drunk," Hannah said. "Do yourself a favor and don't start kissing everyone and telling them how much you love them. As much as I'd enjoy watching you do it, you'd hate yourself in the morning."

Scott came in the back door onto the porch, and Hannah excused herself after greeting him with a peck on the cheek.

“She’s drunk,” she whispered in his ear.

Scott shook off his coat and sat down in the wicker rocker Hannah had just vacated, looking at Maggie with sincere sympathy.

“I’m so sorry about your Grandpa Tim,” he said. “I know how fond he was of you, and how much you loved him.”

Maggie nodded in an exaggerated way and then wiped her eyes.

“I’ve had a little whiskey,” she said. “You’ll have to excuse me.”

“I do,” Scott said. “It’s completely understandable given the events of the recent days and weeks.”

“Not to mention months and years,” Maggie said.

“That too, yes.”

“It all started when Cousin Liam died. We were all just kids.”

“That was very sad.”

“Then Dad fell off the ladder.”

“I remember.”

“Then I didn’t go to college.”

“You could always go back.”

“No,” she shook her head. “Way too late, in all regards. Don’t argue with me.”

“Okay,” he said.

“Then Grandma Rose died.”

“I was scared to death of her.”

“We all were. She hated my mother.”

“They fought, that’s true.”

“Then Sam got his legs blown off outside Kuwait.”

“That was awful.”

“Then Gabe left,” she said. “But you know all about that.”

Scott just nodded.

"Then my house burned down."

"That was terrible," Scott said.

"Then Brian left Ava."

"Yes, he did."

"Oh wait," she said. "Eve left Ed on Valentine's Day. Gabe left me right before Easter. Then you and whatsername broke up. When did that happen?"

"It was May of the same year. Seven years ago."

"That whole year sucked."

"It did."

"So where was I?"

"Brian left Ava."

"Oh, and Brad drowned. Don't forget Brad."

"That was when we were in high school."

"Sean loved him, you know."

"I know; it was sad for everyone."

"Sean left home because Theo blackmailed him. He lives in Pittsburgh. He'll be here soon."

"I just saw him. He's in the kitchen."

"Sean's a good brother."

"Yes, he is."

"Theo was a rotten bastard."

"Yes, he was."

"And now he's dead."

"Yep."

"Why does everyone keep leaving or dying?" she asked him. "You're the police, do something."

"Grandpa Tim was old and sick, so he was going to have to die sometime."

"But why today? Hannah's pit bulls got killed today. Caroline broke Drew's heart yesterday. Sam keeps breaking Hannah's heart over and over and over. Ava broke Patrick's heart. You and I are barely speaking. Brian's such a bastard. Now Grandpa Tim's dead. Why can't God spread it all out a little more?"

"People are choosing to do most of those things, Maggie, not God."

"But God is supposed to send angels to intervene. Why do they show up for some things but not others? Is there a seven-year curse on us or something? Did we forget to invite some bad fairy to a christening?"

"I don't know, Maggie. It's definitely been a rollercoaster this year."

"That's exactly right," Maggie said. "You said a true, right thing, right there, you just did."

"I think it's time for some plain coffee, Maggie, what do you say?"

"Alright, I've had enough," she said but took another sip of her whiskey-laced coffee.

"You let me have that, and I'll go make you a fresh one without whiskey in it."

"You always take good care of me," Maggie said. "You're a good man, Scott, a fine man."

"I think I like her better drunk," Scott said to Hannah in the kitchen.

The crowd had thinned out somewhat. Father Stephen had gone, and Bonnie was upstairs lying down. Hannah was washing coffee cups, and Sean was drying.

"I'm getting her some plain coffee," Scott said.

"She never gets drunk," Hannah told Sean. "Never."

"She doesn't like to lose control," Sean said, "in contrast to our role model in there."

Fitz could be heard in the front room singing a sad Irish folksong, although you couldn't understand a single word. Patrick, on the other hand, had a beautiful voice and wasn't quite as drunk. He was playing an old upright piano that was in desperate need of tuning.

When Scott got back to the sunroom, Maggie was lying down on the glider's cushions, snoring. He set the coffee cup down, covered Maggie with his coat, and then sat in the wicker rocker.

She woke up startled and asked, "Where is everybody?"

"I'm right here," he told her and covered her up as she lay back down.

"Don't leave me," she said.

"I won't, I promise," he said.

Scott made himself comfortable, put his feet up on the wicker coffee table, and sipped the coffee he'd brought out for Maggie. Lazy Ass Laddie groaned and rolled over to expose his other side to the small heater. Banjo moaned a little and looked longingly at the door to the kitchen. Patrick had told him to stay, and while he lived to please Patrick, he wasn't happy about it.

Hannah stuck her head out the back door of the kitchen.

"You want me to sit with her?"

"No," Scott said. "There's nowhere else I'd rather be."

Hannah went back in the kitchen and leaned down close to Sean, who was sitting at the table eating some rolled up cold cuts impaled on toothpicks.

"Ava may not have won the battle after all," she said.

She'd been filling Sean in on every subject.

"Good," said Sean.

Hannah sat down, speared some olives, and ate them.

"I can't seem to get enough olives lately," she said. "Black ones, green ones, with pits or pimentos."

"The food is the only good part about these things."

"I've been talking your ears off telling you all the Rose Hill gossip, and you haven't said a thing about you. How's Pittsburgh?"

"It's fine, I guess. I'm getting to that place in my job where I know how to do everything, I've done it all a million times, and I'm bored to death."

"So do something else."

"I make too much money just to walk away. A few more years and I can retire."

"What is it you do, again? I know it's in a bank, so there's money involved."

"The official answer is that I manage people's money by helping them invest it wisely; by setting up trusts for their heirs, and by finding the lowest cost way to distribute the earnings."

"What's the truth?"

"I manage people's greed, vindictiveness, and unreasonable expectations."

"Uh oh, you're using your powers for evil. Jesus hates that, you know."

"I do encourage people to donate to charity, for the write-off, of course."

"Come back from the dark side, Sean. The force is strong with you."

"I get six weeks of vacation every year, and I can't take any of it. I have to be available every moment of every day to hold hands with jumpy clients. I work at home for two hours in the morning before I even go to work at the bank. I stay until eight or nine every night, and I take work home on weekends. I work for a bunch of conservative backslapping pinheads who love nothing more than to provide each other with alibis so they can cheat on their wives. Then there are the board meetings, committee meetings, and management meetings where no one actually says anything; they just sling around phrases like, 'value-added,' 'core competencies,' and 'performance indicators.'"

"Those aren't real words," Hannah said. "Use them in a sentence."

"We need to re-examine our core competencies to ensure that the end product is value-added, results-driven, and comparable in synergy with the bottom line of our targeted performance indicators."

"What in the world does that mean?"

"Make more money, or we'll replace you."

"That sounds like a soul-sucking job."

"It is. How's your job?"

"I helped someone kill four dogs today."

"I'm so sorry. You win. My job is never, even on the worst day, on par with that."

"Thank you. How's your love life?"

Sean gave Hannah a wary look.

"There isn't one right now."

"A handsome single man like yourself? What's wrong with those Pitt chicks?"

"Um, actually it may have more to do with me being gay."

Sean looked as if he was bracing himself for rejection and judgment.

Hannah did look shocked.

"Jiminy Christmas. Does anybody else know?" she asked him. "I mean, here."

"Maggie and Patrick know. I thought Maggie probably told you."

"No, that little scamp never said a word."

"I haven't told Mom and Dad yet, but I plan to."

"It'll be fine," Hannah said. "It's much more accepted now than it was."

"Sure, Hannah," Sean said as he gave her a dubious look.

"Well, what do you want me to say, Sean? It will shock the hell out of them, they'll be pissed off about it for a while, and then they'll either get over it or they won't."

"You're right. I know."

"But it doesn't matter to me," Hannah said. "I'm a skilled matchmaker, and I'll just have to use my core competencies to find you a value-added boyfriend. What kind of performance indicators are you looking for?"

"No thanks," Sean said. "I'll figure it out myself."

"Well, since you told me a big secret I'll tell you one. I am great with child."

"Hannah, that's wonderful!"

"Nobody else knows about it though, not even Maggie, so don't tell."

"Sam must be thrilled."

"He doesn't know. He's been gone for a few weeks, on business."

"I bet he'll be excited when he finds out."

"We'll see."

Some ladies arrived with more food, so Hannah rose to greet them.

By six o'clock Maggie was awake with a headache. Scott's back was stiff from sitting so long in an uncomfortable chair.

"Hi," she said to Scott. "When did you get here?"

"A little while ago," Scott said.

"Sorry I was asleep," she said. "Being nice to so many nosy people is very tiring. My teeth hurt from grinding them and my face hurts from smiling. It sounds like the piano bar in the front room has finally closed. Where is everybody?"

"Your mother is upstairs in her room; she's had a sedative. Your father is asleep in the front room. Patrick took Doc home. Your uncles went back to work."

"Heaven forbid we would close a business when somebody dies," she said.

"I'm sure your uncles were fond of your Grandpa Tim, but he wasn't their father-in-law."

"Did Mom close the bakery?"

"No, Mandy was there, and now she's over at the Thorn."

"Aren't you supposed to be at Ava's?"

"No, that's done with. The FBI agents are keeping an eye on her."

"Hmph," Maggie said. "Did Ava come over?"

"She called to ask if she should come, and your brother told her not to."

"Figures. Who told you?"

"Patrick called, and I came right over."

"Thank you."

"You're welcome. How are you feeling?"

"Numb, with an aching head. I had some whiskey earlier, which is never a good idea."

"I'll get you some aspirin and a big glass of water."

"Thank you."

"It's the least I could do. You've nursed me through a few headaches."

"How's your head been?"

"Fine. The front room smells like a barbecue smoker, though, so I may leave by the back door."

"Don't go. I mean unless you need to."

Scott smiled at her.

"I'll stay," he said. "I've got nothing better to do."

After Scott went to the kitchen, Maggie leaned back and rubbed her temples.

Ed came by to say how sorry he was, and that he had to get home for Tommy. Maggie thanked him for coming. Sean came out and sat with her.

"Thanks for coming home so fast," Maggie said.

"Thanks for offering to let me stay with you. This house is going to be a drunken wake for several more days to come."

"I forgot I'm supposed to be staying with Hannah. Where is she?"

"She's staying at her parents' house tonight," Sean said. "Don't worry about it."

"Remember when Grandma Rose died?"

"And the drunken sons of the sainted Mother Rose drowned their sorrows for forty days and nights."

"She and Mom were like oil and water."

"More like hydrogen and whatever else you need to make a bomb."

Scott came back with her aspirin and water.

"Anything else I can do for you?" Scott asked Maggie.

"No," Maggie said. "I probably should go do my daughterly duties and put away all the casseroles and pies that are bound to be stacked to the ceiling in there. I'm sorry, that sounds ungrateful, and I'm not. One of the nice things about this town is that there will be many good-hearted, religious women available to form a buffer between my mother and me for the next few days."

"Hannah and I took care of the food. Let me take you home," Sean said. "I need to check my e-mail and voice mail and clear my calendar."

"Any word on when the funeral will be."

"Sunday," Sean said. "Right after church."

"Which means a buffet lunch for two hundred at the Community Center afterward," Maggie said.

"Probably."

"Oh, take me home, Sean. I get tired just thinking about it."

Scott and Sean helped her up, and she wobbled a bit but swore she was fine.

"Thanks again for coming, Scott," she said. "It was very kind of you."

"No problem," Scott said, and brushed her forehead with the briefest kiss before he left.

Sean drove her home and helped her up the back steps to her apartment.

"Excuse the mess," she said. "I've been running around like a chicken with its head cut off for days."

"Don't worry about it," Sean said as he picked up the phone handset in the kitchen. "Hey, Maggie, the light's on. You have a message."

"Oh, that's right," Maggie said. "I had two yesterday and only listened to the first one. It was Mom yelling at me to get my butt down to the bakery."

Maggie took the receiver out of Sean's hand and dialed her voice mail service. When prompted, she pushed the button that corresponded to "listen to your first message."

"Maggie," it began. It was Gabe.

Maggie slammed the phone down, and Sean was startled.

"What?" he said. "Was it Brian?"

"No," Maggie said. She was trembling and had gone two shades paler than usual.

"What was that?"

Maggie shook her head.

"Did somebody threaten you?" he asked.

"It was Gabe," she said. "Sean, I don't want this."

Maggie started crying, and Sean took her hand and led her to a chair by the kitchen table. He sat silently with her while she cried. Then he took a dish towel and made a cold, wet compress out of it, and put it on her eyes.

"Listen," Sean said. "This may not relate to your situation in any way, but it's the only comparison I can make to what you're feeling right now. Brad Eldridge was the love of my life. I've been in love since then, of course, and I've had my heart broken a few times. But no one has taken his place. No one could. I loved him with every fiber of my being. That sounds corny, but I don't know how to explain it any other way. I loved him regardless of anything he did to hurt or betray me. What I want to tell you is this: if Brad was alive and called me right now, I'd get in my car or get on a plane and go to wherever he was. I'd go to him and be with him and help him if I could. Does that make sense to you?"

Maggie nodded, and fresh tears fell down her cheeks.

"I keep telling myself he wasn't who he pretended to be, that it was all a big lie," Maggie said. "How could the love I feel be real when he wasn't who I thought he was?"

"You can love someone and not know all there is to know about him. He could even love you and lie to you. Nothing is black and white in this world. No one is all good or all bad."

"How did Brad break your heart? I mean, other than dying."

"He slept with Phyllis and told me he liked it. He wasn't like me; I knew I was gay before I knew what being gay meant. He was still trying to figure out what his preference was. For awhile that summer before he died, it was both."

"That must have been terrible for you."

"It was, but I accepted it; because we were friends and were honest with each other about it."

"But Gabe wasn't honest with me. He'd been in prison before he met me, and started dealing to Eldridge students for Mrs. Wells so she wouldn't tell me about it."

"He probably thought he was starting over after prison," Sean said. "He probably thought he could be a new person and change his whole life. Patrick said he was a great guy and was crazy about you."

"I thought so, too."

"Hannah told me what happened. I think Scott and Gabe were both trying to protect you."

"Gabe went down to Florida and got a job at some boat business in the Keys. Brian found him there and talked him into going with him to do a drug deal. They sold the first batch in Miami and Brian sent Theo his money. Then they had a car wreck in Fort Lauderdale. Brian took off and left Gabe pinned in the car. Gabe says he was just being paid to drive the car, but who knows what really happened? He got arrested with a boatload of drugs in the car. He wrote that letter to me from the county jail before he went to prison."

"If you'd received the letter, would you have gone to him?"

"Oh, probably; I was such an idiot."

"So, what's different now?"

"I don't trust my own judgment," Maggie said. "I think one thing, but I feel something completely opposite. What should I do?"

"I think if you don't face him you'll be stuck at this same point forever, and might waste the rest of your life wondering what if."

"I'll wait until later to listen to the message. I'm not ready right now."

"Then if you don't mind, I'm going to check my messages and do some e-mailing."

"Go right ahead. I'm going for a walk."

Maggie put on her coat and boots and went out the back door of the bookstore into the alley. The night was crisp and clear; the black sky was filled with stars and a fat crescent moon. She walked down to the corner behind the bank and crossed Pine Mountain Road, then continued down the alley to where it made a T with the alley between Sunflower Street and Pine Mountain Road. She turned up this alley, which went past the back of the bed and breakfast on the right. There were several cars with Maryland and Virginia license plates in the back parking lot next to Ava's minivan, so Maggie knew she had a full house.

Further up the alley on the left was the back door to Scott's house. She knocked, and he must have been in the kitchen because he let her in right away. He was surprised to see her, she could tell. He had paperwork spread out on the kitchen table.

"I'm interrupting," she said.

"I'm glad you did," he said. "Have a seat. Do you want some coffee or tea?"

"No, nothing for me, thanks. I've had enough coffee and tea today, not to mention whiskey."

Scott offered to take her coat, but she declined, saying, "I can't stay long."

Scott gathered up his paperwork as Maggie sat down at the table.

"What's going on?" he asked.

Maggie felt a rush of affection for Scott, who was sitting there looking at her with such tenderness and concern. She realized again how much she missed him, and how good it was to feel how much he cared. It made her feel even worse about what she was about to do.

"I have a terribly rude question to ask you," she said.

"Rude?"

"Maybe rude is not the word. Impertinent, maybe. Amazingly insensitive would be even more accurate."

"Okay. I'll brace myself."

"Before I ask you this rude question, though, I want to say something else. Something nice."

"Alright. I'll brace myself after you say the nice thing but not before."

"You and I have been having this weird, on-again, off-again, whatchamacallit for a year or so now. But before that, what we had was a friendship, a good one. Would you agree?"

"Absolutely."

"The reason I'm going to ask you this amazingly insensitive question is that I trust you to give me an honest answer, as my friend, even if you would rather not say anything; even if you would be tempted to lie."

"I'm prepared to be offended and still answer truthfully."

"I want to apologize in advance for the temerity to even ask this."

"Just ask me, Maggie. I won't lie to you."

"Do you think Gabe really loved me or was he only pretending to?"

Scott blinked and took a deep breath. Then he looked at Maggie, and she could see she'd hurt him.

"I'm sorry," she said. "You were his closest friend. You are the only person I can ask."

"I believed he loved you," Scott said.

"Thank you for that," she said and stood up.

"Maggie," Scott said. "There's something I want to say to you."

"Fair's fair," she said and sat back down.

"I know Gabe is coming back to testify against Mrs. Wells. I know you'll see him and there's a chance you may get back together. I know how much you loved each other. I just want you to remember one thing."

"What's that?"

"I love you, too."

"I know that. I do."

"I love you enough to stand by and watch you go through this next part, and if you don't end up with me, I'll understand. Even though I'll be sad, I won't hold it against you."

"I don't know what to say," Maggie said. "You're either the kindest or the stupidest man I've ever met. Either way, I'm lucky to have you in my life."

"Don't forget what I said."

"I won't."

Scott watched her walk down the alley until he couldn't see her anymore. Then he sat down and spread his paperwork back out on the table. He couldn't read it for a minute or two because his eyes were a little blurry, but eventually, he got back to work.

Ed waited up for Mandy to come home from working at the Rose and Thorn. He knew she would be exhausted after covering the bakery all day and going straight to the Rose and Thorn without a break. When she walked in the door, Ed could see dark shadows under her eyes. He hugged her and helped her take her coat off.

"This is a nice surprise," she said. "You're usually sawin' logs in the recliner by now."

"Can I get you anything?" he said. "Something to eat, maybe?"

"Naw," she said, as she slumped down on the couch. "I did nothin' but pick at the bakery all day, and Delia brung me some soup this evenin'. Did you go over to Bonnie's?"

"Yes, I did. Then I picked up Tommy, brought him home, gave him some dinner, and helped him with his homework. We played scrabble, watched some television, and he was in bed by nine."

Ed sat down and put his arm around Mandy. She snuggled close and rested her head on his shoulder.

"I sure do appreciate havin' you around," Mandy said. "The Fitzpatricks are always willin' to take Tommy when I gotta work, but they've got their hands full right now. It's so good to have a man to look after him. He loves you, you know."

"I love him, too," Ed said. "I enjoy taking care of him."

Mandy yawned.

"I don't think I've ever talked to you about when Eve and I broke up," he said.

"Huh-uh," Mandy said. "You never have."

"We were together six years," Ed said. "From graduate school until the year after my dad died. She didn't belong here in Rose Hill. She tried her best, but it just made us both miserable. I thought after she left that eventually, we might get back together, but I haven't thought that for a long time. The reason I mention this now is that I don't know if I ever told you that we never got divorced. There was no reason to do it, and neither of us ever wanted to marry anyone else. Except now I think you and I should get married and give Tommy a stable home. I think he'd like that. What do you think?"

Mandy was sound asleep.

It had taken Ed a long time to compose that big declaration, and he'd been proud of how he got through it. He guessed he'd have to do it again tomorrow.

CHAPTER EIGHT – Saturday

Maggie spent most of the night picturing various scenarios that ended with her reuniting with or ending things with Gabe. Lying in bed, staring at the ceiling, she dug out all the memories she'd stored in the furthest recesses of her mind, somewhere she never liked to go if she could help it (alongside: her father falling off the ladder; cousin Liam dying of leukemia; and climbing out the second floor window of her beloved house as it burned to the ground).

At the time she believed Gabe had saved her from a sad, lonely life working in her family bakery and living in her parents' house. Like a one-man demolition team, he'd persistently chipped away at the wall of smart-ass she hid behind until she was brave enough to show her true self to him. And then he loved her. A love she could feel, taste, smell, and see, every day they were together. After so many years of feeling like she came first with no one, and that no one would ever love her the way she wanted to be loved, Gabe had wooed her with patience and tenacity and had made her feel cherished.

It helped that he was handsome, charming, and kind. He loved people; he was willing to help anyone do anything. He was the kind of man who made people feel good just by being around. Everything Gabe did he seemed to enjoy doing, seemed to savor more than anyone else. Even ordinary things, like warm, clean towels right out of the dryer; he would bury his face in them, wrap them around his neck and hum with delight. Gabe's deep appreciation for simple pleasures created an atmosphere of joy in their house that was contagious. Maggie realized now that was probably how a man just released from prison might demonstrate his gratitude for the small pleasures in life that other, un-incarcerated people might take for granted.

Gabe made her a better person. He refused to let Maggie hide her fears behind sarcasm and sharp comments. He demanded that she be compassionate when she wanted to judge. He taught her how to be generous without expecting something in return. Maybe most importantly, he made her feel, as Aretha so aptly put it, like a natural woman. Over the three years they were together, he opened her up like a beautiful flower and made her believe her life could be happy and full of love. Then he left her in the middle of the night without saying goodbye.

Maggie couldn't reconcile the Gabe of her sweet memories with the Gabe selling drugs to college students, going to prison for drug trafficking, and lying to her about his past. How could he be both? Her Aunt Delia had once warned Maggie that she idealized Gabe so much that no man could ever replace him. Maggie wondered now if even Gabe himself could replace the man she thought of as the great love of her life.

By morning, after very little sleep, she hadn't come to any definitive decision, but she felt she was ready to listen to his voicemail message. Unfortunately, Sean was using her phone for a conference call. She took a shower and got dressed. She had this irrational feeling Gabe was coming any minute, so she put on clothes in which she felt she looked her best and took some trouble with her hair and makeup. She'd just put the kettle on for tea when there was a knock on her apartment door. Unreasonably, she thought it might be Gabe, and her heart began to pound. It was her mother.

Bonnie Fitzpatrick had been in her daughter's apartment maybe three times in the five years she'd lived there. She hadn't approved of Maggie living in sin with Gabe in the farmhouse up Possum Holler. After Gabe left and Maggie's house burned down, she'd gone back to her parents' house to live, and even though she and her mother fought the whole time, still her mother refused to help her set up the new apartment. She hadn't approved of Maggie buying the bookstore and leaving her job at the family bakery. She took to her bed with "a killing headache" on the day Maggie moved out.

Bonnie had a determined look on her face.

"Is your brother here?" she asked, in an irritated tone.

"He's on a conference call in the kitchen. Do you want to come in and wait?"

Bonnie came in, looked around the front room and sniffed a little.

"I've been trying to call you all morning, and the line's been busy."

"Sean's trying to do his work from here," Maggie said.

"His grandfather died. You'd think they'd understand he needs to be with his family right now."

"Is the bakery open today?"

"Of course it is. If you think I'm going to sit home and watch your father drink himself to death, you've got another think coming. I could have used your help this morning."

"I'm sorry, Mom, how are you doing? Let me take your coat."

Bonnie refused to take off her coat and perched on the edge of Maggie's deep reading chair. She looked all around at everything as if searching for something to criticize, until her eyes lit on Maggie's photo albums.

"Do you mind?" she asked, pointing to them.

Maggie brought over a stack of photo albums and pulled the ottoman over so she could look at them with her mother. There were many photos of Grandpa Tim in them. He was always smiling. You could mark time passing by the color of his hair: bright red, then a little duller red shot with white, then all white, then sparse and white over a bald head. He seemed to get smaller too, and then stooped over. After his cancer treatments, he seemed shrunken and pale, but still, he smiled.

"He was so proud to be Scottish, to have come over as a child so he could still remember what it was like back there," Bonnie said. "I'm sure he romanticized it in his memory, but maybe that's better. If he'd gone back, he might have been disappointed."

"He always said he didn't mind you marrying an Irishman, that they were just refugees from Scotland."

"He asked your father if he would consider taking the MacGregor name. Fitz knew a compliment when he heard one, meant only with the best intentions, but his mother had an absolute fit. Can you imagine? He would have been Fitz MacGregor."

"Grandma Rose told me she felt sorry for me because I had this awful ginger coloring," Maggie said. "She said it was a curse, and that I'd always be looked down upon because I had it."

"She said the same about your brother Brian," Bonnie said. "Did I ever tell you she refused to let your father name our first born after himself? She said he couldn't be sure it was his child because of all that red hair. When Patrick was born, she was beside herself. 'That one,' she said, 'is a Fitzpatrick.'"

"What an awful old witch."

"She was that, our Rose."

"Her three boys loved her, though. You couldn't say a word against her."

"Even though she hated their wives and picked on their children," Bonnie said. "When poor little Liam died she blamed Delia, said she had that French blood in her and had poisoned the boy with it."

"How could they defend her when she was so wicked?"

"Because she raised them without any help. Your grandfather Fitzpatrick was a horrible drunk and was always hopping trains to who knows where. There was even a rumor he had another family somewhere, in California, I think. Rose was left with three boys and no money. Before she opened the bakery, she baked at home all morning and delivered orders every afternoon. The boys helped her clean the bank every night. She worked all hours of the day and night to keep a roof over their heads and food on the table. In return, she demanded complete loyalty. When Fitz married me, she saw me as a threat, a rival for her affections. She never accepted me."

"I don't know how you stood it; working with her every day, living in the same house with her all those years."

"I think your father picked someone who was just as stubborn as his mother was. Neither of us was going to let the other one win."

"Did you ever feel like you won?"

"No one wins a tug of war like that. There's your father, a broken down old drunk just like his father, only too crippled to run off. Brian seems to have gone to the devil. Patrick won't settle down; he's broken the heart of every nice girl in this town. Sean couldn't wait to get away from us, and I can't even talk to my only daughter without making her hate me."

"I don't hate you."

"I'm glad to hear it."

"What was your mother like?"

"Just like me. We fought all the time, too."

"Maybe that's what all mothers and daughters do."

"Father Stephen says we each have to bend a little more. I don't know about you, but bending feels like giving in to me."

Maggie laughed, "Me too."

"Well, I guess we'll both just have to try harder," Bonnie said, "only you go first."

"Mom, I love you, but I'm going to lead my own life and make my own decisions, and I'm not going to do everything on your terms just to get along with you."

"You're a stubborn, pig-headed girl, just like I was. I just worry you'll end up alone, with no children."

"And marriage and children worked out so well for you?"

"It hasn't all been bad. You know, it's the grandchildren who are the real reward. You need a husband long enough to get the children who give you the grandchildren. Brian's given me some beautiful grandchildren, but Patrick and Sean need to get busy."

"Hi, Mom," Sean said as he entered the room. "What is it I'm supposed to get busy doing?"

Bonnie jumped up and hugged her youngest son.

"I need you to help me pick out some clothes for your Grandpa Tim to wear. Then I need you to take the clothes to Peg Machalvie and help me set up the Community Center for the funeral reception. Patrick has to work at the station and pub all day, so he'll be no help at all. I also need some help getting the reception baking done since your sister can't be bothered. Your father has some fool notion of a wake at the pub tonight, but I doubt he'll be conscious by the time it comes to go."

Sean put his coat on and followed Bonnie out the door. She was still telling him all the things she needed to do before the funeral the next day, and he waved to Maggie over his shoulder as he closed the door. Maggie's mother didn't look back or say goodbye to her; when one of Bonnie's sons was present Maggie always felt as if she'd disappeared.

The phone rang, and it was Jeanette downstairs, saying Lily Crawford was in the café and wanted to talk to her, so Maggie went down to the bookstore. On the way over to the café side, Maggie saw a young boy looking through the online role-playing game books.

"Do you need some help?" Maggie offered.

The boy had dark curly hair and big brown eyes. He was at that age that to Maggie seemed so bittersweet; she could see the boy he still was and the man he would become. He had a beautiful smile.

"I can only have one, and I don't know which is best," he said.

Maggie reached around to an end cap and handed the boy a magazine that she kept stocked there.

"Here's a magazine that reviews all the games. If you'd like to look through it, we don't mind. Or, if you can come back after three, Jeffrey will be here, and he's into all this in a big way. He can tell you all you need to know about it. I'm sorry I'm not more help."

An attractive woman came up and put her arm around the boy, then said something to him in Spanish. Maggie assumed it was his mother. She had the same dark eyes and hair, the same smile. The boy said something to his mother in Spanish, and the woman said "gracias" to Maggie. The boy thanked Maggie as well. Maggie thought to herself as she walked away from them that she wished more young customers had such good manners. That woman had done a good job raising her son.

Lily was sitting at a table by the window, looking out. Maggie had been hearing bits and pieces of what had been going on at Ava's, and she knew Lily was involved somehow because Gabe was coming to stay with her, but she hadn't had a chance to talk to her about it. She sat down and tapped on Lily's arm.

"Hey, come back," Maggie said. "You look like you're a million miles away."

"Oh, Maggie," Lily said, as she looked around the store as if she was trying to locate someone. "I need to talk to you, and it's going to have to be quick and painful, I'm sorry to say."

"What is it?" Maggie said.

"You know that I'm involved in this investigation that Ava's involved in."

"Someone told me that, and I meant to come and see you, but it's been super crazy around here the past couple days."

"Forgive me, Maggie," Lily said. "I should have said first how truly sorry I am about your grandfather."

"That's okay," Maggie said. "He never really recovered from his cancer treatments, and we knew it would happen some time."

"Oh, no," Lily said, looking over Maggie's shoulder.

Maggie turned around to see what she was looking at. The young boy and his mother were walking toward them, smiling. They seemed to know her.

"Is this your store?" the woman asked Maggie.

"Yes," Maggie said. "Are you vacationing here or visiting someone at the college?"

"We're waiting for my father," the boy said.

Maggie looked at Lily, curious to learn how she knew these people.

Lily looked aggrieved; there was no other word for it. She reached for Maggie's hand and squeezed it.

"Maggie, I want you to meet Luis and his mother, Maria. They're going to be staying with me for awhile. Maria, Luis, this is Maggie Fitzpatrick. She owns this bookstore."

Maggie held out her hand and shook each of theirs.

"Pleased to meet you," Maggie said.

"My mother says I have to wait to buy something when I come back with my father," the boy said. "He's coming on the bus tonight."

The penny dropped for Maggie, but she looked again at the son to be sure, and immediately saw the resemblance.

"Your last name is Cortez, isn't it?" she said.

"Yes," Luis said. "My father is Gabriel Cortez."

Lily gripped Maggie's hand, but Maggie pulled it away.

"A phone call would have been nice, Lily," Maggie said under her breath.

"Your line was busy all morning. I couldn't very well keep them locked up in my house until I talked to you," Lily said quietly. Then she said more loudly, "Maria and Luis came on the morning bus, although I wasn't expecting them until next week. They're enjoying Rose Hill, but wish they had brought warmer clothing."

Maggie rose, and because she couldn't help herself, she stared at Maria. The woman was lovely, and the son was as handsome as his father.

'Twelve years old,' Maggie thought, 'twelve or thirteen at the most.'

"I hope you enjoy your stay," she said, as graciously as she could manage.

Maria smiled and thanked Maggie again. Maggie didn't look back at Lily as she walked away, and then ran up the stairs to her apartment. She slammed the door behind her and went straight to the telephone in the kitchen. Her hands were shaking as she dialed the voice mail service. She punched the numbers in by rote.

"Maggie," Gabe said. His voice was the same, deep, warm baritone. A shiver ran through her body, and her stomach rolled. She slid down the wall until she was sitting on the floor of her kitchen, stretching out the phone cord.

"I don't know how much you know about what's going on; I'm not supposed to talk about it and definitely not on the phone. I should be in Rose Hill on Saturday night, and I'll come see you as soon as I can. There are some things I need to tell you in person. Things I've had on my conscience for a long time. I know I have no right to say this, but I can't wait to see you."

Maggie dropped the phone in her lap, looked around the room, but saw nothing. She'd thought when Gabe disappeared that the bottom had dropped out of her world, and when she found out he was in prison for drug trafficking she felt like things were as bad as they could get.

Now she'd discovered there was still a distance farther she could fall, and she was falling.

Drew went with Hannah to set the traps for the feral cats. She could tell he was down about Caroline, but she decided to let him bring it up. She gave him the map of the county with the trap sites marked in red. They were setting twenty today.

"We're lucky with the weather right now," Hannah said. "You don't want to trap them only to freeze them to death overnight. A warm front is supposed to come through tonight, and we'll put these in sheltered areas out of the wind."

"So we set the traps today and pick them up tomorrow."

"Yep. And half of them will have possums or raccoons in them. I caught a huge groundhog in one once. He was so fat that he couldn't turn around, so I had to take the darn thing apart to get him out. We'll let those guys go."

"So, maybe ten cats. When do you want to check them?"

"It will have to be early because I have church and then Grandpa Tim's funeral to go to. How do you feel about staying at my place and starting at four in the morning?"

"Fine with me," Drew said. "I have nowhere else to go and no one who cares where I am."

"Sorry about that," Hannah said. "I debated whether to tell you or not."

"I'm glad you did. I don't think Caroline was planning to. At least it didn't seem like it."

"If it makes you feel any better, she always does this. It wasn't something you did. She's very impulsive."

"I feel so stupid. All the signs were there, but I saw what I wanted to see and heard what I wanted to hear."

"At least we got the check."

"It kind of feels like she's paying me off."

"She owed me that money."

"I know," Drew said, "for finding homes for all of Theo's dogs, on your own time."

"With county resources," Hannah said. "Now we can get the grant, the college has agreed to host the Vision workers, and I have tentative agreements with people in ten other states to help us redistribute the cats."

"Who would want feral cats?"

"You'd be surprised. Farmers like them because they're natural predators for vermin, and if they're spayed and neutered there's no fear of overpopulation."

"Isn't that what Anne Marie was talking about? 'Keep some,' she said. 'Keep the balance,' or something like that."

"That lady is crazy."

"So you aren't pregnant."

Hannah didn't answer right away.

"You are?!"

"Yeah," Hannah said. "But very few people know. Maggie doesn't even know."

"Hannah, if you're pregnant you shouldn't be working with feral cats. Toxoplasmosis is a real danger to pregnant women."

"Toxowhatsits?"

"It's a disease you can get from cat feces and uncooked meat. It's dangerous for you and the baby."

"How am I supposed to run this project if I can't get near cats?"

"Maybe you can direct the project, and the Vision workers can handle the cats. Tomorrow I'll handle them. But please don't work with any feral cats while you're pregnant. Don't even scoop a litter box for a domesticated cat. Wash your hands thoroughly if you accidentally come in contact, and keep your hands away from your face until they're washed."

Hannah thought of the litter of kittens she'd recently rescued from under that house, and the local cats she petted whenever she came across them.

"Have you seen a doctor yet?" Drew asked her.

"No," Hannah said. "But I did the stick test thingy."

"I'm sure you're fine, but you should see a doctor soon. You need to be on prenatal vitamins and have tests to make sure the baby is okay."

"You mean that one with the long needle? I've heard about that. No, thanks."

"Just go see a doctor next week," Drew said. "You'll feel better if you do."

"Okay, okay," she said. "I'll go see Doc Machalvie next week. Heck, I think he delivered me."

Ed Harrison picked up the puppy from the pen he'd constructed in one corner of the newspaper office and took it outside to the alley to do its business. Tommy was still trying to decide on a name, so Ed was calling it 'pup.' He cleared an area of snow with his foot and put the puppy down on it.

"Hurry up, pup," Ed said, shivering without his jacket, which he'd left inside.

"Whatcha got there?" Scott said as he walked down the alley toward him.

Ed told him about the puppy and Scott admired it. He followed Ed back into the news office and watched as Ed put the puppy back into the pen. Hank was snoring on his bed by the stove.

"I missed you at the Fitzpatrick house last night," Scott said. "Everything okay?"

"Well, I've got my hands full with Tommy and the puppy now."

"I heard you talked with the FBI agent. What did you think of him?"

"I've never met an FBI agent before," Ed said. "I was surprised. He seems like somebody we'd be friends with. You think it's an act?"

"He does seem like a regular guy," Scott said. "I think he probably gets a lot more out of people that way."

"Do you think Brian killed Ray?"

"No, I don't," Scott said. "Our good buddy Sarah was just in the station, meeting with Jamie in my break room. You know how I can hear everything through the vent in my office. She found out who killed Ray."

"I thought she was off the case."

"She was supposed to be. She went out to the Roadhouse to talk to Phyllis, and Phyllis said the caretaker up at the cemetery told her he killed Ray, to keep him from killing Brian and collecting the fifty grand."

"The Machalvies own that cemetery."

"I checked with Peg, who says they haven't seen him in a couple days. Her worthless sons aren't willing to do his work, which means Patrick is going to have to dig the grave his grandfather is going to be buried in."

"That's awful. Can I help?"

"They have this mini backhoe thing, and you know Patrick, that's like a big toy to him. He says he doesn't mind doing it. I'm going up there to give him some moral support, and I thought you might like to go. We'll be done in plenty of time for the game."

"So was Sarah in trouble for working on the case?"

"Yes and no. Jamie thanked her for the information, and then told her if she stuck her nose in again where it didn't belong he would have her fired."

"I really wish I could have been there for that."

"I couldn't see her face," Scott said. "All she kept saying was 'yes, sir.'"

"So this guy from the cemetery..."

"Duane something."

"He's after Brian?"

"Looks like it."

"Heaven help him, then."
"Which one?" Scott asked. "My money's on Brian."

Patrick Fitzpatrick picked up the keys to the cemetery maintenance shed from Peg Machalvie at Machalvie Funeral Home, and then drove out Possum Holler to the Rose Hill Cemetery. It was a small cemetery, arranged around a figure-eight-shaped drive on top of a gently rounded hillside. From the highest point, where the curving lines of the figure eight crossed, you could see all of Rose Hill, Eldridge College, the river, and the hills on the other side.

Patrick parked at this high point and took a moment to admire the view. It was quiet, with only the wind blowing and a few birds singing as if they believed spring was coming. He walked over the hill to the east side of the property, to a small stone building with a heavy wooden door. He unlocked it and swung the door outward. The stench almost physically knocked him backward. He covered his mouth and nose with the sleeve of his sweatshirt and flipped on the light so he could look inside.

The room was hot from a space heater with glowing red bars, and the man was dead, that was for sure. He was seated in a chair with his head on his chest, and every inch of him seemed to be tattooed or pierced or both. There was no blood on his face or bald head that Patrick could see; it all seemed to be emanating from under his chin. From that point downward there was so much blood that it had spread over his chest and abdomen and had dripped down his legs into a puddle on the stone floor.

Patrick backed out of the room, shut the door and locked it. As he walked back up the hill toward his truck, he saw Scott's Explorer coming up the drive. Ed was with him. He waited until Scott got out of the truck.

"Dead guy in there," Patrick said, pointing his thumb back over his shoulder, as casually as if he'd said, "There's a backhoe in there."

Patrick led Scott and Ed back down to the maintenance shack, unlocked the door, and then said, "It's pretty gruesome. You might want to hold your breath."

Scott's eyes watered as he surveyed the bloody scene in the shed. After they backed out and Patrick once again locked the door, Scott and Ed exchanged looks.

"Throat cut," Ed said.

"Yep," Scott said. "Just like Ray."

"You gonna call Sarah?" Patrick asked him.

"Not this time," Scott said. "This one's for the feds."

They heard a car engine as they walked to the top of the hill and saw Jamie had arrived, saving them a call.

"How much longer do you think we have to stay here?" Patrick asked Ed.

They were sitting in Patrick's truck, with the motor running, waiting for the scene of the crime team to finish with the dead man in the shack. Ed had called Drew to meet Tommy after school at the newspaper office. Drew was going to take Tommy and the dogs home and then hang out with them until Mandy got off work.

"We still have plenty of time before the game," Ed said.

"Yeah, but I have to dig a grave first," Patrick said.

Scott came up to the truck, and Ed rolled down the window.

"You guys can go," Scott said. "Jamie said I could take your statements tonight and then he would follow up tomorrow if he needed to. I don't think he thinks you had anything to do with this."

"What about Grandpa Tim's grave?"

"He said they'd be done in there sometime late this evening, and you could probably use the Bobcat first thing in the morning."

"Cutting it pretty close," Patrick said.

"The alternative is we do it by hand tonight," Scott said.

"Nah," said Patrick. "We have a game to play, and I'm not wearing myself out beforehand. We have to beat those rotten Pendleton bastards."

Scott wasn't surprised that Patrick was more concerned about the game than the dead guy in the shed or his grandfather's final resting place. Patrick's priorities may not have been admirable, but they were consistent.

"What about the wake?" Ed asked.

"That bunch of old farts will be passed out by midnight," Patrick said. "Tonight we kick some Pendleton Pirate ass; then we go to the wake; tomorrow morning I'll dig the grave myself."

By six o'clock the possibility of kicking anyone's ass seemed slight. Two of the Thorns' players were out of commission with stomach flu. Ed was sitting at the bar in the Rose and Thorn, reading the rule book to see if substitute players could be drafted this close to game time.

"C'mon, Ed," Patrick urged him. "We only have an hour."

"Who could we get this late, anyway?" Scott asked.

"My brother Sean, for one," Patrick said and picked up the phone to call him.

FBI agent Jamie Brown walked into the bar. He raised his eyebrows briefly at the corpse in the casket but did not comment.

"Could I have whatever's on tap?" he asked Patrick as he sat down next to Scott.

Patrick tucked the phone into the crook of his neck and drew a pint of Guinness.

"On the house," he said. "After mucking around in that stench, you deserve a free shot as well."

He poured Jamie a shot of whiskey and then Sean answered his call, so Patrick turned his attention away to talk to his brother.

"You get those statements?" Jamie asked Scott.

"Yes, sir," Scott said. "They're on my desk. Do you want me to go get them?"

"Not tonight," Jamie said. "I'll pick them up tomorrow. What's Ed doing?"

"He's reading the rule book to see if we can pick up players this close to game time. Our two best shooters are out with stomach flu."

"This a league game?" Jamie asked.

Patrick got off the phone and told Scott, "Sean's in. What about you, G-man? You shoot any hoops?" He was looking at Jamie.

"I was All-State center my junior and senior year."

Ed threw down the rule book, saying, "All we need is a doctor's signature on the health form and the twenty dollar league fee."

They all turned as one to look at Doc Machalvie, who was drunk as a skunk and raising his glass to the embalmed corpse of Tim MacGregor.

"I don't think that will be a problem," Patrick said and popped open the cash register to retrieve two twenties.

A couple of tourists walked into the bar and Mandy and Patrick both turned and said, "We're closed for a private party," at the same time. The tourists turned and left.

"There's a sign on the door," Mandy said. "It's like they can't read or something."

Ed went to the office in the back room to download the physician's release forms off the league's website. Sean came rushing in and seemed taken aback at the sight of his recently deceased maternal grandfather, who was lying in a coffin, wearing the full dress kilt complete with sporran and a tam on his head.

"That was unexpected," he said, plopping down on a stool next to Jamie. Scott introduced them, but of course, Sean already knew Jamie.

"Do you need a permit to do that?" Jamie said as he gestured at the corpse.

"What? Are you a wake inspector or something?" Patrick asked him.

"No, thank goodness," Jamie said. "I'm not."

"This is a private party, and Grandpa Tim is the honored guest," Patrick said. "You may join us after the game if you want, when Grandpa Tim will be buying drinks for the house until the wee hours of the morning."

"I'd be honored," Jamie said.

"Don't you need to be at Ava's?" Scott asked him.

"I have more agents there now than I have people to protect," Jamie said. "Besides, I'm on the night shift. I can hang out 'til midnight."

Hannah arrived to tend bar, and as soon as Doc Machalvie finished signing off on the physician release forms, the members of the team adjourned to walk up the hill to the Community Center.

"Gooooooo Pricks!" Hannah and Mandy called after them.

At Jamie's questioning look Scott explained, "Our team name is the Rose Hill Thorns."

"Ah, I see," Jamie said.

Hannah tended bar while Mandy attempted to wait tables. A wake was pretty much like every other private party, except the booze was free, and the guest of honor was dead. Mandy quickly got tired of fetching shots for what she called a "rowdy bunch of wrinkled ass-pinchers" and finally put a fifth of whiskey and two pitchers of beer on every table.

"Ain't none of them geezers even gonna tip me," she complained to Hannah. "So what's the point of waitin' on 'em hand and foot all night?"

Hannah put a compilation of World War II and 50's crooner music on the bar sound system. The wake attendees sang along with Rosemary Clooney, Nat King Cole, Frank Sinatra, and all the other singers they grew up listening to, and it seemed to mellow them out into a more manageable if maudlin group. Now that the senior citizens were taken care of, Mandy sat on a bar stool and chatted with Hannah.

"What did Sam do when he proposed to you?" Mandy asked.

"Well," Hannah said. "When my brother Quinn left home to go in the Army, my parents decided to sell the farm and move to town. I wanted to buy it, but my father said I couldn't run it all by myself, so Sam said let's get married and live there together."

"That doesn't sound very romantic."

"Sam Campbell is not a romantic man. He's a smart, hardworking man, but he's not sentimental, not at all."

"Was this before he went to college?"

"No, a couple years after. He graduated from MIT and then worked in Pittsburgh for two years for an IT firm. He decided to start his own company with a couple guys he met there, and eventually, he bought them out."

"Did you know Ed's wife?" Mandy asked. "I never met her."

"Eve? Oh yes, I knew her. She didn't like me, but she tolerated me for Ed's sake."

"Was she a bitch?" Mandy asked, hopefully.

"Absolutely," Hannah said. "She's super smart but has no sense of humor, whatsoever. She doesn't just have a stick up her butt; it's the North Pole."

"Really? I got the idea she was Miss Perfect."

"No, not at all. She was sharp and hard, not sweet and cuddly. That's why Ed loves you so much."

"Cause I'm stupid and soft?"

"No, silly. Because you have a sense of humor and you're affectionate. A man needs to laugh and feel loved."

Mandy looked distressed.

"What's wrong?" Hannah asked her. "You two fighting?"

"No, Mandy said. "We're just going down a patch of hard road."

"You haven't been together that long."

"I think Ed is sorry we done moved in together so quick."

"You're looking for things to worry about. Didn't he buy a new car for you?"

"That ole thing," Mandy said. "Did you see it? It's uglier than sin. He's got this idea of his self as a family man now, and he thinks that's a family man's car. It's an old man's car, is what it is."

"So what's wrong with that?" Hannah said. "As long as you're part of the family."

"Oh, he's crazy 'bout Tommy. They get along great. I couldn't ask for a better dad for him. I think maybe I'm just the fries that go with that hamburger. I think Ed would be happy with just the hamburger."

"You're wrong, Mandy. Any man would be lucky to have you. Ed loves you."

"I'm telling' ya, I got a bad feelin'. It wouldn't take much of a wind to knock this whole thing over."

"Talk to him about it, then. You'll probably find out you're upset over nothing. I know Ed's worried about the newspaper. The price of printing and paper keeps going up, but the subscriptions and advertising revenues are going down. He was talking about that the other night in here."

"I didn't know that. He shouldn't be buyin' cars if he's havin' money troubles."

"Me and my big mouth," Hannah said. "He probably doesn't want to worry you."

"We're gonna have to have us a big talk," Mandy said. "I'm just dreadin' it, is all."

When they arrived at the Community Center, which used to be Rose Hill High School before consolidation, Patrick, Scott, Sean, Ed, and Jamie met the rest of the team in the locker room. Tony Delvecchio seemed especially shocked to see Sean, but soon recovered.

"I'm sorry about your grandfather," Tony said, shaking his hand.

"Thanks," Sean said. "I hope we can talk later."

Patrick was team captain, and retired high school coach Floyd Riggenbach was the team coach. Patrick introduced Sean and Jamie and gave Coach the paperwork and forty dollars.

"You, I remember," Coach said, pointing to Sean. "I never could get you to play ball. Always had your nose stuck in some book."

Coach took the paperwork and fees upstairs to the gym, where he anticipated an argument with the Pendleton coach over eligibility.

Patrick found uniforms for Sean and Jamie, and they went upstairs to run some drills in the fifteen minutes they had left before game time. The Pendleton team members made fun of them from their side of the court.

Barty McNulty, the captain of the Pendleton team, sidled up to Patrick.

"I see you're missing your ringers, Patty Fitzpatty."

"I see you're missing your balls, Farty McNutty."

"Care to make it interesting?" Barty asked.

"Always," Patrick said, who had already thought up a very unusual bet.

When Patrick told him what he proposed, Barty said, "You're crazy."

But he shook on it anyway.

So it came to pass that on a cold March night in the small town of Rose Hill, while the Thorns celebrated their 99/97 victory by drinking whiskey at the wake of Timothy MacGregor, Barty McNulty and the Pendleton Pirates were up at the Rose Hill Cemetery, digging a grave. By hand.

Maggie stood inside the darkened front room of Fitzpatrick's Service Station, watching the eleven o'clock bus arrive in the parking lot of the Dairy Chef next door. She'd come for the nine o'clock bus, but he hadn't been on it. When she returned at ten forty-five, Gabe's wife and son could be seen, along with Lily Crawford, sitting in a dark car she'd never seen before, driven by a blonde man she didn't know.

The bus pulled in at ten after eleven, and only one passenger disembarked. She thought she would have known him anywhere even though she could barely make out his features. Her heart thumped hard in her chest, and she felt short of breath. The doors of the dark car opened and the young boy jumped out and rushed into Gabe's arms. Gabe held the boy close and stroked his hair while the blonde man took his luggage from the bus driver, and the mother of the boy hung back with Lily, who kept a protective arm around her. Then Gabe walked toward his wife, with his arm around his son.

He passed through the light of a streetlamp and Maggie could see his face. His hair was close-cropped, and he was clean-shaven. He looked tired; he looked older. He said something to his wife, shook Lily's hand, and then they all got in the car and left. Then the bus pulled away, revealing Scott standing outside the Rose and Thorn on the opposite corner, watching. He raised his hand, but Maggie turned away.

Ed left the Rose and Thorn at eleven thirty and walked down Peony Street before turning left on Iris Avenue. His two-bedroom, one-bath craftsman cottage was in the middle of the block. As he passed Pauline and Phil Davis's house, he noticed a light was on in their kitchen. They had moved to Florida two weeks before, leaving their house and the diner up for sale. Ed had promised to keep an eye on the place. He walked around to the back door and saw the shadow of someone inside pass by the dining room window. He quickly backtracked to the pub and got Scott to walk back with him to the Davis home.

Scott had not had anything stronger than a soda to drink, so he had all his wits about him. He went right up to the back door and knocked. Pauline and George's daughter Phyllis answered the door and let them in. She was wild-eyed and trembling.

"You didn't bring that FBI agent," she said. "He doesn't know you're here, does he?"

"No, Phyllis, why?" Scott asked her.

Phyllis collapsed down onto a kitchen chair, where it was obvious she'd been drinking vodka straight out of the bottle and chain smoking. She put out her cigarette, nodding at Scott. She knew he was sensitive to smoke, and for once, she cared to have him on her side.

"That chick from the county said she would have someone watching my place, but she lied to me. First, that old witch sent someone to threaten me," she said and rolled up her sleeve so Scott and Ed could see the bruises where someone had gripped her upper arm. "Then that FBI jerk shows up, basically calls me a liar, and says I'm going to jail if I don't say where Brian is."

"Agent Brown?" Scott asked her.

"Yeah," Phyllis said. "He and some other goon told me they were gonna throw me in jail for something; I can't remember the words. Destruction of justice, or something."

"Obstruction," Ed said.

"Yeah, that," Phyllis said.

"Who is the old witch that sent someone to threaten you?"

"The one that's offered fifty grand to anyone who kills Brian Fitzpatrick. I told that county woman that Duane was braggin' about killin' Ray, and now I hear Duane got his throat cut, too. If there's nobody gonna protect me I gotta get outta town."

She gestured to a suitcase sitting behind the kitchen door.

"What did Mrs. Wells want to know?"

"Same as the feds, where's Brian. And I don't know. I haven't heard from him. He called Ray for help, and no one that I know has heard from him since."

"So why are you here in your parents' house?" Scott asked her.

"I'm flat broke, Scott. I need some money, and I was hoping there'd be something in here I could pawn. It's all just crappy furniture. They took everything worth anything."

"How did you get in?"

"I've been sneaking in and out of this house my whole life," Phyllis said.

"You said the agent threatened you?"

"He said no one was going to protect me unless I could tell them where Brian is. Well, plenty of people probably saw the county bitch at my place, and now that the feds have been there my life isn't worth a plug nickel. As soon as they left, I packed a bag and got the hell out."

"Do you know who killed Duane?"

"Mrs. Wells knows the cops are closing in on her and she's knocking off anyone who could point the finger back at her. I heard there's gonna be a lot more killed before this is over."

"Who told you?"

"I know a gal knows a guy who works for her, and they say it's kill or be killed right now."

"Did you tell the FBI about that?"

"No, I didn't hear that until just a little while ago. People are leaving town in droves, you know, not just me. No one who's seen her face is safe now."

"Where will you go, Phyllis?" Ed asked.

"I'd like to go to Florida, where my folks are. Make a new start there."

Ed thought of her poor parents, who'd left Rose Hill to make a new start far away from their problematic daughter.

"They would expect you to go there, though," Scott said. "You need to come up with a better plan."

"I'm not what you would call a planner," Phyllis said. "I'm more of a look before you leaper."

"When Theo was alive," Scott asked, "you and Brian worked for him, didn't you?"

"I don't wanna talk about that," Phyllis said.

"If you want my help you will," Scott said.

"We did some jobs for Theo," Phyllis admitted. "I'm not proud of that."

"I know you and Brian helped Theo blackmail some people," Scott said, and even though it was a lie, he said, "I saw the pictures."

"Gosh, Scott," Phyllis said, looking nervously at Ed. "I didn't know you knew about all that."

"When Theo died he left a safe full of blackmail evidence," Scott said. "And the feds have it. The agent asked you about that, didn't he?"

Phyllis didn't answer, and she didn't seem to want to look either of them in the eye.

"So help me, Phyllis," Scott said. "I'll call the feds right now and have them come get you."

"Alright, alright," Phyllis said, and then looked at Ed. "I'm sorry, Ed, for what I did to your dad. He was a nice fella and didn't deserve it."

"My dad?" Ed said. "What did you do to my dad?"

"Theo didn't want him printing something in the paper, so Brian got him drunk, brought him to my place, and we took some pictures. He didn't do anything, he was just out of it, and we made it look like he did."

"That's probably what killed him," Ed said. "You know he died of a heart attack."

"I'm sorry," Phyllis said. "I was too scared not to do whatever Theo wanted."

"Which blackmail victim did the agent ask you about?" Scott demanded. "Not Ed's father."

"He wanted to know who Brian could blackmail into helping him. He said there were some photos missing, and he wanted to know the names of all the people we set up."

"Did you tell him?"

"I didn't know what pictures he had and what he didn't. I told him all the ones I could remember."

"Who did you name?"

"I told him Ed's dad, the last fire chief, Doc Machalvie, and Knox's dad. I don't remember the name of that judge who lives up past you on the hill."

"Eric Estep was the fire chief, and Bertram Rodefeffer was Knox's dad. Do you mean Judge Feinman?"

"Yeah, that's him."

"And that's all?"

"They're the local ones. There was some I didn't know; they weren't from around here."

"The only ones from around here who are still alive are Judge Feinman and Doc Machalvie," Ed said to Scott.

Ed's dad had died of a heart attack while sitting in his usual spot in the Rose and Thorn, Eric Estep had killed himself with a shotgun blast, and Bertram Rodefeffer had died in a car accident. Ed now wondered if all those deaths were a result of Theo's blackmail.

"So, Duane was also involved in the blackmail," Scott said.

"Sometimes," Phyllis said. "When Theo wanted the pictures to be two men together. You know what I mean."

"Did you tell that to the FBI?"

"No!" Phyllis said. "I just heard about that; I didn't ever see those getting made. Brian and Duane did those at Duane's place."

Phyllis looked wretched. Scott told her to go to the bathroom and clean herself up, and she meekly did as she was told.

"I can't believe they did that to my dad," Ed said quietly. "That must have destroyed him."

Scott took his cell phone out of his pocket, held his hand out for Ed's, and then put them both in the refrigerator. Ed looked at him like he was crazy, but Scott held his finger up to his lips and shook his head.

"We don't have much time," Scott said quietly. "Would you be willing to drive to the bus station in Pendleton? I'd like to get her out of town as quickly and as quietly as possible."

"What about the feds? Aren't we supposed to be cooperating with them?"

"I think we're being played," Scott said. "My cell phone is probably bugged, but I'm not sure if it's the feds or Mrs. Wells. I think all the interested parties know where Phyllis is right now, and that we're with her. I think if we leave her alone she'll get her throat slit or the feds will arrest her."

"So how do we get her out of town?"

"Where's your new car?"

"It's sitting in my garage, why?"

"Go get it, and meet me behind the police station. I have an idea, but we'll have to work out the details on the fly."

Ed went home and Drew assured him he was glad to stay with Tommy longer. Ed backed the Volvo out of the garage and drove the short distance down Iris Avenue, up Peony Street and then down the alley behind the police station. Within fifteen minutes, Sean arrived with his car, and Scott arrived with his SUV. They all got out and met in the parking lot.

"Did you leave your cell phone behind?" he asked Sean, and he nodded.

"Wait with me until the ladies get here," Scott said.

About that time, a group of three women came walking down the alley. They were all dressed in dark coats with scarves wrapped around their heads, carrying suitcases. When they reached the parking lot, they split up, and each woman got into a different vehicle. When Ed got in his car, he recognized Hannah as his passenger, even though only her eyes showed.

She held her finger up to her lips and handed him a sheet of notepaper with Scott's writing on it:

"Go to the Pendleton bus station, leave her, and come back to the bar."

As they pulled out of the parking lot, Ed wondered which vehicle had Phyllis in it, and where it was taking her. Although he kept checking his rearview mirror, he never did see anyone following him.

At just before one-thirty they all met back at the Rose and Thorn. Sean took out his note, showed it to Ed, and then set it on fire in an ashtray. He also sang the "Mission Impossible" theme song as he did so. Ed added his note to the fire.

Patrick and a sleepy looking beagle came back with Hannah at one forty-five. They were bickering.

"The only reason I'm still alive is because I made him pull over so I could drive," Hannah said. "I'm gonna thank Scott with a kick in the pants for sending this crazy drunk to pick me up."

"I'm not drunk," Patrick said. "You just can't stand not to be in charge."

Scott came into the bar alone and sat with his friends. Patrick turned up the volume of the music, and they all leaned forward over the table in the booth until their heads almost touched.

"Everyone okay?" Scott asked, and Sean and Ed both nodded.

"I never saw anyone following me," Ed said, and Sean concurred.

"That's because they were following me," Scott said. "I had a tail all the way to Markleysburg, and then I lost him in the speed trap. I used a public pay phone to call my buddy Karl before I left, and he let me go by but stopped the tail. It was one of Jamie's crew."

"Who was with you?" Ed asked him.

"Delia," Scott said. "I took her to her sister's house. Ian's going to pick her up in the morning."

"How did they know what we were going to do?" Ed asked.

"I left my cell phone at Phyllis's," Scott said. "So either they've been following me all night, or there's a tracking device in my Explorer."

The wake was winding down, mostly because the majority of the participants were passed out or mumbling into their drinks. Sean and Patrick decided to play beer pong. Mandy told them if they weren't going to help, she wasn't cleaning anything up and was leaving with Ed and Scott. Banjo, the beagle, made himself comfortable on his bed in the back office and then fell asleep to the sound of The Chieftains and his beloved Patrick's voice.

Ed and Scott waited for Mandy outside the bar before parting ways.

"Aren't you worried about being on the wrong side of the feds?" Ed asked his friend.

"I'm more worried about the people in Rose Hill," Scott said. "It seems like Jamie doesn't care who he hurts to get what he wants."

"You think Doc is the one who helped Brian."

"I do, and I think Jamie does too."

"You think Doc is safe in there?" he jerked a thumb back toward the pub, where Doc was fast asleep in a booth.

"Patrick and Sean are going to make sure he gets home safely. I'll have Frank stay with him overnight."

"What about Judge Feinman?"

"He's on vacation in Europe. He chose a good time to be gone."

"Maybe he knew."

"Maybe."

"If there's anything else I can do, you'll let me know?"

"I will. Thanks for tonight."

"No problem. It seemed like a spy game we would've played when we were kids."

"If Jamie comes to see you, you'll let me know."

"I will."

"What's going on?" Mandy asked when she came out.

"Where's your cell phone?" Ed asked her.

"It died on me a week ago. I told you that," she said and rolled her eyes at Scott. "It's at home."

Ed said goodbye to Scott and grabbed Mandy by the hand. As they walked home, he told her everything.

"I'm not so naive that I'm surprised about the FBI not being what they seem to be," he said. "It's one thing to read about this kind of stuff going on, and it's another to actually to meet the guy and like him."

"I only just met him, and I don't like him," Mandy said. "He's one of them guys that thinks he's God's gift to women."

"I'm considering printing the truth about all of it and damning the consequences."

"You can't do that, Ed," Mandy said. "Think of all the people you'd hurt–pert near everybody we care about. You need to keep your head down and count your blessings."

"If I don't blow the whistle, then I'm just as bad as the person who broke the law."

"What if it was me that broke the law?" Mandy asked him. "What if I broke the law and I'd lose Tommy if you turned me in? Then what?"

"That's different," Ed said. "That's completely different."

"Well, if you're askin' for my advice I say don't use a shotgun when a pea-shooter will do."

"What's that supposed to mean?"

"A shotgun makes a big noise and a big mess. A pea shooter just stings like the devil."

"So if a news story is a shotgun blast, what's the pea shooter?"

"Something that stings bad enough to stop Jamie in his tracks," Mandy said.

When Drew arrived at the wake, the stamped tin ceiling of the Rose and Thorn was obscured by cigarette and cigar smoke. Fitz Fitzpatrick was passed out in his wheelchair with his chin on his chest. Patrick and Sean were playing beer pong, and Hannah was playing solitaire on the computer in the back office. Hannah was more than ready to go, so Drew declined all offers of a drink and they walked out to the animal control truck.

"They'll all be so hung over tomorrow I don't know how they'll make it to the funeral," she said as she slid behind the wheel.

"All that smoke is not good for you or the baby," Drew said. "I'm sorry, Hannah. That must have sounded like scolding."

"No, you're right. I've been sitting in the office with the side door open, breathing fresh air, but I don't think that helped. I'm going to have to quit working there, too, I guess. This baby has certainly dropped a bomb on my working life."

"I thought there was a state law that all businesses had to be smoke-free."

"Technically the Rose and Thorn is a private club," Hannah said. "They just happen to have an open house for new members six nights of the week."

Drew talked about his evening with Tommy, and Hannah told Drew about the basketball game bet. They talked about the murders, and about Brian escaping. They talked about the grant application and the feral cats that they hoped to rescue and redistribute instead of exterminating.

"I'm to the point where I can't stomach the killing," Hannah said. "I know sometimes they're dangerous and damaged, and not safe to be around. I know it's a horrible life living in a cage, but at least they get enough food and get to breathe the air and see the sky a few times per day. Isn't a damaged life better than no life at all? After all they've been through, don't they deserve some peace and dignity, even if they can't be the cute lapdogs we want them to be? People made them the way they are, don't people owe it to them to make it up to them, somehow? Or at least accept them the way they are? They can't help it if they can't be what we want them to be, and we have no right to demand it."

"Are we still talking about dogs?"

Hannah gave Drew a puzzled look.

"What do you mean?"

"The war made your husband the way he is, and now he can't be the way you want him to be. Isn't that it?"

"That's not the same thing at all."

"I think it is. I think the two situations are very similar. Trained killers, violence, damaged ability to socialize that can't easily be overcome. I'm not trying to trivialize what Sam went through; I'm just seeing the parallels: the psychological damage, physical pain, scars, the stigma, and how difficult it is for you to trust him not to revert back into what he had to be to survive."

"I understand what you're saying," Hannah said slowly. "But I resent you comparing what veterans go through with dogfighting. It especially offends me on Sam's behalf. He joined the Army in order to defend our country. He got hurt while voluntarily ensuring our freedom. That's a completely different thing."

"I'm sorry," Drew said. "I just think part of the reason you feel so strongly about the dogs is because of what Sam's going through."

"My husband is not a dog."

"I didn't say I thought he was," Drew said. "I'm sorry, Hannah. That was a bad analogy; my lame attempt at amateur psychology. I'm sorry I said anything. Let's change the subject."

Instead, they were quiet the rest of the way to Hannah's farm and were almost to the end of the long driveway before Hannah noticed that the lights were on in the farmhouse, and her husband's van was parked outside.

When they pulled into the parking area, someone turned on the porch light, and two men walked out the side door from the kitchen.

"Is that Sam?" Drew asked. He almost added, "Standing?"

Hannah unsnapped her seat belt, threw open her door, and ran into the arms of her husband, leaving Drew to introduce himself to Alan, Sam's friend from MIT.

"Let me show you the barn," Drew said, and Alan couldn't hide his relief at having somewhere to go.

Back in Rose Hill, heavy clouds moved in and obscured the stars, and then the moon. The wind whipped through the trees in the park, and a dead branch fell to the ground with a crash. Scott was keyed up and wide awake, so he made a slow surveillance drive of Rose Hill. He started down by the river, on Lotus Avenue, and then drove around every block all the way up to Morning Glory

Avenue. At the end of that block he saw a man walking out of Possum Holler, so he pulled up beside him and rolled down his window.

"Hello, Gabe," Scott said.

Maggie couldn't sleep, she couldn't read, and she couldn't sit still. At two thirty she was organizing the clutter in the lower kitchen cupboards when there was a knock on her balcony doors. She turned and saw Gabe's face framed in one of the windows. It felt as if her heart stopped beating for a moment, and then thumped hard in her chest when it resumed.

As she stood up, she was painfully aware of her flannel pajamas and robe ensemble, the fuzzy slippers, and what she knew was a wild head of hair. She couldn't look at him as she fumbled with the lock on the doors, and he came in on a blast of cold wind. She could smell him then. Even though there was a different detergent smell on his clothes, and a stale cigarette smell about him, underneath was Gabe's scent. It smelled like home.

"Maggie," he said. His look was tender, and his voice was the same warm voice she used to know. He reached for her, and she took a step back. It was instinctive, and it surprised her as much as it obviously stung him.

"I'll make tea, and then we'll talk," Maggie said.

He looked around the kitchen while she put on the kettle. He picked up objects and set them back down; he looked at everything on her bulletin board; he studied her niece's and nephew's artwork on the door of the fridge.

She didn't want to look at him, and she put it off as long as she could. He finally came to a stop and leaned back against the counter. It was as far apart as they could get and still be in the same room. Maggie had boiled the water but made no move to prepare tea. Instead, she turned off the gas ring.

She turned and made herself look at him, their eyes met, and instead of the longing she expected to feel, or the lust she was afraid she would feel, the predominant emotion was sadness. As he had in the light of the streetlamp, he looked exhausted. He was so thin. His skin was pale, his brown eyes were bloodshot with dark shadows beneath them, and there were deep lines on his stubble-covered face.

He smiled, and Maggie noticed his teeth had yellowed. The youthful strength and vitality she remembered were gone, an old nicotine stain left in its place. He coughed, and it sounded bad, from deep in his chest.

"Are you okay?" she asked him.

"I'm out," he said. "Anything else is beside the point."

"I met your son today," Maggie said. "He looks like you, but also like his mother."

"I wanted to tell you about them before they got here."

"Where were they when we were ... when you were here before?"

It seemed too easy after so many years of not knowing. She could finally ask all the questions she had and Gabe himself would tell her the answers.

"Maria was done with me when I went to prison, the first time, I mean. I didn't think I'd ever see her again; she told me I wouldn't. She was pregnant when I went in. After I got out, her father and brother came to meet me, told me they would kill me if I tried to find her. They brought me a letter from her, telling me to stay away. So I did."

"Why didn't you tell me you'd been in prison? Or that you were married and had a child?"

"If I'd told you I was an ex-con with a wife and kid, would you have gone out with me?"

"No," she said. "I wouldn't have."

"I thought I could leave all the mistakes I'd made behind me. I wanted to start over."

"Why didn't you tell me when Mrs. Wells threatened you?"

"I knew how you felt about lies, Maggie. I'd told so many by then."

"Everything was a lie, then," she said. "All of it."

"Not everything," he said. "I did love you, Maggie. I still do. I didn't want it to end the way it did. When Scott came to our house that night, he gave me the option to stay and be arrested or disappear. I couldn't face you. I'm sorry."

"When you wrote that letter, what did you think I'd do?"

"I hoped to see you and tell you the truth about everything before I went inside. I felt I owed you that, at the very least."

"And now you have your family back."

"A few years ago Luis decided he wanted to know who his old man was, and Maria hired a detective to find me. It turned out the prison was less than an hour away from where they live. They started visiting me, and Luis and I e-mailed each other every day."

"You're still married."

"Yes. Her people are devout Catholics."

"Are you going back with them?"

He looked away.

Maggie felt like he'd punched her in the gut.

"You are," she said. "You never had any intention of coming back to me."

"I've promised Luis to try to be a good father to him, to be a good husband to his mother. Maria's offered me a second chance. I thought I'd be stupid not to accept her offer. She knows me, knows all my faults, but she's willing to try. She's a fine person, Maggie, too good for me."

"Then why are you here?"

He shrugged.

"To explain, I guess. To say I'm sorry."

"Well, thanks for that," Maggie said. "You can go now. Good luck."

"Maggie," he said, and came toward her, reached out to her.

"No," Maggie said. She batted his hand away and opened the door to the balcony. Another blast of cold air came in, and Maggie was grateful for the feel of it on her hot skin.

"Maggie," he said, from so close, and although it was the same Gabriel smell underneath the cigarettes, it turned her stomach.

"Please go," Maggie said, with her hand out to keep him at a distance, but looking him right in the eye. "I want it to be completely clear to you that there's nothing here for you anymore. Nothing with me, I mean. I wish you well, but I don't want to see you again if you can help it."

"Alright," he said. "If that's what you want."

She crossed her arms and stepped back as he went out the way he came in. Duke, the cat, ran in the open door and almost tripped him. She noticed his fur was wet and that a light rain had begun to fall.

"You have a cat?" Gabe asked. "I thought you hated cats."

"I don't hate cats; I'm allergic to them," Maggie said.

She shut the door behind him, locked it, and closed the curtains. If she could have built a brick wall right then, over the whole shebang, she would have; plus maybe a fence with razor wire on top of it. Maggie sprayed room deodorizer to take away his smell, scrubbed the kitchen counters and every surface he'd touched, and then mopped the floor. Afterwards, while the washing machine scalded the clothes she'd been wearing, she took a hot shower and scrubbed her skin until it was raw.

Scott picked up Gabe in the alley and took him back to Lily's house.

"How'd it go?" Scott asked him.

"You know Maggie," Gabe said. "She's not the forgiving type. She never wants to see me again."

"I'm sorry."

"At least I got to say what I needed to. I want to apologize to you, too, Scott. We used to be friends."

"I forgave you a long time ago," Scott said. "As long as you do the right thing now, you and I will have no problems. I hope you and your family will be very happy."

"You're in love with her," Gabe said.

"I am," Scott said.

"Were you back then, too?" Gabe asked.

"I've always loved Maggie," Scott said. "I can't remember a time when I didn't."

The silence grew, but Scott was an expert at waiting,

"I still believe she belongs to me," Gabe said. "But if it has to be someone else, I'm glad it's you."

Scott didn't respond, but they shook hands before Gabe got out of the car.

CHAPTER NINE - Sunday

At four o'clock in the morning veterinarian Drew Rosen and prosthetics engineer Alan Davidson took the Pine County Animal Control vehicle and set out in the pouring rain to check the humane traps Hannah and Drew had set the day before. It was against county policy for anyone who wasn't a county employee to drive the vehicle, and if discovered, both men would certainly be prosecuted, and Hannah would be fired. None of them cared about that this morning. When Drew and Alan left the farmhouse that morning, Sam and Hannah lay entwined in their bed, amidst a tangle of blankets and snoring dogs, exhausted after a night spent talking about Sam's physical therapy experience and the son or daughter that would arrive with the red leaves of autumn.

When Bonnie Fitzpatrick and Sean left the family home, rain was lashing the windows and Sean could hear both his father and brother snoring peacefully in their warm beds. As soon as they were in the kitchen of the bakery, Bonnie tied an apron around her youngest son and showed him how to use the large Hobart mixer. She handed him the recipe for the sweet yeast rolls she planned to serve at the funeral reception. The faded words were written in the hand of her former nemesis and mother-in-law Rose. Sean swallowed some aspirin and strong coffee to combat the hangover that he didn't dare mention. The sound of the mixer scraped the inside of his skull, and he cursed his sleeping big brother silently but thoroughly.

Ed Harrison, Tommy Wilson, and their two dogs arrived at the newspaper office in time to meet the truck that delivered the big city daily papers. Since it was

Sunday, they also delivered the Pendleton paper, so it was double the work to roll each one and drop it in a plastic bag so it wouldn't be ruined in the rain. They talked while they sat at the worktable and rolled the papers, watching the puppy crawl all over a forbearing Hank, who gave Ed a doleful look as the pup, now named Lucida (Lucy for short) bit his ears and shook them with a fierce puppy size growl.

"It's going to be a miserable ride out there," Ed said. "How about we make a big pancake breakfast at home afterward?"

Federal agent James R. Brown received a phone call. He crept out of Ava Fitzpatrick's bed, dressed, tiptoed down the stairs to the kitchen, and quietly let himself out the back door. There he got inside a dark SUV that was waiting in the alley. Ava turned over in bed with a smile lingering on her lips, which were still a bit swollen from the agent's passionate kisses.

Lily Crawford got up, made coffee, and let Betty Lou out to do her business. Betty Lou was followed by the scampering, long-legged young cat Lily called Snicklefritz, who took one step out into the rain and then ran back to the safety of the porch. Lily had heard one of her house guests go out and return in the night and hoped that his wife and child had not. She wondered why the FBI agent pretending to be her nephew would allow a witness to leave the safety of her house, and then reckoned it was just so he could follow him to see where he went.

Brian Fitzpatrick was lying on his back in a deep ravine off a lonesome, narrow track in the dark woods of the Pine County State Forest, having crashed his sister's car and been thrown from the vehicle. He was pretty sure his back was broken because he couldn't feel anything below his waist. He was racked with cold and soaked to the skin; tremors like seizures ran through his chest and down his arms.

Through the trees that towered above him, he had watched the moon appear and disappear behind dark clouds as it seemed to cross to the west. Storm clouds flashed lightning, followed by earth-shaking thunder. He hadn't prayed since he was a boy, but he felt now might be a good time to resume the practice. According to the prison chaplain, it was never too late to be forgiven and saved. As the rain beat down on his face, Brian prayed for someone to rescue him. He heard a rustling noise in the nearby foliage and prayed nothing would come and eat him. As it became clear to him that no one was coming, he prayed for a merciful death.

Brian could feel his life force, a buzzing energy that had hummed loudly in his ears when he first crashed, begin to leak away. At first, he struggled, even though it hurt so much it took his breath away. Finally, exhausted, he lost the motivation to do anything, think anything, or want anything. He drifted in and out of consciousness, so he wasn't sure how much time had passed before he heard someone or something crash through the brush down the hillside, and then a woman's voice calling his name. He tried, but he couldn't respond. He felt a sharp pain in his chest. Then he began to feel lighter, everything was suddenly bright, and it wasn't at all scary. It was actually kind of pleasant.

By mid-morning three inches of rain had fallen, added to several inches of a melting snow base that was cascading down Pine Mountain. The beaver dam blocking Raccoon Creek broke apart, and a flash flood surged down the Little Bear River. River gauges put into place by the Corps of Engineers detected the sudden rise in water level and sent a signal to the man in charge of the operation, who was just sitting down to breakfast with his wife.

Police Chief Scott Gordon received a frantic phone call from Fire Chief Malcolm Behr and alerted his two deputies to meet him down on Lotus Avenue. The volunteer firefighters were arriving as he did and started going door to door, alerting residents of the need to evacuate their homes immediately. The fire station's warning siren began to wail; fire trucks were moved to block Pine Mountain Road and Peony Street, and a crowd began to gather in the darkness.

"If neither of the dams fails, Lotus Avenue will still be flooded," Malcolm told Scott. "If one of them breaks, we'll be flooded up to Marigold Avenue, and the pressure of the water may take out all the houses on Lotus as it goes by. I hate to think what will happen if they both go."

"I'll alert the college," Scott said and ran back to the patrol car.

Although the dorms were high enough on the hillside they shouldn't be in danger, Scott didn't want to take any chances.

"Stay on the radio," Malcolm shouted to his men. "If that dam breaks, I want you out of there."

The Rose Hill Women's Club and Whistle Pig Lodge members were alerted by phone tree and convened at the Community Center to set up a temporary shelter for displaced residents. Elbie brought the church van down to transport the elderly, and Cal Fischer pulled his boat up to Iris Avenue so that it could be used for rescues if needed. His wife and dog had already evacuated their little house on Lotus Avenue.

The sun had not yet peeped over the mountains to the east, but the sky was light enough so they could see the water rise. As the river rose and began to run faster, Scott felt like the whole community was collectively holding its breath. Malcolm's team had begun waking up residents on Marigold Avenue as the swell of water converged on the train tracks and the empty Rodefeffer Glassworks buildings. The old train depot was built up high enough that the water did not quite reach the first floor, but it swirled around the building and uprooted a tree next to it.

Scott felt equal parts terrified and thrilled as the water swept over Lotus Avenue. Felled trees and debris, swept up by the rushing water, slammed into the wall between Eldridge College and the town, but the hundred-year-old stone wall held. Scott helped Patrick carry his father's wheelchair down to the sidewalk, and then Fitz himself, grumpy, hungover, and still wearing his pajamas and robe.

Malcolm listened to his radio and then called out that the two dams were holding. The crowd gathered on Iris Avenue cheered.

"They're holding for now," Malcolm said to Scott. "But they won't hold forever."

Ed and Tommy walked down to where Scott was standing.

"Can Tommy stand here with you for a minute?" Ed asked, and Scott nodded.

Only Tommy's wide eyes could be seen beneath the enormous rain poncho Ed had made him wear. Scott had to suppress the impulse to hold his hand as if he was a small child.

"We won't let anything happen to him," Scott said.

Ed walked down Pine Mountain Road to take some photographs.

"It's still too dark for them to be any good," Ed said after he walked back.

Mayor Stuart Machalvie came strolling down the street holding a big black umbrella, smiling and greeting everyone on his way. When he got to Scott and Malcolm, he greeted them, shook their hands and then looked suitably serious and concerned while Ed took a few photographs.

Afterward, Stuart said quietly, "The governor has declared this a state of emergency. If we're lucky, both dams will break, and then we'll get enough state and federal money to build a hydroelectric dam."

The mayor went on down the street, shaking hands and making reassuring noises, and Malcolm shook his head.

"Count on Stuart to already be figuring out how the town can make money off a tragedy," Malcolm said.

Within the hour Malcolm received a radio transmission that one of the dams had been breached. Through a bullhorn, he ordered everyone to move up two blocks. Pendleton firefighters arrived and joined in the effort to evacuate the homes on both Marigold and Iris Avenues.

Scott left them and his deputies in charge of the scene and went back to the station to call the county sheriff's office. He heard the phone ringing as he closed the door behind him. It was county sheriff's investigator Sarah Albright.

After a brief conversation, Scott hung up the phone, hurried back out of the station, then jogged across the street and down the block to the Fitzpatrick family's service station. Patrick was inside, telling his father and Uncle Curtis about the dam failing. Fitz was propped up in his wheelchair, sipping coffee that Scott assumed was spiked with a fortifying ingredient. Banjo, the beagle, was curled up in the corner, sleeping.

"I remember the flood of 1952," Fitz said. "The water came all the way up to Rose Hill Avenue."

"We were lucky that time," Curtis said. "It was a slow rise and not a flash flood; we had time to prepare. If both dams break, Cal may be fishing bodies out of the river."

Scott asked Patrick to come outside with him for a moment.

"What's up?" Patrick said when they got outside. He crossed his arms and stuck his hands under his armpits to keep them warm.

"They found Brian; he's been in a car accident, and he's in pretty bad shape. They're taking him to the hospital in Pendleton, but they're not sure he'll make it."

"Son of a bitch," Patrick said and looked out over Scott's shoulder. "Damn it to hell."

"I'll be glad to take your mom to the hospital in the cruiser. It would be faster."

"Thanks, Scott," Patrick said. "You go get the car and meet me at the bakery."

Patrick went back inside. By the time Scott got the patrol car and arrived at the bakery, Bonnie was standing outside in her coat and scarf with Sean holding an umbrella open above her. Scott thought she looked as if she'd aged ten years since he saw her last. Sean, Patrick, and Bonnie got in the backseat of the car, and Scott asked, "What about Maggie?"

The words had just left his lips as Maggie rounded the corner and came running down the middle of Pine Mountain Road, her raincoat and long red curls flying out behind her. She got in the passenger side of the patrol car, her ringlets dripping with rain. She turned around to look at her brothers and mother.

"What about Dad?" she asked.

"He's going to stay with Curtis at the station," Sean said.

Scott turned on the flashing lights.

"Wait!" Maggie said. "What about Ava?"

"She's already there," Scott said. "Agent Brown took her."

Maggie looked back to gauge the reaction to this information. Sean looked grim, Patrick looked angry, and Bonnie's crumpled, tear-streaked face broke Maggie's heart.

It normally took a half hour to get to Pendleton, but they were there in twenty minutes thanks to the flashing lights and police siren. Scott let them out at the emergency room entrance and told Maggie, "I'll park and be back in a minute."

The staff on duty would not let Bonnie go back to where Brian was. She was forced to sit with her sons in the waiting room, where she cried into Sean's shoulder. Maggie paced outside the entrance until Scott came back.

"What happened?" she demanded. "They won't let Mom go back."

"All I know is that he was driving your car in the State Park, went off the road into a ravine, and was thrown from the car. A hiker witnessed the accident and called the park ranger, who called the county sheriff's office, and Sarah went out there. They had to use climbing equipment to get him out, and at one point on the way here in the ambulance he had no pulse. The park ranger said the hiker saw two vehicles driving pretty fast, one was your bug, one was an SUV in pursuit, but the SUV seems to have disappeared."

"Why was he out at the State Park? I figured he'd be in Mexico by now."

"I don't know."

Maggie and Scott entered the emergency waiting room just as Agent Jamie Brown came through the swinging doors from the nether regions of the department, following a woman dressed in a white medical coat who had a stethoscope hanging around her neck. Jamie glanced at Scott and nodded, but followed the woman. Maggie and Scott followed him. They all stopped in front of Bonnie.

The woman in white crouched down so that she was right in front of Bonnie, who was still seated. She put a hand on Bonnie's arm. There was real compassion in her face.

"Mrs. Fitzpatrick," the woman said. "I'm Dr. Balaji. Your son Brian has sustained serious injuries, both external and internal. He has multiple fractures and internal bleeding. He had a cardiac event on the way here, and although they resuscitated him, we've had to put him on a ventilator. Ordinarily, we would take him right into surgery, but he is completely non-responsive, and our monitor indicates there is no brain activity."

"What does that mean?" Bonnie asked.

She had to clear her throat to speak, and tears continued to fall as she did so.

Dr. Balaji gripped Bonnie's hand, looked her straight in the eye, and spoke quietly.

"He's gone," she said. "We're keeping his body alive with our machines, but he has, for all intents and purposes, already passed away. Does your son have an advance directive that you know of or anything that would indicate his wishes in a situation like this?"

Bonnie's face crumpled, and she started sobbing so heavily that she could not answer. The doctor stood up and looked at Patrick and then Sean.

"Are you family members?" she asked.

"I'm Brian's brother and an attorney," Sean said. "If there's a living will we have no knowledge of it. I thought in these cases that the spouse..."

"Yes," Dr. Balaji said. "His wife is here, and she is the one who is legally obligated to make that decision. I just need to make absolutely sure first that there is no written record of his wishes before we remove him from life support."

This got Bonnie's attention.

"Don't unplug him!" she cried. "Sean, stop them!"

"No one's going to do anything before you have a chance to see him," Dr. Balaji reassured her. "We're moving him to a quiet place where you can spend some time with him. The social worker will come down here to meet you, and I suggest you ask her to call Hospice. They are very good to help at times like these. As soon as he is moved, we will come get you. I understand from Ava that you'll want to have your priest here as well."

"No!" Bonnie wailed. "Don't let them do it!"

Dr. Balaji told the assembled, "No one is going to do anything right this minute. You should take a little time and process everything I've just told you. If you have any questions, I'll be glad to answer them now or later. Do you want the chaplain to come?"

Sean said that would be good, yes, and he and Patrick attempted to console Bonnie, who was beside herself with grief. Maggie had been clutching Scott's arm, and as soon as she realized it, she let go.

"What do you want me to do?" he asked her.

"Go get Father Stephen," she said.

He left running, and shortly thereafter Maggie could hear the siren as he left the hospital parking lot. Maggie looked over at Jamie, who was sitting a few seats away from the family, staring at his hands in his lap. He looked up at Maggie, and she was surprised at how grieved he looked.

He was shaking his head as he mouthed, "I'm so sorry."

"I'll be right back," she told her family and walked outside.

The sky was dark with heavy clouds, and although the wind was still cold Maggie thought she could smell a hint of spring coming. There were circles of dirt carved out of the landscaping at intervals, with spindly little Bradford Pear trees planted in each one. Although the trees were bare, around the base of each, she could see the green tips of some sprouted flower bulbs peeking out of the mud, like tiny green tongues.

She took out her cell phone to call Hannah, but as she punched in the speed dial number, she caught sight of Sam's van flying through the entrance to the hospital parking lot. He zoomed up the emergency driveway and screeched to a halt right in front of her. Maggie, who hadn't yet cried, burst into tears as soon as she saw Hannah.

Maggie, Hannah, and Sam went to the hospital cafeteria and got some coffee. Maggie told Hannah all she knew about what had happened to Brian, and Sam showed her his futuristic-looking leg prosthesis. Maggie felt better and calmer just having them both with her. Hannah was obviously happy to have Sam home, and Sam kept touching and smiling at Hannah. For an undemonstrative man like Sam, Maggie thought that was an amazing testament to how good he was feeling about his marriage.

When they returned to the E.R. waiting room, Maggie could hear her mother screaming in the nether regions of the department. She and Hannah followed a nurse back to Brian's room, where they met Patrick and Sean practically carrying Bonnie out of it. She was wild-eyed, gasping and wailing, and looked like she might faint.

"Ava's going to kill him," she cried when she saw Maggie. "She's going to kill my boy!"

The nurse told Maggie she was going to see about getting their mother a sedative and gestured to Patrick and Sean that they should follow her.

Inside Brian's room, Maggie and Hannah found Ava with a nurse from the local Hospice. Also present was Father Stephen, who always seemed able to remain calm in the face of any drama, but was now looking a little shell-shocked. He hugged Maggie and Hannah, told them he would be outside if they needed him, and stepped outside the room. The Hospice nurse didn't seem at all phased by the drama, and she gave Ava's hand a reassuring squeeze before she too left the room.

Ava was sitting in a chair next to a beeping machine at the head of Brian's bed, looking pale and small. Maggie knew she should hug her sister-in-law, say some kind words, or reassure her somehow, but found she couldn't do any of that. Hannah stayed back by the door as Maggie went up to the head of the bed and looked at Brian. His face was swollen, and Maggie had to search for some point of recognition. His shaved head and face could have been that of anyone.

'Maybe,' she thought, 'it's all been a big mistake. Maybe this is not Brian.'

Then she recognized the pale red-gold eyelashes and eyebrows, just like her own, and although his hands and arms were battered and bruised, there was no mistaking the long index finger on each hand, longer than his middle finger. Maggie touched each of her own index fingers with her thumbs; she'd also inherited this trait from her father.

She thought about Brian's quick, cruel temper; his ability to lie so convincingly while looking you straight in the eye; his withering contempt for anyone he was able to take advantage of; and his arrogant, selfish sense of entitlement. This is where it had led him. Maggie felt pity for him, and sympathy for the mother and father they shared, but she couldn't honestly say she loved her brother.

Tubes and IV lines were inserted in several places. The beeping of the machine next to Ava demonstrated that the heart still beat in his chest. The respirator attached to his face breathed in and out for him, so his chest rose and fell with each breath. He didn't look like someone who was sleeping, which was what she'd expected. He looked like a life-like human puppet, being made to look animated by some trick. She recognized the container, but the contents were missing.

She looked up at Ava and met her sister-in-law's frightened gaze.

"He's already gone, Ava," Maggie said. "You're doing the right thing."

"Thank you," Ava said, and a perfect fat tear slid out of one of her pretty brown eyes and down her pale cheek.

"Do you want me to stay?" Maggie asked. "When they do it?"

"No," Ava told her. "Father Stephen will be here."

"Call me if you need me," Maggie said.

"Thank you," Ava said.

Maggie and Hannah left the room.

At 11:13 a.m. Timothy Brian Fitzpatrick was officially pronounced dead.

Grandpa Tim's funeral was postponed until the next day. Bonnie spent the afternoon and evening heavily sedated in her bed, thanks to Doc Machalvie. Doc was feeling no pain, either, sitting in the front room with Fitz and Sal Delvecchio, drinking shot after shot.

The Hospice bereavement counselor came by and offered to help in any way she could. Fitz asked if she could play the fiddle and she replied that although she could not play the fiddle, she could play the trombone, and she would be glad to fetch it if that would help. Fitz invited her to join them all in a shot of whiskey, but she declined and said she would come back the next day. Patrick sat at the piano and played every song his father requested until the old man finally passed out. Meanwhile, townspeople came and went.

Maggie and Hannah sat in the kitchen with Sean and accepted more food and condolences. These newer well-wishers had the scent of gossip collectors about them, and Maggie was curt with a few of them.

"Vultures," she sniped after one of them left. "Here's your pierogies, what's the latest?"

"They're not bad people," Hannah said. "They mean well."

"Why do people bring food at a time you least want to eat?" asked Sean, who was trying to find room in the fridge for this latest offering.

Their Aunt Delia came in through the back door.

"Have you seen the river?" she asked Maggie.

It was so pointedly asked to Maggie and no one else that Sean and Hannah exchanged looks. They stayed put while Maggie followed Delia out onto the back porch to look at the flood waters covering Lotus Avenue. The river had stopped rising, and residents of Marigold Avenue had been allowed to return to their homes now that the danger was thought to have passed. Maggie watched as tree limbs and trash sailed by and crashed into the wall surrounding Eldridge College.

"It's nerve-wracking," Maggie said. "Everything feels so out of control."

"I only have a minute, and then I need to get back to Ava's," Delia said. "What's going on with you and Gabriel?"

"I saw him last night," Maggie said. "He's going back to Florida with his wife and son after the trial."

"It may be months before that trial begins," Delia said. "They're going to be around for awhile."

Maggie shrugged.

"I don't mean to pry," Delia said. "I'm just worried about you."

"I know, and I appreciate it," Maggie said. "I'm just numb at this point."

"I think he feels obligated to his wife, but I don't think she means to him what you do."

"Well, how nice for her. She gets her jailbird back, but he doesn't love her. Another relationship based on a lie."

"If she didn't want him, would you take him back?"

"I still have strong feelings, but they're for the man I thought he was," Maggie said. "If I'd known he was married and an ex-con when I met him I never would have gone out with him."

"And Scott? Do you think you can forgive him for what he did?"

"I know Scott had good intentions," Maggie said, "but he lied to me, too. I hate being lied to for my own good. Funny how it turns out it was actually for their own good and not mine. There was actually nothing 'good' in it for me. I didn't need these men to make my decisions for me. How insulting. How condescending. How patronizing."

"I agree it was a bad decision on Scott's part," Delia said. "He made a mistake, and he's paying for it, but is he condemned for life?"

"I cannot imagine a scenario where what he did was okay."

"I agree. But can you imagine a scenario where you both agree that what he did was wrong, stupid, and unacceptable, but you can put it behind you?"

Maggie didn't answer.

"We don't get endless opportunities to be loved," Delia said. "I know young people like to believe that they do, but don't you kid yourself. Don't ruin the rest of your life just because you're angry right now."

"So, I'm going to be alone and miserable if I don't snap up the only available man who wants me, is that it?"

"It's a distinct possibility," Delia said. "You hold your future in your own hands right now, but not for much longer."

"Hannah thinks Ava is going to seduce Scott. Do you?"

"It's entirely possible," Delia said. "I'm sorry to have to tell you this, but it wouldn't be hard for her to do."

"Maybe he'd be happier," she said.

"Don't be stupid," Delia said. "When has Ava Fitzpatrick ever made a man happy?"

"I've never heard you talk about Ava like that before. What's happened?"

"I can't tell you," Delia said. "Just take my word for it, Scott would not be happy mixed up with Ava, and it's up to you to put a stop to it while you still can."

"He's a big boy," Maggie said. "He can decide what's best for himself."

"You're a fool, Mary Margaret," Delia said. "Remember, pride goeth before the fall."

Maggie stared at Delia, remembering what Anne Marie had told her while in a trance.

"How can you tell if a man is really a snake in disguise?" Maggie asked.

Delia gave Maggie a look that seemed to indicate Maggie had lost her mind.

"I don't know what you're getting at, but I'd say if he looks like a snake and acts like a snake, he probably is a snake," Delia said.

"You're right," Maggie said. "Thanks."

Lily Crawford sat at her kitchen table and broke green beans into a bowl. Gabriel's wife Maria came downstairs and sat across from her.

"Gabriel and Luis went with my nephew to look at the river," Lily said.

"I feel sorry for the people who have lost their homes."

"They may not lose them," Lily said. "But they will have a lot of cleaning up to do."

"It feels so safe here," Maria said. "I am grateful to you for letting us stay."

"You're very welcome," Lily said. "I'm sure you must miss your family."

"My family is not happy that we are here," Maria said. "Even though Gabriel is my husband, they do not approve. Because of my religion, I cannot divorce him, but I also cannot live with him and be welcome in my family home."

"What will you do?"

"We will start over in another place, and make our own family. If my parents see that Gabriel is a good man who provides for his family, in an honest way, they may forgive him."

"Isn't that also a part of your religious beliefs?" Lily asked. "Forgiveness?"

"It's supposed to be," Maria said. "If it were not for Luis building a bridge between us I would never have considered forgiving Gabriel."

"Luis is very special."

"He's been sheltered, so he's very young for his age. He has a wish for the kind of father and mother that Gabriel and I may not be able to be."

"I wish you luck," Lily said.

"You know this person Gabriel was involved with," Maria said. "The one who I met in the bookstore."

"Maggie Fitzpatrick."

"Do you think he still loves her?"

Lily paused, then reached over and held Maria's hand.

"I think you can love more than one person. What's important now is that Gabriel has chosen you and Luis and that you both go into this wholeheartedly, giving it your best."

"I am not so sure that Gabriel loves me with his whole heart," Maria said. "I think he may only love me with a tiny piece, a very old piece."

"You're a beautiful, kind, intelligent woman," Lily said. "If he loved you once, he can love you again. Remind him why he fell the first time."

"I don't want to beg."

"Pride won't keep you warm at night," Lily said.

"There is a man in Florida," Maria said, "someone I am hurting very much by doing this."

"Ah," Lily said. "So a part of your heart belongs to someone else as well."

"Yes," Maria said. "Do you think Gabriel and I are doing the right thing to try to make Luis happy when it makes so many other people unhappy?"

"Simon and I never had children, so I'm no expert," Lily said. "But there's no guarantee that you and Gabriel can make Luis happy even if you do stay together. Life has a way of making us pay dearly for our good intentions."

Gabriel, Luis, and the federal agent posing as Lily's nephew came in, and Luis excitedly told his mother all about the flood. Lily listened with one ear while she observed the body language between Gabriel and Maria. They could barely make eye contact and were awkwardly formal with each other. It was painful to watch.

Luis and Maria went upstairs, and Gabriel sat down with Lily. The agent excused himself and went to the front room.

"I saw Maggie," Gabriel said.

"I figured as much," Lily said. "You need to be careful wandering around town when so many people are being killed."

"Maggie doesn't want to see me again," Gabriel said. "She hates me."

"She's hurt," Lily said. "When people are angry they say lots of things they're sorry about later."

"I made a commitment to Luis and Maria," he said. "While I was in prison, it seemed like the right thing to do. I couldn't wait to be with them."

"And now?'

"Seeing Maggie again," he said. "I wanted to confess my sins, say I was sorry, and say goodbye. But seeing her, being near her, it's got me wondering what if. What if she could be persuaded to forgive me? What if we could be together again? Do you think it's possible?"

"It seems to me you shouldn't rush into any decision right now," Lily said. "Talk to Maria, just the two of you. Be honest. If you can't be honest with each other, what chance have you got?"

Gabriel looked toward the stairs.

"It will be hard enough for me to find work to support myself, let alone support the two of them. I don't want them to suffer because of what I have done, but I don't want to hurt Luis."

"What is it we achieve when we sacrifice our happiness for someone else's?" Lily said. "I know there's a lot to be said for putting your child first and doing what's best for him. But what's best for him? Is it giving him what he wants or helping him deal with life as it is?"

"If I disappoint him now, I'll lose him."

"Are you so sure? Can't you be in his life in a way that works for all of you?"

Gabriel looked toward the stairs again.

"I need to see Maggie again," he said. "I need to convince her to give me another chance."

He put his finger to his lips as he got up and put his coat back on.

"Be careful," Lily said. "Remember Mrs. Wells wants you dead."

Scott knocked on Ava's back door, and Delia answered.

"How's Ava?" Scott asked as he entered the warm kitchen.

"She's upstairs with the baby," Delia said, and then shut the door to the family room, where Charlotte was reading, and Timmy was napping on the couch.

"I want to talk with you privately," she said. "But we can't do it in here."

"Okay," Scott said. "Do you want to go for a walk?"

"I'm supposed to be watching the kids," she said. "As soon as Terese gets back, I can go."

A little while later they left Terese in the kitchen and walked up the alley behind Ava's house.

"Do you have a cell phone on you?" he asked.

"No," Delia said. "Why?"

"I think the feds have mine bugged."

"Good gracious," Delia said. "Ian asked me to stay away from Ava's until this is all over, but I thought it was only the drug dealers we needed to worry about."

"What's going on?" Scott asked, as soon as they were far enough away from the house.

"I'm fond of you," Delia said, "and I'm fond of Maggie. I don't want to see you both miserable."

"I don't know if Maggie and I will be able to work it out or not," he said. "Right now her life is turned upside down; it's not the right time to pressure her about anything."

"I know that; I want to warn you about Ava."

"About Ava?"

"She's having an affair with that agent."

"Jamie and Ava?" Scott asked. "I don't believe it."

"You haven't been in the house lately. You aren't seeing what I'm seeing."

"Are you sure about this?"

"I've seen them together, and there's no doubt in my mind."

"I don't believe it," Scott said.

"Then tell me what this means," Delia said. "Jamie goes up to her room late at night, after the kids are in bed, and comes back down in the morning before the kids wake up."

"You don't sit there all night and watch. He's probably just checking on her and the kids."

"I don't watch but Terese does," Delia said. "She's been dropping some big hints."

"It would jeopardize his case if he carried on with a witness," Scott said.

"I don't trust that man," Delia said. "He's way too smooth and charming."

"He's certainly not what he seems to be," Scott said.

The alley ended at Morning Glory Avenue, and they turned left toward the library.

"I'll tell you something else," Delia said. "When the call came about Brian, I was in the room, and Jamie wasn't surprised."

"You think he had something to do with it?"

"Ava's next door neighbor said Jamie left with another agent early this morning in an SUV and it came back covered with mud. The first thing the other guy did when they got back was wash it, even though it was raining. You tell me why that was so important at eight o'clock this morning."

"You think they ran Brian off the road and left him for dead?"

"I'm just telling you what I heard."

"It's possible," Scott said. "Maybe it would be wise for you to take your husband's advice and stay away from Ava's for now."

"Maybe it would be wise for you not to get in between this man and what he wants."

"You think he'll kill me if I try to intervene between him and Ava?"

"Or look a little too hard for the SUV that left the scene of the crime."

"That's Sarah's crime scene, not mine."

"She's already been to see him."

"How'd that go?"

"I couldn't hear them, but they must have come to some agreement. As she left, I heard him say he would commend her to her superiors."

"If what you suspect is true, she must have agreed not to pursue the SUV that left the scene."

Scott and Delia passed the library and walked out Possum Holler toward the cemetery.

"What about the guy who got murdered in the cemetery maintenance shack?" Scott asked. "Do you think Jamie had anything to do with that?"

"I don't know," Delia said. "Ian thinks that was probably just Mrs. Wells warning her employees to keep their mouths shut or get the heck out of town."

"That's the county's crime to investigate as well," Scott said. "In case you haven't noticed, I'm more of a night watchman around here than a detective."

"Don't underestimate yourself," Delia said. "Ian thinks you're doing very well."

"This is going to sound incredibly naive," Scott said, "but I had no idea all this stuff was going on. I knew there was drug traffic, but not that business was being transacted at the cemetery, or that Simon and Lily Crawford were involved way back. I'm not sure what to do about it."

"You can't be everywhere and control everything," Delia said. "If you knew the nights Ian paced the floor, wrestling with his conscience over what to do, or whether to do anything at all."

"Right now I just want to be sure that Ava's family is safe."

"I think Jamie has that covered."

"You'll think I'm stupid," Scott said. "But I thought at one point this week that Ava was interested in me."

"Oh, she's interested," Delia said. "You're not out of the woods yet."

"I don't believe she would have an affair with that agent in the middle of all this."

"No," Delia said. "I can see how you wouldn't."

Scott remembered that the first time he met Jamie, the agent was holding Ava's hand.

"I think you're reading too much into the situation," Scott said. "Ava's a warm, affectionate person and the situation is intense. I think they've probably become close, but I don't think Ava would have an affair with someone she just met. If you'd said Patrick was with her, then I'd believe it. They had a long relationship, and I don't doubt there are still feelings there."

"I'll wager I know Ava Fitzpatrick better than anyone," Delia said. "She's a lovely woman and a wonderful mother, but she's a curse to any man foolish enough to fall in love with her."

At the end of Possum Holler was Lily Crawford's farm. As they approached, Betty Lou came waddling down the driveway baying at them, with the little cat right behind her.

"Gabe said that Maggie doesn't want to see him again," Scott told Delia.

Lily came out the back door to see who it was, and then called to them to "come on in and get warm."

"He may still love her," Delia said. "But she loves you."

After they had their coffee, Delia went back to the bed and breakfast, and Lily took Scott out to the barn. Penny was in her stall and snuffled at them as they passed. Lily gave the pony a carrot from her pocket, and all the feral cats scattered as they approached.

"I want you to see this," she said, and Scott watched her climb the loft ladder. She used a key to remove the padlock securing the trapdoor in the ceiling.

Scott was amazed to see the laboratory and greenhouse Simon had created in the loft. Lily showed him how the panels on the south side of the barn roof slid back to allow the sun to shine into the greenhouse, with supplementary lights to back it up. There was a sophisticated irrigation system and a dated-looking computer system.

"My husband, the mad scientist," Lily said, taking a seat on one of the high stools.

"I had no idea," Scott said. "I'm guessing no one in town did."

"Theo knew," Lily said. "That's one of the reasons he wanted the property."

"What will happen to it now?" Scott asked. "After the trial?"

"I don't know," Lily said. "They've promised me immunity if I testify, but then everyone in this town will know about my scarlet past, so I'm not sure I'll still be welcome here."

"I'd hate for you to leave," Scott said. "Where would you go?"

"I don't know," Lily said. "I don't have any family left, and Simon's brother is in Canada. They fell out over the war, and I haven't talked to him in years."

"Don't go anywhere," Scott said. "Stay here, and your real friends will stand by you."

"Don't you think it will look bad for the police chief to be friends with an ex-drug producer?"

"I don't care," Scott said. "I've been reassessing what's important, and what other people think of me has fallen way down on the list."

Hannah stopped at the service station to say hi to her dad and found Patrick sharing some new gossip.

"Hatch is buying Marvin's gas station," he was saying. "I don't know where he got the money, but word is he came up with enough for a down payment, and the bank is giving him a loan."

Hannah was reminded of what Hatch said when they chatted while waiting for the dog's owner to arrive. She thought about his sister's boyfriend, the drug dealer. She decided to drive out there.

Hatch was working on a car when she arrived.

"Hey, you!" he called out as soon as he saw her, and he looked truly pleased to see her. "I heard about Grandpa Tim and Brian. I'm so sorry for Bonnie and Fitz. You tell 'em I'll put 'em in my prayers."

"I hear you're buying the place," she said and watched as his face changed. She knew him well and could see his troubled conscience.

"Yeah, well, you can guess where I got the money," he said, looking away. "We called it a gift for legal purposes, but it was Patty's man payin' me off for takin' care of Joshie. He ain't Joshie's father, but he cares what happens to him."

"Where's Patty?"

"She's in some jail for people who done went crazy. I guess the drugs finally fried her brain. He figures she's never gettin' out."

"How'd he get the money?"

"Hard to tell," Hatch said and seemed reluctant to say more.

"Is he still working for Mrs. Wells?" Hannah asked him.

Hatch shrugged and said, "I never asked him, and I don't wanna know."

"If it's drug money, or he took that money for killing someone, and it gets traced to you, what do you think will happen?"

"I guess I'll worry 'bout that when it happens, if it happens."

"What will happen to Joshie if you go to jail?" Hannah asked him.

"I ain't going to no jail," Hatch said.

"You need to go to the police and turn Patty's man in," Hannah said.

"Are you crazy?" Hatch said. "What do you think will happen to Joshie if I do that?"

"Tell me this," Hannah said. "Is Joshie officially yours, like, with paperwork through the courts and everything?"

"He is. I had to do that before he could get enrolled in school."

"You need to make a will saying what happens to him if something happens to you."

"I ain't gonna even think about that," Hatch said, shaking his head.

"If you care about him you will," Hannah said. "You want Patty's man to get hold of him, or him to be sent to foster care if no one else in your family will take him?"

"Ain't nothin' gonna happen to me."

"Just like nothin' happened to your mom and dad, I guess."

"Why are you here?" Hatch asked her. "I heard your old man is back; does he know you're out here?"

"I'm here, you stupid man, because even though you broke my heart a hundred years ago, I still care what happens to you. I don't want anything bad to happen to you or Joshua."

"You better get on outta here before you get tangled up in something you'd best not," Hatch said, with real heat in his voice. "This ain't none of your business."

"You know I'm right," Hannah said.

"Go on," Hatch said. "Go home to your husband."

As Hannah left the station and walked toward her truck, she noticed a young boy of about seven running down the sidewalk. Hannah felt her breath leave her body as he approached her, grinning and loping along like the happiest kid she'd ever seen. His clothes were scruffy and wrinkled, and one of his shoes was untied. But more importantly, his head was covered in bright red curls, and his big blue eyes were shining out of a sea of freckles.

"Hi!" he said to Hannah, and Hannah had to blink a few times before she believed what she was seeing.

"Joshua?" she asked him.

"Yep," he said, "Who are you?"

"I'm Hannah," she said. "I'm a friend of your uncle's."

"Nice to meetcha," he said, and bobbed past her into the service station, so Hannah got a good look at the raggedy backpack, patched with duct tape, that he wore on his back.

Hannah stood there, rooted to the spot, as the spitting image of Timmy Fitzpatrick greeted her old boyfriend.

"Another one," she said. "There's another one."

Scott stopped in at Ava's on his way back to the station.

"Hey, stranger," she said, then hugged him and kissed him on the cheek.

A warm feeling spread throughout Scott's body, and he forgot what it was he came to say.

"How are you holding up?" Scott asked.

"I'm just taking it moment by moment," Ava said.

Her big dark eyes were full of tears.

"Is there anything I can do?" Scott asked her.

"Come by more often," Ava said. "I've been missing you."

"It seems like Jamie's keeping you isolated," Scott said. "It makes me wonder if he has an ulterior motive."

Ava looked at him like he had two heads.

"What in the world makes you think that?" Ava said.

"I'm sorry," Scott said. "I just don't want him to take advantage of you."

Ava laughed, grabbed Scott's arm, and gave it a shake.

"You crazy nut," she said. "You're so sweet to worry about me. Agent Brown has been nothing but professional. Actually, he warned me away from you."

"What?"

"He said I was taking advantage of you by making you stay here; interfering with your job. That's why I told you to go, you know, not because I wanted to."

"Are you sure it wasn't because he wanted to get rid of me?"

"I have a feeling Delia's imagination has been running away with her," Ava said. "She doesn't like Jamie, and she's over-protective of me. Believe me; nothing could be farther from the truth."

"Sometimes we read things into a situation that aren't true," Scott said. "Sometimes we think people feel a certain way when actually the situation is completely innocent."

Ava stood close enough to Scott so that he felt enveloped in her warm, floral perfume. He felt drawn toward her. It was intoxicating.

"I think you know how I feel about you, Scott," Ava said.

Agent Dulvaney came in, and Ava stepped away from Scott. If that hadn't happened, he was pretty sure Ava would have kissed him.

Maggie was sitting at her kitchen table, sipping tea and making a list of things she had to do to get ready for the funeral when she heard someone climbing up the fire escape to her balcony. The hair stood up on the back of her neck. She knew the doors were locked, but nonetheless, she tiptoed across the room and took a large, sharp knife out of a drawer. She heard a tap on the glass. She parted the curtains. It was Gabe. Her heart thumped, and she set the knife on the table. She unlocked the door and opened it a crack.

"What do you want?" she asked.

"Let me in, Maggie, please," he said. "I need to talk to you."

"We don't have anything more to talk about," Maggie said.

A pair of headlights shone down the alley, and Gabe gave her a pleading look.

"Please, Maggie," he said. "There are people out here who want to kill me."

"Then why risk it?" she asked as she let him in, closed the door, locked it, and drew the curtains behind him.

"I needed to see you," he said.

He looked a little more rested, and there was color back in his face. The cigarette smell was still there, but not the industrial detergent smell. He looked and smelled more like the Gabe she remembered. Maggie was so quickly overcome by her attraction to him that it frightened her.

He took off his coat and sat down at her kitchen table. He rolled up both sleeves of his shirt and leaned forward, his arms on the table and his hands outstretched toward her. He drummed his fingers on the table and then cracked his knuckles. He couldn't seem to sit still.

"I heard about your grandfather and your brother," he said. "I'm sorry."

"Why are you here?"

"I've decided I'm not going to let you go without a fight."

Maggie sat down across from him, but sat back in her chair, arms crossed.

"We already discussed this," Maggie said. "You're going to testify and then go back to Florida with Maria and Luis."

"I know that's what Luis wants, and I convinced myself it was what I wanted. I love my son, and I want to be a good father to him, but Maria and I were so young when we met, and we're such different people now. I don't have the feelings of a husband for her. I don't feel the attraction to her that I feel for you. I don't love her like I love you."

Maggie's heart beat a little faster, and she could feel her face flush.

"This is about more than feelings," Maggie said. "You're married to her; you promised to stay married to her, in a church, before God and everyone. How can you turn your back on her when she's willing to forgive you and try again?"

"She doesn't love me. Better for us both to tell the truth now than to live a lie."

"I can't just decide the past seven years didn't happen, Gabe. I can't pretend you didn't lie to me about everything."

"There's nothing I wouldn't do to change the past, to make all that up to you. Haven't I served my time for the mistakes I've made? Don't I have a right to be happy? Don't we have a right to be happy together?"

"We can't be together. You're married. It's as simple as that."

"She would give me an annulment. She doesn't love me. She knows I love you."

"Even if Maria doesn't care, I don't want my happiness to be at the expense of Luis," she said. "Besides, how could I trust you when everything you've ever told me was a lie?"

"Not everything," he said. "You know that in your heart."

"It's no use," Maggie said. "It would never be the same."

"It could be better," he said. "Only pride is keeping us apart. You hold my heart in your hands, Maggie."

Maggie was confused by her conflicting feelings. She had every reason to be righteously indignant, but suddenly she couldn't bear to be mean to him. His dark eyes were so intent upon her. She couldn't help but remember how it felt to be with him all those years ago. How safe he made her feel, how loved and protected. Sweet memories began replaying themselves in her mind as she felt herself soften toward him.

"Please, just go," Maggie said, but even she could hear the lack of conviction in her voice.

"Is that what you want, Maggie?" he asked her. "Is that what you really want?"

The timbre of his voice was like smooth whiskey. It felt like everything up to this point had been a dream, and now she was wide awake but intoxicated. This was her Gabriel, the love of her life. Memories of how they were together flooded her mind, her resolve collapsed, and the attraction she felt toward him overwhelmed her. She let herself remember what it felt like to be in his arms, kissing his lips, and, oh my ... all she had to do was reach out, and she could have that again.

"Say the word," he said. "Say the word, and I'll move heaven and earth to be with you."

"My family would never accept you," Maggie said.

"To hell with them, then," he said. "We don't need anyone else. We can go someplace no one knows us. We can start over."

"My mother is going through hell right now; I can't do that to her."

"Then we'll stay here," Gabe said, looking around. "There's plenty of room for me here. Eventually, she will get over it. If we give her a grandchild, she will definitely forgive us."

"But where would you work?"

Maggie knew it would be next to impossible for Gabe to find employment in Rose Hill, where everyone knew everyone else's business. After the trial commenced, Gabe's testimony would seal his fate in this town, reputation-wise.

"I don't know," Gabe said. "Maybe your Uncle Ian would let me work in the Thorn."

"Not likely," Maggie said, trying to picture it and failing.

"Then I'll work downstairs," he said. "I can learn to make fancy coffee drinks."

Maggie pictured the fall off in business from all the local customers who wouldn't want an ex-con and former drug dealer to sell them anything. She'd be ostracized in the community. Hannah would stick by her, but few others would.

He pushed back his chair and stood up. Maggie felt paralyzed as he came around the table and knelt at her side.

"Maggie," he said, and put his hands on her crossed arms.

The warmth of his hands and the proximity of his scent overwhelmed her senses. Their eyes met. There was no denying the feelings that had reawakened between them. Maggie tried to think, but the pull was too strong. It was that familiar drowning feeling, that drowsy, dizzying force field that quickly overwhelmed her rational mind.

"Maggie," he said, and he leaned forward, upward, reaching out to kiss her, to hold her, just like he used to.

A flash of color caught her eye, and she saw he had a tattoo on his outer arm that he hadn't had seven years ago. Only the tip of it was visible under the edge of his rolled-up sleeve. It was the head of a serpent. It was like a bucket of cold water poured over her head. The spell was broken.

"No," she said.

"Maggie, what's wrong?"

She grabbed the knife off the table and held it out between them as he stood up.

"Out," she said.

"What are you doing?"

"Out," she said and pushed her chair back so she could put distance between them before she stood up.

"Maggie, you know I'd never hurt you," he said.

"But you did, Gabriel," she said, her voice breaking with emotion. "You hurt me more than anyone else ever has. You lied to me about everything, and I believed you. Then you left without even telling me good-bye."

"I wrote to you," he said. "It's not my fault you didn't get the letter."

"Since I found that letter, I've been wondering what I would have done if I had received it when you sent it. You know what? I think I'd have burned it. I think I'd have done what I'm about to do now, which is wash my hands of you."

"Don't throw away what we had," Gabe said. "Everyone makes mistakes. Give me a second chance, Maggie. I can prove to you I'm the man you once loved."

"A second chance to screw up my life? No thanks. Look at what you just offered me: to reject my family and everyone that I love, to break your son's heart, and to abandon Maria. She gave you a second chance and look how it's turned out for her."

"Maggie, just listen to me," he said. "I love you."

"You're not the man I fell in love with," Maggie said. "You're just pretending to be him to get what you want. You know all the right things to say, but they're all lies."

Keeping the knife out in front of her she backed up to the balcony doors, opened one, moved to the side, and then gestured toward the open door with the knife.

"Go right now, and I won't call Scott," she said. "But if you ever come near me again, I'll have you arrested."

"Please don't end it this way," Gabe said. "Please."

"Just go," she said.

"I'll do as you wish," he said. "But I'll never stop loving you."

As soon as he left, she locked the doors and drew the curtains. She sat down at the kitchen table and looked at her list, but her vision was blurred. When the first tear dropped on the paper, she crumpled it up and threw it across the kitchen. As if on cue, it started raining again. The tin overhang that sheltered her balcony rang out with every drop; it was a cozy sound that had always lulled her to sleep before, but tonight it gave no comfort.

Scott saw a dark figure walking up the alley ahead of him and called out. Gabe turned and waited for him.

"You shouldn't be out alone," Scott said.

"I don't care what happens to me," Gabe said.

He was soaked to the skin and looked as miserable as a person could be.

"But maybe Luis does," Scott said.

Gabe shrugged, and they walked together up the alley.

"Were you at Maggie's?" Scott asked.

Gabe looked at Scott but didn't answer.

"C'mon," Scott said. "Let me give you a ride home."

Gabriel accepted, and they walked to Scott's house to get his Explorer.

As Scott opened the driver's side door, he felt the cold barrel of a gun pressed into the back of his neck. Gabe was already in the SUV, and Scott heard him curse as he saw what was happening.

"Get in," the man said. "I've got nothing to lose by killing you both, so don't do anything stupid."

As soon as Scott was seated, the man got in the back, and again he felt the gun barrel on the back of his neck.

"Hey, good buddy," the man said. "Long time no see, Gabe."

Scott looked into the rearview mirror, but he didn't recognize the man. He had a clean-shaved head, a scraggly goatee and his pupils were dilated in his red-rimmed eyes.

"Let him go," Gabe said. "I'm the one she wants, not him."

"It would be stupid to leave a witness, though," the man said, smiling at Gabe.

"It would be more stupid to kill a cop," Gabe said.

The man's eyes widened.

"State or county?"

"Local," Gabe said. "He doesn't have a dog in this fight."

"Well, I'll tell you what we'll do. We'll drop him off somewhere, he'll have a long walk home, and you and me will go see the boss."

"He'll kill us both," Gabe said to Scott. "It might as well be here as somewhere out in the woods. Don't go anywhere."

With his eyes on the man in the rearview mirror, Scott slowly moved his left hand across his lap toward his holster, which was on the right-hand side of his belt. The man in the backseat had his eyes on Gabe.

"What's she paying you?" Gabe asked the man.

"Fifty grand," he said. "Dead or alive."

"Did you kill the guy up at the cemetery?"

"Duane killed my buddy Ray, so I killed him. Live by the sword, die by the sword."

"Did you kill Brian?"

"No," the man said. "We don't know who did that."

"She could've paid somebody else to do it," Gabe said. "Maybe she doesn't tell you everything."

"Let's go," the man said to Scott. "Drive down to the river. You make any stupid decisions, and I'll kill this one and then you."

"Don't," Gabe said to Scott. "If he shoots us here, someone will hear, and he'll get caught. If he drowns us in the river, he'll get away with it."

"If this cop doesn't put this car into gear and move right now," the man said to Gabe, "I'll kill you both and then pay a visit to your redheaded girlfriend. I followed you down there. I know where she lives."

Scott immediately started the car and put it in reverse. His eyes briefly met Gabe's; where he expected to see fear instead he saw steely resolve.

"Use the alley by the college," the man said. "There's no roadblock down there."

"What's the old lady gonna do, kill everybody?" Gabe asked him. "They're closing in on her, and she's getting sloppy."

"She's got people everywhere," the man said. "She'll get them before they get her."

"It seems to me she's killing anyone who could be a liability. Why is it any different for you?"

"She trusts me," the man said. "I've never done wrong by her."

"You won't live to see next week," Gabe said. "You're nothing to her but a means to an end."

"She needs somebody she can count on, and that's me," the man said. "We've got big plans."

"She's slick; I'll give her that," Gabe said. "You'll believe that right up until somebody slits your throat and tosses you in the river."

"Ray didn't deserve that," the man said. "He was a good guy."

"She didn't do such a great job protecting him, did she? And yet you somehow think she's gonna protect you."

"I've been with her a long time. She's never let me down."

"If you can't trust a paranoid, drug-addicted psychopath," Gabe said, "who can you trust, right?"

"Shut up," the man said to Gabe, and then to Scott, "Quit driving so slow. You'll draw attention."

"When they arrest her, and they will," Gabe said, "what's to stop her from claiming you acted on your own? Maybe you killed all those people because you're the psychopath."

"Nobody's gonna arrest her. She's got people in high places who owe her big time."

"Maybe locally, maybe even in the state, but not in D.C., pal. In D.C. she's just a roach that's about to get stepped on."

They turned down Daisy Lane. Scott drove slowly down the alley and then stopped where the water lapped up against the backyards of the houses on Marigold Avenue. They were behind Bonnie and Fitz's house, and Scott could see the light in the kitchen was still on.

"You won't survive being arrested if you kill a cop," Gabe said. "They'll call it resisting arrest when they fill out the report afterward. Or they'll give you a head start and then shoot you in the back, say you were armed and dangerous."

"Quit talking about that," the man said. "I ain't gonna kill him."

"But you have to," Gabe said. "No witnesses, remember?"

"You need to shut up," the man said.

Tires spun behind them, headlights zoomed up toward the rear window, and the man in the back seat turned to look back, saying, "What the..."

Gabe launched himself into the back seat, knocking Scott sideways and causing him to lift his foot off the brake. The Explorer rolled into the water. While the two men struggled in the backseat, the vehicle floated a few yards before an uprooted tree carried along on the fast-moving current slammed into it, and sent it spinning. A gun went off, and the back window of the Explorer exploded. Scott grabbed his gun out of his holster and spun around in his seat. Gabe looked back at him as calmly as if nothing had happened, even though he was spattered with bright red blood.

"You might be willing to die for her," Gabe said, "but I'm not."

The SUV hit the brick wall that surrounded the college, then scraped against it as it was swept down toward the fast-moving river. Scott knew they had very little time left. Using his door controls, he rolled down all the windows, thankful the water hadn't yet drowned the electronic mechanism.

"Good luck," Gabe said and climbed out the back window. Scott released his seat belt, climbed out through the driver's side window, and climbed onto the roof of the SUV. Water filled the cabin of the vehicle, and it began to sink, nose first. Scott heard a man yelling his name.

"Here!" Scott called out. "By the wall!"

It was dark and pouring rain, but the headlights of the vehicle up the hill behind them and the lights on the Eldridge College campus illuminated his predicament. As soon as the SUV cleared the wall, it would be swept up by a raging river churning with debris, headed for the dam below town. He wouldn't survive it.

The SUV tipped further and sank fast; Scott climbed backward until the tailgate disappeared into the dark, frigid water. He went under and then bobbed back up. The shock of the cold water knocked the breath out of him, and he found he couldn't call out again. The current slammed him into the wall. Scott scrabbled with his hands against the bricks, but the wall was still high enough that he couldn't reach the ironwork at the top.

He thought about Maggie, and how sad he was he'd never see her again. He heard a boat motor and saw the spotlight. It temporarily blinded him.

"Scott!" Cal Fischer shouted. "We're throwing you a line!"

Scott felt the rope land across his shoulder and grabbed hold of it with both hands. Once again he bounced off the brick wall, felt a sharp pain in his shoulder, and had to drop his left hand from the rope. His right hand was so cold it was almost completely numb, but he was still able to grip the rope and wrap it around his wrist as the current pushed him down toward where the wall ended, a few yards away. Cal's boat loomed up out of the darkness.

"Hold on!" Malcolm yelled. "We'll pull you in!"

As Cal turned the boat and towed him away from the wall, Scott could feel them pulling the rope, reeling him in, and moments later two sets of strong hands hauled him up out of the water into the boat.

"Gabe's out there," Scott said through chattering teeth. "We need to go back."

Malcolm looked out through the torrential rain at the madly swirling currents.

"Too dangerous," he said.

"But you did it for me," Scott said.

Malcolm shrugged.

"He's not worth it."

Malcolm carefully unwound the rope from Scott's wrist. The pain in his shoulder was excruciating.

"How did you know what was going on?" Scott asked him.

"I called him," someone else said.

Scott turned in the boat, crying out at the pain in his injured shoulder as he did so, just so he could see who was speaking. It was Federal Agent Jamie Brown.

CHAPTER TEN - Monday

At noon on Monday, a day after he was originally scheduled to be buried, Timothy Brian MacGregor was laid to rest in a muddy hand-dug grave in the Rose Hill Cemetery. The sky was overcast, and the wind was sharp. A "V" formation of Canada Geese flew over, heading northward, honk-honking as they passed.

Mayor Stuart Machalvie had arranged for a piper, paid for by the Kilt and Bagpipe Club, of which Tim had been a charter member. The mournful wail could be heard all the way down at the Eldridge College campus, and it echoed off the hills across the Little Bear River. The brothers of the Whistle Pig Lodge, of which Tim had also been a member, serenaded the assembled with three verses (a mercifully shortened version in deference to the weather) of a ten-verse Scottish dirge, accompanied by the piper.

Maggie stood shivering between Hannah and Sean while her mother sobbed, held up between Sean and Patrick. Scott, Sam, and Ed stood behind them. Maggie's father had been in no shape to attend any part of the service, so his brothers Curtis and Ian were at home with him. Ava stood off to the side, holding hands with daughter Charlotte and son Timothy. Agent Jamie Brown, his eyes covered by dark glasses, stood behind her holding Little Fitz.

After each family member threw a handful of dirt on Grandpa Tim's coffin, they rode in the hearse back to the Community Center. Patrick and Sean had to help their mother inside. Maggie and Hannah huddled close together for warmth as they waited outside for Scott, Sam, and Ed to arrive.

"How are you doing?" Hannah asked.

"You don't have to ask me that every five minutes," Maggie said. "I'm okay."

"You want to talk about what happened last night?"

"No one bothered to call and tell me about it until this morning," Maggie said.

"I didn't know about it until I got to the church today. Those scanner grannies must've all been asleep on the job last night."

"He could have died," Maggie said.

"They haven't found Gabe," Hannah said.

Maggie shrugged.

"Which one were you most upset about?" Hannah asked. "When you heard the news, I mean. Which one did you think, 'oh woe is me, I can't live without him?' Was it Scott or Gabe?"

"You know," Maggie said, "the only thing that keeps me from throttling you some days is how fond I am of your father."

"You want to hear some good news?"

"Sam's home and walking. I know that."

"Nope, even better than that."

"You got your grant?"

"Nope."

"Hannah, just tell me."

"There's a tiny tart in my toaster oven."

"Oh, I already knew that."

"Who told you?"

"You might as well have," Maggie said. "You quit smoking and drinking, you're sick all the time, and you've found religion. I'm not looking forward to nine months of this."

"Only six more months, but then I have to breastfeed the little monkey. I am looking forward to finally filling out a bra."

Maggie hugged her.

"I'm so happy for you," she said. "Why didn't you tell me when you first suspected?"

"I wanted to make sure it was real first. Telling you makes it real and official."

"Your mother is going to go berserk."

"I know; we aren't telling her yet. If it's a girl, she may take it away from me. She probably saved all those pageant dresses, you know."

"I won't let her do it. I'll keep an eye on her."

"I hate when they put pink headbands on bald baby girls. You know my mother will have one of those waiting in the delivery room to snap on her little noggin as soon as she pops out."

"She'll have lots of books," Maggie said. "I'll personally be in charge of all the books."

Sam and Ed arrived. Maggie hugged Sam and said, "Congratulations."

He hugged her back, and when she looked into his eyes, she was heartened by what she saw.

"How are you doing?" Sam asked her as they walked to the front door of the Community Center.

"I'm just going with the flow," Maggie said. "I'm just accepting what is."

"That sounds kind of new age-y."

"Caroline once told me that's what the Buddhists do. It keeps them from suffering."

"How's that working out for you?"

"It's quite calming, actually," Maggie said. "I do feel guilty about not caring as much as I should. I think that must be what Catholic Buddhists do."

They all made their way into the Community Center, where there was a loud buzz that sounded more like a party than a funeral. Maggie's mother was sitting in a place of honor, receiving condolences.

"I don't know why this reminds me of *The Godfather*," Sam said to Maggie.

"My mother is a force to be reckoned with," Maggie said. "Hannah says Ava's the queen of this town's pity party, but I say there's our new queen."

"I don't think Ava pities herself," Sam said. "I think she's been very brave. It was hard for her to stand up to your mother yesterday. She hasn't had it easy."

"Well, where is this paragon of virtue whom others call Ava?" Maggie asked.

"Agent Brown took her home. After that scene with Bonnie at the hospital, I can hardly blame her for not being here. Why do you and Hannah have to be so hard on her? She only ever says nice things about you two. She could use your support right now."

"Why, when she's obviously got yours and every other man's in this town?"

"Don't be petty, Maggie. She's under an incredible strain right now. You don't even know how much."

"Well, she's free of my brother at last. I wonder if she and Patrick will finally get together."

"Hmmm," was all Sam said.

Maggie was even more irritated by this non-answer.

"You don't have to babysit me, you know," Maggie said. "I'm perfectly fine."

"Okay, okay," Sam said and went to get something to drink.

Maggie found Hannah raiding the olive bowl.

"Leave some for the rest of the town," Maggie said.

"Hey, c'mere," Hannah whispered, pulling Maggie to a quiet spot. "Who was the hunky guy with Ava at the hospital and the cemetery?"

"That's the head FBI agent, Jamie Brown. He's staying at Ava's."

"James Brown? Get out of here! The king of soul? The hardest-workin' man in show business?"

Maggie smiled, which was no doubt Hannah's goal.

"You should have seen the way he was looking at her," Hannah said. "I think he's taking the notion of body-guarding verrrry seriously. I think maybe Agent Brown is on the scene like a sex machine."

"Really? He just seems like a nice guy to me."

"Uh huh. That's just how he softens up the ladies. Then the cape comes out, and it's all, 'Get on up-a!'"

"Ava did tell Scott he didn't have to stay with her now that Jamie's there."

"You know, it's a man's world, but it wouldn't be nothin' without a woman or a girl."

"Hannah. Her husband died yesterday."

"Uh huh, I saw how anxious she was to pull the plug."

"This is my brother we're talking about."

"You weren't that fond of him, either."

"I know, but stop. I just...I don't want to joke about it."

"But now that Ava's a merry widow, don't you think it will be interesting to see which silly ass she ends up with?"

"Well, I doubt it will be Jamie."

"He ain't no drag," Hannah said. "Papa's got a brand new bag."

Maggie thought about how quickly and vigorously every man in this town came to Ava's defense and thought she could probably take her pick.

Hannah was singing, "I Feel Good" under her breath, so Maggie threw an olive at her.

Sam was in the game room; his pants hiked up to show Patrick his new legs.

"Rotational shock-absorbing pylons," Sam said. "They have microchips in them."

"Are you able to leap tall buildings in a single bound?" Patrick asked.

"Not yet," Sam said. "But we're working on it."

"You were never this tall before," Patrick said. "You asked for longer ones just so you'd be taller than me, didn't ya?"

"I did," Sam said. "It's always been a dream of mine: walking again, and being taller than you."

"Hannah said you rode a bike while you were up there."

"It was the best I've felt in a long time," Sam said. "Riding that bike was so easy I couldn't believe it. Remember how good it felt to do that when we were kids? It feels like flying. I only wrecked once; pothole got me."

"I bet you could play basketball in those things."

"Eventually, yeah, probably."

"We could get some bigger pistons added, maybe some huge springs to give you more leverage. Lester down at the station could probably put those in for you."

"I'll look into it," Sam said. "Do you know Pudge Postelthwaite's son Caleb?"

"Sad story. Drunk driver, I heard, totaled his car; Doc said they saved his left leg but not the right."

"I'm going to introduce him to Alan while he's here, then raise enough money for him to go up there and get fitted with something. The sooner he does it, the better, I think."

"Let me know what I can do; we can always have a fish fry or a spaghetti dinner."

"I knew I could count on you."

"Did you hear about our bet with the Pendleton Perverts?" Patrick asked.

"Hannah told me. That was truly inspired."

"The only problem is we set the bar so high I hate to think what will happen if we lose the next game."

"Don't worry. As soon as I get my new legs tricked out, we should be all set."

"Glad you're back, man," Patrick said. "This has been a tough week in a tough year, and we need you here."

"You doing okay?"

"You know me and Brian never got along. He was such a jerk to Ava and the kids. My mom and dad are broken up about it, but I don't feel much of anything."

"Your grandpa was a character," Sam said. "Do you remember the time your Uncle Curtis took us all on a hayride and Grandpa Tim fell off the back of the wagon?"

"He said if we promised not to tell Bonnie he'd fallen off the wagon, he'd buy us all movie tickets. And he did."

"He was a sweet man," Sam said. "After I came back from the Gulf he came to visit me and told me his World War II stories. He said he still had bad dreams about what he saw over there; said it was like living through it over and over every night."

"He would never go hunting with us," Patrick said. "He hated guns."

"He helped me, you know," Sam said. "He understood what I was going through."

"Now, him I'll miss," Patrick said and wiped his eyes.

"I have some good news," Sam said. "Did you know Hannah's pregnant?"

"No! Congratulations! That's great news," Patrick said as he hugged Sam. "Ah, man, that's wonderful. A son, maybe. That's just great."

"I heard Ava has a new addition to her family."

"Yep. Cute kid. Looks just like Timmy."

"You guys still off?"

"Yeah, probably for the best."

"She's a widow now, though."

"That may be true, but to my mother, she'll always be Brian's wife."

Scott cornered Doc Machalvie in the cloakroom, where he was pouring something from a flask into his coffee cup.

"You caught me," Doc said. "The older I get, the more friends I lose. I need a little nip to get through these days."

"I appreciated your help last night."

"You're lucky to be alive," Doc said. "How's the shoulder?"

"Sore," Scott said. "But I'm okay."

"And you're sure you didn't hit your head?"

"No," Scott said. "Amazingly enough, the one thing that doesn't ache today is my head."

"Is there anything I can do for you?" Doc asked.

"Tell me this," Scott said. "Did Agent Brown question you about helping Brian Fitzpatrick?"

Doc's face sagged.

"You know about that, do you?" Doc said and reached out to steady himself on a nearby chair.

"When did he come to see you?" Scott asked him.

"Yesterday. No, no, the day before yesterday," Doc said, rubbing his face with one hand, and sloshing coffee out of his mug with the other. "It wasn't Agent Brown; it was the other one. It was after I got home from the wake. Don't blame Frank. He was asleep in the car out front when the agent showed up. I certainly didn't want anyone else to hear what I said."

"You knew where Brian was and you told him."

Doc sat down on the chair he was gripping. His face was gray, and his hands were shaking so hard Scott took the mug out of his hand so he wouldn't drop it.

"What did you tell them?" Scott repeated.

"I thought they would arrest him and put him back in jail, not kill him," Doc said.

"Did you help him after he escaped?"

"I stitched him up. I gave him some painkillers and antibiotics. That's all. I told him not to call again. I said I wouldn't help him anymore."

"Where was he?"

"Fitz's hunting cabin."

Scott could have smacked his own head. He'd forgotten all about that cabin.

"If those photos get out," Doc said, "it will kill my wife."

"Those photos were destroyed after Theo died," Scott said.

"But the agent said there were photos," Doc said. "They knew Theo was blackmailing me and they found the photos in his safe."

"They found out about the blackmail from Phyllis. Those photos were destroyed before the feds got to the safe."

"By whom?"

"By someone who cares about you," Scott said, thinking of Patrick and Maggie destroying the photos after Hannah and Maggie discovered them in Theo's hiding place. They had also destroyed the blackmail evidence against the former fire chief and Ed's father by burning up the evidence in the burn barrel behind the fire station. He had almost arrested Maggie for doing it. "You never have to worry about anyone seeing them."

"He made it sound like he had them," Doc said.

"He was lying," Scott said. "They would say or do anything to get to Brian."

"I may as well have killed him myself."

"It was an accident," Scott reassured him, even though he thought that it might well have been murder. "They chased him through the State Park, and he went off the road, down into a deep ravine. He was thrown from the car and was almost dead by the time they found him. You aren't to blame for Brian's death. He brought this all on himself."

"I didn't know all that," Doc said. "Thank you, Scott."

"Let's get you some hot coffee," Scott said, offering a hand to the older man.

"You know," Doc said, as he accepted Scott's help getting to his feet. "After Theo died, I thought maybe the dark cloud I was under would disappear. Even though you tell me those photos have been destroyed, I can still feel it hanging over my head. I wonder if it will ever go away."

Scott got Doc some coffee and left him in the kitchen, safely surrounded by doting women. Then Scott went to find Sam Campbell. He took his old friend outside for a chat, and afterward, he went to find Maggie.

Scott found Maggie in what had been their eighth-grade classroom. The desks were all still there, as well as the chalkboards and bulletin boards. She was sitting at the teacher's desk with her head down on her crossed arms.

"Are you okay?" Scott asked her from the doorway.

"Yes," she said, without lifting her head. "I wish everyone would quit asking me that."

"I just wanted to be sure," Scott said and walked to the front of the classroom.

Maggie looked up.

"Are you okay?" she asked.

"I'm alive," he said. "Everything else is just details."

He sat down on the corner of the desk and looked at her with such tender fondness that Maggie felt guilty for every cross word she'd ever spoken to him.

"I didn't find out until this morning," Maggie said. "It must have been scary."

"It was," Scott said. "There for a minute I didn't think I'd make it."

"Malcolm said the FBI agent called and told him to bring the boat before you were even in the water."

"They had the Explorer bugged," Scott said. "He knew what was going on while it was happening."

"Malcolm said you shot the guy."

Scott smiled a little ruefully.

"Is that not what happened?" she asked.

"A gun went off, and the guy died," Scott said.

"Are you saying Gabe killed the man?"

"If Gabe killed someone, he'd go back to prison," Scott said, "no matter what his deal was with the feds. Jamie and I talked about it and decided having Gabe available to testify against Mrs. Wells was more valuable than sending him back to prison."

"If he's still alive," Maggie said.

"I'm sorry," Scott said. "They haven't found him."

"Don't feel sorry for me. It's Maria and Luis you should feel sorry for. If he's not dead, he ran away, and that may be worse."

Scott reached out and pushed a stray curl back from Maggie's forehead.

"I love you," he said.

"I don't know why," Maggie said.

There were tears in her eyes.

"When I thought I was going to die," Scott said, "I thought how sad it was that I'd never see you again."

Maggie took his hand and held it up to her cheek. Tears rolled out of her eyes onto his hand.

"I've been so awful to you," she said. "I'm so sorry. I know when you let Gabe go instead of arresting him you did it because you loved me."

"It was a mistake not to tell you," Scott said. "I'm sorry."

"Just more details, right?" she said. "It doesn't seem to matter so much now."

Maggie brought his hand to her lips and kissed it, held it there.

"Tell me, Maggie," Scott said. "Can we finally let go of the past and be together?"

"It's not that simple," Maggie said and dropped his hand.

"Oh, yes, it really is," Scott said. "It's just that simple."

"I can't," she said. "I don't know what's wrong with me, but I can't seem to change it. I do love you. I know I'll probably regret it, and the thought of you with anyone else makes me want to scream, but I just can't give in."

"Committing to me feels like giving in?" Scott said.

"I know it's crazy," she said. "I can't explain it except to say I just can't do it."

"Okay," Scott said. "It's not what I wanted to hear, but I'll accept it."

"It's not fair to ask you to wait."

"I'm not going to," Scott said. "Not anymore. Life's too short."

Tears rolled down Maggie's face, and Scott gave her a clean handkerchief from his pocket.

"We're still friends," he said. "When you need me you can call me."

Maggie found she couldn't talk.

She listened to Scott's steps across the squeaky wood floor of the schoolroom and the hallway outside. She heard him go down the steps and out the side door; it slammed shut with a bang. She put her head back down on her arms and wept.

Hannah found her there.

"What's up, chicken butt?"

"I have spiritual cooties," Maggie said, as she raised her head. "I may have soul chiggers, too."

"Sounds itchy," Hannah said. "You wanna hear about your old boyfriend?"

"Did they find him?"

"No, but someone thinks they saw him get on a bus in Morgantown."

"Of course he ran away," Maggie said. "He's a drug dealer who just got out of prison and probably killed a man. Poor Luis and Maria are lucky to be rid of him."

"Now, what would Jesus do, Maggie? You're supposed to turn the other cheek, like, seventy billion times or something."

"He came to my place last night before the accident. He climbed up the fire escape."

"And?"

"He has a snake tattoo on his arm."

"So? Sam has an eagle on his bicep," Hannah said. "And I may or may not have a small bluebird on my tushie."

"And they both mean something," Maggie said. "Why would a man pick a snake?"

"I can't imagine," Hannah said. "Snakes are creepy."

"And dangerous," Maggie said. "I was a fool to think he was anything but a snake-tattooed, lying drug dealer who was willing to abandon his wife and son for me. He saw the bookstore and my apartment and thought, 'hey this is a much better deal.' He's no better than my brother Brian. I'm just lucky he didn't marry me and kill me for the life insurance. What an idiot I was."

"Don't get too worked up," Hannah said. "We all do stupid things we regret. Let it go, and get on with your life. You're finally free."

"Except Scott had some epiphany during his ordeal last night and gave me an ultimatum: now or never. I chose never, as usual. I am officially my own worst enemy."

"So what? It's your life, and if you don't want to be with Scott, then heck with him. Scott Gordon's a mama's boy, anyway. Scott Gordon can go suck an egg."

"That's one of the things I love most about you, Hannah. You never hesitate to take a situation back to the sixth-grade level."

"I hate seeing you so miserable all the time."

"I know. Thanks for being such a pain in my butt. I do appreciate it."

"Did you see my big boy Sam walking around on those wacky robot legs?"

"He looks great. He seems, I don't know, healed in some way. I know that sounds corny, but it was something in his eyes. He looks like he's made peace with himself."

"He'll probably always have problems with depression; I'm not kidding myself about that."

"But this is a huge accomplishment."

"I guess because the wheelchair didn't matter to me I thought it shouldn't matter to him. He knew he could probably walk but was afraid to try again. Alan has been waiting for a chance to help him. That Alan; now there's a nice single man for you."

"Oh, no. Stop that right now."

"And Drew's single again."

"I love you, Hannah, but no."

"I love you, too. And because I love you, I'll tell you this: you look awful. You need to wash your face or something."

"I don't want to go downstairs," Maggie said. "All those horrible people."

"There are some nice people down there, too; people who care about you and your family."

"I still think that for their safety I should not be let loose among them today."

"I need to tell you about something, but I'm not sure it's the right time."

"Oh, crap, here we go," Maggie said. "Just say it."

"I went out to see Hatch."

"Hannah."

"He admitted he got the money to buy the station from Patty's drug-dealing boyfriend. I'm worried he might somehow get caught up in this investigation."

"There's nothing you can do, Hannah. Stay out of it."

"I know, I know," Hannah said. "Did Patty ever fool around with Brian?"

"Probably, everyone else did. Why?"

Hannah told her about Joshua.

"Your brother was a fertilizing fool," Hannah concluded.

"Is there anything to be gained by finding out for sure?" Maggie asked.

"Not unless Ava wants to add to her collection."

"That woman," Maggie said. "She's got Scott right where she wants him."

"It's not too late," Hannah said.

"It is," Maggie said. "I just blew my last chance."

Hannah's stomach gurgled loudly.

"You're hungry?" Maggie asked. "You just ate a whole bowl of olives."

"I'm not hungry, but the vessel is starving. Let's go feed the vessel."

"What does that mean?"

"I haven't told you about my Ann Marie séance? Wait'll you hear this…"

Sam and Ed were sitting in the game room of the Community Center watching some men play pool.

"You know, it was Drew and Alan who saw Brian wreck," Sam said.

Ed's head snapped around instantly, and his mouth fell open.

"Why did they call it in anonymously?" he asked.

"They were driving Hannah's county truck. If they got caught, she'd be fired. They were checking feral cat traps and took a shortcut from the old camp on our property to the State Park. Brian and the SUV chasing him almost ran them off the road. Luckily Drew was pulled over in a lay-by looking at a map when they came past. They called me first, and I used an untraceable cell phone to call it in to the park ranger."

"I can understand not wanting to get caught with the county vehicle, but why all the secrecy of an untraceable cell? Why didn't Drew and Alan just use one of their cell phones and say they were hiking?"

"They saw the license plate on the SUV chasing Brian, and I advised them not to get involved."

"Why?"

"It was a government plate," Sam said.

"Holy smokes."

"Uh huh."

"Sam, you remember I run a newspaper, right?"

"You won't print this. You have a new girlfriend and twelve-year-old boy to protect. These people don't care how many little fish they hurt; they're only interested in catching the big ones. If they have to use little ones for bait ..."

"Okay," Ed said. "So why tell me if I can't do anything about it?"

"So you'll be aware. So you won't let your guard down."

"You know about our little escapade the other night with the three vehicles," Ed said.

Sam nodded.

"Lester put Scott's Explorer up on the rack the next morning and found the GPS device and the bug," Sam said. "We left them there so they wouldn't know we found them. It's a good thing we did; it saved his life last night."

"No search warrants were applied for or issued for this surveillance, I presume."

"You should assume your house is bugged," Sam continued. "All your phone calls and e-mails are intercepted, and all of your movements are supervised."

"But how can they do that indiscriminately, without subpoenas or just cause?"

"You're an idealist, Ed, and while that's admirable, it's not very realistic. I recommend you practice being more of a pragmatist."

"How do you know all this?"

"You know, Ed, for somebody who is so smart you're still a bit slow on the uptake."

Ed stared at Sam, whose face was inscrutable. Then he knew.

"You don't..." Ed said. "Oh, except you do. You do security work for the government."

Sam clapped Ed on the back and smiled at him.

"Now you're with me. If any of this starts to get you down, I can recommend a good antidepressant. It has very few side effects."

Hannah came in and sat down on Sam's lap.

"I gotta go, sweetie," she said. "They arrested those dog-fight guys Hatch told me about, and I need to pick up the dogs."

"You want me to come?" Sam asked.

"Drew's going with me," Hannah said. "There are state troopers out there so we'll be okay."

"Be careful," Sam said. "Remember you're carrying our little biology experiment."

"You're pregnant?" Ed asked.

"Yeah," Hannah said. "He knocked me up after we got married. He's old-fashioned that way."

Hannah's truck labored through the muddy ruts and deep puddles that made up the narrow road between two steep hillsides. They crossed a shallow creek in two places.

"I can't believe anyone lives out here," Drew said.

"Brace yourself," Hannah said. "I've been to places like this before, and it's never a good experience."

There were two state troopers standing guard at the end of the rutted driveway, and their facial expressions were grim.

"There may only be two or three worth saving," one of them said.

On the way back to Rose Hill, Hannah and Drew stopped in Fleurmania at Hatch's gas station. Drew filled the tank while Hannah talked with Hatch in the office.

"We saved four," Hannah said. "There were six others so bad off Drew put 'em down right then and there."

"I think them people ought to be chained to a dog house up to their knees in filth," Hatch said. "They ought to have to spend the winter outside, see how they like it."

"You did a good thing telling me about it," Hannah said. "And don't worry, no one knows who I got the tip from."

"I been thinking about what you said the other day."

"I say a lot of things," Hannah said. "Most of it comes out of my mouth before I stop to consider how rude it is. I was awful rough on you."

"No, you were right," Hatch said. "I told Patty's man I didn't want the money and I canceled the loan application. Just in time, too. I guess you heard Patty's man done got his self killed yesterday."

"He was the guy who kidnapped Scott and Gabe?"

Hatch nodded.

"I didn't want him hanging around Joshie, but I didn't wish him dead."

"I'm sorry you won't get to buy the station."

Hatch shrugged.

"Maybe I'll take your dad up on his offer. Rose Hill's got a better school for Joshie anyhow."

Hannah thought about little redheaded Joshua going to class and sitting next to Timmy Fitzpatrick.

"Hatch, have you ever met Ava Fitzpatrick's kids?"

"I can't say that I have. Are they as purty as she is?"

"Charlotte's the spitting image of Ava," Hannah said. "Timmy looks like Brian."

"Well, I guess that's natural."

"Did Patty ever run around with Brian?"

"Not that I know of, why?"

"I just wondered," Hannah said, and then snapped her mouth shut.

"What?" Hatch asked.

"Joshie is the spitting image of Timmy Fitzpatrick."

"Well, he would be with that red hair."

"No, I mean so alike they could be twins."

Hatch stared at her for several seconds.

"Well, I swan," Hatch said. "I guess it's possible."

"I thought I'd better warn you; I hope I was right to do it."

"If that boy's got Patty's and Brian's blood running through his veins, I'm gonna have my work cut out for me. I didn't do so well with Patty."

"You were only a kid yourself," Hannah said. "You did the best you could."

"I always regretted what I did to you," Hatch said. "Not a day goes by that I don't think about you, and wonder how you're doing."

"I'm doing fine," Hannah said. "Sam and I are doing just fine."

"I'm glad for you, I really am," Hatch said, although his sorrowful face belied the words.

Ed was surprised to see Ava Fitzpatrick walk into the newspaper office.

"Hello, Ed," she said. "Do you have a few minutes for me?"

"Sure," Ed said, and then looked away as he realized he was staring.

"I'd like to take a walk if you don't mind," Ava said.

"Sure," Ed said, and then wondered if he'd ever had a more limited vocabulary.

Ed put on his coat, and they walked down to where the barriers were set up on Pine Mountain Road. The water, although no longer rising, was still rushing fast and loud, with occasional crashes as debris struck obstacles in its path.

"You don't have a cell phone on you, do you?" Ed asked.

Ava shook her head.

"I know everything's bugged. That's why I didn't bring my purse," Ava said. "Someone's probably watching us, but I think if we speak quietly they won't be able to hear us over the sound of the water."

"What's going on?"

"I think Jamie was involved in Brian's death," she said. "I think he may have murdered him because of me. I'm afraid of what he might do next. To Patrick, to Scott ..."

"I think you're right," Ed said. "But if we go to the authorities, or I publish a piece about it, it would derail the case against Mrs. Wells. Plus, I don't think our story would hold up in court. So many people would get hurt and what would we have accomplished?"

"So we're stuck," she said.

"Maybe not," Ed said. "Someone recently advised me not to use a shotgun if a pea shooter would do."

"I don't think I could shoot him," Ava said. "Not unless he hurt one of the kids."

"I'm not suggesting that," Ed said. "We have to think of something that would stop Jamie, and get him to back off, but not hurt anyone else in the process."

Ava looked thoughtful.

"I'm sorry you're in the middle of this," Ed said. "I'm sorry about Brian, too. He didn't deserve to die that way."

"If this is about Jamie eliminating his competition," Ava said. "I'm the only one who can put a stop to it."

"You need to be careful," Ed said. "These people are vicious."

"Don't worry," Ava said. "I think I may have the right weapon for the job."

Ed found Scott in the police station, where he was working the phones, trying to get more supplies donated to the shelter at the Community Center.

"What's up?" Scott said.

"We need to talk, but I guess not here," Ed said.

They left the station and walked down toward Lotus Avenue, where the Little Bear River was swarming through the houses and stacking up debris against the brick walls of the old glassworks factory. There were barricades up, but people were hanging out in small groups, some with tailgating tents and lawn chairs.

Scott told Ed what happened the night before.

"After they got me back to the station, Cal left, and Malcolm went to get Doc. Jamie questioned me and then suggested an alternate version of events. I called Sarah to report what happened, and she was thrilled to be involved. She never even questioned my statement."

"So everyone thinks you killed the guy."

"It was clearly self-defense, and I've got the feds and the county to back me up. Once we hit the water, the bugging device shorted out, and they only have my word as to what happened."

"Will there be an investigation?"

Scott shrugged.

"Why protect Gabe?"

"He saved my life, for one thing," Scott said. "Plus, if he went back to prison, he couldn't testify against Mrs. Wells."

"If he's alive and ran off, he may still go back in."

"What's done is done," Scott said. "If all this has taught me anything, it's that sometimes you have to put your ideals aside and do what's best for everyone."

"Sam recommended that same approach," Ed said. "Being pragmatic, he called it."

"I'm hoping that after Mrs. Wells is arrested, tried, and sent to prison, the feds will leave, and everything will get back to normal around here."

"Is that even possible?"

"I'm counting on it," Scott said.

"How's Maggie doing?"

"She'll be fine," Scott said.

"She didn't get back together with Gabe," Ed said. "That's good news, right?'

"It's over between us, whatever it was."

"She's pretty upset right now. Maybe when things settle down ..."

"That's just it, though, isn't it? Things never do settle down, and she's always upset about something. It's time for both of us to move on."

"I'm sorry. Maggie and I never hit it off, but I know you love her."

"Sometimes you have to do what's best for yourself even though your feelings may want something different."

"That sounds pretty pragmatic."

"You know what?" Scott said. "Being pragmatic hurts like hell."

Ed walked back up to the Community Center and found Mandy in the kitchen, washing dishes.

"Take her home," Delia told Ed. "I told her to take the rest of the day and night off, but she won't listen to me."

"I know better than to tell any woman what to do," Ed said. "Whatever Mandy wants to do is fine by me."

The other women in the kitchen laughed, and Delia said, "You've certainly trained him well, Mandy."

"I know a good one when I find one," Mandy said. "He already done been trained when I found him. I oughta write that ex-wife of his a thank-you note."

Mandy dried her hands, and Ed got her coat for her. As they left the Community Center, she leaned against him.

"I'm plum tuckered out," she said. "I don't feel like I seen you for weeks."

"Let's go home," Ed said. "I'll run you a hot bath and scrub your back for you."

"You're a good man, Ed Harrison," she said. "Where's my son, by the way?"

"He's taking care of all the dogs over at Bonnie's house. That boy loves to be helpful. You've done a great job with him."

"Let's leave him with Delia tonight," Mandy said. "You and I'll have a quiet evening at home, just the two of us."

The evening didn't quite go as Ed had planned. After Mandy got out of the tub, he performed his speech again, but her reaction wasn't at all what he anticipated.

"Whatta you mean, get a divorce?" Mandy yelled. "I thought you was already divorced!"

"It's no big deal," Ed said. "I haven't seen Eve in a long time. It's only a legal detail we didn't take care of right away, and then we let it go. Why are you so upset?"

"Why am I upset?" Mandy said as she dried off with a towel. "Because I didn't know I been living with a married man."

"In name only," Ed protested. "Does it matter?"

"Yes, it matters," Mandy said. "I'd never have moved in here if I'd knowed you was still married to her."

"I thought you knew," Ed said, but when Mandy gave him an evil look, he amended that. "I didn't think it was such a big deal. Patrick knew. I can't believe he didn't tell you."

"Well, he'll have to answer for that," she said. "I hate bein' the last person to find out somethin' like this. People have probably been laughin' at me behind my back all this time."

"Mandy, I truly thought you wouldn't care."

"Didn't think I'd care. Lord God almighty, what a load of crap you can talk. I have half a mind to move out of here right now."

"What about Tommy?" Ed said. "Please don't jerk him out of here. He's used to being here. He loves this, and I love this, us being a family."

"Well, you shoulda thought about that before you kept this from me," Mandy said. "Everyone told me it was a mistake, but I just had to have my way. 'He's too old for you,' they said. 'He's too set in his ways,' they said. But never once did someone say, 'by the way, he's still married.'"

Mandy had been pulling on her clothes while they argued. She put on a shirt inside out and backward but Ed didn't think now was the time to point that out.

"I think you may be overreacting a little bit," Ed said. "You're tired, and there's so much going on right now that it probably seems worse than it is. I think if we both take a deep breath and discuss this calmly and rationally we can work through it."

"I know you been thinking you made a big mistake. I ain't completely stupid. I know I don't talk good enough and I ain't smart like your wife, with her college degrees and fancy job. Does she even know about me?"

"No," Ed said, "But ..."

"I'm not surprised," Mandy said. "You're ashamed of me. If you weren't, you would've already told her 'bout me and asked for a divorce."

"I'm not ashamed of you."

"I know you love Tommy, and I know you like going to bed with me, but I'm done kiddin' myself. This ain't exactly the real thing for you, is it? You're willin' to make good on your promise to take care of us, but I think maybe you better be honest now. If I didn't have Tommy, would you be askin' to marry me?"

Ed hesitated.

"That's what I thought," Mandy said. "I think I'll stay at the trailer tonight and move out of here while you're at work tomorrow."

Mandy tugged on her coat and zipped up the front. She stuck her feet down in her snow boots and hoisted her over-sized purse up over her shoulder.

"Please, Mandy, don't do this," Ed said. "Tommy will be heartbroken."

"I think it'd be better for him to know the truth and deal with it," Mandy said. "He'll have to decide for himself if I done the right thing or not."

Ed stood in the doorway and watched her walk away. Unlike him, she was brave enough to act on what she knew was right without worrying about the consequences. He'd been prepared to shortchange her as if he was doing her a favor. He admired her now more than he ever had. And she was gone.

Mandy flung her purse down on the floor of her trailer and looked around in disgust. Patrick wasn't known for his cleaning abilities, and it would take her several hours to whip this place back into shape. Then she needed to go pick up her son and break his heart. First, however, she had something to do that she'd put off way too long. She took the letter out of her purse, unfolded it, and then dialed the number written on the bottom.

"Mrs. Wilson," she said when the older woman answered. "You don't know me, but I knew your daughter Miranda. My name's Melissa. Melissa Wright."

Maggie Fitzpatrick was lying on her bed, staring at the ceiling when the bell to her apartment rang. Her first thought was, "Now what?"

Maggie ran downstairs and found Tony Delvecchio at the door to the street. He was wearing dress clothes under his raincoat and smelled really good.

"Hey, Tony," she said when she opened it.

"I was so sorry to hear about Brian," Tony said. "Right on top of your grandfather dying, that must be difficult."

"Thanks, Tony, I appreciate you stopping by."

"I'm sorry," he said. "Am I interrupting something? I can come back at a better time. I should have called first."

"Look, Tony," Maggie said. "Your brother Paulie told me your family wants to fix us up, and although I'm flattered, I've got too much going on in my head to even think about dating anyone."

"Oh, Maggie, I'm so sorry," Tony said.

"No, don't be," Maggie said. "You're a great guy and incredibly handsome, and any girl would be lucky to date you. It just can't be me right now."

"Actually," Tony said quietly, "it's Sean I came to see."

"Oh, Tony," Maggie said. "Just kill me now."

"It's okay," Tony laughed. "My family doesn't know any of my friends from the city. This is such a small town and my mother, well, you understand."

"Of course I understand," Maggie said. "Sean's staying at our parents' house tonight. You may want to call first; my Dad's probably drunk with no pants on. Please don't tell Sean what happened here."

"Maggie, don't give it another thought. I won't tell him, I promise."

"Good night, Tony," Maggie said. "I just need to go upstairs and die of embarrassment now. I'll see you later."

Maggie closed the door behind her and leaned against it, laughing and cringing at the same time. Then she thought, 'Tony and Sean? Hmmm ...' and ran upstairs to call Hannah.

Ava thanked Delia for coming to get the children.

"Are you going to have a service for Brian?" Delia asked her.

"We'll have a small one for family only. I'm leaving all the details up to Bonnie. I'm hoping that will help her and the kids."

"How are they doing?"

"I've told them about Brian. Charlotte has memories of her dad, and there are lots of pictures of him with her.

She may have a harder time at school, especially when word gets out about what all he's done. Timmy's more upset over Grandpa Tim dying."

"We'll get through it," Delia said. "We'll just hold our heads up and get on with it."

"Thank you for taking them today."

"I'm glad to have them," Delia said. "I miss having little ones around, and Ian's good with children. He'll keep Timmy and Charlotte entertained, and there's nothing I like better than to rock a baby. We'll be fine."

Delia looked askance at Terese, who was putting on her coat, preparing to come accompany them.

"Does she have to come?" Delia asked. "I don't know what I'll do with her."

"Terese's here to make sure nothing happens to them. Don't worry about entertaining her. She's a big reader, and she's got her book reading gizmo with her."

"This is awful," Delia said quietly. "You must be terrified."

"I feel numb right now. I appreciate you giving me this break."

"Are you sure you feel safe alone with them?" Delia asked, nodding toward the family room where Jamie and Agent Dulvaney sat talking quietly.

"Don't you worry about that," Ava said. "I can handle them."

"I hope when this is all over you can have some kind of peace in your life."

"Well, the two men who made my life hell are both dead now. That should help."

Delia looked a little shocked at this statement, but hugged her, gathered up the children, and left.

Jamie and Agent Dulvaney were talking in low voices with grim looks on their faces. They stopped when Ava entered the room, and then Agent Dulvaney went out, leaving Ava and Jamie alone in the kitchen.

"I need to talk to you," Ava said, "but not here, and not with any listening devices present."

"Okay," Jamie said, and put his cell phone on top of the refrigerator, pushing it back so no one could see it.

"You want to pat me down?" he joked, but Ava didn't smile.

"Let's take a walk," she said and put on her coat.

The sky was still overcast, but it wasn't raining. They walked up Pine Mountain Road to Lilac Avenue, and then through the city park. They sat on a bench, looking up at the houses on Morning Glory Avenue.

"That's what I wanted, you know," she said, gesturing at the large homes on the highest street in Rose Hill, "a big beautiful house full of children."

"But you've got that," Jamie said.

"No, I've got a business I live in the back of while strangers enjoy the best rooms in the house," Ava said. "I work all the time, I constantly worry about bills, and I lie awake every night wondering if I'm a good enough mother. That life, up there, would mean no worries about money, no strangers in my house, and no working unless I wanted to. I could live in the best rooms, and I'd never have to smile if I didn't feel like it."

"Is there a man in that dream?"

"Well, there've been two. One who could afford to give me that life whom I didn't love, and one who couldn't afford to whom I did love, for a while."

"Are you going to tell me why Theo left you all that money?"

Ava nodded.

"Why now?"

"Because you're falling in love with me and it's a big mistake."

"Nothing you could tell me will make a difference in how I feel."

"We'll see," Ava said.

"It won't," Jamie said. "I don't have you up on a pedestal. I know you aren't perfect and I find that sexy as hell. You won't budge me, Ava, but you go on and tell me anyway."

She shrugged as if to say, "You asked for it."

"How much do you know about Theo and his brother Brad?" Ava asked him.

"I know Brad Eldridge drowned when you guys were teenagers, and that Theo was suspected of having something to do with it."

"He did do it."

"What do you mean?"

"Theo drowned his brother. He tackled him in the lake and held him under until he drowned."

"Did Theo tell you this?"

Ava shook her head.

"Then how do you know?"

Ava turned and looked at Jamie.

"You saw him do it," Jamie said.

Ava nodded and continued to look at Jamie.

"You saw Theo drown his kid brother and you did nothing to stop it," Jamie said.

"I thought he might kill me, too," Ava said.

"Where were you?"

"I was in the boathouse. I had come to tell Theo I was pregnant. I saw them through the boathouse window."

"Did Theo see you?"

She nodded.

"I ran up the hill to the house, and he followed me. I got in my father's car, but he stood in front of it so I couldn't leave. It was so hot that morning. We didn't have air conditioning in our car, and the vinyl seats were burning the backs of my legs. I had locked the doors, and the windows were rolled up. I had morning sickness, and I was nauseated. He stood there with his clothes dripping, his hands planted on the front hood of my car, looking at me, smiling at me."

Ava was looking over Jamie's shoulder and seemed to be reliving the scene.

"I screamed at him to move, that I'd run him over, but he just stood there smiling that awful smile. Finally, I rolled down the window, just enough so that he could hear me. I screamed, 'I didn't see anything. I didn't see anything.' Then I closed my eyes, covered them with my hands, and kept screaming. It felt like for hours. When I looked up, he was gone."

"Then what did you do?"

"I drove back to Rose Hill and went to the pool, where there were lots of people around. Eventually, we all heard about Brad. I pretended to be surprised."

"Was the baby Theo's?"

"It might have been. I was going to say it was so he'd marry me. His family was rich, and I wanted that life so badly. Then when I saw what he was capable of I had to marry someone, so I married Brian. I lost the baby afterward, but I was stuck. Catholic marriages last 'until death do us part,' you know. Mine lasted over twenty years, up until yesterday."

"Did you and Theo ever talk about what happened?"

"After Brian left me, Theo came to the house one night and offered me money. I refused it. He said, 'You'll never have to worry about money as long as I'm alive. All you have to do is ask.' Only I never asked. I didn't expect the bequest, but I knew what it was when the lawyer told me about it. It was payment for twenty years of silence."

"So Theo didn't pay Brian to leave town?"

"Brian left me because Brian wanted to leave."

"This doesn't change anything. You were just a kid when it happened. I'm not going to judge you harshly for that."

"Then let me make this clear to you: I don't have feelings for you."

"You're lying," he said, smiling that smug smile.

"I'm sorry if it hurts," Ava said, "but it's over between us."

"No," he said. "I don't believe you. I'm the best thing that ever happened to you. What are you going to do, marry Patrick?"

"I love Patrick. As soon as a decent amount of time passes we probably will get married."

"Why would you do that? Patrick can't give you anything. Marry me, Ava. I'll give you the big house and everything that goes with it."

"But I don't love you. I love Patrick."

"Patrick's mother will never allow it."

Ava shrugged.

"You might be right," she said. "In that case, I'll find someone else, someone who belongs here, someone the whole town will approve of. I'm never leaving Rose Hill. This is our home."

"What about us?"

"You didn't seriously think I was going to end up with you, did you? We had a deal: I slept with you so my family would have protection. The sex was good, but it meant nothing more to me than a business transaction. I just did what I had to do."

Jamie seemed to be struggling with his emotions. He was always so cool and controlled that Ava thought it was interesting to see the change she'd wrought.

"Now do you wish I hadn't told you?" she asked him.

"Yes, I wish you hadn't told me."

"You said you wanted to know everything about me," she said. "But you didn't. No one ever does. Not. At. All."

"What makes you think you can trust me with this information about you and Theo?"

"Please," Ava said. "What can you do? You've been sleeping with the star witness in the biggest case of your career. That's kind of risky behavior, don't you think?

Taking advantage of the abandoned wife, now the recently widowed mother of three? You need me to make this case, and you can't afford to do anything to jeopardize that."

"You're as bad as Theo was," Jamie said. "That money he left you has Brad's blood all over it."

"Have you ever heard of the pot calling the kettle black?" she asked him. "Do you think I don't know where you went yesterday morning?"

Jamie looked shocked, and Ava laughed.

"Don't worry, Jamie. I'm good at keeping secrets. You make sure my family stays safe, and you have nothing to worry about."

It started to rain.

Ava stood up and said, "I'm cold. I'm going home."

Neither of them spoke as they walked back. As soon as they got back to the house, Jamie retrieved his cell phone and went up to his room. Ava busied herself in the kitchen. She was washing vegetables in the sink when Terese brought the kids home. She settled the bigger kids in the family room, put Little Fitz down in his playpen full of toys, and then joined Ava in the kitchen.

Jamie came down the hall with his coat on, carrying his suitcase and laptop case. He didn't look at Ava.

"I'm going back to D.C., and I'll coordinate our next tasks from there," he told Terese. "You're in charge here."

Then he turned to Ava.

"Mrs. Fitzpatrick, I want to thank you for your hospitality and for putting up with so many of us at the expense of your business. If all goes well, we should have some resolution within the next few months. Meanwhile, if you need anything, please tell Terese."

He held out his hand, but Ava said, "I'm sorry, my hands are wet," and held up her hands, which were covered in elbow-length rubber gloves.

Jamie dropped his hand and took a deep breath.

"Okay," he said. "I guess that's it."

"You have a safe trip," Ava said and turned away.

Jamie hesitated briefly but did not respond. He said a quick goodbye to the kids and then went out the back door. Ava could hear the car start up and then the gravel crunch as he backed his car into the alley and drove away.

Terese asked if there was anything she could do to help, but Ava said there wasn't. She pulled off her gloves, picked up the phone, and punched in a familiar number.

"Scott," she said when he answered. "It's Ava. I'm making that beef stew you liked so much and wondered if you'd care to join us for dinner. We've been missing you. You'll come? That's great news. See you soon."

Ava hummed under her breath as she set the table. She added place settings for the remaining agents, her children, herself, and then one for Scott, right at the head of the table.

ACKNOWLEDGMENTS

I'm grateful for my parents, family, and friends. I give special thanks to first readers Terry Hutchison, Ella Curry, and Joan Turner; and to John Gillispie and Mitzi Cyrus for proofreading. Love to all my good buddies at Hospice of Huntington, especially Harriette, Mitzi, Karen, Ethel, Linda, Jaimie, and Martha. I wish dogs lived forever, especially June Bug, Henry, and Daisy.

Thank you to Tamarack: The Best of West Virginia, for selling my paper books in your beautiful building.

And last, but not least, I want to thank the people who buy and read my books. Thank you so much.

If you liked this book, please leave a review on Amazon.com (Thank you!)

Find out more on RoseHillMysteries.com

Peony Street

Book 4

Chapter One - Friday

"You! You with the towels. Don't look at me, don't speak to me, and don't touch anything. Stay right where you are. Tuppy! Why is no one monitoring who comes in the door? Where is security?"

A shudder ran through Chance Farthington "Tuppy" Tupworth's body as the shriek of the diva preceded her noon-time appearance in the doorway to his hotel suite, where he was organizing her day. She had a plush towel wrapped around her head, and a peony-patterned silk kimono floated around her whippet-thin body. Her muscles were so tightly stretched and defined they looked as if they might snap and roll up at any moment. Soft terry spa slippers with miniature padded straps between each freshly painted toenail cushioned her tiny, manicured feet.

She glared at Tuppy and then, distracted by a noise, pointed at someone further down the hallway.

"You! What's your name? Speak up! I pay you people a fortune; why can't you just for once do what I hired you to do? Why am I surrounded by idiots? You're supposed to keep these people away from me. Get her out of here and make sure it doesn't happen again or you're fired."

Her perfectly motionless, exquisite face, the one so often displayed on film posters, in fashion magazines, and on tabloid covers, suggested twenty-nine. Every ropy vein in her arms and hands admitted thirty-nine, which was closer to the truth. The lack of any discernable emotion in her facial expression could lead one to assume all was calm behind her sea-green eyes. Tuppy hadn't made that assumption in a long while.

"Tuppy," Sloan said. "Where's Claire? This is royalty we're dealing with; I want everything to be perfect."

"Teeny's styling and Juanita's doing makeup," Tuppy said calmly. "Alexander McQueen sent a selection of couture with accessories, someone from Tiffany's will bring the jewelry this afternoon, Teeny has procured a selection of Christian Louboutin shoes, and Andrew Barton is sending a team to do your hair."

"I don't want a team. I want Claire."

"She's not returning my calls," Tuppy replied in a reasonable tone. "I've left voicemails, texts, and email messages."

"Then why are you just sitting there, you moron," she huffed. "Go find her."

"What would you like me to do when I find her, Sloan? Rough her up? Kidnap her?"

"I don't care how you do it, just get her here. Tell her I'll double her salary."

"You've tried that."

"Tell her I'll have Juanita deported."

"You've tried that as well," Tuppy said. "You might as well accept it, Sloan; that bird has flown."

"It's not over until I say it's over," Sloan said. "Claire just needs to be made to understand. If Stanley were here, he'd take care of it, and I wouldn't have all this horrible stress."

Sloan moved across the room to closely examine her face in a mirror on the wall as if searching for the detrimental effects of the horrible stress. Tuppy realized he was holding his breath and quietly let it out, willing himself to calm down and not let her provoke him. He recalled what Claire always said to him: "Remember to breathe, Tuppy. She won't kill you and eat you; she doesn't eat red meat."

Tuppy was glad Sloan's attorney wasn't with them on this trip. The man dressed like a mobster smiled like a shark and didn't miss a thing. Tuppy tended to stutter and drop things when Stanley was around, and the attorney enjoyed the effect he had on the members of Sloan's staff. Claire was the exception; she just rolled her eyes at everything he said, and for some reason Sloan let her get away with it.

"Why are you just sitting there?" Sloan asked as she continued her facial inspection. "Did I not make myself clear?"

"Claire quit," Tuppy said. "She gave a month's notice. We had a lovely party for her yesterday evening, which you didn't attend, and now she's free to leave."

Tuppy bit his lip; he hadn't meant to let that last bit slip out.

"What do you mean, she's leaving?" Sloan said, turning away from the mirror to look at him. "Where's she going?"

"I haven't the faintest," Tuppy replied. "I don't know, and I don't care. Life stories of the poor and witless bore me to tears."

Sloan tightened the belt of her robe as she came toward him and then stood way too close to him. He struggled not to choke on her strong perfume as she pointed a beautifully manicured nail in his face.

"I don't care what bores you; I don't pay you to have opinions. If you'd like to join Claire on the unemployment line, I can arrange that."

"I'm so sorry," Tuppy said. "I forgot my place. It won't happen again."

"You still have her personal information, don't you? Cancel her credit cards. Cancel her plane tickets. Report her as a terrorist. Do whatever it takes, but don't let her leave this country."

"Yes, Sloan," he said, "right away."

"Was that sarcasm?" she asked him.

"No, Sloan," Tuppy said. "I have your orders, and I'm on top of it."

"You'd better be," she said. "Tell her if she doesn't sign a new contract you'll be fired because you will be."

"Yes, Sloan."

Sloan looked around the beautifully appointed lounge of one of the most luxurious accommodations available in a five star London hotel.

"Is this the biggest apartment they have?"

"It's apartment one, Milestone Hotel," Tuppy said. "It's 1178 square feet."

"I know everything on this island is small, but this is ridiculous."

"I did suggest we take a whole floor in the main building."

"At least in here there aren't so many flowers and stripes," she said. "It's like Laura Ashley threw up all over my bedroom."

"Would you like to move?"

"No," she said. "This is supposed to be the best."

"They have agreed to secure sole use of the resistance pool for you every day at five a.m."

"Good," she said. "I want security to escort me, and not this idiot out here; get me someone competent."

"It's all taken care of."

"Where's my lunch?"

"Three steamed asparagus spears and half of a poached chicken breast will be delivered precisely at one o'clock."

"And spring water, the French one."

"I'll bring it myself."

"The most important thing for you to do today is getting Claire back."

"I'll deliver her in plenty of time for you to get ready."

Tuppy could see she was looking for more things to criticize to provoke him into raising his voice or defending himself. She loved to nick his self-confidence first thing in the morning and then pick at the scab all day.

Tuppy put on his headset, picked up his phone and pretended to make a call, hoping she would leave the room. As she went down the hallway, she screamed for Teeny and Juanita. Doors slammed, people scurried, and another tension- and drama-filled day with Sloan Merryweather entered its seventh hour. Unfortunately, there were at least fourteen more to go.

Tuppy had worked for the award-winning film actress for eighteen months. He didn't know how Claire had lasted twenty years. Claire knew Sloan better than anyone, and she was able to advise the best course of action in every difficult situation, of which there were many. Fresh out of grad school and new to the personal assistant game, Tuppy had needed someone to steer him through the shark-infested show business waters until he could navigate on his own. Claire had done that. He owed her.

Claire was kind of a ditz, and the way she let Sloan walk all over her made him dislike them both, but she didn't deserve what Sloan had just instructed him to do. So instead of ruining Claire's life, Tuppy prepared to honor the reservation he had made for himself on the same flight Claire was taking. At 2:45 p.m. GMT Tuppy ordered car service to take him to Heathrow and retrieved his luggage from where he had it hidden behind the sofa.

When Claire didn't show up for their flight and didn't answer her phone, Tuppy was perplexed. Had she actually taken a different flight, he wondered, leaving the original reservation in place as a decoy? That seemed awfully clever for someone he considered so simple-minded. He left her a voicemail message and sent her a text while waiting at the gate. He continued to ignore all the calls from Sloan, which were now coming every thirty seconds.

At just before 5:00 p.m. GMT Tuppy's phone tweedled again as they called for first class passengers. He didn't recognize the number, so he answered, hoping it was Claire.

"Where are you?" Juanita asked in an urgent whisper.

Tuppy could hear Sloan screeching in the background.

"I'm on my way," he said. "I just have to pick up Claire, and we'll be there in twenty minutes, depending on traffic. Tell her everything's under control. Tell her I'm bringing the spring water and her nicotine gum."

"She doesn't like any of the dresses they sent," Juanita said. "She won't let anyone touch her hair; she says she's not leaving her room until Claire's here."

"Not to worry," Tuppy said. "Tell her Claire and I will take care of everything as soon as we get there."

His first-class seat was in the front row, left the side, by the window. It was Sloan's favorite seat, the one over which she would throw a colossal fit if she didn't get. As soon as he was settled Tuppy turned off his phone. He was done living in reactive anxiety over Sloan's rapidly changing emotional temperature. He was done trying to anticipate her every need and desire only to be jerked this way and that by her whims of iron. He was through being berated and belittled at every turn, until he agonized over every decision no matter how small, sure it would somehow turn out to be wrong. He was done with that part of his life and ready for the next part, the part where he would be the one making demands.

He ordered a vodka gimlet and took a sleeping pill. As he drifted off to sleep, somewhere over the Atlantic, he imagined the scene at the hotel, wondering how long it would take Sloan to realize he wasn't coming. If she had to cancel her appearance at the royal engagement party, she would be looking forward to firing Tuppy in revenge. As soon as she read the resignation letter he had arranged for the concierge to deliver to her at precisely 1:00 a.m. GMT (by which time he would have safely landed in DC) she would call Stanley, her attorney, who would conference the call with Angus, her agent, and Ayelet, her publicist. Damage control, revenge scenarios, and ass coverage would all be quickly and efficiently organized by the various parties involved.

'To no avail,' Tuppy thought to himself. 'I've seen to that.'

He fell asleep smiling.

At the baggage claim in D.C. Tuppy turned on his phone, which tweedled to inform him he had texts and voicemails waiting. He adjusted the time back to Eastern Standard Time, which meant it was just after 8:00 p.m. The phone's calls-received list was full of the various phone numbers belonging to Sloan and her fame preservation league, and his voice mailbox was full, but there was nothing from Claire. The same was true of the long list of texts he'd received. On impulse, he deleted "all previous" in each category.

Afterword, as he stood in line for a rental car his phone tweedled again. This text was from Sloan.

"Yr as gd as ded"

Despite his earlier bravado, Tuppy felt a knot of apprehension clench in his solar plexus. When he rented the car, he listed his destination as New York, NY. Thinking Sloan might have the authorities track him down through his personal credit card, and having no doubt reported him as having stolen her jewelry or something equally heinous, he impulsively decided to drive to Claire's hometown (where despite his protestations otherwise he knew very well she was going) in order to meet her and discuss the situation in person. She must be warned, and he needed somewhere to lie low until his appointment in Manhattan on Monday. What better place to hide than in Lower Podunk, USA?

He sent Claire a text, left her a voicemail, and then used his phone to map the route from Reagan Airport to Rose Hill.

After surveying the driving directions and accompanying map, he decided not to worry about that last thin, squiggly black line until he came to it. It seemed to represent a two-lane road that left a four-lane highway in southern Pennsylvania, wandered south along the Little Bear River, crossed over into West Virginia, and eventually meandered down to a tiny dot labeled Rose Hill. The next furthest dot encouraged him with the news that there was a ski resort nearby. Armed with the largest espresso-based beverage eight dollars could buy, he claimed his rental car and proceeded to rediscover the seventh level of hell, also known as the Capital Beltway.

It took him four hours to reach the start of the squiggly black line, which he quickly decided should be called "the nauseating trail of random wildlife crossing blacktop alternating with sudden fog pockets." On the bright side, fear of a life-limiting car crash joined caffeine in keeping him wide awake.

At one-fifty-five a.m. he arrived in Rose Hill, which the tiny dot on the map had completely oversold in terms of size. His arms and hands were rigid with tension from gripping the steering wheel. A song began to play in his mind, and he smiled as he remembered from whence it originated.

Tuppy was still humming a tune from Brigadoon as he parked the car on the main street and got out to stretch. The weather was exactly like that he'd recently endured for several weeks in Scotland. A bone-chilling misty rain fell, and much of the town was obscured by a low-hanging fog bank. The map on his phone stubbornly insisted on ending at the dot, even though he'd put in Claire's parents' full address. When he zoomed in for a street view of Rose Hill, he was only shown a field of gray with the black Co. Rte. 1/1 squiggle and the aforementioned dot. Beyond the dot, the squiggle took a sharp left and Co. Rte. 2/1 squiggled over to a town named Glencora, where the ski resort was alleged to be located.

There were very few cars parked on the street, and no cars passed through. The only sign of life, a light from the window of a bar on the corner, illuminated his parked car. He could hear what sounded like Irish fiddle music playing inside.

"The Rose and Thorn," he read on the window.

He thought about going inside to ask for directions, estimated the likelihood that he would be welcomed with open arms by the local rednecks, and decided against it. The town wasn't that big, after all. He could probably find it on his own.

The absence of traffic noise and the moisture in the air amplified every sound. He could hear the drip, drip, drip of water from every surface, and the tang, tang, tang as it struck hundred-year-old tin roofs above the brick storefronts that lined the street. There was a steady low roar from the nearby river, with which he'd become so intimate during his journey, having crossed it twice. A street sign informed him that he was parked at the corner of Rose Hill Avenue and Peony Street. He recalled Claire mentioning that every street in Rose Hill was named for a flower.

"How quaint," he'd said at the time, in a tone that indicated it was anything but.

Claire's parents lived on Iris Avenue, so logically he surmised that if the avenues and streets formed a grid if he stayed on Peony Street, he would eventually cross Iris Avenue. He popped the collar and tightened the belt on his Burberry trench and wished he'd thought to pack an umbrella. After a moment's consideration, he crossed the deserted street and walked east, which in Rose Hill meant up a steep hill.

The town was built on a hillside with the Little Bear River at the foot. Tuppy noticed that as he ascended Peony Street, the homes were bigger, were spread farther apart, and the properties were better kept. He crossed Lilac and Magnolia Avenues and ended up at Morning Glory Avenue, where the homes were quite grand, and the architecture was classic Victorian, Edwardian, and Gothic.

He turned and looked down the hill toward the river, where the main street was blanketed in fog. He had yet to see a person. All the homes looked tucked in for the night, with plumes of smoke curling from chimneys and a few windows lit by dim lamps behind sheer curtains. Tuppy had the strange sensation that he had somehow wandered into an Appalachian wormhole and gone back in time. When he returned to his rental car, he noticed the Irish fiddle music had ceased, and the Rose and Thorn was dark inside. He sent Claire a text.

Tuppy walked down Peony Street beyond the bar and the alley behind it and was gratified to see the first avenue on his left was Iris. Claire's parents' house was the third one on the right. The flickering blue light of a television seemed to indicate someone was still awake. Tuppy hoped it was Claire, having taken an earlier flight and suffering from insomnia after crossing time zones.

A large, elderly man answered his knock. He had on a stained sweatshirt, flannel pajama pants, and corduroy slippers. His eyebrows were wild, and he needed a haircut. He was frowning, but there was also an unfocused, fuzzy look in his eyes; Tuppy apologized for waking him.

"I wasn't asleep," the man said gruffly.

Tuppy explained who he was and that he was looking for Claire. This seemed to agitate the man.

"Claire's in California," he said. "She and Pip live in Los Angeles."

Tuppy knew that Pip was Claire's ex-husband, whom she hadn't seen in many years. Then the penny dropped. Claire had mentioned multiple strokes, memory problems. Tuppy felt ashamed of how bored he'd been by the subject, and how poorly he'd listened.

"I won't keep you," Tuppy said. "Claire's coming here to see you this week. Please give her this."

"What is it?" the older man asked.

"A book," Tuppy said. "Will you make sure she gets it?"

"My memory isn't too good," Claire's father said.

"Tell her it's from Tuppy."

"What in the heck kinda name is that?"

"A family name," Tuppy said.

"I probably won't remember it. My memory isn't what it used to be."

"I'm sorry I disturbed you," Tuppy said. "It was nice to meet you."

"You could come in," the older man said. "You want me to get Delia?"

"No, please don't wake her. I've got to go. Goodbye."

Tuppy walked halfway down the block toward Peony Street and then turned to look back. Claire's father had shut the door. His phone tweedled that he had a text; it was from Sloan

"I no whr u r cmn 4 u."

It may have been a combination of fatigue, worry, and the freezing rain falling in this creepy fog-covered town that time forgot, but Tuppy suddenly had the urge to get the hell out of Rose Hill as soon as possible. Sloan's attorney Stanley had sleazy contacts everywhere and enough money to arrange any dirty deed. They must know where he'd gone; the rental car company could have tracked him through the GPS. Someone may have followed him at a distance.

Tuppy called Claire, left a voicemail, and then sent her a text. He had just pressed send when he heard raised voices nearby. A car started up with a roar and tires squealed. Then there were footsteps on the wet pavement behind him, running in his direction. The fog was so thick he couldn't see farther than a few yards in front of him.

Fear raced through his nervous system and adrenaline surged through his veins. He took off, running as fast as he had ever run in his life, only to trip over the curb and fall headlong into the middle of Peony Street. He was just picking himself up off the ground when headlights illuminated him, blinded him. The car roared toward him, and the impact flung him up over the hood of the car into the windshield, rolled him over the roof, across the trunk, and then dropped him back on the street.

Tuppy's head hit the pavement as he landed and a sharp pain radiated throughout his entire body. His ears rang, and a buzzing sound bloomed in his head. He felt so dizzy he became nauseated.

'This is so inconvenient,' he thought. 'I have the most important meeting of my life on Monday.'

Then he could no longer feel the hard, wet pavement, and the pain disappeared. He could see his motionless body on the street beneath him as he floated above it, but he only felt a benign sort of attachment to it. He felt confused, but not worried.

'This is interesting,' he thought.

The dark night evaporated, leaving everything shrouded in gray fog, but lit from above. It was like being on a plane as it ascended through a cloud, just before it rises into the bright sunshine of a blue sky. He realized he wasn't floating up; he was being drawn up.

'I must be in a coma,' he thought.

He heard music; it started out far away and faint, but soon gained strength.

It was "Rhapsody in Blue" by George Gershwin.

In his youth, Tuppy had been a dreamy, sensitive boy who lived mostly in his head, watched black and white classic movies, and listened to songs by Cole Porter and

George Gershwin. His mother, who adored him, took him to Broadway musicals and plays, and always encouraged his creative side. His father, who didn't have a creative bone in his body, ignored Tuppy to the point where the boy sometimes wondered if his father cared if he lived or died.

The music became louder as he rose higher. The piano chords had a curious vibration that overwhelmed him and infused his body with invigorating energy. This energy filled him up and expanded his sense of himself until he felt huge, vast, and couldn't tell where he ended and the music began. As he emerged into what looked and felt like bright, warm sunshine in a brilliant blue sky, the music rang out with raucous, almost unbearable joy.

In the distance, a tableau appeared against a backdrop of brilliant white light. Tuppy felt drawn to this apparition, whatever it was, and as soon as he had the thought that he wanted to get closer, he instantly found himself there.

He was standing on a street corner in midtown Manhattan. The street signs indicated he was at the intersection of 7th Avenue and West 58th Street. The blaring of vehicle horns and throngs of people hurrying every which way was familiar to him if their mode of transportation and dress were not.

The cars were huge, with all the edges rounded; their headlights looked like the popped eyes of cartoon characters. All the men wore suits and hats. If it hadn't seemed so real, Tuppy would've imagined he was on a 40s-themed movie set. When he looked down, he saw that he was dressed just like everyone else, and he could feel the hat on his head. He took it off and stared at the snappy gray felt fedora.

A traffic cop blew a whistle that startled him.

"Are ya crossin' or ain't ya?" he bellowed.

Tuppy hurried to the other side of the street.

"Tupworth, where the hell have you been?" a man said as he approached Tuppy and wrung his hand with enthusiasm. "We've got auditions in fifteen minutes at the New Century, and you're walking in the wrong direction!"

"I'm sorry, do I know you?"

"Does he know me? It's Sam, Sam Spewack. We've only known each other ten years. Did someone drop you on your head or something?"

Tuppy allowed himself to be turned and hurriedly ushered in the opposite direction, while his companion talked fifty miles an hour.

"Don't let the big man intimidate you," he said. "He might bust your chops, but Bella says he's the real McCoy."

"What should I do?" Tuppy asked him.

"What should you do?" the man laughed. "What should I do, he says. How about you do your job, pal, and make us all look good."

Sam led the way into the New Century Theater. There in the lobby stood a slightly-built, middle-aged, well-dressed man who was looking at his watch while leaning on a cane.

"I know, I know," Sam said as approached him. "Is Bella here?"

The man gestured to the theater doors, and Sam went on through. The older man looked Tuppy up and down.

With an arched eyebrow, he asked, "What took you so long?"

"I'm sorry," Tuppy said.

"Never mind," the man said. "You're here now."

He handed Tuppy a librettist's loose-leaf book with the title "Kiss Me Kate" typed on the cover page.

"What's this?" Tuppy asked.

He then looked more closely at the man and finally recognized him.

"That's the baby," Cole Porter said. "Let's hope it grows legs."

Tuppy was overcome; he couldn't speak.

This was heaven.

Iris Avenue by Pamela Grandstaff

Peony Street is available on Amazon.com

Made in the USA
San Bernardino, CA
26 April 2019